THE DECISION

Colleen Ferrary

'What would you do if everything you thought you knew was wrong?'

Rainey Beaufort

A journey of love, obligation, and strength.

To my amazing husband who allowed me to dangle truth and fiction so perilously close to each other that even he was nervous, I love you.

To God, for shepharding us through the many storms and may you continue to do so.

And for Aislinn... because everything in life I do, I do for you.

Have Faith

"He who dwells in the secret place of the Most High shall abide under the shadow of the Almighty. I will say of the Lord, "He is my refuge and my fortress, my God, in Him I will trust."'

Psalm 91:1-2

PROLOGUE

Is everyone's journey in life predetermined? I can't help pondering this question as I sit paralyzed with fear, wondering if this is it.

Is he dead?

The light dances precariously across the walls, only giving me enough light to make out what's happening. As my eyes adjust, his limp body is bounced into the air with a jolt and lands quickly back down on the wood floor. I'm staring at him, unsure of what I should be doing. Do I touch him? I'm not a doctor, but I wish I were at this moment. My brain flashes of episodes of *Gray's Anatomy* and *The Good Doctor* after I berate myself for not being prepared. Damn it! I should be doing something. Why isn't he waking?

As the electrodes shock his body a second time, all I can think is he's not coming back to me this time.

The real question is, do I want him to?

RAINEY BEAUFORT

His fingers lay like heavy wet rags across the bend of my arm. They're warm and moist against my skin, yet they hold me in place like leather bonds. As I look around the room, the freshly painted walls seem lifeless and incomplete. I painted this room a slightly pastel shade of sand and imagined completing its look with seagrass wallpaper, soft driftwood accents, wispy linens and casually entwined rich wovens. My goal was to create a serene oasis where we could escape physically as well as mentally. I haven't been inspired to finish it, which Simon doesn't seem to notice. In fairness, he's got more menacing things on his mind these days.

The morning light is begging for me to touch it as it reigns from the three large skylights across the room. The sunbeams are goading me, challenging me to break free to go to them. But, I can't. Or maybe, the truth is, I won't. His fingers flinch slightly, reminding me they are keeping me from the light, and from so many other things. I have been holding my breath for what seems like an eternity praying for his breathing to return to that deep rumble I hear when he's sound asleep. I've been awake since five, but that was only minutes before he finally fell still. I felt him tossing and turning throughout the night. I'd feel the gentle tug of the covers, the bounce of his turning on the mattress, and even the gentle touch on my arm in the middle of the night as if to make sure I hadn't left him, every movement representing a sign of his pain and fear.

It used to be endearing, his touch and his reaching hand; now it seems so desperate.

I wait longer, constantly longing for the sun to touch my skin, until finally his steady breathing is restored. Hopefully now he'll get some sleep and I'll return to planning my escape. How I wish I could leave not only his bed, but the last several years. Then again, I'm still here. I'm not being held against my will, but by other holds. This is a big day for Katherine, I need to leave soon. Why, I wonder, am I so compelled to coddle this man who's been the source of much of my pain? Is it the vows I took? Is it empathy? Is it fear?

Katherine will be leaving soon. It's her first day of high school, and I want to spend time with her. This is a big day for her. It's another new school in another new town. I catch myself feeling sorry for her, but again, this has become my norm as well. My heart aches for her, especially knowing that I'm completely responsible. I've created this problem. My heartache is replaced with pity and self-loathing. I can barely remember the indomitable woman I used to be.

What Katherine has had to endure, not only this past year, but especially this past year, has been unjust. Every plan I had to give her the right tools leading up to this moment in her life, had disintegrated. There has been so much change. Even her name has changed, she no longer goes by Katherine.

"It's Kate, Mom."

I quickly push emotion aside and try to slink out of bed unnoticed. This time, if I wake him, so be it. Katherine has been through so much. She needs to come first. She will always come first. She is the one true person in my life who means more to me than anything else. Of course, every mother knows this, I would assume. But until you're a mother, I'm not sure you really understand love. Perhaps I'm wrong. Maybe it was just me who didn't understand love? There was nothing I wouldn't do for Katherine, nothing. I would sacrifice my life and happiness for her. I would kill for her.

I make my way downstairs to find Katherine already dressed. Her hair is damp and she's eating a blueberry Pop Tart. I feign disappointment in her choice of breakfast, but secretly I'm filled with envy. That Pop Tart would take two hours on the treadmill to remove from my hips, but for her, she could eat a box of them.

"Do you want me to dry your hair?"

"No," Kate answers.

"Braid?"

"Mooommmmm." She groans.

"I know baby, you've got it." I lean over, touch her forehead with my lips, and walk into the kitchen eager for the welcome smell of French roast coffee. This cup has come too late this morning. It's no different than yesterday or the day before. Simon's sleep has been sporadic for days and when he doesn't sleep, his symptoms flare mercilessly. Like this morning, I have lain frozen in bed next to him for hours in fear of waking him.

"Do you have all your things together for today?" I ask as I walk back into the living room, embracing my aromatic treasure.

"Yes, Mom," her annoyance that I'm treating her "like a child" rising in her tone.

"Do you want me to drive you?" I ask.

"No, I'm going to walk with Eva."

"Nice" is all I say in response. I'm secretly relieved to hear this. Our move here this summer was not a popular decision. No one could have predicted what would happen, but Katherine was adamantly opposed to another new school. Who could blame her? Since Simon and I had married, this would be her third new school. Eva was a neighbor she had just met three days ago while walking our ten-year-old golden retriever, Popcorn. I didn't even realize they were that friendly, but friendships are not created on front stoops any longer. Social media had become a blessing, and a curse, especially for teens. Hopefully, in this case, it has been a blessing.

I keep revisiting my conversation with my old priest in my head.

"Kids are resilient, Rainey," said Father Jon. "She'll adapt, probably better than you." His words still keep me sane.

"On second thought, Mom, can you dry my hair?"

I quickly jump to attention and can barely contain my smile, "Of course!" I recognize that if I'm too eager, it has the adverse effect. I have learned never to find a blouse too adorable or jeans that are just perfect. Words like that guarantee hatred in her response, whether she agrees with my assessment or not. This is how teens flex their independence, I'm told. I'll take this over drugs and alcohol, I keep telling myself. I could lead a team of five thousand people of all ages and intellects in corporate America, but one teen can bring me to my knees.

As I dry her hair as I inhale her scent. The baby scent was gone years ago, but her familiar smell still comforts me. It's these little things you hold onto as a mother in hopes your children never outgrow you. I used to despise drying her hair. Our constant bickering throughout the process was like politicians in an MMA ring.

"You're hurting me!" "Ouch!"

"Stay still!"

It's funny how time changes your perspective. What I used to dread, I now adore. The fact that she no longer cries like a cat in heat with every brush stroke certainly helps.

Katherine's long blond hair is too long, if you ask me. When you blow it out, however, it's like silk. Long luxurious strands of golden honey with natural highlights make me cringe with envy. She and I share the same eyes. Light bluish gray- although hers are slightly bluer. They seem to be just a touch too big for her face. These eyes have certainly helped me get what I want and I know Katherine has lost no time learning the secret of their charm. The subtle act of looking through her long, dark lashes has earned her extra allowance, new clothes, more dessert– I don't want to imagine what else it will help her get.

From her father she took big, plump lips and the ability to make anything funny. Simon calls her our triple threat. She's smart, beautiful, and clever enough to use it all to her advantage.

Katherine once told me she took all the best features from me and her father and she put them together better. You had to laugh at her confidence sometimes, but she was right. That's what I wish for more of these days– confidence, for both of us. I couldn't have predicted how what we've gone through could strip us of our most valued possession.

As I'm drying her hair, I realize she's sprouted another inch this summer. She is officially taller than I. Add tall and thin to her list of attributes. I had prayed for kind and happy when she was in my womb, her beauty and intelligence was a bonus.

It's nearing seven-thirty and Eva shows up at the front door. You can tell Eva is a good kid just from the way she carries herself as she comes to our home for the first time. I wonder if her parents told her to invite Katherine to walk with her? Eva has a natural, New Jersey kind of beauty. Her dark, unspoiled hair is pulled back from her face but bounces across her shoulders as she smiles. Her perfect white teeth are outlined with a light-colored lip gloss, and her eyes sparkle with wisdom beyond her years. Eva has shiny new Converse on, shorts of which I'm sure triggered an argument with her parents before leaving the house, and a cute floral top I refused to buy Katherine at Neiman's last week. Katherine tells Eva how cute she looks and shoots me a glance acknowledging the top. They bound out the door, hardly looking back.

This past year, for various reasons, the business I had started five years earlier started to decline. Simon's salary was not what Katherine and I had been accustomed to living on, so buying a blouse at Neiman Marcus for a thirteen-year-old was out of the question. No one could have predicted the past five years, and because of everything that has happened,

I've had to learn to be frugal.

"You've lived a thousand lives in the past five years, Rainey," a dear friend recently commented. She was right, and I've felt every single one of them. Although there have been eruptions of incredible joy and at much needed intervals, there has also been unbearable heartbreak that has steadily unleashed like Chinese water torture.

"God only gives you what you can handle," so the saying goes. These past few years have tested that theory.

As I watch Katherine and Eva walk up the street, I hear Simon rushing down the stairs. "Did I miss her?" he panics.

"Yes, it's OK. She knows you didn't sleep well."

"Damn," he curses. I know missing her means a lot to him. Maybe I should have woken him. It's a hard call, I think. Is it really worth it?

Simon jumps to the front porch wearing his boxers, nothing else. As he catches her attention and wishes her a great first day– maybe it was the breeze– he realizes that he has just jumped to the front porch in only his boxers. He jumps back in as quickly as he jumped out. He is barely seen in the house without a shirt on, never mind the front porch in only boxers. All this medication is taking its toll on his body and his thinking.

His disappointment in me is quickly replaced with fast eye contact, cringed faces, and then, an eruption of laughter. For a moment, I remember the us I knew.

"I'll go get you a cup of coffee." I offer.

"I must be losing my mind." he says.

"Well you've certainly lost your pants." I giggle.

We laugh off his disappointment and frustration and sit at the kitchen counter bantering a few more minutes about what the neighbors must think of the new occupants on Woodland Rd. I show him the first day of school pictures I took. I tell him about Eva, but not about her two-hundred-dollar blouse. I make a second cup of coffee and then start chopping fruit for our regular breakfast of Icelandic yogurt and homemade granola.

"Will I ever get bacon again?" he asks.

"No."

"You know, Mrs. Bradley, you are getting harder to live with every day."

"I know," I smile.

Today is our 1022nd day of marriage. Someone might think this is a romantic accounting of our marriage, one that I've been counting since our first day. In truth, I figured it out before we knew he was sick, on the day he changed our lives forever– Day 838.

THE BEAUFORT WOMEN

"Mimi, that's not a word!"

"Of course it is. S-O-G-Y-N-I-S-T; sogynist. It's the opposite of misogynist. It's a man who finally realizes that women are the superior beings!" The three women erupt in laughter. As Mimi picks up her letters, I watch the magic of the Beaufort women unfold as it does once a month, when we visit our cousins.

There are four sisters, each one a little more Irish and a little more outspoken than the next. Sometimes this group is joined by other women in our tribe, but not this day.

I'm twelve. I started reading the dictionary, so I could sit at the table and play Scrabble with these women. I needed to be good or I couldn't play. There was no mercy in this family if you were a kid. There was no mercy in this family no matter who you were. I'd have to play with all my younger cousins if I couldn't be competitive with the adults. That was fun too, but what I learned at the poolside table playing Scrabble wasn't going to be taught to me by a bunch of 10-year-olds.

Pilar reached down into an ice bucket behind her chair and grabbed a cold beer. "Whose ready?"

"I am," I joked. Before I knew it, an ice-cold Michelob Light was on the table in front of me. The sweat was beading off the sides as it glistened in the summer sun. I stared in disbelief, my eyes the size of silver dollars. Could this really be happening? I was only twelve. I wasn't sure I had really wanted a beer, but suddenly I knew it wasn't really going to happen as the sisters roared with laughter.

"Does this mean I don't get it?" The question spawned more laughter.

Audrey got up from the table. "I'm going to refresh my gin and tonic. Mimi, are you ready?" My mother nodded, gulped her last sip, and handed Audrey her glass.

"How about you, Rainey?" At that, the three women started laughing with their signature cackle. Sometimes they weren't as funny as they thought they were.

"Rainey, I bet you don't know this, but I was there when your mother was naming you," Pilar boasted. "You know what your name means, don't you?" I told her it meant queen. "You're right. Some people say it's English, some Gaelic. Your mother and I decided you will redefine what it means for the world. You were born a queen and always will be one. One day, everyone will bow to you, but you'll have to earn it." I remember that conversation like yesterday. I wasn't sure what Aunt Pilar meant by it. If I were a queen already, shouldn't they already be bowing? What did I need to earn? Was all the beer she had drunk finally kicking in? She was on her fourth... or was it her fifth?

"Beaufort means a fortress; our family is your fortress. We will all be protected by our strength as a family," my mother added in her gin and tonic haze.

"To the queen of the family, our first born, Rainey Beaufort," Pilar cheered.

"Shouldn't queens be able to decide when they get to try beer?" I chided. At that, Audrey walked back out with two tall glasses showcasing freshly cut limes perched on top of the icy cold drinks.

"Are you ninnies still talking about giving Rainey beer? For God's sake, Mimi, stop corrupting your child and put a real word on the board!"

The women laughed and toasted, "To strong women everywhere."

Growing up, it was those afternoons I remember most fondly.

It always played out the same. We'd make the trek to one of their houses. There was always a pool, a gaggle of cousins, a grill, and Scrabble. For a couple years, they switched to Trivial Pursuit, but it was harder for them to cheat, so they went back to Scrabble. They were fiercely competitive, unwaveringly loyal (except to their brother), and were changing the world over a cooler full of beer and gin and tonics.

The four sisters would laugh into the night as the daytime picnic would turn into a massive sleepover. I can still smell the crisp cotton nightgowns that always seemed readily available for those sleepovers. We'd cram four kids into a king size bed and would spend the next couple hours getting scolded for giggling while the sisters continued to cackle through the night in the next room.

"Go to bed," one would admonish.

"Don't make us go in there," another sister chimed.

"No talking, girls!" The more they told us to stop, the more we'd giggle. It wasn't until years later I'd learn that they were eager to have us fall asleep because they had a motive of their own. Turns out, since they were kids, they'd wait until the rest of the house fell asleep, and then creep out to the pool to skinny dip.

"A fine, cherished tradition," my mother would explain to me when I got older. When I bought my first house– of course with a pool– I would learn how empowering it was to do the same.

I loved these women. Of course, they were my aunts. I had to love them. But more so, I admired them. They seemed fearless and they did whatever they wanted. They were strong and challenging. If you got second place, you were the first to lose. Winning was almost as important as being a woman. I was born in the seventies, and they lived the seventies. They told stories of burning bras and smoking grass. They marched in Washington Square and made posters that would demand better opportunity for them, and for future generations. They were too cool to knit pussy hats. They had work to do, and they all were going to work hard and live up to the articles they read in Ms. Magazine.

Audrey was the matriarch of the family. She reminded me most of my grandmother. Maybe it was the gin and tonics, but it was also the way she just kept this loving group in line. She never drank too much, but she was always drinking. She was a senior executive at Mastercard in Manhattan and regularly boasted that she was the highest-ranking female executive. I often wondered what that meant. I would imagine her sitting at an oversized gleaming boardroom table being the only woman. She'd be telling the men what she needed them to do and how quickly it should be done. She'd be impressing them, I'd think to myself. She was powerful in our family, so she must be powerful at work.

Pilar was the diva of the group. It was hard to be a feminist diva, but she worked it out. Years later we'd learn that she really loved wine, but feminists drank beer. She'd explain years later, "As long as the bartender is good looking, I'll drink anything. By the way, the good-looking ones didn't know shit about great wine, so until wine became vogue, I drank beer. Finally, the world has caught up with me." Again, her logic always seemed a little flawed, but she always had this remarkable gift of being able to talk to anyone. And when she did? They fell in love with her instantly. Men, women, children, puppies, every last being loved Pilar.

Pilar was the first entrepreneur of the group. She owned a shop in town and would go into the city and shop Seventh Avenue for merchandise for the store and, of course, sample sales for herself. She always had the most amazing clothes, and everything down to her toe polish matched. If she was wearing a slick green pantsuit, she had an attaché in matching leather; her Diane Von Furstenberg dresses were paired with smart accessories in complementing shades. My mother would always say, "If any of us wore that outfit, we'd look like two-dollar hookers. Pilar always looks like she just stepped off a runway."

Pilar was fiercely independent and had never been married. There were family rumors about a male friend who always seemed to be around. For years and years, when Pilar missed a Scrabble game, the conversation always came up, "So, do you think Arthur and Pilar are having an affair? She swears they aren't."

"Whatever they're doing, he jumps to her every call."

Regardless, I wanted to be like Pilar. She travelled around the world, had more friends than you could count. She knew everyone, and everyone knew her. Yep, I would be single my entire life and live a life others would envy. That plan would stay with me until my thirties.

The third sister, Mimi, is my mother. She was the Lucille Ball of the family and was more known for her hair-brained schemes than her successes. She would regularly have insane strokes of genius that we always looked forward to exploring with her. One minute we'd be cutting out flowers from contact paper and sticking them to the kitchen walls and the next minute we'd be outside painting her old VW bug. However, she could be the worst nightmare as a mother. She was the mom who embarrassed her daughter in front of friends, but also their favorite parent and party planner. My friends couldn't wait to see what was next, and I couldn't wait to hide from her. She made life fun, and hard, and real.

Mimi's greatest gift was making you believe you could do anything in life that you set your mind to doing. I knew that if I wanted to graduate from Harvard Law School and be the first female president of the United States, all I had to do was try. I'm smarter now, but at the time I bought that package of beliefs hook, line and sinker.

Mimi started selling real estate in the eighties after my

parents divorced. Her fun, spontaneous personality, and her belief that she was always right, convinced enough home buyers and sellers of the same thing. Her business grew and grew throughout the eighties. It seemed as though nothing could hold her back.

These women were my lineage. These were a group of women so strong and so right, what could go wrong? These were the women I would become.

The year I turned twelve was a significant year for Scrabble and only solidified my future plans as an eternally single woman. That was the year the fourth sister got divorced. I sat at the table as Pilar, Audrey and Mimi went into great detail pulling together the pieces of Cecilia's divorce.

"I heard it was Linda!"

"Not Linda O'Malley! She's Cecilia's best friend. She'll be devastated."

Although I was able to sit at the table, the three women tried to shield me from the conversation. Between the beer and the time, I would eventually piece together the entire story. With each clue, my heart broke more. You should never have favorites, but Cecilia was mine. She and Uncle Tony were like second parents to me. I would go for sleepovers at their house, make cookies, ride the train, walk the dog... They were my vision of happily ever after. I had read enough princess books to know that the queen has a king and the princess a prince. When you ruled the land, you got everything you'd ever dreamed, and in my mind, that was Cecilia. Until, that is, I was twelve years old at a table playing Scrabble with the Beaufort women.

In hindsight, maybe Aunt Cecilia and Uncle Tony were the only example I had of a happy couple. My parents had divorced when I was seven and all of my friends' parents fought incessantly. The more I became a staple in their homes, the more the veils would disappear, and we'd witness the truth.

Growing up, my friends and I decided there were four

kinds of marriages: The Castle Marriage, The Jones, The Friends, and The Regulars.

Aunt Cecilia and Uncle Tony had a "Castle Marriage." These are the stories you read in books growing up that always seemed to close with the omnipresent "happily ever after." We'd soon learn never to believe everything we read.

Some parents were just constantly nagging each other. That was something I'd want to avoid because, naturally, queens don't nag; they order. Parents who always nagged were "The Jones." We had quickly realized naggers always complained about what they didn't have, hence their nickname. Perhaps they married for love but somewhere along the line realized love isn't everything. The Jones would nag about their cars or clothes not being nice enough and would start each argument the same way, "Why can't we..." and end it with something to the effect of "like the Joneses have."

Vicki's parents didn't even know what the other one looked like, perhaps why we spent so much time with the grand dame herself, GiGi. Witnessing Vicki's grandmother's posh lifestyle– sans grandfather– made me think. If I'm going to go to all the trouble of getting married, I decided I certainly wanted a husband who would be home. We called these marriages the "friends." This wasn't a bad type of marriage, but why share everything if you don't have to? I now realize, this was a theory devised by self-centered teens.

Then there were 'the regulars.' These were most of my friends' parents.

"Why are you so late? I've been taking care of the house all day while you're out having martinis with people you've been with all day?"

"Where is all our money going? You're irresponsible!"

"Can't you at least just wipe your feet for God's sake?"

We called them regulars because these were the parents who regularly fought. Years later we'd learn of affairs, gambling addiction, alcoholism, and various other sordid marriage plagues. At the time, they were just "the regulars."

After my dad moved out, he returned to build us a great treehouse on the edge of the back yard. It had three stories and was wedged between 3 massive oak trees. We kids could add as many nails as we deemed fit during the construction process. Dad had bought giant boxes of long silver nails which we'd spend hours logging our contribution to his design efforts. I visited years later to find it still standing, presumably due to the thousands of nails the neighborhood kids and I had pounded in. It was our fortress; where we would look at our first *Playboy* magazines, have our first kisses, and share our dreams. When we would dream together, we'd decide what kind of marriage we would have. We'd pretend Vicki married a regular and Melanie was in a Jones' marriage. I would always choose Aunt Cecilia's, until this warm day in June, when I was twelve.

It was on this day, June thirteenth, when I learned that Uncle Tony cheated on Aunt Cecilia with Aunt Cecilia's best friend. He confessed about the affair and told Cecilia he wanted a divorce, so they could be together. They hadn't told my cousins yet, so I was sorry they weren't there with us that day. We could tell them everything would be OK, even better. Of course, my sister Zoe and I knew this because we had been through it, I naively thinking every situation the same.

"What will Cecilia do?" Pilar was concerned. Audrey quickly reminded her that both she and Mimi had gone through divorces and they were both fine and so were the kids. The three women looked at me. I didn't know what to say. Frankly, I'd never been more concerned about what my face had looked like than I was at that moment. It didn't seem like the time for a joke.

"But there's FIVE kids," I reminded them. Aunt Audrey had an only child and I had only one sister, Zoe.

"Rainey, please. Haven't you learned anything sitting at this table all year? We're women. We're family. We're there for each other. I'd be worrying about Uncle Tony. He doesn't know what he's losing."

At that, without saying a word, the three women raised their glasses, clinked, and all hailed "TO CECILIA!" before their hearty, man-sized sips. I would always remember that toast. These strong, powerful women had a different tone. How they felt about Cecelia would change. I would later understand that tone, it was pity.

That was when my decision was made. June thirteenth. That was also the day before Vicki, Sally, Patty, Johnny and I sat on the third floor of our tree house and made a pact never to get married.

I had decided I would grow up to be Aunt Pilar– no husband, only friends to travel and laugh with and neighbors to visit. No headaches, nagging, affairs, or problems to worry about. My heart was officially safe, and I would go on to rule the world.

Today, I was pouring my husband a freshly brewed decaf trying to decide what we would have named THIS kind of marriage.

Dear Diary,

It's Kate.

My mother is so annoying. Seriously!!!!!!!!!!! She just won't give me a break. When is she just going to trust me? When I say everything is OK, everything is OK! Even if it isn't, it's none of her business!!!!

I can't believe we moved to New Jersey for Simon! I hate him sometimes. I'm trying to forgive him, but I can't believe mom agreed to move again - for HIM! What about me?!?! I can't believe I need to start at another new school and make all new friends AGAIN!

Met a new friend, hopefully she turns out to be cool. Eva. Not sure if mom had anything to do with it. She usually does. Who knows though? She's not the same anymore. Maybe this time my friends will hate her. I hate that they always like her because they tell her <u>everything!</u> It's like she gives them truth serum in their iced tea. All she wants to know about is boys, and who's doing what, and what we do after school. I swear all the other moms tell her everything they hear, too. So annoying!!!!!!!!

That's what Mom does. Controls conversations and throws parties. I can't remember a time when she wasn't having people over. She hasn't done that since we moved to New Jersey. I wonder why? She makes friends in a minute, what's she waiting for this time?

In our old house, my mom built this super long counter that thirty people could stand around. We did everything right there. The neighbors would never call before stopping over. Ten minutes later after they showed up it would look as though Mom had planned a party with all kinds of food and desserts. You could NEVER walk downstairs with no clothes on. I made that mistake just once. It's the kind of mistake you only ever make once. It was totally embarrassing! My favorite shirt was in the dryer and I thought I'd just run down and get it. I came around the bottom of the steps and BAM! Mr. and Mrs. Sanders were having coffee with my mom in the kitchen at seven a.m. There I was, NO SHIRT! UGH! She could've warned me! I can hear her now:

'Katherine, we can blame no one but ourselves and can succeed only when we lead ourselves to victory.' Blah, blah, blah.

My aunt Audrey, or is it my great aunt, does the same thing. Sometimes I think she was raised by Aunt Audrey and not Mimi. They have all these words of wisdom I've heard a thousand times. You should hear her now with the #metoo movement, she's all into it! Why couldn't I just have a normal mother???? I have one that needs to be everyone's champion. Lately, she seems to be everyone's champion but her own. I wonder if I should tell her that? Maybe she's homesick. We're pretty far from all of her friends in Connecticut.

Maybe that's why she's acting weird now. I miss her having people over. Before a dinner party it was just the two of us. I'd help her get ready and she'd tell me who was on their way over and what gossip I might hear and why I should ignore it. I never did! She hated when people spoke bad about others in our house. There wasn't a lot of it, especially because mom always changed the conversation. When her closest friends – the "aunts" and "uncles" - would come over, they would just be laughing and telling funny stories. They never talked about others either unless they needed help or there was something exciting to share.

My job was always to greet everyone "appropriately" at the door. It went something like this, "Hi Uncle Trevor. It's so nice to see you tonight. Thank you for joining us. May I take your coat?" I'd get two responses after my aunts and uncles would smother me with hugs and kisses.

Uncle Michael would always say in a funny voice, "Oh no, Katherine, I'll take care of my coat!" and then he'd throw it over his shoulder onto the ground. I laughed every time.

Everyone needed to be addressed as "Mr." or "Mrs." except for close friends. They were aunts and uncles, "Uncle Trevor" or "Auntie Chris." Turns out, they aren't even relatives. It took my being embarrassed by my second-grade teacher to figure that out! We had to draw a picture of our family for art. When I drew the eighth aunt, my teacher started asking questions about how big our family was. You can guess how embarrassing that was. My mother could have warned me.

That's how she is. She loves to have people over and make people feel loved. She is always telling her friends she loves them. I thought she was a little over the top at first, but they really do love each other. My dad always says, "You never know who will show up in your mom's life next. It could be a prince or a pauper. Your mom can make friends with anyone." He told me a story about one time went she went to the bathroom at a restaurant and came out forty-five minutes later with a new friend. He thought she left him there. He must have always known she didn't want to be with him, but somehow, he survived ten years with her. Simon has only survived three, or is it four? Dad wins, I guess. I think he's still heartbroken though, even though I can't imagine mom with him now. I don't know how they ever lived together. I love Dad but he's everything Mom hates.

I'm nervous about tomorrow. Even if my mom made Eva walk with me, I don't care. Being the new kid sucks! Does she even realize how hard it is to find a new friend group? These kids have known each other their entire lives. UGH. I hope my mom is telling the truth. I hope everything is fine with her and Simon. I just cannot move again. Simon would never make me move again.

I know the thing with Simon last year was a big deal. Really, I still can't believe it. I know mom still thinks about it. She's said all the right things to me, but I know my mother. The problem is, everything that happened goes against everything she's taught me. Really Mom, decide!!!!!! Simon is trying so hard. I don't want to move again and you're missing out on the moments! FOMO? Haven't you heard about it? It's time to start living your life again! I hate holding this secret for her.

BEFORE SIMON

Although Katherine's dad and I weren't married, he had lived in my house in Bedford for over ten years. I never wanted to marry him, and although he asked many times, it was nothing I would even consider. I didn't love this man, he was the man I had a child with, and that was it. He knew that going in. The problem was, I'm not sure he believed it.

When I was thirty-three, I still thought I was going to live Aunt Pilar's life. I was single, free to do what I pleased, and on top of my game professionally and personally. I had everything. I had a great job leading a team of several thousand employees for a Fortune 500 company. This also meant a very good paycheck that went along with it. I had an oversized brownstone in Chicago that I picked up for a hell of a deal. I had great friends, a busy social life, and my life's plan was on track. I was making the Beaufort women proud.

One night, after a group of good friends had gone home from what had become a weekly girls' night, I sat in my favorite chair with a cup of tea reflecting on just how good my life was. I looked at the chair I was nestled in. The oversized, pale-yellow, soft, yet robustly stuffed chair had a casual elegance that I had always hoped described my personal style. My two shih-tzus lay next to me on their bed at the foot of the chair, exhausted from the neighbor's boxer who also attended our girls' night. I looked around the room. It was perfect. The colors of the room, the conversational art, treasures from my global expeditions, the furniture... they were all perfectly placed. The last few small reminders of an evening well-spent surrounded me as I marveled shamelessly at my own life. Despite having everything I had planned (I didn't wish – I was a Beaufort woman – I made things happen), I asked myself what I would be missing or regret if I were sitting in the same chair forty years from now.

"Grandchildren." That was the answer that came streaming in my head. Of all things! You can't have grandchildren without having a child. I guess I wanted to have a baby? A month later that nagging thought didn't leave. I decided to step forward and put my Beaufort brain to action and I created a plan.

I had this guy I was dating, he would do. He has an incredible family, he was a lot of fun, hot as hell. "Yep, good sperm," I thought. I wasn't getting any younger. I had the conversation with him the next time we went out about my epiphany and what I had been thinking. Surprisingly, he was all in. He would certainly be a sperm donor. Hmm. That was easy. Too easy. I should have known better.

Shortly after getting pregnant I was transferred to Connecticut. My baby's father wasn't anywhere near Connecticut which was OK with me. I had every intention of raising Katherine as a single mom. Unfortunately, what I didn't predict was that he was not really in this thing to do me a favor, as originally agreed.

Shortly after arriving in Stepford, Connecticut, I received a knock on the front door of my new home. The town wasn't Stepford. That's what I called it, though. Everyone looked so perfect in front of their perfect colonials on their tree-lined streets. They had two-point-five children and the wives stayed home and took care of the house. I swore I watched my neighbors secretly peer through the curtains to see what I was having delivered or to see what new car I was driving up in. There was a curiosity about me. Single woman, big house, just she and her two dogs. I'd laugh. Little did they know about the bun in my oven. I quickly met the neighbors and was invited to a few barbeques. Stepford is where I'd build my new life. I had grown up in Connecticut, so returning home meant returning to friends I've had since grade school. It was as if I had lived in this little town of Stepford my entire life.

A few weeks after having settled, I opened the door to find the shock of a lifetime. There he was. Five hundred miles from home on my front stoop. I looked past him to my driveway. In it sat an old Chevrolet Suburban– gone was his cool old convertible Mustang. On the back of the Suburban, he had hitched a large rental trailer.

Oh. Shit.

"What a surprise. What are you doing here?" I mustered. I wanted to shut the door as quickly as I had opened it.

"We're having a baby and I want to be here with you. I'm not going to let you raise her alone."

Her. I remember getting all weird when he said the word. "This was not the plan," I stammered.

"Well, you owe it to her to try. What kind of kid grows up without both parents?"

After agreeing on a few contingencies– he would have to get a job, find a place to live, and that I would in no way support him– I allowed him past the front room of the house. A few days ended up being a few months. As we got closer to Katherine's due date the excitement distracted me from my adamancy. A bunch of family vacations later and a hectic work schedule let ten years slip by. He asked me to marry him a hundred times. I said no two hundred times. Never did I love him.

I may have had a baby out of wedlock, but I swore I would never get married unless there was no doubt that I would be with that person until the day I died. I believe in the sacrament of marriage. I vowed to only marry a man I would never divorce. Based on my experience, marriage was not a gift the Beaufort women were blessed with, and I knew that Katherine's father would not be the exception.

I said those words many times to him and others, "If I believe for a moment that this relationship might, at any time in the future, end in divorce, I have to say no." I did have a caveat to my till-death-do-us-part beliefs; "If your husband did something truly egregious and the church would annul your marriage, there is no way you should stay." I'd say this to the large handful of women who had worked for me over the years, whom I had recognized as battered or who had confessed to me some other truth from their marriage that was causing their pain.

At the time, I wasn't sure there was a love that could be that sure or that pure. After giving birth to Katherine, I didn't believe I could love anyone as much as I loved her. I thought I had that undeniable love once when I was younger, but I was wrong. I know better now.

For ten years, Katherine's father and I were roommates. He was my date when I needed him. He was a babysitter. Every time I encouraged him to leave; he'd find a reason to stay.

Eventually, I started to visit attorneys to see how I could get him out of my house.

"You could say he beats you," one said.

"I know a guy," a slightly seedier attorney, told me.

Ultimately, this was Katherine's father. Those weren't options.

Turns out, even though there's no common law marriage in Connecticut, you can't just kick someone out if they don't want to go. You must evict them. For six long months they can stay there willfully. So that was it. Six months of hell and now he was finally moving out, somewhat forcefully. He would not make it easy on me, but why should he? He had been living a pretty great life for free for almost ten years. He never really worked, minus the occasional odd job. I had traveled an extraordinary amount. He was masterful at leveraging that as an excuse for not getting a full-time job.

Finally, he was gone.

A funny thing happens when you end a relationship in a town like Stepford. You find out that not everyone in your little town is as happy as they seem.

"You were the happy couple," parents with children close to Katherine told me.

"I was?" I thought. Well, it is true. When you don't care, you don't fight. I suppose we appeared happy. After being persistently goaded by some less happy women I knew in town, I agreed to host a celebration of my single status. I have always loved a good party and it was as good an excuse as any.

After announcing the gathering, I got busy with invites. A good friend announced her pending divorce - she was invited. I met two women on the lacrosse field that "didn't have the courage to leave" their husbands and proceeded to invite themselves to the party. I had a couple girlfriends who regularly complained about their husbands– they made the list. Of course, the several women who did the initial goading were the first to RSVP. Each of them, disappointed women looking for a way to spice up their social calendar. This little soiree had officially become the feminist equivalent of the He-Man Women Haters' Club. Ten women who hated their men.

That's where it all started.

I recall pouring the first glasses of wine thinking that at this counter there were seven women who were fiercely successful and equipped to live pretty amazing lives without the help of a man. Two could comfortably live on alimony if they had to. One just could not give a damn and was painfully unhappy. But only two, Laurie and I, had actually done anything about it – or would.

Laurie had just announced her divorce. Much like me, she was the breadwinner. She was a hotshot corporate lawyer with three kids. She was, in a word, fabulous. Sadly, much like me, the quest to be a good mother and great at our job outweighed the importance of dumping the dead weight of our relationship. Her marriage had gone on for thirteen years.

"As a Jew," she boasted, "it is my obligation to celebrate the number thirteen. Only I choose to do it with divorce." Then she raises her glass.

The day Katherine's father finally left was exhilarating. Laurie, I knew, would soon feel the same. I have never been so happy or felt so free. Guess what? So was Katherine. Turns out, the more you try to hide it, the more your kid's Spidey-senses kick in and they know. Katherine knew it was an unhealthy relationship. I never fought in front of her. She would never accidentally walk in on a conversation she shouldn't. I was too careful. But still, she knew. Perhaps it's female intuition at its earliest stages?

In my quest to be the perfect mother and erase any possibility of emotional scarring, we would talk about the separation ad nauseum. Of course, I'd find clever ways to start the conversation, or would jump on a topic she'd mention, but I needed to make sure she was happy. On April Fool's Day, I told her that her father was moving back in. Cruel, I know.

She screamed in horror. "No, Mama! Please don't! That is not a good idea. But we're so happy!"

There is was, "We're so happy." I no longer felt guilt. I had done the right thing.

Katherine was perfectly fine.

FEMALE MAN HATERS' CLUB

Here I was, 6 months after being freed, and I was the happiest I have ever been. Katherine was the happiest I had ever seen her. Had I any idea during the previous ten years that it would affect her this way, I would have pushed this outcome sooner.

I tell you this because, the very last thing on my mind was bringing another male into my house. I was now exactly where I wanted to be my own, updated version of Aunt Pilar!

At the Men Haters' Club party I was hosting, the drinks started to flow faster. I realized that this group I had assembled was not my usual oenophiles; they could not handle their wine. Thankfully, I had put Katherine on a plane to visit her father that morning, and I could allow them to get as loose as they wanted. I was already arranging who would sleep in which guest room.

Laurie became extrospective. "You know, Rainey. You and I have known each other since our girls were little. Rainey, you knoooowww you're fabulous. You deserrrrrve happily ever after, Rainey."

Sometimes Laurie would pop by after she put the kids to bed. I'd always grab a bottle and we'd go out in the hot tub or around the outdoor fireplace and talk till all hours of the night. I always knew I was in trouble when she started extending her syllables like a drunk socialite. It was coming. And even with a buzz, Laurie could persuade even the firmest adversary to give her exactly what she wanted. These women were no match for her and, as I would soon learn, she would use them to have a little fun with me.

"RRRRainey, darling. It's time that you found your Prince Charrrrrrrming. What do you think, ladies?" She looked around my kitchen island at the eight women who were clearly enjoying the evening. "Ladies, you knoooow, Rainey has never been in love. Real love. You know the kind of love where you'd strip off alllll your clothes and run down the street compllllleeeeetely naked just because your tall drink of water asked you to?" At that, the women pounced.

"What!" "Rainey, really?" "Oh please, there must have been someone?" The barrage of questions ensued. Laurie wasn't done.

"You know ladies, I'm not sure Rainey believes she's worthy of happily ever after. Tell her she is." This created a frenzy. The truth, or wine goggles, whatever they were wearing at the time, made my worthiness the source of much fodder. I must admit; it was nice. While I was smothered in love by some newer friends and told how I could have it all, and told how I do everything for everyone else, Laurie made her way to my office.

What I didn't share that evening was news I had just received from my mother's doctor earlier that afternoon. It made what they were about to do so much more important.

Laurie emerged from my office with my laptop. What was she up to? "Ladies, let's help our good friend write her match dot com prrrooofile." Based on her tone, she could have just been telling them that they were about to embark on a ten-day all-expense paid cruise to the South Pacific. She didn't say that, but you wouldn't have known from their reaction. They enthusiastically got right to work. More wine.

Someone grabbed the bottle of vodka from the wet bar. By 2:00AM, they had written a better profile than I could have ever dreamed. They had added pictures and they were now focused on the perfect man.

In Tinder-fashion, it became a game. A face would show on the screen and we would give him a thumbs up or down. Every time a wink or instant message would pop up, we'd giggle like school girls. This was surprisingly great fun. Sometimes a little about the potential suitor would be read to the group. Always, their handle would be shared. Simon's handle was "SeemsLikeANiceGuy." I wonder, if I had to do it all over again, would I turn my thumb in the other direction? I do know now that I should have paid better attention to that handle.

This game continued until half past three when some of the women realized their husbands had been calling and texting all night with worry. Not one of us noticed. The group started nervously to disperse in embarrassment. I wondered what they were expecting when they returned to their angry spouses. Most everyone lived within a few blocks away and walked home. Laurie fell to the couch before I could walk her to the guest room. One other stayed in a guest room upstairs. Both women were gone before I woke up at seven, presumably to ensure their children didn't realize they were gone all night.

I pulled out the French press. There was nothing more decadent than making yourself a pot of French press coffee when you're alone, I thought. I was alone. It was the strangest feeling. Momentarily, I wondered what Katherine was doing with her father right now. It was the beginning of summer and she would be staying for a week. The timing was probably good, I thought. This will allow me to take care of Mimi.

Then, a strange unsettling feeling came over me. I was, for the first time in a very long time, completely alone.

Yesterday's news was a huge blow. This month had been

full of surprises. Yes, the timing was good for Katherine to be visiting her father. For me it wasn't because right now I needed that little girl desperately. The pain of her absence was vibrating through my body. I had a pain in the back of my throat. It was surfacing, and I was about to lose control at any second. For the past week I had kept everything so close and hadn't shared it with anyone. I didn't want anyone to slip up before I had decided how best to tell Katherine. I wanted her to leave happily. Although she was only nine, she had an old soul. For some reason, all I wanted to do was hold her and cry my biggest, fiercest cry. That cry was about to happen at that moment. "Focus on the coffee, Rainey," I said to myself, "just make some coffee." I kept talking to myself, right in front of the kitchen window. "Rainey, you can handle this." Pat Schwartz stared at me from the other side of the window.

I was embarrassed at first glance, but then could care less. Pat, my sixty-year-old neighbor, just happened to be miserable. She had orange-y wavy hair that always seemed undone but always looked remarkably the same. She was tall and wore her clothes a bit awkwardly. It was common to see her outside in the garden with her apron still on. Her apron was off white with large rust colored flowers and olive-green leaves with a thick ruffle that framed the top of the squared bodice. Each time I saw this I tried to guess its age. I'd feign my adoration for it and ask probing questions like, "Did someone make that for you?" or, "Was it a gift?"

She never fully answered with much more than a "Yes," or a "No," before she'd say something like, "Oh, I noticed you had friends over again last night."

It was a passive aggressive war waged over a five-foot fence that, in hindsight, I should have replaced with one a foot higher. She spent her days judging others and pointing her finger at wrongdoings. She was Gladys Kravitz with an attitude, and her husband was no better. They tried to be good neighbors, but it just wasn't in their nature. Prior to the fence, her husband once showed up at my front door with a small bag. I opened the door and he handed it to me. I'm not sure why, but because he put it in a Ziploc bag and I could see the contents, I just couldn't stop myself from laughing. He was not pleased. This sixty-two-year-old Boy Scout – yep, he had the shorts, the tie, the badges – the whole gamut – was holding a Ziploc baggie containing what I could only guess was my dog's poop.

I mean, come on. That's funny, right? Apparently, Bentley– my fourteen-year-old, blind shih-tzu– had stepped too far over the property line when I sent him out to do his business. I mean, that's funny shit, right? It was also the perfect excuse to build a fence.

So, I'm about to burst out in tears while nosey Gladys Kravitz stands twenty feet from my window staring right at me. Oh, I couldn't give old Pat the luxury of talking to myself <u>and</u> crying. What is wrong with me? I wondered about my motive as I gave her my best fake smile and waved at her like Queen Elizabeth. Simon once said that I was hard to live next to if you were miserable because I never was. I took that as a compliment.

I decided I would see what damage was created during last night's debauchery. This would definitely get my mind off my parents. I grabbed my coffee and made my way into the sunroom. I loved this room. It was surrounded with three walls of windows and was always a skootch warmer than the rest of the house. The hardwood floors were worn with age but added a fitting complement to the more contemporary seating I had placed on them. The room overlooked what I called my "Serenity Garden." It was a lush, private, small backyard but the garden was an even smaller private nook off to one side. To enter the serenity garden from outside, you'd pass through a rose covered trellis into a small space covered in pea stone with large stepping stones. The roses and shrubs made it a private sanctuary with a stone fountain as its visual centerpiece. The antique wrought iron bistro set matched the trellis that hoisted the roses above the entrance. Flipping on the fountain, I sat on the sofa with my laptop and coffee, staring at the simple but elegant garden. This was a luxury in this neighborhood. Near the city center, most homes were very close together. This was the only room in my home that I didn't need to draw the blinds for privacy. The sun drenched the room and the smell of the flowers someone brought last night filled the air. I flipped open my laptop.

Twenty-seven messages? This must have been some profile these women put together. I read it again without my wine goggles. It was beautiful and demanding and honest. I would never have written it, but I also wasn't going to change it. I loved it and I loved them for writing it.

I started scrolling through the messages. "Ugh, trolls." I said out loud to myself in frustration. I was already on the tenth message and had already been propositioned for sex three times. Many of the men well, I just couldn't see myself dating. Message number thirteen was from SeemsLikeANiceGuy. I remember our sending him a message the night before. Why did I think he was a thumbs up? I wondered. His pictures were not very good. In one picture he sat on a bench with a goofy grin, wearing an old man's coat. The next was really more of his nostrils than his face. This was a forty-year-old man trying his hand at the art of selfies. Not good. The third was his view from his kitchen window. Pretty, but was he just trying to show off his address? The last gave some hope. It was of him and a friend on a volleyball court. It was a bit harder to make out his face, but of course I did have the nostril shot. He didn't look as unattractive as he did in the other photos. He wasn't ugly per se, but he didn't seem my type at all. He seemed... nerdy.

Then I saw it. I know we didn't read this last night, and, frankly, I'm not sure why we winked at him now that I was reviewing his pictures. I saw the reason why I would write him back. SeemsLikeANiceGuy was a research scientist working for a major cancer research center.

Fierce tears began, this time in the sanctuary of my sunroom. Gasping for air as my swollen nasal passages shut down had become a regular occurrence. I needed time to process everything before telling Katherine, before telling anyone.

Last week, my dad told us that he had stage four pancreatic cancer. My father was my light. My father was my daughter's light as well. All men would forever be held up to his example and no one, I was positive, would ever come close. My father was, in a word, extraordinary. Even when he shared the news of his cancer, he found the light in his situation.

Yesterday, before my gathering of male-hating women, the news got worse.

Several years ago, I started caring for my mother. She suffered from MS and was losing her mobility – and her mind, some might say. It required a lot of work to care for her, and although I loved her, my being a single mom and starting a new business with a mortgage over my head demanded more than I could handle. It was pretty common to get emergency calls at two-thirty a.m. from her asking me to pick up cold medicine and bring it over "right away." Her dementia and her persistence were a challenge when combined.

Now, it would become even more challenging. I received a call from her doctor telling me he saw something that looked suspicious in her esophagus and stomach. He didn't need to tell me he thought it was cancerous, I already knew. Both of them, I thought. Both of them are dying at the same time.

My mother was fragile. When I received the call, I realized Katherine would be leaving for Chicago in a few hours, and a few hours after that I would have a house full of angry women stopping over. I decided not to share the information with anyone, including my mother. What would she do in the days between now and her next appointment? She was happy, making friends, feeling fine with the exception of some "heartburn." She would be all alone worrying about it if I told her today, all alone for days, worrying about it. "I had a lot to do just to get through today," I thought, "telling her today would just make her suffer more." I had already shed a million tears this week and needed a break. This party was the perfect distraction.

Two parents, one week. It had been an incredibly long week and here comes some guy who is focused on cancer? It was the right time, it was the right place, and he had the right job. He may not be the guy for me, I thought, but I needed at the very least, to talk to him.

I made a few carefully tailored jokes based on comments in his narrative. I had to read between the lines to really capture who he was so I could effectively capture his attention. I succeeded. He wrote back. I was thrilled when he suggested talking on the phone versus spending a week going back and forth via text. Perfect! We would talk tonight. "Was ten too late?" I messaged.

The phone rang at nine fifty-nine. His voice was dusty, deep, and sexy. It was not what I had expected. He was a scientist after all. I quickly summoned the image of Barry White and George Clooney playing a sexy scientist on the big screen as he introduced himself. Simon's voice fell directly between the two. It caught me off guard. I hadn't even thought to be nervous. Then, I picked up the phone.

"Hi Rainey, it's Simon." My heart stopped for a moment and I caught my breath when I heard his voice. I suppose it was at that moment that the reality of what I was doing struck me.

The conversation was easy. It was like the ones you'd expect to see in a romantic comedy. The hero and heroine talk the night away, you don't hear all of the dialogue, but witness the glorious rapture they're experiencing in each other's company. The director eclipses time to show the passing of hours while the lovers' relentless interest in each other never fades. I always thought they did that because no couple could really talk that long. But Simon and I, we were really talking. We couldn't stop talking. We were learning all about each other. Silly things were coming up like sand under your toe nails and being attacked by killer seagulls because of a ham sandwich.

We shared the colors of our favorite sunset and worst roommate stories. We couldn't finish a sentence before another popped in our head. I looked down at my watch and it was midnight. I wanted to know so much more. I had forgotten about his goofy picture and old man jacket. We had just talked for two straight hours without taking a breath, but it felt like ten minutes.

Here was the problem. Despite God's plan to throw a wrench into my happy existence by killing off my parents, I knew death was an inevitable occurrence which I would manage. I didn't need help to do this, I was happy on my own. I really didn't want to be on Match.com and go on a bunch of dates with desperate men. I already had happily ever after with Katherine and was fulfilled, really fulfilled. I wanted to go on, take care of my parents, help them live their best lives, and find a cure or experimental drug to ease the pain and keep them with me longer.

I was not in the market for a husband.

Six weeks went by. Every night I waited by the phone after Katherine was put to bed and my work was wrapped up around the house. Ten o'clock never came soon enough. It was our time– Simon's and mine. We shared everything. We talked about my parents' cancer. I told him of my initially selfish motive for talking to him. We talked about God, about children, how he didn't want children. Then, the inevitable words shot through the phone after six glorious weeks:

"Are we ever going to meet?" Simon asked.

MY KNIGHT

Simon and I will have been married for four years this spring. When we married, he was my knight in shining armor. I didn't even know I needed one. As I look at him now, his chiseled jawline and piercing eyes still turn me on. He's got this way of looking at me that speaks a million words, although most of them are used mainly in the bedroom.

I remember when I first set eyes on him.

I was sitting at a bar with Marguerite. Margo, she prefers to be called, is one of my dearest friends. She was named after Saint Marguerite d'Youville, the patron saint of difficult marriages. Margo's mother fell in love with the story of this strong woman who found out her husband had cheated on her, yet she stayed true to her vows and never left him or strayed. Rather, she rose after his death to change the perception of women.

Margo would - in her mother's exaggerated tone - tell her own story, "She was one of our earliest Power Women, Marguerite."

In the early 1700's - after her dirty, rotten, cheating husband's death – Marguerite was left penniless with six children and opened a store in desperation. As the story goes, she not only fed her children but also helped many of the less fortunate in town as well. Margo would continue the imitation, "St. Marguerite may have been one of the first successful female entrepreneurs." And she would always end with, "...proof that my mother was watching a Gloria Steinem speech while deciding on my name!" Margo laughed. Margo and I always knew our greatest bond was the women who raised us.

Margo and I could laugh about anything. The evening I met Simon was no exception.

That late summer night I had suggested to Margo that she and I meet for happy hour, so she could meet Simon. I knew she couldn't refuse. I had been telling her about this man who had slipped into my evening routine now for over a month. As we drank Champagne cocktails and celebrated Friday, I slipped and toasted to Simon's arrival, "May he be as good looking as he is funny and smart."

Unaware that I had not already met Simon (we had been talking on the phone for almost two months,) Margo froze. Color rose in her face as she spoke one decibel lower than a shout, "What!?!"

I couldn't contain my laughter.

Margo continued, "I thought I was finally meeting this mystery man. I had no idea you are finally meeting this mystery man as well! I'm leaving! I can't believe you invited me on your first date."

After mumbling something about killing me, Margo grabbed a twenty from her Louis Vuitton clutch, threw it on the bar, and mumbled "I can't believe you!" as she laughed her way out of the bar.

There I was, surrounded by strangers and a cadre of eager young women hoping to catch the wealthy, after-work crowd. A dashing young bartender asked if everything was OK as Margo fled the bar. "Fine," I laughed, imagining what the scene Margo and I had just created must have looked like.

There I sat; me, myself, and my nerves. Until that moment, I didn't know I had such nerves.

I realized then, while sitting at the bar, waiting to meet this man for the first time, the man I had spoken to every night for almost eight weeks, that I was nervous for one of the first times I could remember.

I had a lot going on at the time, so only when he said, "Are we ever going to meet?" did it dawn on me that I should. But there I was, sitting anxiously at a bar, waiting for this man with whom I may have had already fallen in love.

No one was as surprised as I was to find I had grown dependent on our late-night phone calls. We spoke every night for at least two hours after I put Katherine to bed. I say surprised, because I couldn't ever really remember needing anyone. Sure, I had boyfriends in the past, but I didn't <u>need</u> them.

Dependency was something I was taught never to allow. My earliest memory was sitting at my grandmother's table with a piece of meat and a knife and fork. I may have been three or maybe four at the time. My uncle reached over to cut my meat for me and my mother, her mother, and her sisters almost yelled in chorus.

"No! Let her do it!"

My grandmother continued, "How will she learn to be strong if she doesn't learn first to do it herself?" I'd hear those words thousands of times after.

The Beaufort women– a collection of power women, half Irish and half French– of whom no man could harness, not even the only son. My uncle sat speechless after his admonishment and relinquished my knife and fork back to my awkward little hands. My grandfather had passed before I was born, and my grandmother seemed effortless in her leadership. I couldn't imagine what the dynamics were while he lived, but I imagined not much different after his death.

I had been raised by these women and I would raise Katherine the same. We weren't told about glass ceilings; we were born with ice picks in our hands to break through them. Independence was our birthright.

For the weeks preceding our first date, Simon and I had talked for hours upon hours. I realized I had broken a Beaufort golden rule the day our nightly streak of calls would first be broken. Simon had plans to go out with friends after playing volleyball after work. He wouldn't be home in time for our regular call, and I missed him. I missed a man I had never met. I missed a man I had only talked to on the phone. I was embarrassed by the streak of jealousy that rang through me. Was he spending time with someone else? He had every right to, I had no claims on him. I spent the entire night wondering what he was doing and longing for his usual call. I had become dependent on his voice rocking me to sleep each night. I had become dependent, a curse for a Beaufort woman.

I thought of this rule moments before he would arrive. Suddenly, a thought screamed its way into my brain, "What could tonight bring if he turned out to be even just a little bit attractive?!?"

There were a couple false alarms. Men fitting his description, but, not him. But then; it was.

When he showed up at the doorway, I knew it was Simon in an instant. He had a commanding presence, six foot three with big broad, athletic shoulders. His dark, wavy hair had a soft silky bounce to it. He looked like a surfer in a Robert Graham button down yet had style oozing out of him. I admired the way he wore his jeans and the trendy tee under his navy and white embroidered shirt. I knew I was in trouble almost instantly. His tee pulled slightly across his strong, bulging chest; yet, the way he downplayed his muscular frame made him even more attractive. More than anything, it was the way he carried himself that drew me to him.

He was crushingly confident as he crossed the bar toward me.

His dark green eyes grazed the audience. Yes, every woman noticed his entrance. He had an audience. And then, he shot me that look. The second we made eye contact we knew we were here for each other. It took every ounce of decorum to keep from jumping in his arms and begging him to take me back to my house. That was the first time I had asked myself if I was enough for him.

He let a gentle smile escape as he moved toward me. Over the last few years I've seen that smile many times.

As he walked across the bar to me, he never broke his gaze. I was hoping our thoughts matched as well. I couldn't help watching the other women in the bar turn their heads as he walked past them. He was coming to me, I kept thinking. This gloriously, handsome man was here to see me.

I'm not sure how long that forty-foot walk seemed to him, but to me, it seemed as if he were walking in slow motion. I noticed each movement; I noticed each set of eyes – men and women - that followed him as he strode across the room. When he turned sideways to maneuver through a group of patrons, I noticed again how his strong chest bulged forward and then the curve of his bicep as his sleeve pulled against it. He was more than just a little bit attractive, I was definitely in trouble.

When he finally got to the empty seat I was saving for him, I rose nervously to greet him. My legs felt as though I had just finished a marathon, shaking as they held my weight.

"He's definitely not ugly," I thought proudly.

The next twenty minutes were a blur: I heard a drink ordered, he said something about our downtown, he had never been there before... "Have you been waiting long?" he asked.

I can't even remember my answer. I assumed it was "no," but at that moment, I couldn't even recall the current day of the week. "He's not ugly," I kept hearing in my head. Suddenly, GiGi sprang to mind. It was another moment reminding me that I might be in trouble.

My childhood friend, Vicki, had been like a sister growing up. Her grandmother, "GiGi" was this fabulous woman who wore Chanel and brought us to R-rated movies when we were twelve. She made it her purpose to teach us the way of the world. She was the first real business woman I had ever met, the Beauforts excluded. Gigi lived up to her nickname, she was fabulously elegant and fierce. I never saw her with a man but always imagined hundreds following her, begging for her attention. Gigi would regularly teach us about men.

"Only marry a man who loves you more than you love

him," she would preach.

Could this fine specimen ever love me more than I love him? Was this a recipe for disaster? Now, as I recall that moment, I should have listened to my instincts.

I hadn't even been looking for a man when we started talking. I was busy. I was a single mom with amazing friends, a growing business, an active social life, and a storm of shit brewing. I wasn't looking for more, but there he was, one of those eruptions of incredible joy I mentioned. From what I knew about him so far, he was everything I had hoped for at the worst possible time. Yes, I knew that fact on our first date, although fear would keep me from admitting it until much later. I was intimidated by the possibility of him.

As we sat talking, I knew I needed to snap out of this head game I was playing with myself, wondering if he'd like me. I had never been that girl. Of course, everyone wants to be liked, but I was never derailed if I didn't connect with someone. Why did it matter this time? I started telling myself that I was a catch. I was feeling good that night, and I needed to remember that.

I had started running again. Running does something amazing to your body, I always felt leaner and stronger when I was running regularly. I told myself that I looked fabulous. My friend, Lisa, and I had gone shopping together the weekend before when I bought the dress I was wearing. It was a warm honey silk simply strapped dress that reminded me of Katherine's golden hair and hugged my body perfectly. I had spent too much on the dress but knew I had to have it. It seemed to bring out the natural color in my tanned skin and blonde highlights. I could see Lisa's envy when I stepped out of the fitting room with it on. It was sexy, somehow in a conservative way.

The dress worked. Nine months and 1022 days later, here he is, at the kitchen counter complaining that I've cut bacon out of his diet.

The phone rang, interrupting my trip down memory lane.

Simon pretended to jump to get it but I knew better. I signaled him to stay put as I walked over to the phone.

"Yes... oh... he is... well, I'm not sure... it's been days... can you hold for one moment?" I was responding to the steady stream of questions from Dr. Agazzi. I had left an email on his portal while I practiced not moving in bed earlier this morning. I asked for Ambien for Simon. These restless nights were not good for him, or me. He was crankier, didn't feel well, and his work was suffering. Even this morning, he was already an hour late and didn't have the energy to get in the shower yet.

Simon hated when I mothered him, this I knew. I had wished I let the phone go to voicemail and retrieved the message after Simon left. Turns out, Ambien wasn't in the cards for Simon.

"Melatonin," Dr. Agazzi suggested.

I was never a drug pusher. Quite frankly, I have never been one to take medication for anything. This past year, however, I had learned there's a time for everything.

I put the phone to my chest and looked at Simon, "He wants to know if you'd be interested in talking to him about incremental mortgage insurance?" I smirked. Simon hated solicitors. Since we had moved into the house, he had been bombarded with phone calls, emails, and flyers of every shape and size. In the back of my mind, I wondered if he would call my bluff and take the call. I looked at God for forgiveness as I picked up the receiver and stated, "I'm sorry, you just missed him. He's in the shower. I'll have him call you if he has any questions."

"Next time let it go to voice mail," Simon scowled.

"No shit," I thought to myself.

After nine months and 1022 days of marriage, we were finally beginning to communicate. Too bad he had fucked it all up.

THE PURSUIT OF MORE HAPPINESS?

I was so happy, yet couldn't help thinking of what happiness meant. How is it measured? When should you stop looking for more and just appreciate what you have? I thought of Aunt Cecilia and her dissatisfaction. Happiness seems to be the dish du jour these days. The *Happiness Quotient, How To Be Happy, The Pursuit of Happiness, 10,001 Reasons To Be Happy...* All great advice for those struggling with happiness, I suppose. Last month, scientists reported a study showing that people who made a conscious effort to be happy were less happy than those who just do things that they enjoy. I wonder, is it that people who worry about happiness are simply less happy to start? Maybe those people who read all those books just came to the realization that if they just do what they want to do, they will be happy and therefore don't need to worry about being happy? Maybe, and I hope this is true with Katherine, that those who are truly happy are raised in an environment that appreciates life and all its gifts and therefore never feel obligated to seek happiness because they know they have it? Is this a gift from our parents or something we all must learn – hence the plethora of books on the subject? I believe my happiness evolved as I learned to appreciate what I had already been gifted. Watching my mother and sister struggle with Multiple Sclerosis – and now my mom and dad with cancer - has made me thankful for my own health. Is it natural for us to always want more?

The quest for happiness seems like sun dried tomatoes in Chicago. When I lived in Chicago, they were on every menu. You weren't a chef unless you had a signature entrée ablaze with sun-dried tomatoes. Today, replace "sun-dried tomatoes" with "quinoa" or "farro." Same thing. It's a trendy new dish that promises you happiness for forty-five dollars. Happiness shouldn't be a trend, but our current world tries to make it such. I have lived a happy life. Was bringing someone else into it going to change things? I wondered, was I adding unnecessary complication to my already complicated, but neat, and happy world?

All my theorizing could not dismiss the fact that this pretty happy woman was now, well, even happier. Simon and I had seen each other three times that week. We talked every day. Only three dates, and I was feeling like a giddy school girl. I might even say I was, happier. Who knew that was even possible?

Our first date was brilliant. We met at Treva, talked until we were late for dinner, had an amazing dinner, and then walked back to my car where I mouth-raped him.

We still giggle about this today. Our first date was everything I had hoped. We met for cocktails where our newly introduced appearances didn't slow our ability to engage in rich conversation. We had to rush down the block to make it to our impossible-to-get dinner reservation. Arugula was a quiet, quaint restaurant in town with five-star meals created out of their tiny kitchen and sidewalk herb garden. It was small and purposefully un-marketed with no bar which allowed them to avoid all the noise of the more populated haunts in town. After dinner, Simon walked me to my car. On the way, he asked if we could walk around the block a bit more. He "didn't know our little town," of course, "and wanted to see it." I knew he just wasn't ready to say goodbye. I felt it, too. We walked until we wished the city had more sidewalk. Eventually, it was time for me to go.

As my girlfriend Lisa always says, "leave them wanting more."

We got to my car. I had just received my special-order BMW 650i convertible, a turbo convertible that had a conservative but sexy, mom-feel to it. It said, "let me bring your kid to soccer practice with us, but after I drop them off, I'm going to burn the rubber off these wheels on the way to the country club." I allowed him to walk me to it. We stood at the rear bumper saying goodbye. It was one of those long, unspoken good-byes where you can tell no one really wants to say goodbye. It was the first time we had stopped talking. We had casually brushed each other "accidentally" while strolling through downtown but we hadn't touched yet. Besides the initial kiss on the cheek when we met at the bar hours earlier, we hadn't even as much as linked arms. As we teetered awkwardly saying goodbye, my body screamed for him to kiss me.

He and I stood eighteen inches from each other. I thanked him for a nice dinner and told him what a wonderful time I had. He seemed as though he wanted to lean in.

Kiss me. Damn it! Just– Kiss– Me.

I felt our bodies swaying. It was as if we were so busy trying to hold back, that our emotions were creating a magnetic field forcing us closer. I could feel his body pulling me toward him, like the earth to the sun. We were close. The heat of summer could be felt as sweat beaded between my breasts. His pull was so strong, yet Simon seemed to be moving in slow motion. His body was swaying toward me, he started to lean over my shoulder, I could now feel his breath on my face. We were getting closer and the anticipation of what was next was torturous. That's when I kissed him. I leaned forward and kissed him. Yes, right on the lips. Not anything crazy, but I definitely was the one who made the first move.

This event would become known as the Great Mouth Rape. Apparently, good girls don't kiss on the first date. This little-known fact had slipped my mind.

Even today, he tells unsuspecting friends about the mouth rape. It starts innocently.

"Oh, how did you two meet?"

We tell about Match.com and cancer bringing us together. The next story is Margo's abrupt pre-date exit, and then, BAM! Simon ends with the mouth rape. Everyone is screaming. It's one of those stories that never gets old because unsuspecting future friends will always ask the same thing.

"How did you two meet?"

At first, I described my feelings as lust. Lust for something new, for a distraction, for the touch of a man. I came up with every excuse I could to disqualify what I was feeling for Simon. After our evening at Jen and Trevor's house, I couldn't deny that it was more than that. Let me remind you, I'm forty-five at this point and have never been in love, at least not in love enough to sacrifice my future. This also means I have friends who have been with me a very, very long time. Jen and Trevor are two of those friends. They know me. Whoever showed up on their doorstep– as long as he was in my arm– they'd welcome. But, they had only seen me smitten once, years ago, in college. Now, they'd see me smitten again.

There is that thing that happens when you bring a new person into old territory. They either fit in or they don't. Jen and Trevor were always my test. Men either passed the test or they didn't. Something happens when someone is around people whom you're so comfortable with you could pass gas and they'd think it was cute enough to comment on. It's also that environment where conversations are so safe that you never know what the next one might be. You can say anything or ask anything in front of these friends without judgement. Once I even asked them about anal sex. I was dating someone who desperately wanted it, and I, well, it didn't seem like a path I ever wanted to go down. Jen, Trevor, Michael, Margo and Lisa were all there. They were honest and caring; some gave tips, some told about embarrassing moments, but no one judged. Of course, everyone laughed. I guess this was a surprising curiosity they didn't expect from me. These are friends. However, when you love someone– or think you do– the moment you bring them around someone else who can finish your sentences, or the conversation gets questionable, one of two things will happen. You either know this person is a keeper because he seems to befriend them so easily you think it was a setup or it's just uncomfortable, really, really, uncomfortable.

I hadn't brought anyone around for a long time. It was fun to monitor their expressions as I walked in with Simon.

We drove a half hour to their place. This is a good test. Does he complain? Does he ask about them? Is he getting nervous? Would he get mad because I let him pass the street that I have turned on at least once a week for the past ten years on the way to their house? That thirty minutes can be revealing. Test number one? Simon passed with flying colors!

Test number two. You introduce him to someone you love. You know, these are your protectors. Like the Sirrush Dragons guarding the Gate of Ishtar. The gate it guards protects the ancient city of Babylon and is aptly named for the Goddess of love, war, fertility and sex. The dragons were named after Marduk, the chief god of Babylon who was later associated with judgement and magic. Passing their ominous positioning is a small price to pay to enter one of the most splendid and powerful cities of the ancient world. I always imagine my friends as the silent dragons helping me see people through a different lens and guarding and protecting me. Stepping away from the lust and seeing my suitor navigate my guardians helps me see them with fresh eyes in a setting that is not blinded by my desires. Like the dragons, my guards stay silent and non-judgmental. It would only be my vision that would be changed. My lovely dragons protect my Babylon. Isn't that what love should really be? Splendid and powerful like Babylon was to King Nebuchadnezzar, its creator?

Simon sails through with flying colors. It turns out that Jen and Trevor were so excited that I might be bringing a date, they invited our entire crew. Friends I have had for over twenty-five years. This group was the family I made, not the one I was given. This was a lot of pressure and Simon passed. There would officially be a date number four.

I have a ten-date rule. I won't have sex with someone until the tenth date. It shows me they are serious about me, and more importantly, sex complicates things. No matter how independent I am, I am a woman. Being intimate means something more personal. So yes, I wear ugly underwear straight up until date ten, so I won't be tempted. The real person, not the guy on his best behavior, starts to shine through before then. Funny, no one has ever dumped me because of this rule. I have stopped seeing them, but something about the hard-to-get girl and potentially virtuous vixen intrigues them, I think. I may have not wanted to get married, but this rule has earned me many proposals.

On the way home from Jen and Trevor's, I realized this rule might be very difficult to keep. Simon walked me to the house and I offered him a cup of coffee before he drove home. Katherine was at a sleepover, so we were alone, and I was feeling emotion far more intense than mere lust. I wasn't sure I believed in love at first sight, but if there was a time, it was now. I was falling hard for this man. As we walked in the house, Popcorn greeted us anxiously at the front door. There was this excitement about your return that no other breed can rival. Goldens, especially Popcorn, would greet you like a volcano about to erupt. Her good manners were barely maintained, and she'd cry with a mixture of love and excitement while waiting for you to bend down and receive her hug. When you'd lower to your knees, she'd gently put a paw on each shoulder and nuzzle her nose into your neck with her tail flailing wildly. It was a ridiculous thing to witness, but when she hugs you, you could feel her body finally calm and you just know that her love for you is unconditional and pure. I think that's why we love our dogs. They deliver true, unconditional love from the day they're brought into our home to the day they leave it. It's like a mother's love, unwavering. Popcorn moved from me to Simon. I always thought her a good judge of character.

"I guess this is just another test you've passed with flying colors," I giggled. "If you have Popcorn's vote, you're definitely a keeper." Simon looked at me with a funny hint of relief, as if he had wanted to ask how it was going but now wouldn't need to.

I led Simon to the family room at the back of the house. The house was dark but the light streaming in through the French doors lit the way. I opened one of the doors and Popcorn dutifully marched to her assigned area. I stood in awe at the doorway watching her as the moon shone so brightly it was as if the sun hadn't set that day. I'll never forget how the yard glistened as the moonlight sparkled off the dewy grass and thick foliage that created my backyard oasis. It was hard to imagine we were only steps from our bustling downtown. Simon appeared behind me in the doorway, dangerously close. Looking out into the yard, the secret steps to the hidden hot tub beckoning beyond the granite outdoor countertop. The perfectly potted planters framed the brick patio with dewy blooms and the firepit and loveseat sat waiting for company. How I wanted him to stay. Would we make love in the hot tub, hidden precariously from view of the neighbors in my urban oasis? I could feel the heat of his body as he stood close behind me. We had only kissed at this point. Not the groping desperate kiss that preludes sex, but we shared intimate kisses that were respectful and loving. He would softly hold my face, tell me I was beautiful, and kiss my lips so slowly I could feel the creases in his lips fall one at a time on mine. His eyes would melt me as he would steadily hold my gaze, as he reached in for each thoughtful kiss. Minus our lips and occasionally linking arms, our bodies hadn't yet touched. It was all about the unspoken words and promise of what was to come. Tonight, as the moon lit up the back yard, I couldn't stop thinking about his kiss. How I wanted it, and how tonight, I wanted much more of him than his lips.

I was warm from the wine. I had had a bit more than usual and was feeling somewhat uninhibited. Forget that ten-date rule, I thought. We had spent more time talking in the past month than I had with any of my past lovers, even after a year. I would have him tonight, I decided. He passed the test. I wanted to be with this man.

I was thinking this when I felt his arms come around me from the back.

"I've got you" he said sexily.

"What ten-date rule?" I thought. Against my body, I felt the muscles I had only been admiring until now. His arms felt like giant tree limbs winding gracefully around me making me feel small and protected. They were strong, yet in gentle control. I was losing myself to him. His chest was muscular and wide against my back. I turned quickly in his arms. I wanted him. I surprised him with my turn. I could feel him wanting me now as well. His pants were growing. His urge was getting stronger. Mine was as well. My hands moved to his strong chest. I had been fantasizing about putting them there for days. It didn't disappoint. I moved my hands down his chest toward his pants. I wanted him to know I was ready for him. His hand slowly followed mine and stopped me.

"We have a ten-date rule," he reminded. Did I mention that to him? Why did I mention that to him? That is a stupid rule. He pulled my hand away from his bulging groin before I touched it. I was so close. I wanted him and could tell I wouldn't be disappointed.

"No, babe. Let's wait." I couldn't believe my ears. I felt like Popcorn silently begging for the last piece of filet. "I'm crazy about you. Let's not do this when you've been drinking." Ouch, I thought. Had I really drunk that much? He moved my arms to the sides of my body and gently kissed my forehead. "I'll call you tomorrow?"

I was speechless. Had anyone ever turned me down before? I wanted this man, and tonight, made me want him more.

A LOVE AFFAIR

I didn't know this feeling existed, but then again, had I ever allowed myself to be open to it before? I wondered if it was my vulnerability that had opened the door. Since I can remember, I was in control. That's how I had been raised. When my mother first started to get sick, I was just starting college. *Family is your fortress.* I rearranged my plans to attend Boston University and stayed close to home to take care of my mother and Zoe. I worked two jobs, went to school, paid for college, and helped my mother and Zoe financially. That's what Beaufort women do. As I climbed the ranks of corporate America, I was able to give more and do more. I had become my Aunt Audrey, keeping my family unit in check. I was the one my family came to. When family members lost their job or were hurting financially, they'd mysteriously find five hundred dollars in an envelope with their name on it from an anonymous donor or they would receive a call from a prospective employer. *That's what family does; that's what Beaufort women do.*

When I met Simon, I was balancing on a log in the middle of a river, desperately trying to keep my footing. The tides had shifted for me suddenly. On one side, there was love and happiness, comfort and joy, and new opportunities. On the other side of the log, there was death and illness and pain and a river full of things that were out of my control. Simon would say, "I got you" regularly. Did he really know what he was getting?

I'm not sure how he could because, at that moment, I didn't know that over the next two years the side of the river I was trying so hard to avoid would become even more violent and dangerous.

Simon's words, "I've got you," made me feel invincible. He was more than I expected and every day he became more important to me. We would continue to talk nightly as Katherine slept - I never got tired of talking to him. We could talk about anything. He helped me navigate my parents' care. As my parents got sicker, my sister, Zoe, seemed to become more and more fragile and angry. It was understandable. She and Mimi both struggle with MS. Watching our mother deteriorate would only stand as a foreshadowing of her own fate. Simon would listen through my pain and frustration. When I would spend my nights in the ICU wondering if my mother would survive the night, Simon drove an hour to meet me there and hold my hand. When Katherine's father returned from Chicago angry and drunk, Simon showed up to answer the door. As my life became more like a soap opera than the idyllic world I had painstakingly created, Simon never passed judgement.

He simply said, "I've got you."

I was vulnerable, and Simon made me feel safe.

I decided it was time for him to meet Katherine. She was about to leave for my cousin's lake house for three weeks, and Simon had been careful to mention that he hadn't ever seen kids in his future. This had changed, he was willing to accept mine, he told me. Before our tenth date, I decided I should know if there was a future for both Katherine and me in his world. Loving Katherine was non-negotiable. He could be the sun and the moon, but she would always be my universe. Even though he said he was prepared, you just never know if they're a good fit until you see them together with your child. Katherine was confident and precocious and rarely managed her filter. I had only been single for seven months at this point.

I wasn't sure if anyone could accurately predict her response. What would adding an unplanned ingredient do to our perfect family recipe?

I sat down with Katherine. I was a little nervous about bringing a man into her life and probably more nervous about how she would respond to this conversation. What would I do if she wasn't receptive? We had talked freely about her father and me not being a good fit, but this conversation might be a little too soon or bring out a response I hadn't expected. Kids can be funny little creatures and this nine-year-old was no different.

I had been dating since her father left, more for entertainment than for a relationship. I've always enjoyed dating and have rarely had expectations of something becoming serious. Once you're single, almost everyone you know has someone they want you to meet. Katherine, of course, didn't know this. It was this other life I lived while she was visiting my dad or spending time at a friend's house. When I told her about Simon, I was cautious. I told her we had been talking on the phone for quite a while and I had been on a couple dates with him. Of course, she asked what we did.

"Where did you go, Mommy?"

"Was the meal good?"

"Did he have good table manners?" I found her line of questions tickling.

"Well, Katherine, before I decide if I really like this man, I think I need your opinion," I said. Was I giving my nine-year-old too much power or was I playing her like a fiddle?

"OK, Mommy. I can do that. When should we go out with him?" I laughed at the Beaufort in her.

"Well, I have been telling him about your riding. He doesn't know much about being an equestrian and he'd love to learn. Would that be a good place?" Yes, I was playing her like a fiddle, I thought.

"Yes! Could he come to my show Saturday? Could he?" She was legitimately excited. The barn was her safe place. She had been riding for two years and her walls were already littered with ribbons. "Well, I'll see."

I couldn't wait to text Simon. "Saturday,seven a.m., wear jeans. Katherine wants you to see her horse show." I saw the three little dots on my screen signaling his response was coming. Was he as excited as I was?

"Really?" was his response.

"Yes, really!" I typed back.

Silence.

"Are you still there?" I typed, starting to get nervous. Was this really a good idea?

Finally, the three little dots returned.

"We need to talk. I want to hear what she said. I can't believe she wants me there."

He was nervous. All good. Nervous is good. It shows he cares.

"Don't worry, I've got you." I used his catch phrase. He responded with a smile emoji. Then three dots. "I miss you," flashed on my screen. I smiled and went back to Katherine.

I'm not sure Simon was accustomed to getting up so early. From Mystic, it was an hour and a half drive. He showed up promptly at seven. I saw a text telling me he had arrived, to which I responded, "We are by the entrance of the barn." I waited, my nerves rising faster than the sun. As I looked over the meadow toward the parking lot the morning fog still caressed the grass. I should have warned him not to wear those Italian boots I've seen him wear. There was no way they'd survive a day at the barn.

Just like in a movie, I saw him emerge from the blanket of mist. As he came into focus I could feel my nerves pulsing. I stood silent as he walked toward us. I watched as his silhouette came more into focus. I could tell by his walk that the super-confident Simon had a few nerves he was trying to slay this morning as well. His outfit was slightly overthought. He was wearing designer jeans and a sweater with a zipper at the neck. It was a cool morning and his signature tee popped above the zippered opening. He had those boots on. Damn he's sexy. Katherine was standing next to me, already mounted on her prized Pumba for her practice ride.

"Look whose here," I whispered up to her.

"Is that him?" she giggled back.

"Yep. That's him all right. I guess he made it in time for your practice ride." In his hand was a small bouquet of flowers.

"Do you think those are for me?" Katherine said nervously. "Oh Mom, that would be so embarrassing."

I giggled. In a few years it won't be, my love. Just you wait.

Simon walked up to us with that mischievous grin he loved to sport. I could tell he was nervous. He held out the flowers.

"Are those for me?" I asked as I batted my eyes. Hoping for Katherine's sake he'd say yes.

"They're for both of you," he bettered me.

"Hi Katherine, that's a beautiful horse you have." She was toast.

"This is Pumba," she boasted. I started leasing Pumba, a meticulously trained, fifteen hand, chestnut pony a year ago earlier. Once Katherine fell in love with riding, the idea of her falling off a horse was unbearable. They say that you're not a real rider until you've fallen eight times. That was eight times too many for me. Pumba and the best trainer was my version of controlling everything I could. Luckily for me, Katherine's love for Pumba made Romeo and Juliet seem like high school acquaintances.

"Well it's very nice to meet you Pumba." Simon said as if having an intellectual conversation with her pony.

"I don't think he understands you," Katherine giggled. More than her funny bone had just been tickled.

"Well, it's nice to meet you, too, Katherine." He raised his hand to shake hers and Pumba startled. You could tell he hadn't been around horses much.

"Oh no! I'm sorry." You could see his embarrassment. Katherine giggled more. At that, her trainer walked over to escort rider and pony inside.

Katherine looked back, "It's nice to meet you, Simon. I'll teach you about horses when I get back. I don't want you to get hurt." Shocked by her response, Simon laughed.

"Hopefully her mother will be as gentle."

The two of us spent the day together at her show, and Katherine popped over regularly, each time with a different friend, to introduce them to her "mother's new boyfriend." Each time Simon smiled wryly and looked over at me warmly. Amidst her stream of introductions, she went on to win four blue ribbons and two red. It would only be a couple years longer before the second-place ribbons would infuriate her and become her fuel to push harder. After almost eight hours at the barn, Simon seemed no less drawn to Katherine. Had I told him to expect to be there all day? He handled it graciously, but I'd later learn it was one of the least favorite of our activities we'd make him endure. We went back to the house and showered while Simon used the time to try to salvage his Italian handmade boots. Once off his best behavior, Simon would tell us how they still "to this day," reek of horse poop. We walked downtown for dinner, stopped at Ben & Jerry's on the way home, and then returned to the fire table in the backyard while Popcorn bounded around gleeful that we'd finally returned. As we sat around the fire, Katherine's head rested on my shoulder. Eyes half closed, Katherine looked at Simon and said, "OK, I like him. Now can I go to bed, Momma?"

Knowing that was what I needed to continue our affair. As I walked him to the door, Simon sang, "Date number nine was even better than the first eight."

Oh, the idea that the next time we met would be our tenth date was not lost on me. I had wanted him no less that day than I had wanted him every other date before. Our kissing had become closer. Feeling his body against mine was more regular. The anticipation of our next date was already in the air. What would we do?

TENTH AND GOAL

For our tenth date, Simon decided he would do the cooking. We chose a weekend when my dad offered to watch Katherine. Dad lived about forty-five minutes away where we had been visiting him every Tuesday. A Saturday was a treat for us all. He had always loved taking Katherine since the day she was born. When she was an infant, she'd fall asleep on his big round belly until my stepmother would pick her up many hours later and put her in bed. She called him "Pa." I never liked it but there was nothing that child could do that her Pa didn't adore. Nothing would make him happier than to take her overnight, even while he was battling this toxic demon. Katherine couldn't wait to "take care of him like a king." She was, and still is, the most caring being I know.

I dropped her off at Dad's. He was looking a little thinner these days. He had his legs folded up on the chair. Funny, I thought, his sister– who is very thin and quite petite– always sits the same way. They must have been sitting that way their entire lives, I thought. It's funny how important every little detail is to you when you know someone is dying. I guess in the absence of a belly, the seat now had room for his feet once again. My father may have been shrinking but his smile was as big as ever when Katherine walked into the room. She always had that effect on him.

"You don't have to worry about her being here. We'll have

a nice time. Susan will be here as well." I knew what he was really saying. Truth was, Katherine was a Beaufort. Fiercely independent at nine, she could cook, clean and take care of herself better than most adults. Regardless, I knew no matter what happened, my father, even on his death bed, would keep her safe.

"Well, why would I worry about that?" I tried to answer nonchalantly as I moved over to push Katherine out of my way, so I could get my kiss. Katherine had already launched across the room and was sitting on his frail lap barraging him with what they were going to do. "First, you can watch your car shows on TV while I make us chocolate chip cookies. Thennnn, I want to show you what I learned at camp. You do have some string, don't you?" My father, all smiles, leaned his head toward me and kissed me hello.

He smiled at Katherine and boldly announced, "Of course I have string. What kind of grandfather doesn't have string for the most wonderful girl in the world?" I sat on the couch and watched them. Katherine snuggled into his chest as he asked her all the things she was doing on "that horse of hers." Sitting in the corner I saw a small gift bag. Another new horse shirt, undoubtedly.

I smiled. Growing up, I earned a dollar from my father for every A on my report card. Straight A's would mean a shopping trip with dad for something extravagant. It always seemed to be batons. Batons with ribbons, batons with beautiful wooden cases, sparkling batons... It was never really about the batons. It was that special trip to the store with my dad, just the two of us. He always looked at you like he was the proudest father in the entire world and now, Katherine would be awarded that same loving gaze. I had shared with him about Katherine's show this past weekend. I'm sure she'd receive a dollar for every clean jump, and, seeing as they were all well-placed, something extra. Her weakness was anything with a horse on it. Her "Pa" adorned her in equines. She had shirts, statues, pictures, purses, blankets and pillowcases - all from her grandfather and all proudly displaying some horse. My favorite was a brass statue of a unicorn rearing proudly. My father had painstakingly removed the horn and filed it down to look like a horse. I couldn't imagine the time it took.

I made a mental note that I would need to talk to Katherine about sitting on his frail lap in the future and took a seat on the adjacent sofa.

I sat with my father and Katherine while Susan puttered in the kitchen. I'm sure she needed a break. I couldn't imagine how Susan was suffering. I'm sure she had seen more than my father would ever want her to share with us. The pain, blood, vomiting... I didn't want to imagine what else. I couldn't get enough of my father. I especially couldn't get enough of my father and Katherine together.

"Well you look ravishing, Rainey. Where are you off to tonight?" I blushed at the thought of giving him an honest answer. He chuckled. He knew I had started to see someone new. As I wondered if I really wanted to tell my father that I was going to Simon's house, the goddess of honesty herself popped up.

"Pa," she sang, "Mama's got a new boyfriend." Her voice lilted. "And I told her she could go on another date with him. I approve." My father's eyes lifted comically, he turned his head toward Katherine and puffed out his beard.

"You approve?" He didn't miss the comment.

"Yes, I'm teaching Simon all about horses. He's reeeeally nice. Kind of has a big nose. Maybe Mom could bring him to visit you next Tuesday when we come back?"

I choked on her words. My dad laughed jovially. I wasn't sure in the absence of his big belly that he could still be jovial. I guess he can.

"Sounds like a great idea, Katherine," my dad raised his eyebrows toward me this time.

"Rainey?"

I had been beat. "Sounds great, dad."

I stayed and chatted for another thirty minutes or so before I excused myself. I made plans to come back tomorrow and have lunch with them when I picked up Katherine. My dad, in all of his good fun, left me with a knowing smile.

"Feel free to bring Simon with you when you return."

At that, Katherine now looked at her grandfather sternly, "Pa. I said they were having a date TODAY, not tomorrow."

My father flashed me a knowing smile.

"Ohhhhh...." he apologized, "I must have forgotten."

I smiled all the way to the car. I love that man.

The ride to Simon's was fifty minutes from my dad's house. I decided that I had been in the car far too much today and I would stop at a rest area to freshen up before my final few miles. I thought about how funny that sounded and wondered if I'd still be so concerned how I looked (and smelled) when I walked in the room five years from now.

Simon has a well-appointed bachelor pad on the Mystic River. He is in the center of all the action and could see the yachts cruising to their final destinations from his dining room table. It was a breathtaking view. After seeing it, I understood why he posted it on his Match.com profile. I was looking forward to sitting at the table having coffee with him and staring at it in the morning.

I was surprised when I showed up that there was no smell of food. He did say he was cooking, didn't he? I clutched the bottle of wine I brought with me as he opened the door. He seemed sexier than he did last Saturday. The week between visits seemed like months. He was dressed casually. Jeans, a short sleeve button down, and barefoot. His hair looked as though he spent all day on the water. It was wavy and full and slightly damp.

"Hi beautiful." That voice. He opened the door and leaned against it, gazing at me dreamily. It was a funny thing for a man to do but it made me feel like a princess. I let his lips touch mine. There was a different energy between us. Expectant? Anticipatory? Anxious?

I smiled and entered the room. I handed him the wine and he looked at me embarrassingly. "I've changed our plans." Really? I thought he wanted tonight as much as I did. "Babe, I only know how to make a turkey panini," he confessed, "so I made reservations at my favorite restaurant. We can walk there." Relieved that no one was joining us, I exhaled and smiled.

"Perfect. Don't think you're getting off cheap tonight."

"I wouldn't dare." he smiled.

He excused himself to finish dressing. He had made our reservation early so we wouldn't be tempted to rush, I would later learn.

"No overnight bag?" he suddenly noticed.

"I didn't want to be presumptuous." That smile shot back at me.

We walked to The Oyster Club and the hostess was awaiting us eagerly. She knew him; she was waiting for us. Was this his usual routine I wondered?

"Sir, as requested." A polite waiter showed up with an ice bucket and a 2001 bottle of Le Montrachet Grand Cru Comtes Lafon.

"What?" I gasped. "I have dreamed of this bottle. How did you know?" This was an eleven-hundred-dollar bottle of wine. I'm sure I hadn't shared this with him. How could he afford this?

He lifted his glass and answered my unspoken question, "You're worth it. And tonight? It may be the first, but I know it won't be the last. I have loved having you and Katherine in my life these past two months, Rainey Beaufort." Well this was one hell of a way to make an impression.

I would later find out that Michael, my dearest friend and wine director, called in a favor for Simon. He arranged for the bottle at cost, but still. I loved that he went to all that effort for me. I love that he dropped the bottle off earlier in the day to be chilled. I loved that he went out of his way to make tonight special.

"To tonight." I sipped his opulent purchase. The grapes burst into my mouth. The grape was huge, rich, but remarkably tight. I tasted pear, no, apricot and jasmine. Oh, that signature Montrachet spice. What an amazing way to begin our tenth date.

I'm not sure why I didn't respond with similar adulation about him. I was in over my head and was not prepared for these emotions. Was this love? I'm usually so forthcoming with my emotion, too much so.

Simon ordered a piece of meat that covered his entire plate and juice ran from it as he slipped his knife through. A faux pas with Montrachet, but I still couldn't help thinking of how Popcorn would welcome a meat eater into our home. It had been years since she had juicy leftover steak. My sea bass was flaky and tasted as if the chef had stuck a rod off the back porch and caught it himself. The lighting was dim as the small candle on our table joined several others in a subtle light show across the aged, but polished, wood paneled room. The paned glass highlighted the charm of historic Mystic outside the windows. The streets were already alive with boaters and tourists and, most of all, romantics. It was an incredible evening in a quixotic alcove in a quintessential New England Seaport with all the trappings of romance. Despite the anticipation, we never ran out of things to say. Simon has this incredible way of looking at me that seems to peer past my skin and through to my soul. I could see his adulation in his eyes and it warmed me even more than the conversation. We shared an enormous molten lava cake and ordered cognac. This evening had an amazing start.

It was late summer, but the sun hadn't yet set. When we left the Oyster Club it was dusk, and the sky showcased a deep, purple hue mixed with bright orange. Simon grabbed my hand and led me away from his apartment. This was not the way I wanted to go. He led me through the small streets of Mystic to the drawbridge. He held me close as the cool breeze from the ocean whipped across the bridge. We sat on a bench by the river, closer than we had sat before. As the majestic hues of the sunset screamed for our attention, our eyes kept wandering away from the grand stage and toward each other. I could feel the warmth of his body. He had a big strong body, and when he held me in his arms, I felt safe. Who would make the first move? Who would start us back toward the apartment? I knew Simon had a plan, tonight had been well-orchestrated thus far. My breath was getting heavy. I could feel it. I was trying to control my breathing, so he couldn't hear me. It was ludicrous that I thought he might, but I could feel the energy inside me mounting. My body responded to him like it had no other. The sun completed its final bow and, as if reading my mind, he grabbed my hand and motioned, "Shall we?"

My legs shook as we walked back. I heard me telling myself which foot to thrust forward next. Why does this man make me so nervous, still? It's because you're in over your head, Rainey. You are in over your head.

We returned to his apartment. He held the door open for me and watched me as I walked past. I turned as soon as I cleared the door. He grabbed me. His grasp was firm and powerful. I melted in him as he kissed me passionately, "Follow me," he whispered. He grabbed my pinky and led me to his bedroom. I barely noticed him push a button as we walked in. Smooth, silky jazz filled the room. He had done this before. I didn't care. He was mine now.

Simon's hands ran over my dress as if he were straightening the fabric from my waist to my hips. We were standing next to his bed with our bodies so close we could feel the heat from our mouths. He moved his hands slowly to my bare shoulders and then around to my back, softly touching my skin as they moved. Both hands moved in symphony with each other. They moved under my shoulder blades, to my waist where they were as he pulled me closer to him, and down to my hips.

I could feel my body shutter as he moved around to my back side. He grabbed my buttocks toward him. I felt my pubic bone push against him and heard him moan slightly. I felt him dip his knees and gently move his groin upward and closer to me again. He liked that but I knew he wouldn't give into his urges more than this once. It was subtle, but I could feel his growing member through my dress. He wanted more but was holding himself back. He was in control. I don't think I was. I know I wasn't. I don't remember where my hands were. I just remember his arms sinking to my thighs. I wondered if his hand would find its way around my body, to my womanhood. I was longing for it to find its way there.

He moved his hands up the front of me. He carefully avoided my breasts and kept to the outside of each while his hands, grazing the weight of each breast as he passed, moved to my neck. His hands were too big for my neck. He grabbed my jaw and drew me near for a passionate kiss. This kiss was like no other I had experienced with him, it was rapturous and complete. His hands retreated to my shoulders. The spaghetti straps that held my sundress up easily slipped past my shoulders. The dress fell to my breasts where it clung in anticipation. He pulled himself back and adored what he saw. His eyes stayed on my body, his playful smile admiring the work he was masterfully executing. He gently took one finger and circled my right breast allowing the thin crepe dress to slide to the floor. His fingers rounded the bottom of my breast. He was delicate. He was tempered. I was erupting.

He finally grabbed both of my breasts and pushed them up to him. I couldn't suppress my moan. His head lowered to them as I stood there with only my lace thong to protect me. When his tongue touched the first nipple, I squirmed. His patience. His touch. I was in over my head. He devoured my breasts. He was becoming animalistic and I loved it. I couldn't push them to him enough. He grabbed me and pulled me up and around him. My legs circled his waist and my vagina was sweating in anticipation. I could feel his largeness near my opening. Like everything about him, he was a man. He pushed me to the bed and started kissing my neck. I stretched up in ecstasy. What was he doing to me?

I wanted him. I wanted him more than I had ever wanted anyone or anything. I needed him inside me. I was begging now. He went back to my breasts. Oh, how I loved how he suckled my breasts. He kissed my stomach. Every insecurity stepped away as he made me feel more beautiful with each kiss. His finger was on the hip of my panties. This was it.

I realized that, as he was devouring me, his clothes were still on. It was my turn. Before the panties. It was my turn. I tried to take control but he wouldn't give it.

"Soon enough" he whispered as he touched my mouth. I playfully tried to bite his finger. He made a noise as if admonishing my impatience. His finger pulled at the string on my hip. He slowly lowered one side barely an inch. His finger then rode the inside edge of my panties to the other side. It went so slowly across that I thought at any moment he would stop and move below them. He didn't, the teasing continued. The other side of my panties finally slipped below my hip. My pubic hair was creeping above my panty line. I wondered if he liked hair. Mine was neat, trimmed. I could never wax the entire area.

He grinned as the curls popped out. His finger grazed my hair as it went back to the other side of my pelvis. Lower. More hair. The other side. Again. My panties sat high on my thigh and my vagina was pulsing to be seen. He lifted my legs up gently and moved his head between my legs. I'm not sure how, but in one smooth move he had rid me of my panties and exposed my vagina. It was inches from his face. I could feel his breath on it. I felt his hand start behind my back and creep forward. His finger glided into my pussy. It was wet. It was so, so, wet. He started exploring. I felt as if he was inspecting every inch. His finger moved carefully around my lips as he studied my face. He kissed my belly as his finger found its way inside. I was on fire.

He pulled back and slowly stood. He was domineering standing over me. As he unbuttoned his shirt I could see the lines of his muscular build. That chest I had been longing to have for months was being exposed, one painful button at a time. We wasn't putting on a show, he was undressing himself while he pawed at me with his eyes. I was wondering what was next. The music filled the room. He wasn't wearing underwear and his physique was even better without clothes. I giggled in delight. Why was that so sexy?

After he undressed he lowered himself back to me. He pulled me up like a rag doll to the middle of the king bed and slowly entered me. I could feel him throbbing. He wanted me just as much as I him. We made love for hours. In between sex we'd roll in each other's arms feeling each other. I felt every muscle. I put my hands on every inch of his body. I couldn't count the orgasms. I fell asleep in his arms that night, ravaged. Complete.

There was something impenetrable about our relationship. It was as if we were going through all the hard stuff together first. My mom. My dad. Building a business.

Katherine suggested he stay over on the weekend instead of driving home one night. That was all it took. He'd start staying on the weekends and we'd pretend to sleep in separate rooms for Katherine's sake. I'm thankful for her being a heavy sleeper.

At three months, I was met at his apartment with an expensive hair dryer I had admired with a note attached.

'Happy Three Months. You blow me away. – Simon'

We were getting serious and both of us knew it. I wanted to be with him all the time.

Katherine and I were enjoying her favorite mom-made meal – Caesar salad and grilled sticky salmon. She'd gladly replace it with pizza or McDonald's, but sometimes she had to stick with healthy. This was our least healthy menu item so she always asked for it. As we finished dinner, the phone rang. I usually don't pick up the phone during my time with Katherine. Life can wait. I have always been like that, but now, with two parents with cancer, my time with people I love seems even more priceless. I glanced down to make sure it wasn't the hospital. Even my parents knew to text if it is an emergency. I knew it wasn't them. They knew I would only respond immediately in an emergency. When I'm with someone I love, the phone and texts can wait. It was Simon. Why was he calling? I was thrilled to hear his voice, but, hadn't I told him my rule. Maybe I hadn't. I know he's noticed me ignore the buzzing nuisance while I was with him. I went to silence the phone but couldn't, I was longing to hear his voice.

"Hi Simon." Katherine looked at me as if I had just stabbed Popcorn. Well I guess she remembered the rule.

"Is Katherine there, please?" His sultry voice surprised me with his question.

"Um. Why, of course." I looked at my disapproving daughter. "Katherine. It's for you." Katherine's face immediately lightened. Apparently, I could not break our no-phone rule, but she could. She bounded over to take the phone from my hand.

"Hello?" she started. She was animated. Her small body mimicked that of an adult. She moved into the living room with my phone and threw her legs over the arm of my favorite chair. "Yes, I did!" she squealed. "He was uh-MAZing." I was assuming she was talking about Pumba. She rambled on about her lesson earlier that evening and confirmed my suspicion. Simon had called an audible and she was putty in his hands. God, I thought, he has a way with women. Katherine and Simon spoke for almost twenty minutes. I had not seen her talk to anyone but my father for as long. As I watched her tell him all about her lesson and every horse in the barn in great detail, I imagined what he was doing on the other side of the phone. I'm sure he was pleased with himself.

"Here Mommy, Simon would like to say good-bye to you

before he hangs up." She handed me the phone and waltzed into the kitchen where we had just started to open one of Katherine's twenty versions of Monopoly.

"Well played, Mr. Bradley." I said as I raised the phone to my head. Simon Bradley, I thought. Rainey Beaufort Bradley, I thought in my head. It had a nice ring. I was shocked by where my brain had just led me. Or did my heart lead me there? These days, I didn't know what was leading me. He told me he would call at our regular time and apologized for interrupting our mom and daughter time. He did know. As I hung up, the words that I say so easily to close friends and family before disconnecting started from my mouth, "I l.." I stopped myself. I was embarrassed by how naturally it started from my lips. "I'll talk to you tonight."

It was then that I decided to plan a coup. I would be the first to say, "I love you." He had already given me a multiple of clues to how he felt about me. He'd say things like, "I love spending time with you," or "I love how you make me feel." Apparently, he would be in control until the very end. If someone had to go out on a limb and say those three monumental words first, it would have to be me.

I told him I had the night free and would drive down to his place. I picked up a picnic of finger foods; a small assortment of hard to find cheeses, crackers, bursting end-of-summer strawberries and various finger foods. I didn't want his appetite to keep me from my agenda. There was only one appetite I was interested in tonight and I could barely keep the smile off my face as I meandered around the market finding the perfect solution. I came up with a small lie, so I would have an excuse to be there when he got home. A meeting, nearby. He believed me and gave me the code for his door. I knew he had a four o'clock meeting so I could safely prepare for his arrival. The plan was in play.

I walked in and started to set the stage. I could smell him everywhere. I walked uncomfortably through his bachelor pad. A black leather sectional faced an oversized television. He had a pillow placed on the floor next to the couch. I imagined him lying on the couch, at night, watching Top Gun for the fourth time and missing me. I opened cabinets and found not much more than protein shakes and K-cups. The predictable bachelor's bottle of vodka sat in his freezer next to various flavors of half eaten Ben & Jerry's. His vice, I thought. I hadn't even thought of ice cream.

I wondered how many other women had been here before me as I really inspected his apartment for the first time. On previous visits I had only inspected him, I thought. I wonder if he had played that same slow jazz number for many others. Jealousy started to overcome me. I didn't know this emotion well. The last time I felt this was with Jaime, my first true love. But that was many years ago, too many years to count. I cried for days after Jaime and I split up, even though it was my idea. Stupid Beaufort genes, I would sob. I shook myself out of this trip down memory lane and smelled the pillow of the man with whom I was now, clearly in love. Unlike my love for Jaime, this was grown-up love, I thought.

It was time to get busy with my plan.

I would arrange the tartines and a few pretty finger sandwiches on the counter in the kitchen. Next to the bed, on one side, I placed the strawberries and whipped cream. Who knows, I thought slyly to myself. I splurged on a bottle of Cristal and put it on ice next to the bed on the other nightstand. I'd plan to be sipping it as he followed the sex jazz into the bedroom where he'd find me, almost naked in the middle of his simply made bed.

I slipped off my clothes and headed to the bathroom mirror. In red lipstick I wrote "I love you" backwards across my bare chest. I imagined him staring at my breasts as he read the words. I started to get aroused. This man aroused me. Sex had never been important to me but sex with Simon, started to consume my thoughts on a regular basis. He had awoken something in me.

I slipped my favorite silk robe carefully over the message and walked to the bedroom. I set the stage on his bed and placed myself in the perfect position in the center.

As expected, he joined me in the room thirty minutes later and my robe was opened in seconds. He stopped. I wasn't worried, I knew he loved me back. "I – love - you" he pointed as he read. He smiled. "I knew you'd be the first one to say it," I giggled. "I love you, too!"

Our lovemaking was tender and passionate that night.

This was a love affair. I loved him and I knew he loved me. I could see it in how he looked at me. He said it over and over.

It started Thanksgiving weekend. Katherine had just left for Chicago that morning and we spent the rest of the day naked and avoiding open windows and nosy neighbors. We laid spooning after a marathon day of lovemaking when he asked me to marry him for the first time.

His arms were firmly around me.

"When will you marry me?" He was casual.

"Well, would tomorrow suffice?" I joked.

"I'm serious. I've never met anyone like you. Marry me."

This conversation came every weekend following. I wasn't sure. I played it off casually each time.

"Tuesday?" "I can't, I have nothing to wear." "Someday, Simon." It had become his way of saying "I love you." I knew he was being sincere, but we had only just been dating for five months. My father was dying. My mother, an unlikely candidate to fight stage four cancer, was determined to beat it. My business was new but finding time to make a living was getting increasingly more difficult as my mother's needs grew. Marriage seemed, complicated.

I was sure I was completely mad about him, but I had a plan, right? I would be Aunt Pilar. That was my plan. This was not at all my plan.

THE BEAUFORT WOMEN

I missed being twelve and sitting around the table with these women. Today we were sitting around a different table. We sat in the hospital cafeteria with trays of uninteresting food in front of us. Audrey, Pilar, Cecilia, Zoe and I. My uncle was on his way. He promised to arrive before Mimi got out of surgery, but this didn't make anyone at the table very pleased. This would become just another way a man had let them down. I can hear them at Scrabble next month, "Didn't he know she had a thirty percent chance of dying on the table?" No one said those words sitting at the table in the cafeteria. They didn't have to, it was an ominous dark cloud blocking the sun today.

I loved my uncle. I knew his wife really controlled things. He grew up with controlling women, so he married one. It had to be that way. He could act tough and like the big brother, but these women right here? They were in charge whether he liked it or not.

"Your mother is amazing," Cecilia started. Please, please don't let this be a eulogy, I thought. Cecilia started sharing stories of how Mimi would always get her in trouble. How at thirteen she had bought her first pack of cigarettes and brought Cecilia into the woods to corrupt her at the tender age of nine. Katherine's age, I thought to myself. "Mimi never got caught. Your grandmother beat me with a spoon when we got home because of the smell of smoke in my hair. Your mother pleaded the fifth and smirked while Gammy punished me. I know she purposefully blew her smoke in my hair that day just to get even with me." I waited for the rest of the sentence as Cecilia got lost in her own memories.

"Cecilia, you deserved it." The eldest sister reminded.

Audrey continued, "Mimi is amazing. Even with everything she has gone through over the years, nothing stops her. And she's a handful, Rainey, I don't know how you do it. We all know how difficult she can be." I could tell Zoe was infuriated by my aunt's passive aggressive statement. Zoe sat right next to me, but Audrey ignored her as she looked in my eyes and applauded my efforts, not Zoe's. My mother had been in a wheelchair for the past eight years. She had a cane and walker before that, but the MS had made her wobbly. I finally convinced her a scooter was a better option – and faster. Faster was key for Mimi. Nothing could happen fast enough for her. For the past nine years since returning to Connecticut I tried to take on the physical burden of my mother as well as the financial burden.

Zoe shook off Audrey's dig and started telling the group about showing up to visit Mimi last week at her new apartment. I had arranged for her to move to an assisted living facility, closer to me, so she would be safe. She could no longer manage on her own and her disability had taken over much of her mobility. She now had a cute, handicap-accessible apartment with nurses on-call, steps away when needed. I was proud of it. I bought her all new furniture and helped her decorate it. It had taken close to a year of strategic conversations and help from her sisters to convince her of the decision. I'd hear from relatives and friends how Zoe was letting me handle everything because "Polly Perfect can do no wrong." I hated to indulge gossip so I never knew exactly whom Zoe was angry at. Was she angry because she couldn't financially help? Was she angry because my mother was constantly comparing her to me (a bad habit from our childhood that could never be undone? Did I in some way make her feel bad? I hoped it wasn't the latter, but regardless, it still hurt.

Zoe continued her story by telling us how she found her when she arrived. The sink was leaking in the bathroom and she was on the floor, her wheelchair to the side, with her plastic orange tool box next to her. She was trying to fix the leak, Zoe explained.

"The super said he'd be there *tomooorrow*," she added, imitating my mother. Everyone at that table knew tomorrow was always too late for Mimi.

"She must have been outraged!" Pilar added playfully.

"How the hell was she planning on getting back in her wheelchair?" Audrey chimed in.

"How on earth did she get down there! That could not have been pretty." Cecilia laughed.

Zoe continued, "She said she knew I was coming so I'd lift her back in. Later she confessed that she was going to pull the emergency string in the bathroom, so the staff would come and pick her up."

"You know her intention the entire time was to pull that string to make them pay for not jumping to attention and fixing that sink immediately. She's always been a princess like that!" Pilar added.

The table laughed and shook their heads. The chorus erupted, "Mimi."

"Should have known!"

"That's why we call her McGuyver."

"She'll never change."

"God, she's stubborn!"

"This is why she'll be all right."

The last comment quieted the women.

It was true. She always had some crazy plan to get what she wanted. They all did. They were different variations of the same woman: strong, determined, stubborn. The Irish and French heritage made them stubborn but persuasive. I watched the sisters convince themselves that Mimi was too focused on beating this cancer for anything to go wrong. I listened as the conversation moved dangerously close to the topic we were all avoiding. I looked over at Zoe to gauge her mood. She was still angry for not getting credit. Good, I can handle anger. Anger is easy, it's her fear and irrational behavior that I struggle to manage. Zoe was at the table with us all for the first time that I could recall. Zoe was four years younger than I, but we couldn't be more different. Most of her attributes were from my father. Thick dark, wavy hair and glowing brown eyes. Her frame was smaller than mine so when she'd lose weight she'd look half my size. Sadly, the only features she took from my mother was a little bit of crazy and Multiple Sclerosis. They shared the same disease and the same lunacy. I used to think, when Zoe was first diagnosed, that they had formed a secret club. They bonded over their disease. Over the years, the bond shifted to anger. My heart broke for her, but she could also be a royal pain in my ass. I was glad she was here, though. The past few years she had distanced herself from the family, but she was still a Beaufort.

I sat at the table watching my three aunts. How life had changed since I was twelve. They were still strong in spirit and determination, but now they were all grandparents, all except for Pilar, of course.

I looked at Pilar. The woman who was once a strong, fierce, entrepreneur had been replaced with a frailer version. Pilar had gone from my idol to someone I would often wonder, "Was she really as happy as she had claimed?" She would go on and on about whom she knew and who did what, but they weren't her stories. They used to be her stories, but they no longer were. Was she OK with observing others' lives? She was no longer jetting off to Paris at a moment's notice. Arthur, her "friend" with the private island and great adventures - and a wife - had passed away. She was alone in her perfect townhouse now.

She'd always over-indulge at family gatherings and when

I'd drive her home, would insist I stop on the way. She always seemed to need some wine for the house in case someone stopped by. I knew it was wine for her. I suspected she'd drink herself to sleep at night. Was she pining for Arthur, her unrequited love? She'd deny it if you asked. She was close to his wife and his family; they were her second family, she'd say. She told us she was happy, but that's what all Beaufort women do. A Beaufort woman would never trouble you with her burdens. So, was she? Was seeing this chink in her armor what had allowed me to explore a new definition of happily ever after with Simon?

Cecilia was the opposite. She would easily tell you how hard her life is. She was open about her daughter's pain killer addiction and her son-in-law's affairs. I'm not sure of either, by the way. She had this amazing little cape on the coast that she had taken a loan to restore. She complained of the loan and her job, but that little cape was adorable. She would sit on the front porch with friends drinking homemade wine and watching the boats come in. She had these amazing gardens in the back that delivered a bounty of ruby tomatoes and mature asparagus. She would can and dry and cook all year from that garden. She'd cook for her grandkids and her neighbors. I wondered why she thought her life was so horrible? I wish I could just knock some sense into her and help her realize how wonderful it was. Was this discontent because she used to have more? She had a thriving business in the eighties with an eight-bedroom home in Greenwich after Uncle Tony left. She was determined to show him she didn't need him, so she built a business and then built a bigger house than he had. I wish I could help her see how her stupid little job with annoying supervisors was still affording her a spectacular life. What was her real regret, I would wonder? Was it still Uncle Tony's betrayal? Love?

All these years later the sisters were still single. Audrey was no exception. She had retired from her job at Mastercard and was living a quiet life in a nice home in Stamford. She had three grandchildren whom she doted on endlessly and she was omnipresent in our family fiber. Audrey visited everyone and truly kept the family together. She doted on her daughter and spent half her time cooking and caring for her daughter's family. She had her weekly bridge club, her travel group, and her old work friends. She was busier than anyone I knew, too busy for any man she would meet. We had laughed about some dates she had gone on recently.

"They are so old!" she complained. Audrey was a chronological seventy-five but looked closer to being in her early sixties with the energy of a thirty-year-old.

"That's what keeps me young," she'd say. Even now, I laughed in amusement at the idea of a seventy-year-old man thinking he could keep up with her. That might kill her, trying to stop and relax, even if it were for love.

Surgery was expected to be at least six hours. Pilar suggested we might get a proper lunch at the restaurant down the street, but none of us felt comfortable leaving the hospital grounds. I'm not sure why. Her doctor had my number, I would be called when the surgery was over, ...or if there were a problem. Speaking for myself, I just wanted to be as close to her as possible. If I couldn't be in the operating room, I wanted to be outside of it.

Dr. Flanigan was top in his field. When Mimi decided she wanted to fight the cancer, the original team at Yale refused to perform the procedure. "It was too risky given her current health." The survival rate for esophageal cancer was nineteen percent for an otherwise healthy person. My mother not only had MS, but also a rare blood disease, and rheumatoid arthritis. Yale was right, she was not a good candidate. Dr. Flanigan was referred to me by her Yale oncologist. The day Dr. Flanigan met my mother, he immediately attached to her Beaufort strength and agreed to do the surgery.

"Mimi," he would say, "those other doctors turned you down because they didn't get to know you. I know you're a fighter, and if anyone has a chance of beating this, it's you." He'd later tell me that he had never met a woman so determined. Welcome to the Beaufort clan, Dr. Flanigan.

The procedure today, an esophagectomy, would remove the several inches of cancerous esophagus and the top of her stomach that was too aggressive for the past months of radiation and chemotherapy to resolve. Dr. Flanigan would then use healthy stomach tissue to rebuild her esophagus. My mother applauded when she learned her stomach would be permanently shrunk in the process. It was a sure way to lose that weight, and of course, her weight she believed was the source of her immobility. "I'll be walking again, soon," she boasted. This is when you wondered if years of medication were affecting her thinking or was she purposefully putting a positive spin on this for the family? One thing I knew about my mother: she refused to go down without a fight. Even if she was a little confused, as her power of attorney and appointed guardian, I couldn't take this opportunity away from her. She's been a fighter her entire life and now, at sixty-five, nothing was going to change that. Despite the potential outcome, I knew my mother. Fighting and proving people wrong was who she was. She and I had been alone in the pre-op room with the constant stream of doctors, interns, nurses and anesthesiologists. I had to answer questions about her medication, teeth, past surgeries and worse – her wishes if something went wrong. The last visit before they took her in to surgery was Dr. Flanigan.

"OK, Mimi, this is it. Are you ready to slay Goliath?" he asked. His words ricocheted through my brain. This is Goliath, I thought. This is Goliath and Mimi doesn't even have the manual dexterity to use a slingshot.

"Let's get him!" She reminded me of a freshman who was jumping on the football field for the first time with a turf filled with seniors and a stadium of peers and parents – it was excitement laced with fear she'd never show. Dr. Flanigan sat down humbly next to her hospital gurney.

He spoke quietly, "Mimi, I need to review these risks with you one more time. You know it's not too late to change your mind?"

"Why would I do that, honey?" She said this to him. She always called her doctors 'honey.'

"Mimi, you need to know, there's a small chance you may not come out of this surgery. There's also an equal chance you may come out suffering a fate worse than death." He looked down as if imagining the worst.

Then Mimi broke the silence, "But there's a ten percent chance my MS will be better."

"Yes. It has happened." He responded, trying not to give her hope but being practical.

He continued, "It's highly improbable, Mims." I loved how he was so comfortable with her.

"Well, I've beaten every odd my entire life. Let's get this going before I die of old age on this hospital bed!" she barked. There she was. The real Mimi. The hurry up and get me better, Mimi. It was the first time I had seen any semblance of fear since Zoe was hit by a car riding her bike and rushed to the hospital when she was seven. To the common eye, she wasn't showing it now, either.

"All right, Mims. Let's hurry up and get this shit out of you." We all laughed at him swearing. It was so grossly out of character, even he laughed at himself.

My uncle texted me when he arrived. I told him to meet us in the cafeteria.

I shared his text with the sisters. I wouldn't want them to say anything they'd regret as he walked in. You could never be too sure with this group. That was the one characteristic, I was glad, didn't carry to me. My father never spoke a harsh word – not even to us kids – not even when he really should have. He was gentle, and he found the good in everyone. This was not a Beaufort trait and nothing that came naturally to me, but something I've worked to emulate since I was in high school. Now, I found myself cringing when they would gossip ceaselessly. I wanted to honor my father with the right behavior. I must admit, I still enjoy listening from time to time, but I try never to encourage it.

Before my uncle arrived, I sat and watched these women. Zoe had jumped right back in. I'm not sure why she didn't enjoy family gatherings because once she was there, she was quick to let her wit and fabulous stories flow. My aunts kept rattling on and the stories of my mother got funnier and funnier. I knew the mood would change when my uncle arrived. He was so serious. He'd want a full breakdown of the events. I'd have to repeat every conversation with every doctor over again. He loved his sisters and I often thought my mother was his favorite. She was the broken wing in the family and it gave her brother purpose.

Little did I know how much today would change my life.

YOU'RE LIKE THE MOM

Two months later, Mimi lay angry and helpless in the hospital. The atrophy had taken away the rest of her mobility, and the pain would only be interrupted by seizures giving her periods of mental lapses that she wouldn't recall but would terrify the hospital staff. The cancer was gone, but she wasn't improving from the surgery. Any mobility she had prior to the surgery had abandoned her, along with her sense of humor. Worse yet, she had a permanent catheter and could no longer eat or drink. I had set up office on the window bench in her hospital room listening to her cry in pain day after day. I knew every nurse and aide by name, either because they didn't meet my standards of care or because I had gone to them asking what else we could do to relieve her suffering. In two months, Mimi had been in ICU four times. She was stable, but miserable.

"A fate worse than death," I could hear echoing in my head. Dr. Flanigan had warned her, he had warned us both. Having the ability to see things from a non-medical perspective and possessing some leadership talent– I became the hospital's squeaky wheel. I recruited friends and family in the medical field to ask questions and help me see the standard of care from another perspective. "The squeaky wheel" soon became the "quality control partner" as I was greeted daily by a stream of administrators working to fix everything from continuity of care to power of attorney processes and eliminating return visits through the ER. I became a fixture at Saint Francis and was thankful for the distraction.

Concurrently, Dad now had a hospital bed in his living room as his pancreatic cancer seemed to consume his entire body. He was getting smaller and smaller before our eyes. This man, whom I loved and trusted beyond all others, was leaving me. Beaufort women didn't trust any men, except for my father. Sadly, even their own brother didn't make the cut. Despite my parents' divorce many years earlier, Dad still showed up at parties and picnics and holidays. He was the only man the Beaufort women loved and trusted, and he was the only man they ever asked about. I didn't need my dad; he had raised independent women, but I wanted my dad. He kept things balanced. Even while fighting his own cancer, he helped me navigate my mom's care and Katherine's need for a strong father figure.

Simon and I had spent far too much of our time at the hospital, and far too much time sad.

I asked my dad what he thought of Simon after confessing my love to him. My father gently covered his hand over mine and said breathily, "He's quiet." I was surprised by his answer and immediately defended him.

"I think he's a little nervous around you; you've set the bar high for all men." If that was my father's answer, I wondered what he would have said if he knew him better. Could this be his "nice" answer because he didn't like him? The thought left my mind as quickly as it entered it. No, he would love Simon, he just needed to get to know him better. I hope he had time to do so.

I could see the pain in my father's eyes, but he never complained. My stepmother, Susan would tell us, even when they were together alone, even when she knew he was riddled in pain, not once would he complain. His nurses pulled me aside one evening and shared how they had begged my father to call when he needed something. They knew he was in pain, but he would wait until they were there to say, "Well, OK, maybe I will take a little more morphine." He would never put the nurses out or make them uncomfortable. Zoe and I would joke that our father was the only known man in history who had no enemies nor anyone who disliked him. Even my mother couldn't speak poorly of him. I think I was asking for my father's permission to accept Simon's proposals. What did he mean, "He was quiet?" It would nag me. The proposals kept coming, although my responses never changed. How could they? How could Simon expect me to think selfishly when my parents were in these life and death fights?

Simon had planned a weekend getaway for us in Vermont. As the date neared, my fear of leaving my parents would grow. Both of my parents were so fragile. How could I leave? Katherine and I were visiting both of my parents more regularly now and it was clear that my father didn't have much time left. This next visit would turn out to be the hardest.

When Katherine and I walked into the room today, my father looked over at us. I saw his lips tense. He was trying to smile. He didn't need to, his eyes said it all. I knew he was happy to see us. He looked so small in this big hospital bed. I couldn't help thinking how strange that seemed. My father was six foot two and had the biggest, softest, hands when he was well. When he'd hug you, you'd feel as though your body was dwarfed by his love and his protection. There was nowhere safer. He had not been considered 'fit' in many years, but he was a big imposing figure who was part teddy bear and part linebacker. Although never a drinker, he proudly carried a belly created not by beer but by the finest foods and in his lust for great restaurants. Now, he seemed to be vanishing before my eyes. I can't stop crying. I don't want to cry in front of him, but I love him so much. I knew my father well enough to know that the most painful part of his death would never be the unknown; it would be knowing that we would mourn his loss. I wanted to be strong, but the only one I really knew who could help me right now was lying in this huge bed struggling for air. I may be a Beaufort woman, but my father is my rock. He was always there for everyone, but for me especially. I'm sure everyone in his life felt similarly. Katherine watched me cry. She started to cry, too. I'm not sure if she understood why my tears flowed so much more today than yesterday, but I know her tears were also for fear of losing her "Pa," whatever that might mean to her at that moment. I knew by the look in his eyes, after his initial smile, that he was heartbroken that we were seeing him this way. In my heart, I knew what that meant. Susan ushered Katherine into the kitchen for cookies and milk. What had been my father's solution to life's challenges were now hers.

I sat down next to my father's bed and started to tell him funny stories about Katherine. The usual things you say when you're trying to avoid what you really want to talk about. He knew that. Of course, he knew that. I felt his hand move to my arm.

His weak limb tried to pull me closer. I knew what he wanted and leaned in obligingly yet reluctantly. I didn't want to hear what he would say next and instinctually knew so. It was getting harder to hear him. As he said the words "I love you," I cried. I knew what this was.

"I will always be with you. Right here." he whispered as he struggled to lift his hand up to my heart. I had been there every day now. I knew his time was close. His face was skeletal. His full, jovial, face was replaced with sunken cheeks, and his coloring was changing. It was getting darker, and the yellowish tint reminded us of the cancer attacking his organs. As I sat there, I silently begged for a miracle. My insides churned and ached.

"Dad." I couldn't form words. "Dad. I love you so much." I struggled to make the words. I kept repeating what Jesus said,

"Heaven is an eternal wedding feast." These were words I have clung to since my years in Catholic High, every time I feared death or consoled a friend.

I had to remember that. I kept chanting to myself my faith and my need to be selfless right now. It's an eternal wedding feast. Dad loves to eat. He loves a good party. He would be happy in Heaven. It's a better place. It's our reward for a life lived in faith. Heaven will be lucky to have him. Please God don't allow him to suffer any longer.

Rainey, you must let go. He won't go until you let him. The conversation in my head made me want to convulse.

"I know it's a better place Dad, but I don't want you to leave me." I couldn't control my words. I love this man so much. "Dad." His name trailed off. I was losing him. Although he was the one gasping for breath, I couldn't breathe. He looked up at me. I had never noticed his eyelids before. His eyes always twinkled. Today, his round eyes were half covered with dark lids. He looked so sad. He maneuvered his hand to mine again and tugged for me to come near.

"Go– Vermont." Did he just tell me to go to Vermont? He continued. I could barely make out his words now. He was gasping for energy to send the words my way. "I don't– " he muttered.

"Dad, you don't what?"

"Don't want– you– to see me die." He used his last breath. He was exhausted, but he forced the words out. Those were his last words to me. I couldn't believe what I was hearing.

"You want me to leave?" I was incredulous. Did my dying father just tell me to leave and go to Vermont with Simon?

"Dad, are you asking me to leave?" His frail hand was covered in age spots. I hadn't noticed these before. His skin was changing rapidly. I watched him use his strength to push his hand on mine again. He looked up at me and nodded slightly. His look was so full of love. He wanted to protect me from the tears I could no longer hold back. This was so typical of my father. His look told me it was okay to leave.

I walked into the kitchen, my eyes red and swollen. I knew the time was close and had been preparing Katherine. I thought of not bringing her, but I knew Katherine was too much like me. She needed to come with me. She needed to say her good-bye. Today would be the time to do that.

I knelt down, "Pa would like to go to Heaven now. Do you remember what I told you about Heaven?"

She nodded.

"I think it's time you said good-bye."

I had this conversation with Father Jon. Thank God for the church. "Let her see you cry." We talked about how I would handle this moment with Katherine, if it were to come. I had taught her not to let words go unspoken. We would never leave without kissing each other and saying good-bye. We would never leave each other without saying "I love you." When someone made you deliriously happy, you would tell him. This was her moment, I needed to allow her to have it. I understood what my father saw a few minutes ago. Now, I was watching my own daughter's pain.

"Children are more resilient than you think, Rainey." Father Jon always knew what to say.

Katherine bravely walked into the living room and made her way to the hospital bed. Dad's eyes were barely open, his eyelids were now covering more of his eyes. Katherine put her hand inside his still large, but very thin, hand. I had warned her that he probably wouldn't be able to speak.

"I love you, Pa." With that, tears streamed fast down her cheeks. I saw his hand tighten around hers. His eyes opened wider and looked at her. True love. The love screamed from his eyes. I could tell he was devastated that he was the reason for her tears.

"Pa. Mom said there's lots of food in Heaven and you'll be able to eat again when you're there. She said you'll be able to dance again, too. I bet they have lots of lobster and clams. All the lobster and clams you can eat, Pa. Don't be scared, Pa. You're going to have so much fun. Guess who will be there?

Your mom and dad! I bet you miss them. Uncle Jack will be there, too." She ran out of words. This angel. Was she talking herself into being okay with his fate, or him?

My father's eyes stared at his granddaughter. He was proud. He missed her already. He would look after her from Heaven. This, we all knew. Katherine threw her head on his chest. It was the same place her head had rested when he had his big belly that rocked her to sleep. My father closed his eyes. They stayed that way. I wasn't sure how much time had passed.

I walked up to the bedside and carefully lifted Katherine off my father. "I love you, Dad."

Katherine repeated, "I love you, Pa." We walked toward the door, never taking our eyes off each other.

LOVE AND SNOWFLAKES

Vermont was like a dream. Margo insisted that she take Katherine for the weekend, and I obeyed my father's dying request. I wasn't sure how I would enjoy my time with Simon knowing my father was home fading into the sunset. I watched my phone endlessly on the drive north.

Simon knew not to say much. He didn't demand anything of me. He asked for no conversation, no decisions, nothing. He was there for me, however I needed him to be. We drove in silence the first couple hours of the drive. Not even the music was playing. This is what I wanted. I'm not sure how Simon knew this, but I just wanted to be quiet. His hand crossed the seat and held mine for the entire trip.

As we got off the thruway, it started to snow. "So beautiful" I quieted.

"The innkeeper told me they are expecting over a foot of snow," he said as if he had planned that as well.

"It's so romantic," I whispered. I decided I could not mourn my father the entire weekend. First, he was still alive. Next, every word had been spoken. Lastly, he wanted me to be here. He wouldn't want me to spend the weekend mourning him. I decided I would make the best of it. I would put my steely resolve to the test this weekend.

Our GPS had us driving through the center of a typical small town. Exactly what you'd expect Vermont to offer. The white clapboard buildings still had their holiday décor even though it was closer to Valentine's Day than Christmas. We were instructed to take a right at the old mill. It tried to sit stoically on the corner of Main Street, yet tilted precariously, with its red clapboard siding charred by age, leaning slightly over the sidewalk below. Charming. Weston was a beautiful town just outside Ludlow, VT. We followed the small winding road for almost a mile when we saw a big white snow-covered farmhouse with a simple wooden sign in front. The sign matched the dark green shutters. "The Inn at Weston" it read in gold paint. "No vacancy." It was a scene out of *Holiday Inn,* and we were Bing Crosby and Marjorie Reynolds.

The Audi SUV slid into the parking lot. The snow was thick in the air and covered our shoes when we stepped from the car. We followed the signs to the lobby. The path had been shoveled not very long before, but the heavy snow still coated it with a thick inch of fresh fallen romance. As Simon held my hand for love and for safety, we stepped into the lobby of the Weston Inn. It was warm and welcoming with book-lined walls and lovely worn sofas and a sitting area surrounding the giant open hearth. The fire blazed with warmth and made the room smell, not of smoke, but of comfort and warm cookies. The caretaker's office was right off the lobby to the left. Simon stepped in the office, which was small and stacked with papers on every horizontal surface. He encouraged me to sit in the warmth of the fire, to which I willingly obliged. I had nearly forgotten the past two days as the charm overwhelmed me. The innkeepers were in their mid-sixties with soft, rounded edges. Nancy greeted me in front of the fire and brought me a tray of cookies and tea on a pretty platter. Norman Rockwell couldn't have painted a more predictable scene.

Jim and his wife Nancy were expecting us and were

pleased finally to meet Simon. This was my first inclination that more thought had gone into this weekend than I had known. I had been thankful my father had told me to go, and Simon was the perfect distraction. Our love had matured over the past months and Simon had a wonderful way of knowing when words were needed, when they weren't, and when a distraction was in order. He never robbed me of my emotions. He was kind and patient and present for my grief. It made me love him more.

We followed Jim to our room. We weaved down narrow, crooked hallways as he introduced us to the breakfast room and evening lounge. The halls smelled of warm burnt wood and warm cookies. I started to wonder if they were forever baking cookies or if I was missing hidden chocolate chip incense burners placed throughout the inn. Jim opened the door to our room and gave us a tour without moving his feet.

"The switch for the fireplace is right over thar, those shutters open so you can see it from the tub, the..." He rambled on, proud of his inn. In the corner he pointed out Simon's special order; Champagne and chocolate covered strawberries sat on a small antique table.

Simon smiled and thanked him. As Jim let himself out, he stopped to ask Simon what time he thought he'd like the sleigh ride tomorrow. I smiled. Simon beamed back at me. Was he planning to formally propose? This was all so romantic, it would be the perfect setting. I decided not to ask questions. It was crazy to think we'd get engaged after only six months of dating. I still wasn't sure marriage was even something I wanted. I would catch myself telling past suitors when they started bringing up the future, "I don't know many idiots and I also don't know many happily married couples. I'm not sure I was designed for marriage." Minus Jen and Trevor, I struggled to bring to mind many couples I knew with a marriage I'd want to emulate. Even they have had their challenges over the years. And Jen, she's had to make sacrifices for their love, and some of those sacrifices, I'm not sure, I would ever had been willing to make. I'd keep telling myself over the years that if the sacrifice is worth it to her, then it's none of my business. As I mentally talked myself out of marriage, Simon popped the Champagne.

The weekend was off to a perfect beginning, especially considering the circumstance. We ate strawberries and drank Champagne in the jetted tub while gazing at each other and noticing how the colors of the fire bounced off our skin. We'd make love tenderly that night and I'd sleep naked in his strong arms.

"I've got you," he'd say. How I loved those words. How I loved this man. Every hour or so I'd check my phone for service or messages, waiting for what was the inevitable to surface. Each time I'd look, the relief and sorrow would dance in my throat. I'd shake off my emotions and focus my energy back toward Simon and the moments alone we were sharing.

The next morning, we were greeted in the breakfast room by Nancy, with a tray full of homemade pastries. Simon devoured them. Jim had left Simon a message about the horse drawn carriage, where, I was sure he'd propose. We drove to the barn where we were to meet the sleigh master. I think Simon was a little surprised to see how commercial this all was. The parking lot was huge and already filled with out of state plates. The typical Vermont commodity, the General Store, highlighting maple syrup and candy sat center stage in the lot. A crooked open sign that hung by a rope attached to jingling bells got as much action as the departing sleigh bells from the team of horses pulling up for their next riders. There was a ticket window for horse-drawn carriages, and I could tell this was not something Simon had expected.

When we checked in, we were directed to a roped area with a crowd of people. The romantic horse-drawn carriage ride he planned would include twelve other people. I didn't mention my disappointment but feigned excitement, "I have always wanted to do this!"

"I know," said Simon, "I remember. I was thinking it would

be just the two of us."

"Next time." I smiled.

We would laugh later at dinner at the rowdy group who joined us on the ride. "I can't believe you drank Goldschlager out of that bottle with them, Rainey!"

"When in Rome," I defended myself.

Yes, there had always been a little bit of that free-spirited girl inside. I laugh too loud, can drink too much, and can make bad decisions as well as the next girl. A few years ago, after my friend Linda and I became closer than neighbors, she showed up at my house with a bottle of wine and a plaque that read, "Well-behaved women rarely make history." It was a quote from Harriet Beecher Stowe. I cherished it because I knew that I had made mistakes along the way and regularly beat myself up for them for years after. This gift came after I had made one of my biggest.

I guess it's better he learned that I'm not perfect now, I thought.

Before dinner, Simon has arranged for a nice bottle of wine and cheese and crackers to be brought to our room. The wine he had personally ordered, but we chuckled when he saw the Ritz Crackers and familiar block of Cracker Barrel cheese.

"I suppose these were meant to be paired with the Goldschlager?" he said with great comedic timing. I loved that he was not taking things too seriously. Everything around him was so perfect. He was perfectly groomed, his shoes stood neatly like soldiers in his closet, and every detail was painstakingly planned. This could have gone terribly wrong if he had not been so easy-going, especially considering his anal-retentive tendencies. It reminded me of how much I didn't really know about him yet.

That night we stopped by the evening lounge after dinner. It had a beautiful window, sixteen window panes wide and eight panes high. The massive wall of glass highlighted the rolling hills leading to a row of trees that welcomed the next mountain. The moonlight bounced off the freshly fallen snow while the glow of the fire flickered against the glass. The hearth was so big that you could fit entire tree trunks in there if it pleased you. There were no bartenders or patrons. We sat by the hearth and noticed a small handmade sign on the bar that read, "Help yourself." So, we did. When Simon returned to the table with our drinks, we relaxed in the warmth of the fire.

Jim and Nancy would soon join us, along with a couple other guests visiting from New York. Jim and Nancy had quickly grown fond of us after our short stay. When the New Yorkers left, Nancy went to the bar to retrieve her "special bottle" of wine she reserved for her favorite guests. As Nancy unveiled the Sutter Home Cabernet Sauvignon, Simon shot me a knowing but loving glance as I graciously accepted her offering. As they poured the wine for us, Nancy told us how she and Jim were both Justices of the Peace and could marry us.

Jim said he "knew we were meant to be."

Nancy told us how she and Jim could always tell the couples who would make it. They were quick to share how we were definitely that couple. They invited us back to get married at the inn. Good business, I thought.

The next day we woke early and went snowshoeing. I loved this about Simon. During our time together, we were active. We would hike all day, or walk, or go running. This day we would snowshoe. Our trip lasted a lot longer than expected as my Beaufort confidence and horrible sense of direction would get us lost. Although we survived, I may have left my pride in the woods. Being lost in the woods for a couple hours left us closer than we were when we went in.

It was sad to leave Weston. I knew it meant going back to reality. Dad struggling in his final days, Mom fighting to rise again. Somehow I was also trying to pay my bills as I built a new business and managed a very full plate. I wasn't the kind of person to complain or be overwhelmed, but I certainly was praying for strength on a regular basis these days. This weekend had been just what I needed. I felt rested, reenergized, and thankful… so, so thankful.

Simon said this was the weekend he knew he would marry me. I thought he had decided two months earlier. His weekly proposals had not been proposals? Caught up in the romance, I didn't stop to recognize our communication breakdown. I assumed this was a sign of his ego waging war with my polite dismissals of his proposals.

My father died two days after we returned.

When we returned, I couldn't obey his request to stay away any longer. I went to the hospice where he was now. I entered his room, but he wasn't there. His body was there but his spirit was gone. His breath was unsteady as I gently kissed him on his cheek and touched his hand. I looked for the crucifix his priest had given him when he gave him his Last Rites. It was nowhere. I asked Susan about it. She told me she hadn't seen it.

I'm not sure if I believed the importance of the crucifix, but his priest had told us when you enter the Kingdom of Heaven, the crucifix would open the gate and you'd be greeted by Jesus himself. I knew my father to be a good man. The gates, I knew, were already open for him. The priest had given Zoe, Susan and me a silver crucifix that day. Simon had purchased a silver chain for me, so I could wear it around my neck. I promptly removed mine and asked Susan for a safety pin. Susan always had things like that. I had yet to reach that pinnacle of mature motherhood. I pinned my crucifix to my father's hospital gown. I was taking no chances.

I knew my father wasn't in his body any longer. I don't know why I felt this way or how I knew this. I reached down and kissed him. I whispered in his ear, "I'm sorry I couldn't honor your request, Dad. I just had to see you one last time."

I left his brother and Susan in the room with him shortly

after. My father died that night while Susan slept in the recliner next to him.

The hospice nurse would tell me later that this was common for men of my father's generation. They always allow themselves to go when no one is looking. Women– we were completely different. We wanted everyone we loved nearby.

The next month was filled with services and managing my mother. Her delirium had risen to a new level and we would soon decide to move her into a permanent nursing facility. I was still showing up at the nursing home every day. While Katherine was at school, I continued to build whatever business I could from her room. I could no longer stand the smell of St. Francis Hospital and was thankful for a change of scenery. The gray walls had started to protrude past the balloons, childrens' drawings, and get-well cards that littered her room. She wasn't going to be able to care for herself again. She would probably never taste food again. I had just lost my father, and right now I wanted some semblance of a mother to be there. I looked at her now, she was as gone as my father. Sadness came over me. I knew I would be there for Zoe, but I wondered who would be there for me? It had always been my father, at least for the past thirty years.

Mimi was strong when we were younger. She took care of everything. She ruled with an iron fist and made me tough and independent along the way. She had remarried a couple years after the divorce to the love of her life. Jean had a dominant presence and was the life of every party. Unfortunately, the love of her life was also an alcoholic. His alcoholism grew and grew, and with his drinking, their fighting grew louder and more hurtful. They were married, but Jean lived in *her* house with *her* children and *her* rules. I often wondered if a man like Jean could live like that. She never let him pay the mortgage and never allowed him any control. Eventually she kicked him out. I'm sure it was for the sake of us girls, but it broke her heart. Mimi spent the next two years crying behind her closed door. That's when she stopped being my mother and started being my charge. Had love ruined her? Where was that woman I remember? Didn't she know Zoe still needed her? As she suffered in silence, it manifested in her business and her health. I was only fourteen when I started using my babysitting money to buy food and clothes for me and Zoe. Like everything else, this was our family secret. It wasn't to be shared outside our walls, not even with other family members. By sixteen, I had started working at Friendly's after school and after sports. I'd go to the ladies' room before my shift and take a bath with baby wipes and underarm deodorant. I worked straight through until midnight each night, doing homework in one of the booths when it slowed down. I'd drive home and get everything ready for the next day. I'd leave one hundred dollars a week for groceries in an envelope for my mother and set my alarm early, so I could be ready before I had to wake Zoe. I may have thought I needed her, but whether it was her broken heart or her disease, I realized much later that I became her parent when I was fourteen. Now, thirty years later, nothing had changed.

I stared at her IV that was hoisting a cocktail of Oxycodone and antibiotics to complement her Fentanyl patch. Her body was constantly fighting pain and infections, and the doctors were doing everything they could to make her comfortable. I had become an expert on her needs. I became her advocate, was on a first name basis with the nursing supervisors, chief of staff, and hospital president. Even though the infections subsided, her delirium continued. The day after our father died, Zoe and I went to her room to tell her together. We couldn't help crying as we told her that he had passed. She looked at us blankly and asked,

"When am I going to have Starbucks? I keep ordering Starbucks but the nurses won't bring it." She couldn't comprehend that her ex-husband and dear friend had died. It was painful. Simon told me she wasn't strong enough to hear it, so her brain was protecting her. I wish someone protected us.

Zoe and I had to tell her several times and relive the pain each time.

My mother and father divorced when I was seven but always remained friends. We'd have birthdays and holidays together. When my father was in a bad accident and couldn't walk up his stairs, he stayed with my mother. It was a strange relationship. Their bond started because of us kids but stayed trusted and true long after we were on our own. I knew when the news finally made its way to her brain, it wasn't going to be easy for her to accept.

Simon was there for me at every curve. I don't know how I would have managed without him. I don't say that lightly; I've never needed anyone. I've never let anyone pay a bill for me, I've never asked for help. If I couldn't do something, I would find a way to make it happen. I had come by that honestly, apparently. I am my mother's daughter, and until she became sick, she made her own way. Allowing Simon to be there for me was new. It felt good. I was falling more and more in love with him every day and so was Katherine.

Katherine, Simon, and I sat at dinner together, a couple weeks after my dad's funeral. When we were done, Simon reached for the check. I'm not sure why it hit her at this particular moment, but Katherine looked surprised. She put her small finger in the air and thought pensively for a moment, and then said to Simon, "Oh. I get it. You're like the mom."

Simon didn't know what to do with that information. I wasn't sure where she was going with this either. "What do you mean, Katherine?" Simon had perked up. Was she calling his masculinity into question? Of course, a man would think that, I thought.

I chuckled to myself.

"Well you are taking care of things, like a mom. You paid for dinner. You bought be a present today when we were at the store. You like to make sure everyone is okay. You're like the mom." Simon wasn't sure how to respond to Katherine's explanation.

I guess this is what I've taught her, I thought.

Simon explained that a man and a woman should both do all those things. Katherine listened, clearly impressed, but was sure he must be mistaken. This was not how her father acted. She would verify this information later with me, it turns out. When she did, I couldn't help being impressed– and concerned– about her Beaufort genes.

"It's nice to have you doing these nice things for us, Simon." I agreed with what Katherine articulated so well.

"Yes, thank you, Simon. We love having you in our life." Katherine repeated.

It's always funny when words I regularly say come from her lips. "We love having you in our life," was one of them.

"Well, Katherine, do you think it would be okay if I made it more permanent?" Simon asked. Katherine seemed puzzled by that question. Simon corrected himself. "Katherine, I wonder how you would feel if I asked your mother to marry me."

Katherine squealed with joy. "Really? Yes! Yes! Mom, can I be the flower girl?"

"Well Katherine, I'm not sure he has asked me yet."

At that, Simon reached across the table and took my hands, "Rainey Marie Beaufort, will you marry me?"

AN UNCONVENTIONAL WEDDING

Katherine helped us set the date. We would be married that spring. It seemed sudden, but we decided that we were older, more mature, and why should we wait? It would be close to nine months since our first date and we both knew what we wanted.

We went to New York to choose the perfect ring. There was no chance of Simon taking the chance on the wrong one. It was a two-carat emerald cut surrounded by a carat's worth of smaller diamonds. We picked out our bands, too. Mine was a simple diamond band that complemented my engagement ring, his was manly and platinum.

Simon was careful with his money. I knew he had grown up with nothing and was proud of the savings he had grown. Parting with it was a point of pain for him. He didn't need to tell me that, I just knew. I should have paid closer attention to that point, it would turn out.

I asked to be excused when he talked to the jeweler about money. I told him to make the ultimate decision and I would meet him across the street at Del Frisco's.

Del Frisco's was one of my favorite spots to people watch.

It is a five-star steakhouse with ten-thousand-dollar bottles of wine on its menu. The elegant, dark wood walls rise fifty feet above and reek of good taste and money. The bar was long in matching wood with brass shaded lamps every four seats, casting the perfect ambiance. You never knew whom you'd see at Del Frisco's, but I was forever entertained to see power brokers and tourists mix. Tourists could be whomever they chose on vacation, and Del Frisco's seemed always to inspire them to be someone else. Being there before 4:00PM would allow a great seat at the bar for prime people watching before the standing room only crowd ascended. I chose a seat at the bar next to two Midwesterners here on vacation. I could already see the looks on their faces as they took stock of the early crowd. I couldn't wait to start a conversation and learn more about them as I awaited my fiancé. I giggled at the thought. Who would I be if I could be anyone? I laughed at myself as my mind pondered the question.

I wouldn't be anyone but me right now.

When Simon arrived as I was learning about the Midwestern couple seated next to me. Being pretty good at reading people– I took them for school teachers, maybe– I learned about the inheritance that recently changed their lives. Apparently, they were the only heirs of their long-lost uncle. Turns out, he invented the wind turbine and had amassed a great fortune. They were celebrating his life by visiting his favorite city. When they'd leave, I'd double check my skills. I had asked them just enough questions to allow Google to decimate their story without ruining their fun. I allowed them to be whomever they chose with me and shared my true delight in their story. When Simon walked in, we were toasting Uncle Jim. Simon smiled, not surprised by my already talking to people but looking like a man at least twenty-five thousand dollars lighter. The color had washed from his face. Probably not a good time to let him look at the menu. I'd pick up tonight's dinner. I suddenly wanted to ask him if this is why he had never been married. Was it just too expensive? I laughed at myself. I had always taken care of myself so how much money he had in the bank wasn't something I was worried about. I thought he might need time to digest this all, so I turned to the bartender and asked him to bring over a Manhattan with extra cherries for Simon and a shrimp cocktail. Simon laughed at my cherry comment and snapped out of his shock.

"I take it that's the biggest check you've ever written?" I chided. I knew he had never owned a house, so this was probably close to the truth.

"You're worth every cent," he toasted and raised his Manhattan. "So, we have a lot of work to do before April," he continued.

"What if we elope?" I shocked him. I'm not sure he was ready for my response, but I couldn't help noticing his relief. My guess is he was thinking he had to write another big check and I just solved that problem.

Life had been filled with chaos lately; I didn't want to add more. My mom wouldn't be able to attend, my dad was gone, my business still needed me... I wanted to marry him, desperately, and I wanted to start our life together as soon as possible. I didn't want to see him pack up on Monday mornings and head back to Mystic each week. I wanted to wake up in the same bed each morning and allow Katherine and Popcorn to jump in it with us. It had taken me so long to push past my fear and admit this. April wasn't soon enough. Once I had made the decision, my mother's impatience came out in me.

He worried that I suggested an elopement because I didn't have time to plan the wedding of my dreams in less than two months.

"Was that really why? Are you worried you don't have enough time or money to do it right?" he'd challenge.

No, I had planned my friend Terri's wedding in one day from her kitchen table. She had just found out she was pregnant, so we pushed up her wedding so her old-fashioned family wouldn't notice her showing at the wedding. It was flawless. I can plan a dinner party for eight on my way home from work and a Parisian vacation on the way to the airport.

No, I'd explain, I just didn't want to add anything to my plate. Who knew what would happen with my mother. "Besides, let's not spend a lot of money before my company starts making a lot of money." Sold.

We decided Margo and her husband would be our witnesses. We trusted and loved them more than anyone and Katherine would be fine being left in their capable hands. We would take Jim and Nancy up on their offer and return to the Inn at Weston. It was decided– a simple elopement.

God, I loved this man. Why couldn't life have just stayed so simple?

Dear Diary,

I rule. I didn't get anything for Mom and Simon for their anniversary. Totally forgot. (That part was stupid.) I wrote them a note instead. My mom cried she was so happy, and Simon gave me a giant hug. He kept looking at me as if he didn't deserve me. It was Mom and Simon's second anniversary and I meant everything I said. I don't think Simon expects stuff like that from a kid. He's not as good at showing the love.

So much has changed in two years. I thought I'd hate moving to Mystic but now I love it. I get to ride still, but I also have three best friends. Mom lets me have sleepovers all the time and everyone loves coming here because of the beach. Sometimes we sneak out in the middle of the night to go sit on the beach and talk about boys.

I was happy my note made mom so happy. The last couple months have been hard on mom. I can't believe the house I grew up in is sinking into the ground. She's on the phone with lawyers all the time now. I heard her tell Margo she's lost everything. She can be so dramatic. Simon still works. We still have Simon to take care of us.

Besides, she's been working around the clock to build her new business. She always takes time for me when I get home from school and for Simon when he gets home. But then, nine o'clock and she's right back to work. I'm not sure she even sleeps anymore. I'm proud of her. I miss how much money she used to make but I know she's going to do it again. I hope so. It sucks being broke. Caroline has two horses and rides every day. Imagine how good I would be if I had my own horse? I need new riding pants. I better remind Mom. The dance is coming up, too. I need a dress for that. I hate dresses, but everyone is wearing one. I hope I get asked to the dance. We all decided we'd say "no" if any boys ask, but it would be cool to be asked anyway. Maybe the boys heard what our plan is and that's why no one's been asked. I'll have to ask Kiki about that.

Simon and Mom go for walks after dinner. I'm glad they love walking on the beach because that means I have the house to myself! I finally get to stay home without a babysitter. I know they're only at the beach, but it's nice they finally trust me. Their walks last forty-five minutes. Sometimes they last a little longer. That's forty-five minutes of freedom!!!

One day, when I'm married, I hope we love each other as much as Simon and Mom do.

Mom and Simon,

I cannot begin to describe how blessed I am to have amazing parents in my life. Seeing true love through you both makes my heart happy. As your daughter, I see perfection in both of you.
Happy Anniversary.

Love,
Katherine

BILLIONAIRES

Remember *Sliding Doors*? Gwyneth Paltrow misses the train in one scene and makes it in the next? One door opening created a completely different outcome that affected her entire life. Maybe that's what The Atlantic Club was, a sliding door. You can't go back in time, of course, but had I, maybe life would be different right now.

My consulting business was getting busier. It was comfortable, but boring. I knew the reality was that if we all did our jobs well, eventually our clients would leave us. This meant we'd also always have to be on the hunt for new clients. This constant hustle was nothing I ever enjoyed; I started the business to help business owners, not sell to them. I had watched my mother go from power broker to pauper. She made a lot of mistakes, and my years climbing the ladder in corporate America taught me business owners just don't have access to the same tools. I created a business where I could help people, but I constantly reminded myself that the constant selling was the cost I had to pay for that right.

A year into our marriage, the big idea landed in front of us. I say us, because even though it was my idea, it would take a huge risk and Simon would need to be a part of the decision-making process. I had an army of supporters, but going after this meant taking a financial risk. I was already concerned about money. There had been some permitting headaches with my house in Stepford. I had sold it a few times, but the buyers could never get financing because of the permits. I had to keep dumping money into it to fix problems I didn't even know existed. I knew we'd eventually get it sorted and I had a lot of equity after living there all those years– we'd just have to be patient. It would sort itself out eventually.

Simon agreed. One year, let's give it a shot. If at the end of summer next year, it wasn't earning money, I would start looking for a job. That was our plan. The upside was that if it did work, we could be billionaires.

It was stressful at first. When I shifted all my income from my first business to my second, and then hired someone to run the consulting firm, there was nothing left for me and Katherine. Simon would have to support us for the next year, and I reluctantly agreed to that. It would be the first time someone supported me in thirty years. Simon did OK and we wouldn't live lavishly, but we wouldn't starve. Katherine could still ride. Her deadbeat dad would have to start kicking in. He always said he would, but he never came through. I'd have to force the issue now.

It was exciting. We were doing this together. I knew it would be stressful for me, I have never fully depended on anyone in my life. I would have to check my pride and trust that when Simon said, "I've got you," he really meant it. I trusted him as much as I trusted my father. I believed that God had sent Simon to me to help carry me when my legs were too weak to walk. In return, I would give him the world.

The first time I had to ask him for money, I spent the morning crying. It was part of the deal, I know, but I had hoped it would never come to that. We were paying for a program to be built and I couldn't make the next installment. Simon held me. "We talked about this. It's OK. I expected to have to help." He was amazing.

Simon was getting a little stressed, too. Work was getting to him and living on a budget was nothing either of us was good at. We'd walk on the beach alone after dinner, so we could decompress and have quality time together. Katherine was thrilled to be home alone. During our walk, we'd dream about which house we'd buy when The Atlantic Club hit it big. Occasionally, Simon would bring up Katherine's dad, "Did he send you a check?"

"No." Simon's fury would seem directed at her deadbeat father.

Occasionally, he'd start to stress, and I'd ask, "Are you sure you want to do this?"

He'd always answer, "I can cover us through September. That was the plan. Let's make it work." He always told me the stress wasn't because of me.

I couldn't work any harder at this. I was barely sleeping. I had recruited a team of fourteen to help and they were amped up. We all believed it would be the next big thing. We worked around the clock. My first conference call was at five a.m. with India before everyone woke up. My team in California would rally at nine-thirty p.m. after Katherine went to bed. Simon knew I was killing myself. I had to. I knew watching his bank account dwindle was painful.

He'd say it, but always follow his words with, "Don't worry, I'll cover us through September."

That was the total extent of any stress in our relationship, so I thought.

Sunday's we'd go to the village after church and have breakfast. We'd walk through the historic Borough that seemed romantically frozen in time. We'd dream out loud of how we would live there eventually. Waterfront, of course. Would we live on Water St. for the sunsets or would we rather wake to the morning sun on the opposite shore? We'd hold hands through town and dream non-stop. Simon would tell me how beautiful I was and how much he loved me, and I would tell him how I've never felt this way before. We'd walk on the rocks of the jetty and sit right above where the waves would crash. We'd talk about buying a boat, vacations, our love for each other the entire morning, every Sunday morning, over and over.

During the week we'd walk Popcorn on the beach before he left for work and again after dinner. We'd always hold hands. It was as if we couldn't get close enough to each other. Popcorn would splash in Fisher's Island Sound every day of the year, she loved these daily walks just as much as we did. Some afternoons we'd meet at S & P Oyster for lunch. It's a beautiful restaurant in Mystic, right under the drawbridge. The outdoor patio is on the river and was a lush garden of potted plants and flowers. During lunch, his gaze never broke mine, even with all the beauty around us. Our love affair was flourishing and getting better every week. It was not at all what I had expected from a marriage; it was so much better. Then again, I was sure no one had ever loved each other as much as Simon and I.

Katherine was becoming a teenager quickly. Boys were starting to call, and she was becoming a handful. Normal stuff, as I understand it. We were united in our strategy. Simon was becoming more a father to her than her own, and she seemed to respect him more. She and Simon would study math and science together after dinner. She'd bat her eyes at him to get him to play a board game with her or for a trip to Seaview for ice cream. Our days and nights were magical.

Simon loved our house in Stonington. Mystic was a fire district, not an actual town. Mystic was half in Groton and half in Stonington. We lived on the Stonington side. When we had found it, it was going to be temporary until my house in Stepford sold. We'd then take the equity and put it toward a house in the Borough. Renting here would allow Katherine to start in the right middle school and stay there. That was our plan, at least. Simon loved Lord's Point. We had ocean views from our window and could sit in our back yard and watch fisherman and birds fight over the same fish. We could never find a house that was better than the one we were borrowing from our landlords, so we stayed there the first two and a half years of our marriage. We had made friends here, entertained, and started to build a life in this sleepy shore town. Now we were getting ready to move again. This one would be a big move, especially considering how much we enjoyed the water and how easily Katherine had adapted.

This past year, however much he loved Stonington, Simon had been miserable at work. He had been unable to sleep at night. He started playing spa music, and getting more and more massages to release the stress. He said his company undervalues him. He had been at his company since college, so he believed they still saw him as the smart-ass graduate who thought he knew everything. They didn't see him as the evolved scientist he had become. He was ready to lead a bigger team and the timing was right for him to be recruited. Some old college friends had been goading him to join their company since we met. He finally started to listen to them. Now, in two weeks, we would be packing up the house and moving to New Jersey.

I wasn't thrilled by the prospect of moving, but I'd follow this man anywhere. That I knew.

This summer we had a modicum of success with The Atlantic Club. It gave us hope. We took down the site at the end of summer to revamp it, but this meant, it would be time for me to get a job. I had promised Simon and I would stick to that.

I was invited back for my third interview for a local company when Simon called.

"I got the job in Summit, babe."

My heart sank. It was October. Katherine was a semester into her last year of middle school.

"When do you report?"

"November first."

I was speechless. I decided to wait until I talked to him that evening before I called my prospective new employer back and told them the news. Could I work for them out of the city, I wondered? Doubtfully. This was a prideful New England company and New York City was not New England. Crap. I lost a job I could have fun with and a waterfront house in one fell swoop. I wasn't in love with living in a small town, but the ocean made a difference. New Jersey was nowhere I had ever imagined living but I would make the most of it for Simon. I loved New York so an easy commute into the city might be fun.

I needed to make it work, however, for all of us. I needed to start with Katherine. This wasn't going to be easy. Katherine had fallen into her groove and was loving life. She had great friends, school was easy, and she was burning up the horse world. I was praying for Father Jon's words to be true, especially now. "Kids are resilient." I would do anything for Simon, but this was not just about me.

Katherine wasn't easy. As expected, it didn't go over well but she rose to the occasion quickly, considering. Over the next month I would get her excited about our adventure. We planned a house-hunting and horse-riding weekend in North Jersey. I wouldn't say it worked like a charm, but she was receptive, finally. The outpouring of love from her friends the next few weeks took my breath away. Still, she was in. She knew what this meant for our family, for Simon.

The next week I worked like a magician to organize the move. I had my mother in a nursing home to manage school, doctors, and of course, horses to organize. November first would be no small feat. I was proud of Simon. It would be easier to get a job in the city for me; there was much more opportunity there than in our sleepy town in Southeastern Connecticut. I polished up my resume with a new address and started sending it out. I was selling this move to both Katherine and myself, I realized. We would leave in two weeks. Movers were set. Hopefully, Simon would sleep better now.

I sat on the bed on day 837 staring at Simon. I only know now that it was day 837. His dark hair flopped across the pillow. It was longer than it had been. I loved how the slight wave in his hair made him look. I wanted to run my fingers through it. He hadn't been sleeping well for months so the last thing I would do is disturb him now. His eyelashes were all I could see of his eyes. I looked at his body, half covered with sheets, stretched across the bed. I would wait before I climbed in next to him. Right now, I would just look at him sleep.

I loved this man, I thought. I have never loved like this. For once in my life I have no doubt about my love. I didn't question if we would be together in twenty years. For the first time in my life, I knew that this human being was going to be with me for the rest of my life. I would never get bored. I would never be tempted to stray. What I would never expect was that I loved this man as much as I loved my own daughter. When I had Katherine, I didn't know a heart could love anyone as much. I had loved before, but not like that. This man. I love him that much. I stared at him as he slept. I had never imagined being this happy or this in love.

And then it happened. Everything changed.

DAY 838

I don't know why Vijay decided to tell me this tonight. I had been picking up dinner at the House of India for over a year. I'd go in, order dinner and wait in the dingy dining room. It was a particularly small restaurant with Bollywood movies always playing on the old television hoisted above the tables. The maroon table cloths were covered with glass tabletops and candles in bulbus glass cups that were never lit. It was one of those hole-in-the-wall places where locals go. If it fit twenty patrons that might be a lot.

"Best Indian food in this hemisphere" I'd tell tourists as they stumbled in the front door.

I knew Vijay got a kick out of me. Sometimes I'd bring Katherine in to wait with me, but often, it was just I. The House of India was my go-to joint when I didn't want to cook. They didn't have a liquor license, but Vijay always took my order and came back with a cold glass of chardonnay. I didn't have the heart to tell him that the wine was awful, I just sat and drank with him while my order was prepared. Despite the wine, Vijay was rather cosmopolitan for the sleepy town of Mystic, CT. His mother still cooked in the kitchen, but he spoke boarding school English and dressed like a New Yorker.

Tonight, I had just made my way to Mystic after a long day of talking to the Beaufort women about my move.

"What did that mean for Mimi?"

"You're moving again?"

"You're not going to move Mimi, are you?"

"I can't believe you're moving to New Jersey, of all places."

I told my mother about my move. She was oddly happy for us. She told me to congratulate Simon and seemed fine. Twenty minutes into my ride home my aunt called me telling me Mimi had fallen to pieces. I was looking forward to that bad glass of chardonnay tonight. Vijay obliged as I went to my regular table to wait for my carry out.

A new customer entered. "Table for two?" The place was empty, and I chuckled when Vijay asked if they had reservations. Vijay shot me a look, then bounced his eyebrows playfully. We all laughed, and Vijay told his new customer to order Chicken Tikka Masala. I laughed again, because that's all he ever suggested. "Everybody gets it. Trust me, you'll love it," he assured them, just as I've heard him say a hundred times before. I got the feeling they really didn't want tikka masala. One night I was counting takeout orders. Sixteen orders, forty-two meals, thirty-nine were chicken tikka masala. It dawned on me that this was not only his best dish, but a brilliant way to stay extremely profitable.

That night my order seemed to take a little longer than usual. As I finished the bad grape juice, Vijay quickly rushed over with the bottle to refill it. "No, thank you." I smiled. "Are you trying to get me drunk? What would my husband say when I stumbled in with cold tikka?"

"Leave him." Vijay replied. I choked. Something told me this was not random.

"I have a beautiful home downtown. It's too big for me. There's plenty of room for you and your daughter. I could be a good father, I could give her everything she needs. I'll give you everything you need."

I was tempted to scan the place for cameras but didn't. If I made a Candid Camera joke, I'm not sure he'd understand it anyway. Besides, he was almost kneeling. This was more of a proposal than Simon gave me.

I pointed to my ring, "Vijay, I'm married. You know this."

"Leave him." He was serious.

"I love him." I said somewhat defensively.

"I will make you happier. I am in love with you," as though his love was all that mattered. Had I led him on? I was nice to him, I enjoyed his company, but no, I didn't give him any reason to think more of it.

"I am happy. I'm so sorry, Vijay. I thought we were friends. I didn't mean to give you any other impression." The silence was painful. As if on cue, the woman who had just sat with her husband spoke up. I had caught them watching this unfold and was thankful for her sisterhood at that moment.

"Vijay, we're ready to order now," came her broken syllables. I think she was more uncomfortable than I. Of course, they both ordered chicken tikka masala.

At that moment I realized my food had been ready the entire time. He had held it behind the counter purposefully. "Vijay, thank you." I grabbed his hand. "You made me feel special tonight. I wish I weren't married because I'd take you up on your offer right now. Same time next week?" He bowed his head as I kept myself from bolting out the front door.

I couldn't wait to get home. Katherine was at a friend's house and I was ready for a night in front of the television watching bad movies and eating spicy Indian food straight from the container. I couldn't wait to share with Simon what just happened.

Our sleepy beach community was dark when I pulled in. A funny thing about October, once the New Yorkers pack up their summer homes, it feels like the neighborhood automatically darkens with the dim of porch lights and firepits. In December the winter lights come out, but October and November are unusually dark. You have this intense feeling of being alone.

As I drove over the bridge to Lord's Point, the tiny peninsula on the sea seemed even darker. Our house was on the far end of the peninsula – a nice treat in the summer as beach peepers creep up and down the main streets looking for views of the rocky shores. The most traffic we see on our street is golf carts carrying drunk weekly renters or our neighbors yielding raised glasses as they scoot past.

I pulled into our driveway and all the lights were off in the house. Not even the front porch light was lit. I grabbed dinner from the passenger seat and made my way into the house. Simon's car was there, but where was he?

"Simon?" I opened the door. Our golden retriever came bounding toward me. Always a good sign. "Happy dog, happy home" I thought. "Simon?"

"I'm in here."

Simon was sitting in the master suite looking out the window. The ocean was lapping the beach and the moonlight glistened on the cresting waves. He was oddly sitting straight up in bed, back up against the headboard, feet straight ahead. He was still wearing his work clothes.

"You're NOT going to believe what just happened to me!" I couldn't hold it in. "Come on! I've got dinner. I'm starved. I'll tell you while we eat." Simon didn't move. I wasn't sure what to do, wondering if he was sick. I kissed him on the forehead. "You OK?" I asked. A strangeness fell over me. Something was not right.

Simon finally spoke up, "I need to tell you something." Then, a long pause.

"Yeesss..?" I said.

"I had an affair."

I laughed. This was obviously a joke. Was he in on this with Vijay? We were blissfully happy. Last night I was watching him sleep, counting my blessings. How could this be happening? "I'm sorry, babe. I wish I could undo it. I love you so much." He kept babbling. I'm not sure I heard much of what he said next. "Something... blah, blah, blah... he was angry with me... thought I was lying to him... wanted to escape but then was trapped." My brain was in overload. Of course, this was a joke. We were so happy. I would know if we weren't happy. We never fought. Damn it! I am Rainey Beaufort. It took me forty-five years to get married, I've turned down six other proposals, this couldn't be happening to me. I'm Rainey Beaufort. I was frozen in shock. This can't be real. What will I do?

"Babe, I'm so sorry. Please don't leave me. Please forgive me." He pleaded.

"Is this real? This isn't real. Simon, tell me this is a joke." I was dizzy and the room, no the whole world was spinning.

"It was a mistake– " I could no longer see Simon's face as he spoke. He kept talking, my phone kept ringing, and ringing.

"What the hell! Who keeps calling?" I ranted. I looked down as if to momentarily escape this nightmare. It was Zoe. My sister and I didn't talk on a regular basis, but for some reason, she was blowing my phone up now. What horrible timing. I no longer know what room I'm in; I'm no longer in my own body. All I can hear is Simon giving bullshit excuses and that she's crazy. I look down at my phone.

Zoe texts, "Are you OK?"

What? I'm not sure what's going on. All I want to do is throw up. I'm walking in circles now. Am I in the bedroom? I walk out to the dining room and see the Indian food. I hit it. I'm not sure why, I just sent my fist flailing into the stack of aluminum dishes and crushed that beloved tikka marsala out of the containers and into the plastic bag containing it.

I had to leave. I couldn't breathe. Simon reached out trying to grab me, to hold me. FUCK THAT! I didn't want him to touch me. Just yesterday I was so happy. Just yesterday I was having a conversation with myself about never wondering about the future, because it included Simon. I gave up everything to be here and broke every rule I thought I had. I did something I swore I would never do, I trusted a man. I couldn't breathe. I needed to get out of there. I wasn't sure where I was going, I just knew I needed to leave.

I started to walk out and stopped. "Why did you tell me?"

"She told Zoe and Zoe told me I had to tell you before tonight or she would."

"My sister knows!?!" I screeched. I didn't know I could

screech.

"I'm sorry babe. I fucked up. I love you, please don't leave me. It was only a few times and the moment it happened I regretted it. She started threatening me right away. I didn't know how to fix it. I love you."

"She told Zoe?" I said it out loud to myself. My world was spiraling out of control.

"I'm sorry," Simon confirmed.

Zoe and I weren't particularly close. I had been the bane of her existence for most of our lives. I was the captain of teams, the leader of clubs, an A student, the teacher's favorite and she was Zoe. Beautiful, funny, slightly overweight Zoe. As Mom grew sicker and incapable of caring for herself, resentment started to grow about who would take care of her. I had been in Chicago when the reality of my mother's needs hit and transferred back east to take on the burden. I didn't say a word, just did it. Before I moved back to Connecticut to care for her, she lived next door to Zoe. But I know Zoe heard the passive aggressive wrath from the Beaufort clan. As Zoe tried to avoid someone who was becoming a demanding presence in her life, and a constant reminder of the disease of which she herself was stricken, my efforts to help seemed to be taken as a passive aggressive message to Zoe saying that she wasn't capable. It wasn't, but we were used to passive aggression, so it was easily assumed.

The Beaufort clan can be the most supportive, loving group of women. They have been there for both Zoe and me on numerous occasions. After I returned, the comments wouldn't improve. They would just add in how doting I was.

"Have you seen your mother lately, Zoe?" "I noticed Rainey was there every day this week. When are you going?"

That passive-aggressive thing done by so many families was not lost on mine and, unfortunately, Zoe bore the brunt of it. I always wondered if she thought I put the family up to it. In their own way, they were trying to help me by guilting Zoe into showing up more often. Regardless, our relationship was... tense. We loved each other dearly, but let's just say, Zoe finding out may have been worse news than the actual affair itself. I worried, who else already knew? The Beaufort family was faster at delivering news than any wi-fi network I've found. Simon not only devastated me, but also made me a laughing stock. Wasn't this year hard enough?

"Give me her number." I demanded of Simon.

"No. Why?" Simon was nervous.

"You have her number. Don't play fucking stupid. Give me her number. What is her name?" He'd never seen this version of me. At that moment, I didn't care if he liked it or not. I didn't even know who I was at that moment, or, what I would do when I had her number in my hand, but I was going to get it.

He texted me her contact information. The devastation took over my limbs. I could barely hold myself up. Our move to Stonington had left me an hour drive from my closest friends and I wasn't even sure I'd be able to keep myself on my feet long enough to get back to my car. Same feeling in my legs as the day we met, but a completely different reason why.

There were thirty steps between me and the car. I wasn't sure I could make it. What was happening? My perfect little life was crumbling before me. I have a twelve-year-old and am her sole supporter. We just told her we were moving, disrupting her life again, and moving to New Jersey. How could I do this to her? The night before, her friends in Mystic threw her a second going away party. What would I tell Katherine? She just told me last week that she saw Simon as more of a father to her than her own. She wrote that beautiful note on our anniversary. Damn it, Simon! We are still newlyweds!! Fuck You, Simon! Fuck you!!!! I needed to get away from him and could feel him behind me.

I kept chanting in my head, "Move your right leg. Now move your left leg. Right leg. Come on, Rainey. You can do it. Twenty more steps."

The car seems a mile away. I whipped open the door. I didn't know where I was going, I just needed to escape. I couldn't see Simon from the car. Was he still behind me? He didn't try to stop me from leaving. Or did he? I can't remember.

THREE WOMEN AND A WHORE

I drove out of the driveway and headed toward the highway. I called Margo.

"Hi, you've reached Margo. Please leave a message and I'll call you back as soon as I can."

I crumbled when I spoke to her machine, "Babe, it's me. I need you. Call me back." The caller ID will alert her to my call, I assured myself, because there was no way she understood what I just said.

I pulled over at Seaview, an iconic ice cream stand that sells soft serve ice cream and always has a line. They had closed for the season, so I had the parking lot to myself. I picked up my phone and opened my text messages. What was I doing? I slowly pushed the link Simon sent me and the phone started dialing. Portia. Her name is Portia No going back now. Her name is Portia, but who was I? The more control I lost, the less I recognized Rainey Beaufort.

"Portia. It's Rainey. I understand you've been having an affair with my husband." The line was silent. I could hear her breathing. "Well, apparently you wanted me to know so this is your opportunity to tell me."

Silence.

A couple seconds later I heard a voice, "I already told you."

I could feel her trying to gain her courage. It was clear that having to talk to me was not something she expected, but I didn't care. If this woman was evil enough to knowingly pursue and sleep with a married man– according to Simon's story– then she could have a conversation with his wife. Her nerves aside, the response itself surprised me.

"What are you talking about? I have no idea who you are." I stated angrily.

"I sent you a message on Facebook two days ago." She became righteous.

"What? What do you mean you sent a message on Facebook?" I demanded.

"I sent you a message telling you that I've been having an affair with your husband." She was getting her courage back. I must have given her the upper hand. Did she think this was a contest? My husband is home begging me to stay. The war she was waging was won, and it belonged to me, yet there's no victor in this war. I quickly registered what she just said and figured out that Jordan, my assistant, had probably received it. The only access she would have had was through a business account. It later turned out that Jordan did receive it. I had been getting weird message– now we presume they have all been from her– and he just dismissed it. The amazing thing about Jordan is I knew I didn't need to say anything to him. He would take this secret to his grave.

"My assistant must have received it. So, what did you want to say to me? I'm on the phone now, I'm all ears."

"You don't have an assistant. Simon told me you're a big fraud. You're taking all his money." Her words made no sense. Jordan had worked for me for almost two years. What did she mean I was taking all of Simon's money?

She continued, "You are ruining the Audi. He's only with you because of your daughter. That's why he chose you over the other girl he was dating when you met." I was overwhelmed. She had some particles of the truth. What had Simon told her? She continued, "I know your business is failing. You're a fraud." She kept finding more and more evil in each word. Then she spun out of control and it was like speaking to someone trying to mask a mental illness. They try to keep themselves composed and tell you what you want to hear, but then, the more comfortable they feel, they start to unravel. I was in such shock, trying to piece together the "why" from her words, that my silence must have given her the illusion that I was crumbling and seceding. Her banter became more illogical and crazier with each new sentence. This was not a healthy woman I was talking to. Frankly, this woman was bat shit crazy. What the fuck had Simon got us into? The most upsetting part? He did share things with her. A lot of things. I could hear pieces of the truth in what she said and was getting sick to my stomach. God, it hurt so bad right now. Was I driving? I didn't even know where I was. Oh, Seaview. I was in the parking lot. Thank God I wasn't still driving. Simon and I had decided to spin off my main company for a huge risk. We had a pretty kick ass season for a new company, but money begets money, and we were running out. This is true, but a fraud? I had stuck to my end of the bargain. I would get a job and continue to build the company in my spare time.

I decided to take back the conversation. "When did Simon first tell you he loved you?" I asked. Silence, again, finally. I couldn't bear the sound of her voice any longer. It was white trash dialect combined with self-righteousness.

I grabbed my dagger, "Simon told me that he couldn't get it up with you after the first time and kept making excuses."

I heard a silent gasp. "You should know, he has no problem getting it up for me, ever," I continued. She couldn't speak. I wondered who I was at this very moment. The words I was using were stooping to her level, and now my message had as well. Why did I choose to attack? I took a big risk. What if Simon had lied to me about that in his ramblings after confessing? If they were lies, silence would not have been her answer. She would defend his love for her and try to hurt me more. Every word that flowed from the phone's receiver for the past few minutes had been bathed in hate and vile. She was attacking me. Answering with her truth would have helped her fight back and hurt me more, but she couldn't. I had the truth. She was Simon's revenge.

As I asked more questions, easy ones she'd been dying to answer, the evil adulteress re-entered the conversation. I asked when it started. I asked when it ended. Her story and his were different yet the same. I decided they were both telling their truth. I truly didn't care about this woman. I knew all I wanted was the truth. I could no longer trust Simon and I needed to piece together the truth out of what was being told to me.

She told me her motives were pure. She didn't want me to move my daughter for a husband who was unworthy. Sadly, before she could end her sentence, she couldn't help casting every ounce of ammunition and vicious intent in my direction yet again. She was easy to discredit because she was clearly imbalanced. This wasn't an unhinged, broken heart. This woman had created her own reality. Amongst other things, she mentioned that she had to save him from me because I was casting evil on him. She mentioned she could tell after seeing my pictures online that I had an evil aura and she knew me better than I knew myself. My aura had come to her in her sleep, apparently. I didn't know it could do that. I couldn't help smirking at her lunacy. Lucky for Simon, I suppose.

I wish her words didn't hurt so much. Even though I could easily discount her as unstable and believe that Simon was in this *Fatal Attraction*/work situation that he couldn't break free from, her words hurt more than Sharon Stone's ice pick. The truth was, my business was struggling. I had everything but the money I needed to be successful, to do it the right way. On top of it all, eight months ago I found out my house of 13 years, one that I had faithfully paid the mortgage on for all those years and invested over a hundred and thirty thousand dollars in improvements, was sinking into the ground. My friend and real estate attorney told me to file bankruptcy. I was too proud and kept seeking a solution. Portia was quick to tell me my husband didn't believe me. She said I knew long before about the house and trapped him. I was stealing from him. I was spending all his money. I lied to him. He sought her for refuge.

Was she twisting it, or was he?

She knew too much about me. She knew Katherine's school. She befriended Zoe on Facebook, and she followed everything I did. Four years earlier, I left a Democratic fund-raiser for Senator Joe Courtney and slid on black ice. I thought I was fine to drive but hit a pole, backed up, and started to drive home. I was promptly thrown into the clink. In the spring, right after their affair started, someone took a web-page out in my name and posted the DUI. I always thought it was my competition or someone I had fired. Now I know. It's still up today.

She was creepy. It was weird to hear the interest she took in my life. She was standing on some moral high ground as she spoke, but who knowingly sleeps with a married man, stalks his wife, and then believes they are anything more than a piece of dirt?

Margo called back before I was done with Portia. It was my sign. Staying on the phone was only devastating me more. There was enough of the truth in her words and I realized my world – everything I knew – was a lie. When I switched over I couldn't even speak.

"Rainey?" "Rainey? Girl, are you there? I got your message. Rainey, it's Margo."

I whimpered. Still unable to make a word.

"Shit. Where are you?" Margo commanded, "I'm on my way."

Friends. I smiled a weak smile and softly said, "I'm here."

Margo continued, frantically, "I got your message. Are you

okay? I've never heard you like this. What's going on? How can I help?" She hadn't ever seen me like this. I was the calm one. I was the one in control. I was the eternal optimist.

I caught my breath.

"Simon cheated on me."

"What? No! He wouldn't." said Saint Marguerite d'Youville.

"He did," I stated.

"Come here right now. Where's Katherine? Do you want me to pick you up? You shouldn't be driving." I chuckled at her communication style. She was as upset as I was. She couldn't stop asking and answering questions.

"I can't believe this is happening to me, Margo." I started crying hysterically. I couldn't hold it in one more second. Even though she was sixty miles away, I finally had a safe place to let it all go. She listened as I sat on the side of the road and wailed. I couldn't stop myself. She was so patient with me.

"It's okay. Let it out. I'm getting in my car now." Margo had never had kids, but she'd be an amazing mom. Katherine and I always have the "whom would you go to" conversation if she couldn't come to me. Margo and her father's sister were always her go-to gals.

Zoe kept texting, "I just talked to Simon. I know what happened. Call me. I'm here."

"Don't come. I'm on my way there," I paused, "and Zoe knows, too!" I continued crying in Margo's ear. She knew what that meant. Over the years we had shared crazy family stories. She had been there when I first moved back to Connecticut and Zoe would show up at my dinner parties and disparage me all night to my guests. "Gotta love those younger siblings," she'd laugh.

Margo listened as I regurgitated everything that had transpired that night. After hearing all my pain, walking through all my plans to leave, and listening to me discredit the very whore whose voice was still echoing in my ear, Margo simply said, "I've never seen love like yours and Simon's. You'll get through this somehow."

That was the last thing on my mind.

Several years ago, my friend Melissa was struggling in her marriage. She had two kids; her daughter was Katherine's age at the time. She had found various evidence of her husband's betrayal and would endlessly ask me what she should do. "I found a bottle of massage oil under the seat of his car; do you think he's cheating on me?"

The problem was, Richard was an old friend. I had met Melissa through Richard. Richard, Michael (another friend) and I had been thicker than thieves for over thirty years. I knew what Richard was doing. The longer we knew each other, the closer I got to Melissa. One night, my conscience got the best of me. Melissa KNEW Richard was cheating. With the amount of evidence Melissa had, it wouldn't have mattered if the glove didn't fit, OJ would have been hanged. Worse yet, he was making her feel as though she was crazy, and her daughter was starting to act out. I confirmed her suspicions. One quick sentence changed our lives. They split up. They both hated me for confirming Melissa's suspicions, and then... they got back together.

I didn't understand this. Richard was a dog. I have known him for eons and he is a leopard with permanent spots. I knew it. We all knew it. But, they got back together.

This was a non-negotiable for me. Cheating wasn't something I could forgive. Although my role was to be supportive, I tried to hide my opinion. I was confident that she should run as fast as she could. So, when she asked, I told her. Melissa was weak. I love her, but she's weak. She's turning a blind eye to someone who is a dog.

Staying with Simon was not an option. He was also a dog.

As I was talking to Margo, I realized that during my pep talk to help me remember how to walk to the car, I had left my wallet at home. Katherine would be home at eight in the morning for a lacrosse game. I couldn't leave tonight. I had to go back to the house.

I headed home. I called Zoe once Margo had calmed me.

"Are you okay?" Zoe was charged. I know she wanted to be there for me, but wouldn't she know the last thing I'd want to do is jump on the phone and talk to her about it? Zoe was calling for herself.

"No." I said honestly.

"That bitch."

"That asshole," I added.

"I'm coming over and we'll move you and Katherine in here tonight." Zoe was flexing her Beaufort genes.

"That's not very realistic." I tried to stay calm, managing Zoe the best I could.

I proceeded to ask her how she found out. She told me about this woman and confirmed her craziness. She told me how she stalked her dog's Facebook page. Zoe opted for dogs instead of children. Her pocket pooch was the stuff stars were made. She created a Facebook page for him so her non-dog-loving friends wouldn't have to deal with a barrage of "baby pics" daily. Portia had been trying to befriend Zoe for months. Zoe innocently made her a friend on her dog page and the flood gates opened.

"I wanted to believe Simon, I love him. You and he make sense. But Rainey, this woman is a whack-job. She's a whack job with proof. We need to take her down." This is what I loved about Zoe.

We grew up in a comfortable, middle-class family. Some might even say upper-middle class for our community. But Zoe, she just defined her own style. "Take her down," "Whack-job," I'm not even sure I heard that word before. She always loved the Connecticut mafia boys and had a crush on Tony Soprano. Now seriously, James Gandolfino was an amazing actor, but what thirty-year-old woman has a crush on him? There was something about living on the edge that thrilled Zoe. I know her heart was genuinely breaking for me, but this kind of thing? She loved it. She was ready to take care of this crazy person and Simon for me. I wouldn't dare ask what she meant by that.

I listened to Zoe. She sent me copies of text messages between Portia and Simon. Sexual texts. Dirty, horrible, grotesque texts that I would be turned off reading if they were sent to me. As I received Zoe's feed, Portia decided to show me how she was adored by my husband with more of the same. I blocked her after receiving the following feed:

Simon: I'm on the way over to give it to you in the ass.

Portia: We have a connection that can't be denied.

Simon: I'm on the way over to connect with that ass all right.

Portia: I'm waiting. Are you excited to see me?

Simon: I'm excited to tap that ass.

My inbox was filled with an unending supply of lewd texts between the two lovers. Sadly, the more you read, the more you realized she was infatuated and had no self-esteem. He was a fucked up married guy pissed at his wife but never, ever, gave her what she was asking for in return emotionally. It was strange she didn't see that. She was so eager to send me these messages, but did she know how pitiful she sounded? I couldn't imagine Simon even saying those words to me.

I was furious for so many reasons.

But what I didn't know was that things would soon get worse.

I drove home. I don't remember what was said. I just cried. I wept hysterically in a ball on the bed and wondered how I was ever going to face the world the next day. Simon was there, trying to console me. I told him to leave me alone. He fought it but eventually knew he had to go in the other room.

Eight in the morning would come soon. How would I put on a human face for Katherine the next morning? As I started to ponder my strategy, I gained my strength and stood up.

The Indian food sat in an orange heap inside the white

plastic bag on the dining room table, exactly as I had left it. I was angry that Simon didn't clean it up. I was angry Simon didn't follow me. I was angry at the way his hair was parted. I couldn't see anything but anger, betrayal, and pain. I was mostly angry at me.

I walked into the kitchen, grabbed a fork, walked into the dining room, grabbed the mess of a bag and carried it carelessly into the living room. 'Under The Tuscan Sun' was on. Ironic. I pulled back the edges of the bag and grabbed the round, cardboard cover that sat atop the mess of thick yogurt sauce and chicken. I carelessly moved it to the glass coffee table. I started eating tikka masala straight from the shopping bag while watching Diane Lane be obliterated by her cheating husband. Maybe Katherine and I should move to Tuscany?

What do I do next? *What the hell will I do next?*

Into each life some rain must fall
But too much is falling in mine
Into each heart some tears must fall
But some day the sun will shine
Some folks can lose the blues in their hearts
But when I think of you another shower starts
Into each life some rain must fall
But too much is falling in mine

Ella Fitzgerald

I SHOULD HAVE KNOWN

I'm not sure exactly how the next few days went. They are still blurred by a river of tears. Simon didn't go to work the next day, and I'm not sure he went the second day either. I couldn't look at him. The minute Katherine left for school, I'd start crying and wouldn't stop until two-thirty p.m., when I knew I'd have to compose myself again for her return. I kept Googling things like "Why does a loving husband cheat?" and "Fast divorces." It was as if I was hoping the answer to my problem were going to come to me through Mother Google. I forwarded Simon a copy of an article written by a psychologist that encouraged him to answer every question truthfully, no matter what he perceived the consequence to be. It claimed this to be the only way to move past the breach and save our relationship according to the tabloid psychologist. I needed answers, so I leveraged his current motive to get what I needed. I'm not sure when I started asking the questions that would continue to turn my stomach a year later, but I knew I wanted the truth. What did she have that I did not?

Margo and Zoe called several times to check in. I would just text back, "I'm okay. Just spending time alone thinking right now." For Zoe I added, "Please don't tell anyone."

I pulled up Portia's Facebook account. She was overweight and frumpy. She was hideous looking, lonely looking, lots of cats. She was even worse than I imagined. Her posts were visible to everyone as she droned on with quotes convincing herself that she was righteous. Her conversation made more sense after I tortured myself with her profile. You can always tell a person is damaged from her Facebook posts. If someone is posting about being strong and getting through something, she needs to be strong to get through something. Portia's Facebook page was a continuous stream of confidence affirmations, how to treat people who do you wrong, how she sees things others don't, and how you're not alone in this world. It was pitiful and sad. It said she was insecure, delusional, and lonely.

"You reap what you sow in this life, Portia," was all I could think.

Couldn't she had been gorgeous? That would have been easier. Instead, he chose a broken individual– a sad, lonely, broken, and vile individual. And then he fucked it.

Simon told me, "I wanted to hurt you. It didn't matter whom it was with. You were taking something away from me and I wanted to hurt you. Do you think normal people sleep with married men?"

This is what he's going to say? He intentionally had an affair because he knew it was my non-negotiable and he wanted a divorce? But he didn't. He was begging me to stay.

"I can't believe what you're saying. I caused this?" my fury rose.

"You weren't listening to me. I tried to tell you." He responded.

"What did you try to tell me, Simon?"

"On our walks, I told you I was stressed about money. My bank account was diminishing; you didn't care."

"I didn't care? How many times did I ask you if I should get a job sooner? How many times did you tell me we had until September?" My mind tried to make sense of what he was saying. Did he tell me this? I can't remember one bad walk. There was never a fight, always hand-holding, and always loving words. He always left me feeling as though I was the most loved woman on earth. He always reassured me. How did I not hear what he was saying?

"I didn't want to let you down." He answered my question for me.

"Well, how did that work out?" Rage flew out of me. I didn't understand this emotion.

Then he continued with a different approach. It was "his flight or fight response." We were burning through his savings too quickly and he thought if he couldn't save us he had to save himself. I was going to bring us all down. As he rambled, his truth came out.

He thought I lied about my house.

"How could you be so successful and not know your house was sinking into the ground?" He thought I was deliberately using him to support me and my daughter. I reminded him that he had lived there after we got married.

"Did you know the house was sinking?" I reminded him of how he watched me pour money into it, getting things fixed as they surfaced– a bad electrical panel, a missing vent. Why would I pour money into a house that was not going to pay me back? It took a foundation contractor to come with lasers and tell us what was wrong. It took them ripping up the ground curtains to see the footings.

"How could I have known that?" He told me he knew that now, but it was the straw that broke the camel's back. It was what made him show up at her house at lunch. After the first time, it was too late to pull back.

I was repulsed. She worked with him. She was a secretary in another department and started talking to him at the gym. Their lunchtime bitch sessions about me opened the door for her.

I hated him right now. I really hated him. I kept thinking about my watching him sleep on Day 837. I was so in love. It's amazing how fast that emotion can pivot.

You never know how you're going to respond when things happen.

Simon was crying as hard as I was. I didn't expect that. He was calm the first night, the next two days he cried. I stayed in bed all day until I had to put on a face for Katherine. He would be next to me crying, begging for forgiveness, and telling me how he would make this up to me. He constantly asked what he could do. Other times I would kick him out of the room not able to bear the sight of him. He truly disgusted me. When he went to change in front of me for the first time after learning of the affair, I noticed every piece of fat, his ugly feet and his imperfect posture. I was disgusted by his body and far more disgusted that I shared it with another woman. Suddenly, I couldn't even imagine how I was once attracted to him. I would hear him crying in the next room. It was strange to see a man cry. Was he crying because he can tell I now find him grotesque? I didn't care.

Time was running out. I needed to make a decision. We had to be out of this house in two weeks, the new residents would be moving in. The third morning, while Simon was leaving for work, I told him that Katherine and I would be leaving. His hand grasped the front door knob, not expecting me to follow. Our normal ritual included my hands straightening his collar and then touching his freshly shaven face while I professed my love and wished him a good day. He'd return the affection and say, "I'm going to miss you, today." As he walked down the front walk, he'd glance back at me when he got to the end, smile and mouth "I love you." Today, I walked him to the door with a different agenda.

"We will move to Audrey's house. I need you to have the movers pack our things separately. Mine will go into storage in Stamford."

His face dropped. "I want you to come with me. We can start over. I'll make it up to you." he pleaded. I turned and walked back into the house, not responding to his appeal. I felt him stand frozen for a minute, watching me walk away, before resigning to leave. I watched, out of his sight, as he took the last step on the walkway. His disappointment broadcasted in his expression as he looked back as he did 837 times before. This time, I wasn't there.

He got home that night and he had a ten-thousand-dollar cashier check in his hand. I'll get you more later. I know you don't have anything. The minute I said I was leaving, he went to get me a check??? My emotions ricocheted furiously between my heart and my brain.

I didn't know how I was going to share this with my family. Once I did, there was no going back. Beauforts don't forget. Uncle Tony is still a horrible person thirty years later. They still hold a grudge about something their own brother did to them forty years ago. I wondered if Zoe already spilled the beans?

A bigger problem was Katherine. She loved Simon so dearly. They had become closer than I would have expected over the past three years. They would sit and watch *Friends* reruns together, talk about every play in the last lacrosse game. He started to bring her to the beach to play volleyball with him. Just last week I saw her sit on the couch with him and snuggle up in the wedge of his arm. At twelve, she hardly ever did this with me any longer, to see her with him melted me. This was going to be hard.

Margo was my rock, blindly optimistic, who told me not to make any rash decisions. She kept repeating her comment about how much love was there. Saint Marguerite, I'd think, each time we spoke. But she knew me, and she knew I didn't fall easily. She had faith in us, and in marriage. Her faith seemed to dwarf mine.

I had to decide quickly, the movers were coming in two

weeks. But hadn't I already decided? I had the infidelity clause clearly laid out before we married. Why was I waivering? Katherine had finally geared up to move, and school was all set. It was mid-year, which would be hard enough. After I had talked to the teachers, Katherine coming in as the "new kid" in eighth grade was better than having to acclimate to all this change her first year of high school. Simon was bending over backwards to make everything right. Everything he had told me about the affair added up. Of course, I did have some ownership in our problems. We weren't communicating, I didn't hear what he was saying. Even now, I can't remember one moment when I thought our marriage was at risk or he was angry with me. Could I forgive him?

I decided I'd talk to Rebecca. I needed an unbiased opinion and Rebecca and I had known each other for ten years. She knew what made me tick, but she also knew my fears better than anyone else.

I had had a therapist since I was in my early twenties. When my mother was diagnosed with MS, I started resenting her and knew this wasn't healthy, especially considering how much she and Zoe needed me. Don, my first therapist, wasn't going to allow me to have training wheels. Despite my pleas not to discuss my childhood, Don asked anyway. A box of tissues later and my idyllic childhood was transformed into a life full of not-being-good-enough. He did say something valuable that I keep with me today, however.

He said, "Remember Rainey, your mother was sick before she knew you. It has no bearing on who you are or who you will become."

He helped me see my mother for who she was, so I could find more empathy. He also helped me find my own voice and create my own path. Until then I had been reacting to circumstances and fate.

Now, I create both circumstance and fate.

Could I do this now?

I knew I needed to, but felt my ability slipping from

me. I needed a major tune up and Rebecca would be just the woman to help me. Rebecca was a better version of Don. Her office in Stepford was comprised of two small rooms in her upright colonial. She was on a main street, but the home was nestled behind hundred-year-old oak trees and rhododendrons. When you pulled into her driveway, it would curve around slightly so that your car would be hidden behind the mature plantings. I met Rebecca while trying to convince Katherine's father he'd be better off without me. I had offered him money, had begged him to leave, and met with attorneys. Rebecca was my Hail Mary. I'll never forget our first office visit.

"You're telling me you are hiring me to break up with your boyfriend for you?" She was clearly shocked.

"Well, when you put it like that, it sounds ludicrous." I laughed.

At the end of our first session, I had a sister. Sadly, she wasn't able to get Katherine's father to do anything but promise to change, but along the way, she and I formed a healthy relationship. I called and told her it was an emergency and drove an hour and a half to her office.

I walked into the office I had entered many times before. I would regularly visit for quarterly "check-ups" to keep my focus and decompress. Occasionally, I'd visit when I'd feel my confidence waning or when I was tackling something challenging at work. I always left feeling recharged and invincible. Somehow, her visits made me feel powerful and confident. I wasn't someone who generally lacked confidence but having my own personal cheerleader and honest feedback partner was invaluable. She, like me, never pulled any punches. Her office smelled of comfort. I've never been able to truly describe the smell, there is no specific scent, no lilac or rose fragrances, incense or even cleaning products. Perhaps the smell of comfort was her well-coifed shih-tzu who sat on your lap during sessions combined with the plaster and molding of an old home. I never asked Rebecca, but I assumed her home was the result of a divorce or perhaps a family home. I couldn't imagine her owning such a grand home on what she charged for sessions. As you walked in, the old wood screen would bounce noisily off the door jamb in all four seasons. My guess was this was her cue to look at her clock and wrap up her current session. You could count on Tibetan chimes or meditative spa music playing while you took your seat on the well-appointed but worn leather sofa in the waiting room. Today, I sat in the waiting room with red stained eyes which she had never seen. As predicted, when she opened her office door and saw me in the waiting room, she approached me with a firm, long hug. I felt I was in the loving arms of a parent for a moment, not because of her age or demeanor, but because her hug was safe and asked nothing in return.

"Rainey, don't make a decision for six months. It's too soon." I trusted her, but she had no idea the consequence her advice would have a couple months from now. She knew I had been madly in love. "Rainey, you and I have been talking about forgiveness for ten years. Maybe this is your test?" She continued, "Listen, I know you don't believe in divorce. I know how firmly you hold God to your heart. I guess it never dawned on either of us how conflicting your beliefs are when it comes to infidelity."

She was right. I couldn't run out the door because of my faith. That's why I was still in the house. If we weren't married, I would have moved out and not looked back the first night. I wouldn't have told anyone why. I would have just gone. Katherine wouldn't miss a few extra days of school as we transitioned. She was a great student. But, Katherine is also why I wouldn't move in with him until we were married.

Rebecca continued, "How long have you been married now?"

"831 days." I answered. Her surprise at my giving her that number stayed on her face as she asked,

"When did he tell you?"

"828 days into our marriage," I said quietly.

She decided not to ask about the days and went with it, "Rainey, how did you feel about him on the 827th day?" I started sobbing uncontrollably. She reminded me of our conversations, how I wanted to be like my aunts. Then, when I met Simon, how that had changed. She was right. I had to understand more before I made a life-changing decision for Katherine.

Rebecca reminded me, "A life changing decision for you, as well."

We took out some paper and started identifying options. She started appealing to the practical mother in me. Where did I want to work? What did I want to do for work? Where was the best place to raise Katherine? At the end of the session I made decisions that, no matter what choice I made about Simon, I would be poised to have what I wanted in life for Katherine and me, as well. I had always wanted to work in New York. I wanted Katherine to be in the best schools. Surprisingly, the decision was New Jersey.

"You can do anything for six months, Rainey," Rebecca encouraged, "just allow your emotions to be set free so you can truly understand them. Don't just go through the motions with Simon; talk, be honest, dig in, figure out how it broke down. It takes three people to have an affair, not just two."

I drove home from her office with my answer. I wondered if I knew my answer all along but needed someone to tell me what to do. If she had told me to leave, would I? I knew my vulnerability was wreaking havoc on my ability to make a decision.

"I can do anything for six months," I started to chant when I left Rebecca. Katherine was going to a friend's house after school, so I had time. I had realized the day before that my phone tracker was on and Simon could see if he wanted where I was. He had lost that right. I disabled the location feature the night before and when he realized today, he became unhinged. I looked down at my phone when I left Stepford, I had sixteen texts. They all were from Simon either begging for forgiveness or asking if I was okay or asking where I was.

I refused to answer. I screamed in the car, "FUCK YOU, SIMON!!!!!!!" It felt surprisingly good. I needed to stop thinking– and crying– for a few minutes. I decided to call a couple clients and old friends I knew who had always had a crush on me. I was going to allow them to make me feel good about myself for a little while. They would inevitably flirt. It was one of those things I hated about being a female in business, but today it was just what I needed. I started with Jim.

"Hey gorgeous!" he answered. Right first call. I silently patted myself on the back.

As I built my ego, I could never imagine what the evening would bring.

TECHNOLOGY

The drive was just what I needed. I made three phone calls in the car. It was as if God were shining down on me through all this chaos. Was that why Vijay chose to profess his love to me just before Simon told me about Portia? The calls today were oddly similar. They were helping to remind me that I am liked, and loved, and wanted.

"You know I'm still here for you if you ever decide to leave that husband of yours," Jim predictably reminded me. As the words hit my ear, I thought, he has no idea how close that was to becoming a reality.

"You know Rainey, that Simon is one lucky bastard. I just ran into Adam Cushfeld from school. Remember him? He could never take his eyes off you. Well I told him you are just as beautiful today as you were when we were in college. That Simon, he's one lucky bastard.' Andy had no idea how lucky and how much of a bastard Simon was. I was happy to let Andy build my ego.

"Let's run to New Orleans. No one has to know. I'll send you a ticket." Jeff was an old boyfriend who kept in touch over the years. He was always trying to get me to run away somewhere with him. I was so close to saying "yes" this time.

I hung up the last call feeling wanted again. Simon was telling me he wanted me, but he didn't at the beginning of last year. I heard someone in a movie say after her husband cheated, "Why am I so unlovable?" It's true. Finding out your husband cheated breaks a piece of you. Maybe he just wanted his money more? Could this whole thing really be about money? Was money that precious to him? Regardless, he didn't want me enough to respect our vows or to respect me. My temporary, manufactured self-assurance was replaced again with diffidence only seconds later. Nothing can prepare you for the emotional hit you take when something like this happens. Is that why women stay? I wondered. Are they now too broken to start over?

My mind could not stay away from the pain. The temporary relief I felt from my calls was almost immediately revoked when I looked at the steering wheel of my car. My car? It wasn't really my car. The Audi I was driving was Simon's car when we met. It was a few years old. We decided to turn in my BMW when the lease was up to save money while we were building The Atlantic Club. Simon bought a four-door Jeep for the beach. My mind quickly jumped from how sexy he looked driving it to wondering if Portia rode in my seat next to him. My anger and devastation returned as quickly as it had left. Having a kid who rides horses is tough on a car. Kids are tough enough on cars, but the stink of a barn made it impossible. That must be what Portia was talking about when she said I ruined his car. Did his car mean more to him than I? Clearly it meant enough that he would tell his lover about it. How could he share so much about me with this woman?

This is what my brain now does, moves compulsively back and forth in its cage. Katherine came home from school and told me about Gus, the bi-polar polar bear at the Central Park Zoo. Gus started swimming compulsively in figure eights for twelve hours a day. He'd constantly be changing direction and crashing his head against the glass. When not swimming, he'd lurk underwater and stalk children watching through the glass, trying to attack them. Zookeepers eventually had to put up barriers, so the kids wouldn't be afraid, and he'd stop hurting himself. The zoo spent twenty-five thousand dollars on Prozac and behavioral therapy. He was diagnosed with zoochosis. With zoochosis, even common house dogs can become raging, unpredictable, dangerous animals. I wondered if my zoochosis could be harmful? Maybe I should have asked Rebecca for some Prozac. I would never hurt myself or anyone else, but my head already was screaming for relief.

The ride back to Stonington was long. I didn't want to go there. I knew what Rebecca and I had discussed, I knew what I had decided less than an hour ago, but my ultimate decision now vacillated with every turn of the road.

Ultimately, I needed to decide. Time was running out. If I left, the consequences for Katherine were emotionally scarring. There wasn't enough time to ease into everything with her as I like to do. I would decide to listen to people who were more rational right now, any person who hadn't just had her heart blown to a hundred million bits by the love of her life, who was the only man besides their father she ever trusted, would be more rational than I right now. I had read not to make a decision for six months during my scavenger hunt for answers in Google, and Rebecca just confirmed it. I would listen to Margo, Rebecca, and Mother Google and prolong my decision for six months. Besides, it let me get Katherine settled in her new school before I made any other changes in her life. She was a teenage girl whose emotions were ruling her brain these days. Besides, how much does this child need to be put through before she gets a break?

I can do anything for six months.

As I drove up to the house, Katherine was just getting dropped off. I waved politely at Linda, her friend's mother. "Please drive on, don't wait to talk, just go. Please, Linda, for the love of all things good, just drop and dash," I whispered to myself. Yet, despite all my silent pleading, she didn't. As she waved enthusiastically and opened her door to give me a hug, I made an excuse about allergies and itchy eyes to mask the true reason for my red eyes.

Obligingly she agreed, "everyone is suffering from allergies right now, Rainey. You're not alone."

I thought about Linda's words and wondered how many people were suffering from these particular kind of allergies right now. I thought about the Male Hater's Party I threw several years ago and all the women who had been holding back their anger until they found out I was in the same situation. Maybe Linda did know a lot of people with my kind of allergies but, I quickly concluded that it didn't matter. This was not something I would share.

Katherine was well on her way into the house with not as much as a wave in my direction as she passed me. Linda kept me in the driveway for twenty minutes. She always did. Normally I would embrace her warmth, but not tonight. I even let her gossip and took no control of the conversation. Linda knew everything about everyone in town and complained about "townies" but after twenty years in Stonington, it was hard to tell the difference between her and them. I wondered if she would be telling the other moms about me and Simon one day.

Finally, free, I made my way inside. I walked up to Katherine's room where she had barricaded herself – this was becoming a regular thing. I barged in to find her sitting on her bed with her phone.

"Mom, can you knock at least?" she crabbed.

"Hi baby!" I was genuinely happy to see her despite her angst. I needed a hug.

"Hi." I hated that response. It was more frequent these days.

"You okay, lovebug?" I asked knowing she's just flexing her independence but asking anyway.

"I'm fine." She kept staring down at her phone. Damn phone. Why did I buy her that?

"How was Chelsea's?"

"Fine."

"Is your homework all done?" She shot me a glance to leave her alone. I hated teenagers and she was quickly becoming one.

"Well I'm ordering pizza tonight. I'll call you when it gets here." I kissed my moody teen on her head and went downstairs. I hadn't cooked since I found out. I wish that meant I wasn't eating, but I'm a stress eater, I was doing completely the opposite.

As I waited for the pizza, I thought about what I needed to do next. I looked at the ten-thousand-dollar check. I guess I would have to tell Simon I would stay. I'll leave out the part about six months. He can't know I have a plan. I'm not sure I'm wired to forgive, but I remember a quote I read somewhere.

'Powerful people forgive; average people don't.'

Sadly, this is not a new battle for me. I've been praying for the ability to forgive since junior year when Jane, my then best friend, told my history teacher I didn't deserve the "A" I had received and proceeded to share my secret about making my research paper up the night before. Meanwhile, she had been researching hers for weeks and had only received a "C." I looked at the sky as it set over the ocean and repeated the passage from Matthew 18:21. I knew it by heart.

> *'Then Peter came to Him and said, "Lord, how often shall my brother sin against me, and I forgive him? Up to seven times? Jesus said to him, "I do not say to you, up to seven times, but, up to seventy times seven."*

Sorry, God, but that will never happen. Maybe, just maybe, I forgive him once– for You. I haven't prayed or meditated since everything happened. I didn't feel forsaken when my father died, when Mimi was diagnosed with cancer on top of everything else or when I lost my life savings, but I felt forsaken now. Why this test, oh Lord? Why challenge– in such a short amount of time– everything I hold most dear? I sat in the dining room thinking about forgiveness and God and Katherine and myself while I waited for our dinner to be delivered.

Simon goes to the gym after work– or so I once thought– so he doesn't get home until seven. This gave me two hours to figure out what to say. We normally eat when he gets home, I believe it's important to eat together as a family. I would no longer do that, I decided. There, finally a decision I can firmly make! The pizza would be here at five-thirty p.m. Fuck Simon.

At that, headlights appeared in the driveway. Simon had skipped the gym.

When he walked into the house, he looked horrible. His face was pale, and he looked like a seven-year-old kid whose puppy had just been killed right in front of him. I'm sure I looked no better. I couldn't stop myself. "Did you see Portia today?"

"Babe," he said sadly. "I didn't know if you'd still be here." He looked at the check in my hand as if he just saw the dead puppy breathe, "You didn't cash it?"

I raised my finger to my mouth to quiet him and pointed upstairs. I didn't want to talk to him right now. I knew Katherine couldn't hear us where we were standing, but it was a convenient excuse.

"I love you." It sounded so sad coming from his lips. Was I starting to pity him? No, I still hate him. I would never pity him.

"Pizza will be here in a few minutes," I responded.

Katherine came down, ate her slice quickly and asked to be excused to do homework. Usually I'd make her stick around the table longer to talk. Tonight, I was relieved. When she left the table, so did I. Simon stayed seated as if I were coming back. I walked into the bedroom.

A few minutes passed, and Simon opened the bedroom door. He put his head in the door as if he was no longer welcome, "Can I come in?"

"Yes." I was cool.

"Rainey, I haven't been able to concentrate all day. I can't lose you. Please forgive me. It was one mistake. I will never do it again. I made one miserable, horrible, mistake. Please babe, please don't leave me." I was glad to hear him say this after handing me the check yesterday, but I still said nothing in return.

He grew solemn. He sat on his side of the bed and looked out at the ocean. He looked devastated, and I was glad for that. We sat in silence for minutes and I felt his head turn toward mine. I'm not sure how long we sat there - I ignoring him and looking outside as he sat facing me, begging for my attention. I thought about all the excuses he had given me. How he said it was over as soon as it started. How she would keep showing up at the lab. How he was afraid she was going to make things at work a nightmare and how she kept threatening to tell me. He said he knew I would leave him, so he had to protect his secret.

He said the text messages she had sent me were to quiet her. When she'd start getting crazy at work, he'd send her dirty messages because, apparently, it quieted her. Then he swore to me that he would never show up. That was, oddly, confirmed by her. She had mentioned in her hurtful rant that I was so controlling that I would interrupt him on his way to see her regularly and he would have to cancel so I wouldn't get suspicious. Funny thing was, I wasn't controlling. I had never called him before seven. I trusted him. I had never been suspicious. I trusted him. Damn him. I trusted him.

He had used me as an excuse not to follow through– just as he said. He disgusted me right now, still. But somehow, I remembered how I had loved him. I thought about Jack Twist in Brokeback Mountain.

"I wish I knew how to quit you," Jake Gyllenhaal said to Heath Ledger.

I wanted to quit Simon right now, but I easily agreed to Rebecca's suggestion. Why?

As I stared at the ocean, I thought about our wedding. Saying our vows in front of God.

"I don't believe in divorce," I had warned him, "there's no

backing out now."

I really didn't believe in divorce, this was true. Infidelity was my one exception. I thought about how just a few nights ago I had been watching him sleep. I realized that he had been sleeping soundly since he told me, again, confirming that he was making himself sick trying to cover up "his mistake."

I whispered. "Okay."

His body spun in the direction of his head. He had a look of disbelief. I could tell he wasn't sure if he had really heard me correctly. "Okay? Okay??" It was endearing but I was still so hurt.

I told him I'd stay. I'd move to New Jersey and we'd try to work it out. There was no second chance, I would warn him. He went to grab me in his arms, but I wasn't ready and pushed him away, "I just need time."

"I love you, I love you so much. I'll give you whatever you need, Rainey. I'm so happy. I love you."

There it was, my decision. I told him in one simple word, "Okay." Now I would have six months to live with that decision. So, I thought.

I needed to start thinking about what those next six months would look like for us, for all of us. Pema Chodron tells us to move toward pain in order to heal. I was doing the complete opposite as I sat in the bed next to Simon. I was trying to figure out how to move away from the pain. I didn't want to feel it anymore. I had felt like a crumpled rag doll left behind by Popcorn. The stuffing of the doll all out of its original casing and strewn across the floor, limbs either torn off or left dangling by a string. And the heart? Well, the heart would be completely chewed to bits. I was Simon's chew toy, and it was time to sew myself back together.

We sat mostly silent. Occasionally Simon would burst out "I love you so much," or "I'll make this up to you, I swear." All the time, I didn't hear a peep from Katherine upstairs. This was not completely unusual, but sadly, tonight I was relieved. It was almost nine-thirty and I would go up and tuck her in. I promised her I would tuck her in every night for the rest of my life, even when she was an adult. I don't care how ridiculous I sounded to her. I would never let her fall asleep without her knowing I loved her and was there for her.

What would happen next could never have been predicted.

I walked up the stairs to her room and noticed the lights were already out. I quietly opened her door to see if she had already fallen asleep and was relieved to see I hadn't missed saying goodnight. She had my old iPhone on the bed in front of her.

"Whatcha doin with that?" I asked.

"I use it when my battery dies because my power cord doesn't reach all the way to my bed." Something was wrong in her tone. Had she been crying?

"Is everything okay, baby?" I asked, already knowing the answer would be different than the one she gave just hours ago.

She looked up at me. Her eyes were so big. She had this horrible look in her eyes that I couldn't read. I couldn't imagine what would come from those beautiful lips next, but fear was raging through me. Did something happen? The internet is so cruel. She looked down at my phone and back up at me. These kids could be horrible. Until now, she had escaped the horror stories I had heard, but why should she? What was she about to say? Her lips parted, and she was trying to form words. Oh God. Please God, please let my baby be okay. I could bear anything in life, but I'm not sure I could manage if she wasn't okay. She was my air.

The words finally came.

"Mom. Did Simon... Did Simon cheat on you?"

I didn't expect those words. Dear God, not those words. I was frozen. "Why would you ask that?" My words stumbled through my lips now.

"I was using your phone and I went to Google and saw a

bunch of stuff."

Oh shit. I remembered some of my search topics:

Why do husbands cheat?

Why do husbands cheat with ugly women?

Why do men cheat with ugly fucking crazy women?

Will I ever love him again?

Crap. I was angry. This poor angel. I cannot believe I did something so stupid.

If there was one time I wish I had lied it was going to be this moment. "Yes, baby. He did." I couldn't lie to her. She threw herself into my arms.

"Why, Mama? Why?"

I had asked myself the same thing so many times over the past few days. I usually loved when she called me "Mama." She started doing it when she was five. It was so endearing, and she'd soon learn that it melted my heart and it would become her deadliest weapon. She could get almost anything she wanted when she called me Mama. I was weak. At that moment, the word "mama" almost broke me in two. I thought I couldn't hurt any more than I did five minutes ago, but the pain was flaring through me. My throat was full. I could no longer see through my open eyes. I had never imagined that things could get worse. They did. They just did.

I moved my hand across her forehead and stroked her long, tousled hair. I slowly dried her tears with my fingers. I had caused this. I was the reason these tears were falling. Simon had broken my heart and I had broken hers.

I thought about Father Jon again, "Let her see you cry." There was no choice right now. I couldn't stop right now if I tried. She couldn't either. I kissed her forehead. I needed to help her heal, quickly.

"Jesus, give me the words," I prayed silently.

"Simon made a mistake and he's very sorry. I wasn't innocent. I wasn't communicating very well. It's a little complicated. It was a long time ago and we're working through it. It doesn't change anything between you and him, baby."

"Are we still moving to New Jersey?" she asked through her tears.

"Yes, baby. Nothing has changed. I'm sorry you saw that."

"Okay." She stayed in my arms for a few more minutes holding me tight. That felt so good. I could feel the sobbing stop. She had rolled into a gentle cry. A couple more minutes passed. She pulled her head up, "Are you okay, Mama?"

Oh, God, I love this child. I was overwhelmed by the emotion of that simple question. Are you okay, Mama? I would be now, I thought.

"Yes, I'm okay. I'm hurt, but Simon loves us very much and has begged for my forgiveness."

"Did you forgive him?"

I figure out how to lie, "Yes."

"Well I'm not going to forgive him yet," she said matter-of-factly. I chuckled at the word "yet." She was so smart. She already knew she was going to forgive him, but she was going to make him pay for it. I wish I were so certain.

I sat and held her for a while longer. I thought how I am the worst mother ever. How could I be so careless as to allow her to see this? We talked a little more about forgiveness and God; I listened to my words as well. When telling her how God asks us to forgive, I heard the Beaufort rise in me and added, "That doesn't mean we allow people to take advantage of us, though." I told her there is no forgiving Simon a second time. I made that perfectly clear.

"I want to talk to Simon" she whispered.

Her words took my breath away. I told her I'd send him up and then quickly gave her an excuse to buy some time, "I think he may still be on the phone with his new company." Simon had no idea what was about to happen. Neither did I. "What do you want to talk to him about?"

"I want him to know I'm mad at him, too." She was my daughter, all right. I tucked her in, told her how much I loved her, and went to retrieve Simon.

Simon was in shocked horror. "She what?" "How did she find out?" "What should I say?" I took control of the situation. I told him what I said to her. He interrupted me with, "You forgive me?"

"No. I lied." I brushed his question aside.

"I understand. I hope you will." Tears filled his eyes as he said the words. He knew the conversation was over.

I ignored his last statement and gave him orders. I told him what to say, what to do, and how to act. I was leaving nothing to chance. This is my daughter and I was not allowing him to screw her up. This poor child didn't deserve the craziness she has witnessed and had to manage in her young life: an irresponsible father, a messy divorce of sorts, dying grandparents, moving twice in three years, a bankrupt mother who risked everything only to lose it all, and now an affair after I had promised her happily ever after? No child deserved what I had allowed the last five years to bring to her life. He would go up there, he would follow my direction, and he would start fixing this.

They were up there for over an hour.

MOVING ON

"Rainey, some couples become stronger after an affair." I kept reviewing Rebecca's words as I lay in bed. Every time she said them I got angry.

Why is it therapists always lean toward recoupling? Why not figure out what will really make me whole, figure out who I am, and then tell me to lose the bastard if it's the right thing for me. No. They are all predisposed to forgiveness. I had one therapist who was honest. Frank. Frank told me Katherine's father was an extreme narcissist and borderline sociopath. He quickly followed up saying my exes' extreme narcissism would create a severe conflict for Katherine if I were forced to share custody. Since sole custody wasn't very realistic in our state, he said I should just stay with him until Katherine was a teenager so I could control her environment, for Katherine's sake. Whether his advice was right or wrong, I appreciated his candor. How I missed Frank now. I just wanted someone to tell me what to do and what the future would look like when I did. I wanted control back and I was having a hard time finding the reigns.

I figured if I was going to make it through the next six months, I would need a new therapist. I surely couldn't bring Margo with me, although somehow, I felt she might go if she thought I needed her.

Let me get through the next few weeks first, I thought.

I had decided to tell Simon that I would forgive him in four days; Thursday. I don't know why I randomly chose that day. I convinced him that I was a strong woman and I would allow myself to "go through the process." Then, come Thursday, I would force myself to move past it. "I wasn't ordinary." I believed those words when I said them, I have never thought of myself as ordinary. Everything else I said? Well, I think I was trying to talk us both into believing it.

Someone I didn't know emerged over the next several days. I demanded sex. I demanded a lot of sex. I wanted hard, passionate sex. I didn't want to make love to him, I wanted him to fuck me. I wanted to fuck him.

He asked, "Are you sure about this?"

I told him to shut up and do what I say. I told him to kiss me like he was ravaging me. Harder. I needed to feel it. I had no idea where this was coming from. When he went to work, I masturbated. He came home, I could barely wait for Katherine to fall asleep. I wanted more. I wanted all of him in me. He was my puppet. I was his master. He was exhausted and I was disgusted. He would tell me he was exhausted and couldn't get it up, I would ignore him and make it rise.

What I was doing was unhealthy. I'd cry after sex, thinking about how I had unknowingly shared him with someone else and then would force him to have sex with me again.

Simon wanted to make love to me. He begged for it. I only wanted sex. So, he did what I asked. I was insatiable. Maybe it was the only thing I could control? I had read how some women will go on sex rampages with strangers after finding out their husband cheated. Maybe this was my rampage, one that fit neatly within my Catholic parameters? Perhaps, for the same reason women sleep with men on the first date, I was forcing him to have sex with me. I was confusing sex with love or my desirability. Maybe, if I wasn't so ashamed of my actions and had shared them with my therapist, I might know the answer.

Thursday came. I told him I forgave him. I lied. I made him fuck me again. I think he was hoping to make love. We had never had makeup sex before. Based on the situation, you would think we fought about money all the time. We didn't. Simon thought we did, but I don't remember one fight. He had never raised his voice or asked me to do anything different. We had definitely never had makeup sex. Was this it? No, this wasn't it. Makeup sex would require love. This was one hundred percent pain.

Simon went to work at his old company on his last day. In his pocket he carried a small recorder. I don't know what inspired him to do this, but he decided he would record his goodbyes with his two supervisors. The ultimate scientist, he would ask them for feedback which he would record. He would use this as a tool not to make the same mistakes in his next role. He was also prepared to give one of his supervisors a piece of his mind. She had let him down and was the reason he was leaving the company and he wanted to make sure she knew this. I'm not sure why he felt he needed to record the conversations, but I was glad for it later.

That night, he played the recording for me. It was a reprieve from his begging for forgiveness constantly. Although I appreciated his apologies and doting, they couldn't keep the pain away. This would be a nice break. Before playing the recording, he told me how he "gave his boss a piece of his mind" and how he told her she had "let him down." He also bragged about telling her she wasn't a qualified scientist.

"Wow, Simon, that sounds harsh." I no longer called him loving names.

"It was. I was brutal," he assured me. He played the recording.

I heard him thanking her for everything. The recording was over thirty minutes long. We were fifteen minutes in. I wondered when we would get to the good stuff. Five more minutes passed.

"Simon, you left all the negative messages for the end?"

"What do you mean? I just told her she was a bad scientist."

"What? Rewind it." I demanded. How had I missed it? Simon backed up the recording and he listened this time, too. He really listened. He asked his boss if she remembered when she challenged his thought process on a particular theory and he turned out to be right? She remembered. He then went on to tell her some of the things she did well. None of them were science related, but he showered her with compliments.

"Oh," he grumbled. I didn't say a word. He rewound the recording and listened to it again. "She was happy that I said all those things," he said to himself. Again, I didn't speak but silently nodded. He rewound the recording from the beginning. He listened to it again. His face was different this time. I went to the kitchen to get a drink. When I heard the recording still playing I decided to go up and check on Katherine.

Surprisingly, Katherine was awake. We talked about the affair again. I reminded her not to share this with anyone. It would hurt me. She asked why I didn't leave Simon. Why had I decided to give him another chance? I couldn't tell her the truth. I didn't want her to think I was staying with him just to make her life better. No child should feel that burden. I decided to make up a lie that would become something of the truth.

"I have friends whose husbands have cheated– and no, baby, all men don't cheat. When they did, I was the first one to tell them to leave. What I didn't realize, maybe because I loved my friend so much, was that it takes two to make a marriage. It takes two to break one, as well. Sometimes, the hardest and bravest thing to do is not to listen to your friends at all. Sometimes you need to listen to your heart. I always thought staying was taking the easy way out. What this has taught me is that leaving would be much easier." I thought of Melissa. I owed her an apology I would never give. I could tell her, but

I knew she wouldn't keep my secret. She was a terrible secret keeper. Right now, I didn't want the public humiliation on my plate as well.

Satisfied with my answer, Katherine started to relax. Her eyes drooped slightly as she fought to keep them open. I tucked her in again and kissed her goodnight.

"I love you, Mama." She beat me to it.

"I love you."

I walked into the office where Simon was still listening to his recording. I was with Katherine a long time. He must be on his third go around, I thought. He pushed the red square button and looked up. He stood up and faced me. His hands moved to each side of my face. I jumped a bit. I was not ready for him to take the lead yet, I was still his dominatrix.

"Shhhhh." I steadied myself as he tried to quiet me.

He continued, "I never told you how I felt." What did he just say? He looked at the recorder. He rambled as if in disbelief himself, "I never told Cheryl how I really felt, and I never told you. All this time I just thought you didn't hear me. Cheryl didn't hear me today because I never really said what I thought I did. I beat around the bush. I thought I was giving brutal and direct feedback, I thought I was harsh with her, but as I listened back, I put so many other positive things around my message because I don't want to hurt you that you probably never did know." He switched the conversation from her back to me unknowingly.

"Oh my God, Rainey, I'm so sorry. I'm so fucking sorry."

I loved him right now. I was surprised by this. Margo's words jumped in my head, "I've never seen love like yours and Simon's. You'll get through this somehow." For the first time in two weeks, I thought there just might be a chance she could be right.

Seconds later I would be angry again. Does this mean he wasn't sorry before? My emotions had been a roller coaster and I needed this to stop.

The movers showed up on schedule. The first day they packed everything but our beds. The next day they loaded everything into a massive tractor trailer. It used to amaze me that my whole life could fit into a truck. I had moved so many times for business that I finally realized my life was not in that truck at all.

We'd load up the cars with the clothes and essentials we had set aside and would stay at a hotel tonight. The idea of driving three hours with a dog through New York rush hour and then having to unload the car into a hotel was overwhelming. Simon suggested we go to our favorite restaurant and spend our last night in Mystic the right way. Katherine was thrilled to adjust her plans and go to hibachi with her gaggle of girls one last time.

After dropping Popcorn at the hotel, we walked downstairs to Red 36. It was winter, only days before November would start. Our restaurant on the pier normally had a two hour wait, but tonight we would stroll in without a reservation and get riverfront seating. Red 36 was across the river from Simon's bachelor pad. It made me think of our first time and of writing "I love you" on my chest. I reminded him of the time I was making dinner for him and had to go borrow a can opener from his neighbor. He had lived there a year and didn't know his neighbors. For a moment, I forgot this was a man that I hated.

"Would you do it all again?" he asked. Although I knew my answer, I stayed silent.

The hotel in New Jersey was nice enough. We would be living there while we waited to close on our house, so I was thankful it was as nice as it was. It had one bedroom, a pull-out couch, and a full kitchen and dining room. It would have to do, and I could make the best of any situation. After checking out our new digs, we started dragging in suitcases and plants.

We had stuffed a lot more into the cars than I had expected. Between houseplants and various things the movers couldn't take, we had several trips if all three of us worked together.

Our second trip to the car, Simon was missing. When Katherine and I got to the room, Simon was sprawled across the bed.

"What's this, lazy bones? You're going to let the girls do all the work?" I teased but was not really teasing.

"Come on, Simon!!!" Katherine roared as she and I headed back to the car. I was irritated. I was surprised when he didn't meet us at the car. We walked back into the room with our next load and I noticed Simon sitting against the suitcases we had placed by the bedroom door. Katherine had a box labeled "bathroom" and she stepped right over his legs and passed him without flinching. Something didn't look right. His face was beet red and sweat clung to his cheeks. "Are you okay?" He couldn't answer me. Was he having a stroke?

He nodded his head that he was okay but still didn't speak. I bent down in front of him and touched his chest. I was surprised to feel his heartbeat so easily. His heart felt as though it was trying to escape his body. It was fast, yet his body was sweaty and limp. He had only rolled in suitcases so far. This didn't make sense. Simon worked out at the gym at extreme levels, he wouldn't even break a sweat if he had had to carry them up the stairs all at once. He still wasn't talking.

"Are you sure you're okay? Your heart is beating so fast."

He was disoriented. I saw him trying to look at his Apple watch. I touched the face of his watch and his heart beat showed on the face. He was so proud of his heart beat. As an athlete, his resting heart rate was close to fifty-five beats per minute. Today his watch read one hundred eighty-eight.

Now Katherine was standing next to us. "What's wrong, Simon?"

"Nothing kiddo," he mustered. "It must have been something I ate." That was his answer for everything. Too much flatulence? My cooking was the culprit. Bad breath? Something he ate. The dog is sick. Can't sleep? Someone's grouchy? Always the same answer. Katherine walked away satisfied with his answer.

"What's going on, Simon?" I asked.

"I don't know. I was feeling weird, so I laid down on the bed. "Feel this, feel this!" He interrupted himself and brought my hand to his neck. His pulse was still throbbing, and his neck was saturated in sweat. He looked down at his watch again. "One-fifty. It's slowing down."

"Keep going, babe. How did you end up on the floor?"

"You called me babe," a smile came to his face as he said the words, "you do still love me."

I ignored his comment and was more assertive with my tone, "Simon, how did you get on the floor?"

"Well after you and Katherine left, I thought I should follow you. I knew you were irritated with me. So, I got up, I started walking to the door, and it hit me. I started to get dizzy and thought I was going to pass out. The room started to spin, so I sat down."

I looked at his position. His back was slumped against the suitcases and his legs were spread in a V away from the wall. It wasn't as though he looked comfortable there. I decided he had probably fallen there. Why else wouldn't he have gone to the chair, only inches to his right?

"I can feel my heart beating. I'm not sure I have ever felt it like that before." One thing about Simon. He was incredibly in touch with his body.

"What was happening when I was talking to you?" I asked, "you didn't answer right away."

"It was strange. I could hear you, but I couldn't get my mouth to make words. I don't know how to explain it."

"Do you think you had an anxiety attack?" I asked. He had been healthy and always bragged about his outstanding physicals.

It seemed reasonable. We had both been under a lot of

stress.

"Maybe. I guess. What do I have to be stressed about now? You're here with me. I'm excited about my new job. I got a nice big sign-on bonus." I was thinking that he should be worried that I wasn't going to stay but refrained from mentioning that. Instead I ordered, "I think you should go check that out."

"I'm fine now, babe. You're right, it's probably some weird panic attack."

Simon got up and seemed quite fine after that. We monitored his heart rate and it continued to decline. After a couple minutes he declared, "Fifty-seven! I'm back to my old self again." I told him again to get it checked out and started unpacking.

Things started moving along week one.

I was pleased that I found a job as quickly as I did. I would start after the first of the year. This gave me a month to get Katherine settled in school and figure out our new logistical challenges.

Pushing aside the affair had not been difficult to do our first week there. I was busy doing things for the new house, buying new clothes for my new job, finding pet sitters and doctors, and shopping for Christmas presents. But then, about ten days in, I finished all that. I tried to throw myself into work, but the silence was deafening in the hotel room when Simon and Katherine were gone.

I started worrying about Christmas Eve with my family. What if Zoe told the family? They would surely be cold to Simon. They would be extra cautious with me. I've watched them before. They would sidebar in other rooms to gossip. I would know if they knew and it would be horrible. Could I find an excuse to keep Simon in New Jersey? No, not on Christmas.

The funny thing about an affair, you don't only have to worry about your own emotions, you must also deal with all of those around you as well. Zoe was angry. Zoe read all those texts. Zoe made it clear she believed I should leave. Zoe was the living version of that little red-faced emoji with the inward facing v's for eyes and a zig-zag mouth. Zoe had missed the last few Christmas Eve gatherings with our family. I wondered if she would be there this year because of what happened? We would certainly see her at the nursing home the next day. What would she do? Zoe can sometimes be rather unpredictable. Lord help us.

My head got the best of me. I couldn't separate the pain from my loneliness. In New Jersey I felt completely alone. I know I was only two hours from most of my family, an hour farther to my friends and mother, but it may as well have been a twenty-hour drive. It was even becoming more painfully obvious that I had only shared my heartache with one friend. Unfortunately, Margo had her own challenges with Jon right now and I couldn't burden her every time I needed to talk. Their marriage had been tumultuous, I needed to be there for her.

This was when my crazy began.

CRAZY

Being alone with nothing to do was torturous. I started tracking Simon's every move with an app I purchased to keep Katherine safe. It told me not only where he was but also where he went when I wasn't watching the app or checking his location.

He'd go to lunch with a colleague and I'd seethe with anger all day until he returned. "What did you do today?" I'd interrogate. He'd always tell me it was Mike or John but how would I know? The hotel was thirty minutes from his work so if I happened to drive by he would probably be gone by the time I got there.

I could never trust this man again, I thought.

I started remembering things from before the affair, little things I had simply ignored at the time due to my misplaced trust. These memories would begin to plague me. I realized how foolish I had been, and now looking back, I couldn't believe I had ignored the signs.

I remembered one night before dinner, Katherine pulled up my sharing app to see if Simon had left work yet. She was starving and didn't want to wait until seven. "I don't know if he's on his way home or not. It looks like he's at someone's house."

I dismissed her comment. The app was a little unpredictable and would sometimes show him in the middle of the ocean. I'm sure that was the case. Twenty minutes later she repeated, "No mom, he's still at someone's house." Simon came home predictably at seven and Katherine greeted him at the door. "I pulled up your location and it said you were at someone's house. Whose house were you at?"

I couldn't see his face from the kitchen, but I heard him pause and ask, "Did you tell your mom?" He immediately changed the topic to horses and I heard him go into the bedroom before joining me in the kitchen. His hair was still damp from the gym, I thought. Nothing unusual. He'd say, "I just wanted to get home to you, I didn't want to waste time drying my hair." Now I thought, how many others had there been? Katherine bounded back into the kitchen ready for dinner. "So, whose house were you at?" Simon nonchalantly rendered the program as faulty and reminded us it regularly showed him working at the bottom of the sea.

For days after, Katherine teased him of having an affair. I'm not sure if she knew, but I had not even a clue. I told her to knock it off. Simon was uncomfortable with her little joke. It didn't dawn on me why he'd be uncomfortable.

Another time Simon came home smelling of perfume. I asked him who he had hugged at work today and teased that next Christmas he should buy her a better bottle of perfume. I had no clue. I believed my husband was madly in love with me. We hadn't even celebrated our second anniversary yet. Now I wondered, was this the day he wanted me to smell the perfume? Had he wanted to be caught that night? He told me the first time he had gone to her house he was having an affair because he knew it was my non-negotiable and he was angry at me. He wanted to flee and wasn't man enough to just tell me. He wanted me to leave him. Having an affair was how he was going to save himself, leveraging my own rule against me. Was he going to save himself or his bank account? I couldn't stop the court case being tried in my head.

Sitting alone in the hotel room, I wondered about the perfume and his motives. Did he want to be caught? Portia surely wanted him to be caught. After reading some of what she had written and listening to her insane monologues, I didn't doubt she sprayed her cheap perfume on his collar herself. She was incredibly lonely and unhappy. You could see that from her Facebook posts. She had certainly created an entire illusion around who I was and what she believed Simon thought of her. It pains me to think some of her illusion was based in truth. I wondered how much of the illusion was mine? During my sex rampage with Simon, I was the puppeteer. I now realized Portia and I had been his puppets all year.

My heart broke more with each memory. I felt stupid, naïve. Everything I hated in other women, I had become. Now I was sitting in a hotel room and my husband was probably having lunch with Portia II.

My heart fractured more every minute. I imagined small chards splintering off with each memory and falling next to me on the freshly made bed. As I tried to remember who I used to be, Rainey Beaufort was quickly fading from my memory. Rainey Bradley sat on the white linens of the hotel bed feeling like a whore.

Last month I would have described myself as a broken bird. Life had been breaking my right wing for the past several years. Struggling in business, my father's heartbreaking passing, the daily care I needed to give my mother until finally having to make the painful decision to put her in a nursing home at only sixty-six, leaving my friends and my family and my incredible neighbors behind, my house sinking and the insurance not covering it thus leaving me penniless... These were strong wings, I thought. It took a lot to break the first one. But the second wing? That wing took only four little words, "I had an affair." Nothing would ever be the same.

Last year I was bad-ass Rainey Beaufort– intelligent, risk-taker, confident business woman, and beloved friend. Today I was replaced with a sniveling, self-deprecating, useless whore named Rainey Bradley. My last hope at redemption was to protect my last treasure in life, Katherine, by staying with a man who had betrayed me. Mrs. Bradley was staying with a man who proved to this once arrogant, happy go-lucky, power player that she wasn't immune to ignorance. I needed Rainey Beaufort back. Where was she?

I would get myself so upset I'd vomit. I'd keep eating to make myself feel better, then I'd vomit involuntarily. Sadly, I thought, I ate far more than I vomited so the pounds kept coming. The only way to distract myself from eating was to go buy more Christmas presents. Katherine would get spoiled this year. She deserved it. I tried to go to the gym to work out but all I could think of was Simon's wet hair when he came home. Why did I not realize that he was showering off the sex? I was making myself sick. How could anyone get past this?

I had to know more. I had to know if Simon was sincere–now.

Before I knew it, I had created a gmail account under the name Portia Lamont. During the days before Forgiveness Thursday, I had asked Simon everything about Portia. I knew what made her tick. I knew he couldn't get it up for her and how she would give him endless blowjobs to arouse him. I knew that he said his penis was broken and he had to use Viagra with me. He didn't. Most importantly, I knew how she communicated. He told me of the long, drawn out emails she would send him at work, telling him she could feel my aura and it was heinous. I was a lying fraud, she'd tell him. She claimed herself to be psychic and to be able to read people. She knew that he and she were put on this earth together for a reason. They were soulmates. Apparently, while cyber-stalking me, she had channeled my inner evil. She regularly told him he needed to get away from me as soon as possible. I knew she thought they had a connection because she regularly tried to get him to say he felt it in the text messages she sent me. He never said it back.

He gave me all the answers to the test I was about to create.

I put every nuance into play in my first email to him. As-

Portia I would tell him I missed him, and I knew that Rainey went with him to New Jersey. I told him she would be in New York in a week. Could he meet her there? I hit send before I realized how crazy I had become.

I waited for a response. None came.

Well what would "Crazy" do? Simon and I regularly referred to her by the name "Crazy." Seemed fitting and it was oddly less painful, not much less painful but somewhat.

Crazy would write a follow up email. And Crazy did. Our nicknames were now interchangeable.

"Don't turn away from me now. I need you, and I know we have a connection..." it started.

I hated this version of me. As soon as I hit send I ran into the bathroom. I was so disgusted by myself that I was allergic to my own insides. I vomited again. My nerves were a mess. That wasn't the only thing that was a mess. I passed the mirror on the way back. I had just turned forty-four and had always prided myself on looking younger. Today I was fourteen pounds heavier and looked closer to sixty. My skin was like wrinkled crepe paper and the circles and bags under my eyes worked hard to show how much I didn't sleep. I saw this hideous woman looking back at me in the mirror. "No wonder he cheated," I said to myself. I noticed my double chin. Nice. How did I never realize I looked this old before? I reached to the counter and slathered on face cream. I put it on twice as thick as anyone would dare in hopes that I would be prettier by five.

I went back to the bed and checked to see if Simon had responded back to Portia. He hadn't.

"I need to make sure Simon is getting these emails from Portia," thought the crazy woman who was now inhabiting my body. Simon deletes everything from his phone immediately. I wouldn't find them there. Another sign of a serial cheat, I thought. Another clue I had conveniently ignored. Love is blind, they say. I now believe love eats away at healthy brain tissue and slowly makes you incredibly ignorant. Maybe

Portia was a normal human being before she fell in love with my husband? No. No, she wasn't.

I couldn't help myself, "Simon, have you heard from Crazy lately?"

"No, babe, I haven't. Let's stop talking about her. I told you I would tell you if she contacted me."

Maybe he didn't get them? My mentality took a closer step to insanity as I devised a strategy. At night, Simon would lie in bed next to me and play games on his phone before going to sleep. Before he'd put his phone down, he'd always check his email and clear it out. I would send an email to him while he was lying next to me. I'd have to be discreet; he could never know it was I. He had made me crazy, and I wouldn't give him the luxury of knowing he had that power over me. My lack of sanity needed to be guarded. I should have listened to my aunts. Why did I ever allow myself to give a man the upper hand?

I typed another email and put it in my draft folder. That night, while Simon was in the bathroom, I would open the long email I had drafted to Simon earlier and get it on the screen and ready to send. I'd only need to tap "send" as the final step. I would place the phone next to the bed face-down, and scurry back out to the living room with Katherine. When he would get in bed, I would casually stroll in, look for my phone, let him know I found it, turn it on and push send the second it opened. I'd then jump into bed next to him and wait for him to check his email.

My plan was working perfectly. I snuggled closer than I have been to him in the few weeks and he was pleased. "Baby, I love you so much," he said. He was moved by our closeness as he said the words. "We're going to be OK, right? I am so sorry." He was still apologizing four weeks later. He had done and said everything you would want a man to say who really screwed up and really regretted his decision. I couldn't have advised him any better. There was a part of me that wished I could forgive him.

What happened next was unexpected. A slight ding on his phone alerted him of a notification. "Email from Portia Lamont" it read. His face changed. I quickly started moving my fingers over the face of my phone, pretending to play Word Chums. I saw his eyes dart to my phone to see if I was paying attention. He didn't look at my face for some reason. I suddenly remembered that he hadn't slept well last night. It all made sense, I was sure he received my other emails as well. This confirmed it. The next surprise was that he immediately switched to email and glanced at the email. He didn't look at it long enough to read it but spent enough time to capture its gist. He immediately deleted the email. Then, earlier than most nights, he emptied the rest of his emails and then went to the trash and deleted his trash file.

I couldn't breathe. I tried to find my legs and got up. "Where're you going?" "Shower" was all I could muster. I walked to the bathroom, shut the door, turned the music on, then the shower, and I cried. I wasn't sure I could hold back my tears long enough to get the music to play. I didn't want to have to lie to him when he asked what was wrong. Katherine was still awake, so I needed to avoid her seeing me cry. I got in the shower and fell to the floor in tears. The true test would come tomorrow when I asked him if she contacted him. This one I was sure he saw.

We had a pact. If she tried to contact him, he would let me know. No more secrets. I was now sure he had received the first two emails. Of course, I was pleased he didn't respond, but I was also tragically sad to find out he broke his promise. I would ask him tomorrow night after I knew Katherine was sound asleep. Just in case, I would buy her some noise cancelling headphones. She could listen to music and she could have privacy when she was Face Timing in the small hotel room, I'd tell her. She'd be delighted.

Six months, I thought. I could do anything for six months. Five more to go.

We would be moving into the new house in a few days. Simon told me he wouldn't buy it if I wasn't going to stay. He was buying the house to show me his commitment, "I don't want a house if you're planning to leave me," he said. Was he on to me? I wondered this more than once. He had desperately wanted to buy a house before he met me, so I'm not sure if I believed his words. Then again, after something like this, you stop believing most people's words. Buying a house was not going to be something I would feel guilty about if it didn't work out. I was suddenly surprised by my own thoughts. "If," I said. If it didn't work out. There was a part of me that still loved him and wanted to stay but I hated who I had become. I hated what he had done to me. I hated that I wasn't good enough for him not to cheat on me.

Every once in a while, I would start thinking. Maybe, just maybe, Margo was right. Maybe we could work it out. What would he say tonight when I ask him about Portia?

Why couldn't I just let it go? I was like my mother. When I wanted something done I wanted it done now. I needed to get his response to that question, now. I couldn't wait for Katherine to fall asleep.

Katherine was in the living room with her new headphones on. Thankfully, she liked us to close the bedroom door. I wouldn't wait until she slept.

"Have you heard from Crazy?" I asked, watching him intently as he responded. Research, I thought.

He paused. His look was different. His face shifted slightly, and he looked down at his phone. "Nope, not a peep." He lied, he fucking lied! Bastard! "Really? You'd tell me?" I asked again. "Yep," I studied his face, "I told you Rainey, no more lies." His face was different again. Well if anything came out of this, I know what he looks like when he lies right to my face. He also called me Rainey. He never calls me Rainey.

Six months. My mind was set. I would be a fool to stay

one minute longer. I was getting ready to start creating my plan to leave when my emotions took hold of me. I couldn't stop there. "Why are you lying to me?" He was shocked by the question. His face shifts. He looks down. "Rainey... I'm not lying to you."

FUCKING BASTARD!!!!!!!!!!!!!!!!!!!!!!!!!!!! My insides explode with rage, or is it devastation?

"I know you are. I saw the emails." Face shift, looks down, stutter– this was new.

"What emails?" he asks innocently with his traitorous characteristics on full display.

"Simon, I saw the emails. I pulled them up from your trash." Now I was trying to control my face. I always laugh when I lie. It's the most ridiculous, uncontrollable, response. I grab a pillow to cover my smirk. I'm not sure if he knows about this quirk. I've never had to lie to him before finding out about Portia

I try to never lie to anyone. I think back to the night I told Katherine I had forgiven Simon. I lied. No smile or nervous laugh, though. I'm not sure why. She knows about my quirk when I lie, she calls me out on it every time. You know all those mom lies? Your face will freeze that way? You'll lose your arm out that window? Yep. Took her hardly a minute to figure out I laugh when I lie. I wonder if she knew I wouldn't lie when she asked me about the affair? How I wish I had.

He continued denying that he had received emails.

"I saw it flash on your screen when you were playing your game in bed." Busted, I thought, as if I were eight again. "I'm not sure what (stutter) you're talking (face shift) about. I didn't get an email from her last night." Simon stammered, clearly uncomfortable. WHAT?!?! He's going to continue the charade even after he's caught? He's completely pathological. "I saw it, Simon. What is wrong with you?"

"Oh, you must have seen the email come through from Portia from our travel group." A full sentence of stuttering. Liar.

"Oh really, what did she say?" I asked as if there might be a chance I believed him.

"She's trying to get something going in the spring."

"Oh really? Where to?" I asked, unable to stop.

"Morocco." The lies were rolling off his tongue faster now. He was looking right into my eyes and lying. I've never been so angry.

"Great, you know I've been dying to go to Morocco, let me see the email." I challenged. He starts fumbling with his phone. I can tell he's nervous.

I think at any moment he's going to say, "I'm sorry babe, I didn't want to bring her name up, I should have just confessed." But no, the charade continues. Unsurprisingly, he can't seem to find it. What a complete idiot.

"Let me see if I can find it for you." He starts to hand me his phone. He's confident knowing he deleted it out of his trash. I don't take his phone. I pick up mine, open one of the emails I had sent as Portia and start reading it. He's speechless. Now you're really busted, I thought.

He recovers. "What are you reading?"

"I'm reading the email that was sent to you last night. The one I saw you open in front of me. The one from Portia Lamont."

"How did you get it?" his shock apparent in his words.

"I found it in your email." I now lied effortlessly.

"But I looked in my email just now. I didn't find it." He didn't find it. I watched him. At least one sentence he would utter would be truthful tonight.

"Well I did." I scolded.

"What else did you find?"

"One other." I was getting good at lying, but who wants to be good at lying? Simon now needed to get better at lying.

Head shifting, his eyes down, Simon started stuttering again. "Well, I never got them. I don't know what they say. Anytime I see the name Portia I delete it immediately. It's my defense mechanism," he defended.

"I see two problems with that. First, I saw you skim the email last night. Second, you just told me you read Portia's email from your travel group." He answered quicker than before. Had he anticipated this challenge or was he just getting better at lying?

"Well, hers was a group email and someone else's name was listed." I wanted to ask him what he had responded to Portia from the travel group. I had always wanted to go to Morocco and had shared this with him several times. I had even showed him a brochure with a planned trip. Surely this wasn't a trip we'd want to miss, I'd say. Instead, my bullshit-o-meter was in overload. I was so done listening to his lies.

"Fuck you, Simon. I wrote those emails."

He slips, "How did you do that? You were sitting right next to me when I got it. Well... er... when you said you saw me get it."

"It doesn't matter. Why the fuck are you still lying to me?" I spoke harshly, finding it difficult not to scream. Now would surely be the time he confesses, right?

"Well I didn't respond to them, did I?" He questions matter-of-factly. He deflects, "Why would you do something like that to me?"

I couldn't believe he would turn this toward me. I heard him mumbling about how I had created a new problem. I stopped listening. He wasn't apologizing. He was talking in circles trying to make this about me.

"Simon." I stopped him. "Stop." I demanded. My head was spinning. Why hadn't I taken that check? Could I still move Katherine? Oh my God, this poor kid. I wanted so badly to run out of the room, grab Katherine, and get in the car. It wasn't my reality.

Simon was silent until he could no longer be silent. "Baby, I love you. I can't let that psychotic woman back into our life. I can't allow her to hurt you again."

"You hurt me, Simon. She didn't hurt me, you did."

He kept talking. "I love you. My life would end if you walk

out that door. Please believe me. I never saw those emails. My brain protected me from seeing them. I deleted them as soon as they popped up and I didn't even look at anything but the first name before I deleted them." He seemed oddly sincere.

I didn't know what to do. I had destroyed my own plan. Why couldn't I make a decision for six months? This was not who I was. I needed to start working fast. Idle minds are dangerous. January fourth could not come soon enough.

I stuffed my good sense in my throat and told Simon that I would forgive him, again. He grabbed me frantically in an embrace. I let him. He started kissing me, thanking me for another chance. Still not admitting he saw the emails and throwing scientific mumbo jumbo at me to solidify his lie. He was begging me to forgive him for his "mistake" and telling me he knew he was responsible for my behavior.

Exactly the power I didn't want to give him, I thought.

He always calls it a "mistake." I hate when he says that. Mistakes are done once, decisions are conscious choices that are repeated. His was a decision to cheat. He deserves mistrust.

I stared at the door as he held me. Five more months. Tonight had solidified my decision.

Dr. Rebecca Harpin could never have known what the next one hundred and eighty-two days would bring. I couldn't blame her for my decisions or what would happen next.

Dear Diary,

This year sucks. We celebrated New Year's Eve with "the family." Ugh. Last year I had my friends from Stonington over for a huge party. I wish I could go back. This is so boring. My mom still cries, she doesn't think I know. Does she think I'm stupid? Her eyes are always puffy now. Doesn't she hear Simon? He's trying so hard. He does everything for her. I mean, I get it, but I don't even think she realizes the effect her being mad at him is having. I catch him holding his heart all the time. I think it's literally breaking.

I hate my new school. The first week was cool. So many people came up to me and friended me on Snapchat. Some of the girls told me that a bunch of the boys were talking in English class about me. They said I was hot. I now have over six hundred friends on Snapchat. That's more than anyone I know. I guess that's the good thing about having to live in three different places.

Yesterday Kitt was so mean to me. Alyssa told me that she thinks I was flirting with her boyfriend. I didn't even know she had a boyfriend until she was mad at me. By the way, he came up to ME at MY locker. I didn't even know him before. Now Morgan and Brianna are being mean to me, too. The worst part is there's nowhere to sit in the cafeteria. The tables have six seats that don't move, and every table is full except for the one with my first day "Buddy." Thanks Mr. Woodland, I'm permanently stuck at the irrelevant table.

I hate English. It's so hard here and my teacher hates me. He's always calling on me, always trying to embarrass me, I just hate him. My mom is going to kill me when she finds out I'm failing. I have to take tests on stuff they learned before I even got to this stupid school.

Now my mom is crazy. I hope she just gets over it, like tomorrow! I knew she didn't love my dad, but she definitely loves Simon. They were meant for each other. She told me she forgave him. MOM! Open your eyes!!! He's doing everything you ask. He apologizes non-stop, even in front of me. You keep telling me that God tells us to forgive, just forgive and move on already! He's not going to do it again. I don't want to think about it anymore.

I see her giving in a little. I get it, it was hard for me to forgive Simon, too. I'm not really sure what my mom did to make him cheat, they seemed so happy before we found out. It must have been really, really, bad because that man worships her.

Ugh. Time to do homework. I can't believe we didn't buy that house. I can't wait to get out of this hotel.

LITERAL SLIDING DOORS

"Let's just get an apartment for now," I challenged. "We can't stay in this hotel. It's too expensive, too small, and too far from Katherine's school."

"No, I need to buy a house for you," Simon pushed. "You need to know I am committed and I will never do anything stupid again. I almost lost you, I'm not willing to risk that, Babe," he continued.

"I'm working now, let's just find something. A house isn't going to prove your love." The words came out of my mouth and I wondered if I believed them. He would have to empty his precious little bank account for it. For me. Maybe it would.

Simon grabbed his heart again.

"Simon, are you okay?" He was quiet but nodded. "See, anytime I think of losing you my heart starts beating too fast for my chest. It's the stress of losing the best thing that has ever happened to me."

"You know babe," I started calling him Babe again but can't remember when that happened, "you should go get that checked out. I don't care if it's just stress. Maybe they can give you some valium or something. That can't be good."

"Okay, we'll get a temporary apartment, but we keep looking for a house," he answered after he caught his breath.

No comment about the doctor. Why were all men so stubborn? Ultimately, I knew he'd get the apartment for me. I couldn't go through with the last house, it didn't seem right. If he was really just doing it for me- and I'm not even sure I want to be with him in four months- well, it just didn't seem right. I got lucky that an undisclosed insurance issue with the homeowners' association came up at the last minute. My conscience would be clear, and Simon wouldn't lose any of his precious money.

The temporary apartment was a relief. We had an extra bathroom and Katherine had her own room. I can't decide if she's just becoming more of a teenager or if this move is tougher than we expected. There are so many unexpected challenges. I don't know how we could have planned for them, but my super-confident teen was starting to struggle. Could school be the only problem? Friends? The affair? My working outside the house again? I think it's a combination of it all. I worry about her endlessly.

"Dear God, please let me have made the right decision. Hopefully, now that we're settled she can find her groove– like Stella, I thought. I'm no different, I need to find my groove again as well, soon!"

I was a robot these days. I joined the daily herd of commuters as they walked silently to the train, a slight nervousness in their step that they might be behind schedule and miss the express. As we'd all enter the station, a crowd of well-dressed men and women would stand next to each other in silence staring up at the twenty-year-old display. The white analog lettering simply announced departing trains yet entranced the travelers. Although the room was a beautifully arched atrium filled with sunlight, the hundred or so city-bound executives stood as though they were waiting for a door on an elevator to open onto their floor. They are all here at the same time every morning, yet no one gave a hint of recognition– toward me or anyone else.

This would have tortured me a year ago. I would have struck up conversations with anyone standing near enough to me who looked reasonably interesting. These days, I appreciated the silence. I would take the forty-five-minute commute in silence and dwell on my present circumstances.

More than once, I'd tell myself to rise above, choose my attitude, and create my new future. I listen to motivational and hypnosis recordings before bed hoping to find the woman who once was in this body – this body that was now a whopping eighteen pounds heavier than it was two months ago. Who knew you could gain weight so fast? Just like that, I take my temporary high and crash and burn into insecurity.

I was eager to start this job. I thought it would be the perfect distraction. My first day, when managing through a giant mistake the founders made, one founder turned to me and proudly announced her stance.

"Apologizing is a sign of weakness," she boldly announced. "We will do anything but apologize."

Who are these morally bankrupt women? I wondered. What have I got myself into? No big deal, I thought. It was a job I could love. Who cares if the two women who owned it are working hard to manipulate each other and their team. This was easy.

But it wasn't.

I began to find rage in their manipulations and their selfishness. I had led people like this, hundreds of people like these women, but today I couldn't set my emotions aside to manage them. Every time I saw a fake smile or caught a small lie, they reminded me of Simon. My disdain grew, but so did my depression. I started sleeping on the train, in both directions. If I slept, I didn't need to think, and my thoughts now only led me in one direction: How could this be happening to me? I started to drink wine regularly at night, so I could sleep. I could no longer read more than a sentence or two and still find comprehension in the words. I couldn't even re-read my own sentences. I was a living zombie moving through the routines of life with my eyes open, not seeing anything.

The only thing I did see was the need to be happy. I thought of all those books on happiness again. Was I doing what I wanted to? I don't recall any of them mentioning gaining control and rebuilding your self-esteem after some idiot smashed both into smithereens. How did I give him that power?

I'd start to plan weekends with friends back in Connecticut. It would make Katherine and me happy to be with friends and to laugh. I'd lose myself in the life I used to have, before my heart broke.

Simon never wanted to let us go alone. "I don't want to be without you," he'd whine, "I'll miss you too much." Didn't he know I was leaving to escape the pain he brought into my world?

He didn't know. I had been the master of the ruse.

Men and women are different. If you tell a man everything is okay– they'll believe you– especially if it's something they want to hear.

"I know you love me, Simon. I've forgiven you. Let's work on building happily ever after together now."

He would thank me profusely for this amazing life we were now creating. He shifted from incessant apologizing to bending over backwards to make every one of my dreams come true. Of course, he was cautious. I warned him that the emotion floods back in occasionally and he would have to be prepared for it. I told him to expect a little bit of a roller coaster– so he did– and that's exactly what I delivered. He believed and did exactly what I told him.

Katherine, not so much. She was on to me. I saw the way she looked at my eyes sometimes. She was trying to tell if I had been crying.

"Onions," I'd say. "Allergies," sometimes.

She knew. She's a woman. Women always dig deeper. How I wish I had dug deeper when he came home with perfume on his collar.

I wonder if Simon knows, too. I don't think he knows I'm planning my escape in four months, but I wonder if he's still worried? He's still having those anxiety attacks. He finally went to the doctor last week and she is sending him to a cardiologist just to make sure everything is okay. I couldn't help but notice, great women think alike. I think I'll make an appointment with her for my physical.

As my emotions continue to affect every part of my brain, I decided to tell Simon I thought I needed a hall pass. He reluctantly agreed. I'm not sure if I really wanted to sleep with someone else or did I just want him to feel the pain when I did. Melissa told me she demanded a pass from Richard and it empowered her. She quickly took off to Boston and reconnected with an old flame. I laughed at how easy it was for her. She knew who, when, and where. She never told Richard she had used the hall pass. She told him she was visiting her parents and instead, spent the entire weekend "naked and rolling in the sheets." As she described it, I suspected the guilty pleasure of it all helped her better understand what her husband had done. She said it made her feel better. She said it helped her move on, but I suspected that wasn't the entire truth. Like I said, you can't always take what a woman says at face value. It's not that women lie, it's just sometimes we are tired of hearing our own whining.

The train rides changed after I was granted my hall pass. I was reminded of the eighteen pounds I was now carrying. I had been this heavy before after having Katherine, but it never seemed to affect my sexuality. Now, I wondered if I could even find a lover. I wondered how many men were in my position. I decided to explore Ashley Madison. Ashley Madison was hacked a year ago. That's when I had first learned of it. It was a discreet website for married spouses to escape from their partner. When there was no one to peer over my shoulder on the train, I explored the trove of cheats in my community.

I was glad I was looking in New Jersey, where I knew no one. Nothing would have been as devastating as to see someone's husband trolling for an affair. I was shocked at how many men were looking to step out on their wives. It started to repulse me. Could I do this? I stared at the pictures with their blurred faces aimed at protecting their sins, or future sins. They all had buff bodies, which they willingly photographed. I wondered whose wife wouldn't recognize her own husband's body, especially when he donned a tattoo with a Superman cape or the words "Party Here" with an arrow pointing down his pants. Besides bad tattoos, there were other clues to identify their personality: the messy room, the wife-beater tee, the one room apartment donned with Walmart prints... none of these men were particularly enticing. I felt dirty just looking. I would wash the scum off me when I got home, I thought. The hardest part of the hall pass would be using it. Not just because I knew it would hurt him, but because it might just hurt me more.

It was late January when the heavy snow started.

New York is incredibly beautiful in the snow. When it starts, the traffic continues as if nothing has changed but the snow forces you to look up toward the lights that make the city so recognizable. Staring at the ubiquitous Calvin Klein billboard, I watched the snow as the wind forced it to cling to the naked model proudly usurping eighteen floors of a well-placed skyscraper. The traffic lights became muted but glowed in the thick veil of snow. As the veil thickened, the streets slowly received a beautiful blanket to cover up careless cigarettes and trash left behind by ignorant tourists. I noticed the snow from my office window. I knew if I simply waited an hour, with snow this heavy, the streets would magically clear and I'd have the false comfort of walking down Seventh Avenue with no cars, feeling as though I owned this glorious city. New York is magical when it snows and when I left the office that evening, there would be no exception.

I must have worn that glow into Grand Central that evening. As I looked up at the train schedule, the Gladstone-Peacock line only stated "DELAYED" next to each upcoming time. I knew what that meant when I looked around the crowded terminal. It was almost standing room only in the promenade as people called their families telling them they had been delayed. Little did many of them know, those "DELAYED" messages would soon change to "CANCELLED." Tonight, would be a long night.

When you live in New Jersey, you quickly learn there are only five ways to get over the Hudson River. They include New Jersey Transit (less predictable than the last choice,) the Path train, driving, the ferry, or swimming. To drive the eighteen miles to my house would mean Uber or renting a car. Both may take four times longer than swimming across the river in January, and success might be equally as unpredictable. The ferry would probably be closed already, leaving the last option - the Path train. Even with the subway, it's something of a trek. I decided to take the first train out of Grand Central that would get me over the river.

I ran as quickly as I could to a shore bound train. I just made it into the crowded car as the doors were sliding closed. I thought of Gwenyth Paltrow again. Where would this sliding door bring me?

No one takes this route in the winter, but it was standing room only with seasoned Jersians tonight. I'd quickly navigate my NJ Transit app to find the station closest to Summit, and from there I'd take an Uber. As I looked at the list of stops, not one of them was familiar. When the conductor checked my ticket he simply said,

"You're on the wrong train." I laughed. I had heard him say this at least four times before he repeated it to me.

I asked, "Can you tell me which stop is closest to Summit, New Jersey?"

He looked at me as if I had asked for his first born while wearing nothing but executioner's garb. "You can just say "no,"" I shocked myself with my rudeness. At that, I heard a man laugh. The man signaled to me that he would help me and to free the conductor from embarrassment. I apologized, said I was stressed with the weather, and thanked him. I looked at my phone, it was at six percent. I'd need to save that for Uber.

The man approached. If I had to guess, I'd say he was ten years younger than I. He had an athletic build that was complemented by his tailored suit. I would predict him to be a lawyer but would never ask. His dark hair was perfectly coifed despite the snow and he smelled slightly of olives and gin. His face was darkened by new growth which was clearly well shaven this morning. An Italian with piercing blue eyes, I guessed. I wondered if his mother or father was fair-skinned.

"I don't think the conductor had any sense of humor this evening. Probably the first time since summer he's had to put in an honest day's work," the blue-eyed stranger said as he smiled. He became even more attractive when he smiled. Could that have been possible? "I can help you," he continued.

He told me I had two choices but encouraged me to take Newark Penn Station because of the police presence. He spoke to me as if he was the steward of my well-being and instructed me to call for Uber before leaving the train and ask an officer to escort me to pick up.

"A beautiful woman like you shouldn't be in Newark at this time of night alone."

I needed that, I thought.

He stood next to me and we talked about random topics for the next twenty minutes at the train moved across the river.

"You should come with me," he said casually. I giggled youthfully and went to answer as he moved closer. Did he still smell of olives? No, mint, now. He must have slipped a mint into his mouth. We were face to face. "I'm getting off at the stop before, I live in Paramus, but my car is here from an earlier meeting. We can have a drink together. Maybe get dinner? I can drive you home after?"

Flattered, I showed him my ring.

"I noticed." His tone was serious and tempting.

I laughed nervously. It took everything I had to not undress him with my eyes. Maybe I did, but tried not to. I could feel the heat rising under my coat.

"You should come... with me." I wondered if the double entendre was purposeful. Seconds later, his smile told me it was.

"Thank you, but I can't." I giggled again, completely involuntarily. A little voice in my head was now calling me a "fucking idiot" and reminding me of my hall pass. My thoughts were playing ping pong in my brain.

The train started to stop. "Please come. Dinner, no commitment." He threw his two hands in the air next to his head as if to gesture, "What do you have to lose?" His eyes pleaded playfully, while the temptation rose quickly. The doors behind him opened slowly and he never broke his gaze as he stepped backwards through the door. My muscles tensed as if to propel me from my seat, but my conscience glued me to the plastic mold. He stood in the closing doors, they bounced off him and opened again. "Last chance..." he teased.

"Thank you." I waved and smiled as the door slid shut. Regret filled me. I couldn't, I thought. Or could I?

It didn't matter. I would never see that man again.

I followed his direction as I exited the train at Newark Penn Station. I ascended to the main floor and found it bright and, although there was some riff-raff, I found it very nonthreatening. I had managed worse, I thought. I asked a police officer to point me to taxi pickup and made my way to the oldest, most beat up used car I had ever seen. Not as nice as the picture on Uber, but the driver was a congenial old man with a smile that could melt icebergs. I hopped in. On the ride to my car I wondered what my handsome stranger would have driven me home in. I had missed my own sliding door, literally.

As I used the driver's cord to charge my phone, I wondered

if Melissa was right, an eye for an eye and all that. Would an affair make me feel better, or could I feel worse? I needed to feel better. The regret of not getting off at the last stop nagged me. I deserve to feel better.

I decided to be more self-destructive and opened Facebook. "Let's see what all the happy couples are doing this snowy evening," I taunted myself. The app opened with Jen and Trevor drinking wine in front of their fireplace with the caption "Snowed in with my honey!" Lisa was next, smiling with her two boys. She had long left her husband and did everything well except date. The boys were throwing snowballs at her with the caption, "It's sticky!" I laughed out loud at the ridiculous caption. Lisa was my queen of selfies who always celebrated her glorious boys. She should, I thought, she's worked hard. I wondered if Katherine and I were still alone in Connecticut, would we be doing the same? No doubt, Popcorn would be involved. That dog loved the snow.

It was then I noticed a message. I never paid attention to Facebook messages before. Considering the last one that I read blew up my life, I couldn't avoid staring to the lower corner of my screen now. The number two lit up. I clicked the message to see if they were from the same person, Jaime O'Brien. Jaime, my first true love, had befriended me several months ago out of the blue. I couldn't help scrolling through his photos and noticing he had only got more handsome. He wore glasses now but still took care of himself. There were pictures of his family, whom I missed dearly. The hardest part of breaking up is not the one person but the group of people that you leave behind. His was a big Irish-Italian family. You couldn't help loving his father and you knew Jaime would grow to be just like him. He had the same rugged good looks and sense of humor.

"You're still as beautiful as ever," the first message read. It was from two days ago. When it went unnoticed by me, he followed up with, "Rainey, I can't get you out of my mind. I'm about to get remarried this summer but if there's any chance there might be hope for us, I need to know. Maybe just dinner to help me forget you? I'll go anywhere."

My breath left me. How I loved Jaime. Jaime was eight years older than I. When you're twenty-four, that's a big difference. I was just starting my career and he wanted me to give it all up, get married, have kids, and stay home. I walked into Jaime's apartment on our last night together, as I had every other night. I had no idea it would be our last. He told me to put my overnight bag in his bedroom, he'd be right in to show me something. When I turned the corner, I saw a small box in the center of his bed. I felt him behind me.

At the time, who I was going to be was more important than who he wanted me to be. I loved him, but I never looked back. I knew I couldn't be happy as a housewife. I had no plans of being a mother at the time. But I loved Jaime. I wondered if I could give it all up for him. We made love while I wore his grandmother's engagement ring. It wasn't until the excitement of his proposal wore off that I knew what I needed to do. He couldn't wait for five years and he wanted children – an entire baseball team. I could never guarantee I'd change my mind and he was "too old to wait" to see if I would. I ended the relationship for both of us that night and cried for the next month while I licked my wounds.

Jaime was married one year later to a woman who was my twin. She had even taken my old job after I had left it. They divorced right after having their second child. Had he gotten what he wanted and waited for me after all?

One sliding door had just closed fifteen minutes earlier. Was I being presented with another one right now?

I replied, "Jaime, I have never stopped loving you. I'm married but it's not good. I'll explain when we talk. Do you still have your old number? I'll call you tomorrow."

I hit send before I could even think of what I had written. Before I could beat myself up the messenger icon lit up with the number one. Jaime's message simply included a new phone number followed by a heart and the words, "till tomorrow."

I didn't feel guilty for some reason. After I turned down my first offer this evening, the universe knocked again. It must be a sign. I wondered, however, a sign from whom? Surely God wouldn't be tempting me to have an affair?

I shook off the snow as I walked into the garage where my car was parked. I called Simon to see if there was anything we needed on my way home.

"No, just please get home." His tone was strange. Was he worried about me out in the snow? Had something happened? I couldn't place his tone.

I carefully drove through the unplowed snow to our temporary home. It was nice to pull into another covered garage. I couldn't help thinking of Popcorn staring out the window waiting for someone to release her from her prison, so she could be free to roll about and eat snow. It sounded as if Simon was just as eager to see me. I took the steps up four flights versus waiting for the elevator. If I was going to see Jaime again, it would make sense to drop a few pounds. Why not start now?

I took a couple deep breaths at the top of the stairs. I was out of shape. I walked down the hallway of our "luxury apartment" complex to find Katherine happy as a clam watching reruns of *Grey's Anatomy* and Popcorn almost knocking me over with delight. She cried when she saw me and then quickly ran to the window and back again to me. Yes, even in this apartment, Popcorn knew this was her night and she wanted it to start right now.

I petted Popcorn and gave her a treat to buy myself some time. I walked over to Katherine and kissed her.

"Where's Simon?"

"In the bedroom." My heart sunk. What now? Maybe I was wrong, but last time he waited to talk to me in the bedroom and didn't greet me at the door, he changed my life. Our lives, I thought.

"How was school?" I was clearly interrupting her show.

"Fine. We got out early because of the storm."

"Lots of homework?" I asked.

"It's all done."

"Anything excitin–" I badgered.

"Mooom!" She was annoyed.

Damn teenagers. It was getting harder and harder to get her attention. I decided to cut my losses, tapped her on the nose, asked her not to speak to me like that, and then made my way to the bedroom after she apologized.

Simon was in that dreaded pose. I had seen it once before and I'll never forget it. Turns out tonight would be no different.

I wasn't sure how to react. I didn't want to ask what was wrong because I really didn't want to know. We had enough bad, I didn't want more. What could it be now? Did Portia return? Was there a new woman? How many fucking women could there be? The less he spoke, the more my imagination ran wild.

"Simon?" I asked.

"Hey babe." He looked numb.

My words didn't want to come out, "Is there something... you.. want to.. tell me?" My heart was already breaking. Despite my planning, I knew there was still a part of me that loved him. I wanted so desperately to believe he loved me, too. I wanted to believe everything he told me about realizing his mistake and trying to cover it up because he never wanted to lose me. I wanted to believe he loved me despite what his actions were telling me. I wanted him to love me enough never to be unfaithful again. I'm not sure I could handle this a second time, I was barely holding it together now.

He patted the bed next to where he was sitting upright. I started to lean over, and he grabbed me. He grabbed me so hard and he hugged me. I couldn't tell if he was hugging me like a mother or a lover. I pulled myself away, I was angry. "Babe, what's going on?"

He started apologizing, "I am so sorry– You should never

have married me– I love you so much–"

Fuck me.

I started to cry as if I knew the next words were going to rip what was left of me out of my insides. I pulled away. I didn't want him to touch me. The room was darker than it should have been. Why was he always sitting in the dark when he is about to give me bad news? I will never walk into a dark room again.

As if reading my mind, he left out a quick laugh. "No, it's not that!" He smiled. "I had my appointment with the cardiologist today." With all my sliding doors and the snow, I had completely forgotten.

"What did he say?" I asked, oddly relieved despite knowing it wasn't going to be good.

Simon's face was apologetic. "It's not good, babe. I'm sorry. I've put you through so much pain this year and now, I don't want to put you through my being sick."

"What do you mean, Simon?" I asked.

Simon was a scientist. I'm sure the doctor gave him a few different potential problems and he went into full research mode to identify which one made sense.

"I may have had a heart attack." My head was spinning. I mean, this was bad news and Simon seemed too healthy for a heart attack, but this was controllable. I started to tell him how it's great that they caught it and how people go on to live happy, healthy lives after a heart attack when it hit me. Simon would not be this upset over a heart attack. He was trying to shield me. My next question would have to be careful.

"What is the next step?" I asked.

"Well, they want me to have a heart MRI and a PET scan." I knew what PET scans were used to detect. I had been with my parents every step of the way. PET scans were used to determine cancerous cells. I also knew Simon wasn't ready to give me more.

"Okay, babe," I grabbed his head like a baby and pulled it to my chest, "Whatever it is, we'll get through it together. You're strong, you can overcome anything."

He allowed his head to stay on my chest longer than I expected. I could feel him gently crying inside although no tears fell. He needed me right now. He didn't need his family, he didn't need Katherine, he didn't need Portia; he needed me.

I looked at the phone in my hand. It was lunchtime. Last night had been exhausting. We decided to share only the bare minimum with Katherine so she wouldn't worry. She's so smart, though. She always knows. I went into the kitchen after leaving our bedroom and she promptly joined me. "What's wrong with Simon?" she whispered.

"I'm not sure, love. It looks as if there might be something wrong with his heart. They might have to give him some medicine to control it or something. I think he's just a little bit unnerved. And to think he blamed it on my cooking!" I tried to keep it light.

"Well Mom, your cooking is not very good," she smiled. "Is he going to be all right?"

"Yes, love, he's going to be just fine." I responded. I then challenged her to think about how healthy he eats, how often he works out, and everything he does that is heart healthy. She agreed he'd be fine and observed that men could be big babies. She then shifted topic almost immediately to a "stupid boy" at the YMCA who fell down the stairs today.

"I have to be careful I'm not raising a man-hater," I noted quietly as she walked away.

I looked at the phone in my hand. Jaime. Life seemed so much easier back then. I ultimately hoped he would wait, but when he didn't, I just talked myself into the idea that I had dodged a bullet.

A year after he married, I ran into him at Westside Lobster House. It was our regular after-work haunt. My group of friends always met there after work on Fridays and had been doing so for the past three years. That evening, I was sitting at the bar laughing with Melissa and Lisa when I felt his warm hands on my shoulders. He was the only one who has ever caressed me like that. His hands would lovingly cup each shoulder, slowly sliding toward my neck, and guide my head toward his lips. Two years and I didn't have to look to know who it was. His lips came toward mine, but I pushed my cheek forward.

He whispered, "I miss you."

"You're married," came from my mouth matter-of-factly.

"She's pregnant," he said.

My eyes welled up, I could barely control my sadness. He continued, "I'd leave her in a minute if you'd take me back. You wouldn't have to have children. We could be happy."

At that I stared back at him, "Congratulations, Jaime. It looks like I dodged a bullet. I never took you as a cheater."

"I'm not. I'll leave her. You know you're the one." He corrected me.

He never greeted Lisa or Melissa. It was an intimate moment where the world around us stopped and there was no one but us in the crowded bar. He spoke so softly but his words were so loud. I wanted to kiss him so badly. Despite my anger that he was here, with me, at a bar, when his wife was expecting a child, I still wanted him. As he walked away I talked myself into believing I had dodged a bullet.

I would never want a man who could do such a thing. The irony was not lost now.

As I tied together what was left of my ability to focus at work the next day, I felt the vibration of my phone in my hand. "Hi, this is Rainey!" I said cheerfully. My work voice.

"I took a chance you hadn't changed your number." It was Jaime. My mouth filled with cotton and my knees weakened. How could this man still have this effect on me twenty years later?

"I'm glad you responded to my message. I wasn't sure you would after you didn't respond to the first one." Jaime said.

"I'm sorry, I'm not good with Facebook messaging," I stumbled.

"I've missed you." Those three little words meant so much more coming from him.

"How have you been? How are the boys? I can't believe you're getting married again!" I covered my mouth with my hand. That's what happens when I get nervous, rapid-fire questions.

"I'm nervous to talk to you, too, Rainey. It's been a long time." He said, calming me.

I couldn't believe he remembered I did that. It would turn out, he remembered much more than that. The memory of Jaime seemed as vivid for me as well. In an instant, with nothing but the sound of his voice, I remembered him joining the Beaufort women at our monthly Scrabble game. I remembered the silly way we'd entwine our legs while we'd watch movies and the way he'd brush my hair off my face as we'd lie in bed together. I smiled as I thought of Rangers games and how, when they scored, he'd look at me first as if I were a lucky charm before he'd jump out of his seat to cheer. I always felt like his lucky charm when we were together. I could see his chiseled jaw and cleft chin clearly through the phone line as I moved to the stairwell where I could talk more freely. I didn't want to be interrupted. For one moment I just wanted to pretend life was simpler, back in his bed wearing his grandmother's engagement ring.

He asked about my marriage. "Are you okay, Rainey. Are you safe?" he quickly got to the point. What? I thought. Is he assuming Simon beats me? I chuckled at the question.

"I am. We're just going through some stuff." I responded.

"I can feel you holding back a laugh, what's really going on Rainey?" He remembered everything. At that, to my surprise, I told him everything else. I told him how Simon cheated. I told him how he's got a heart condition now. I told him how I have been thinking of leaving in three more months because I can't seem to forgive him. I even told him I get a hall pass. I haven't even told all that to some of my closest friends. But here I was– after one minute on the phone with my old flame– spilling my heart out.

He hesitated before asking, "Do you love him?"

Silence.

"I don't know, Jamesy, I did." I slipped into my old nickname for him.

"He's a lucky man if you do," he said.

We spent the next thirty minutes talking about our families and how he had cyber-stalked me on Facebook. He shared how he cried when he found out I had a child, and again when I married. I imagined him crying. It wasn't something Jaime did, so it sounded strange hearing his words. He told me how beautiful Katherine looks and how her smile reminds him of me. He told me about his girlfriend and how he's getting older. He told me how he really loves her, but the ghost of me keeps taunting him. The time went so quickly. He was still so easy to talk to.

"I have to go," I finally got the courage to say.

I didn't want to go, I wanted to stay in that stairwell and talk to him until we couldn't find any more words.

"I know, baby. Can I see you?"

"Yes." This was one sliding door I would walk through. "Yes, you can.

Into each life some rain must fall
But too much is falling in mine
Into each heart some tears must fall
But some day the sun will shine
Some folks can lose the blues in their hearts
But when I think of you another shower starts
Into each life some rain must fall
But too much is falling in mine

- *Ella Fitzgerald*

WHEN?

The next two months are filled with doctors' visits and tests. My broken heart has been put on hold for the time being; his had taken precedence. Simon's heart is going into V-tach rhythms, or ventricular tachycardia, several times a day and it seems to be worsening. This means his heart speeds up faster than his body can handle. If it doesn't come out of these rhythms on its own, he could go into cardiac arrest and die. He's now been referred to two other specialists and a dizzying array of testing. Two months later he is diagnosed with the lottery of all diseases: Cardiac Sarcoidosis. Our "sarcoid specialist" we're referred to has a total of two patients with the disease - one in London, and Simon. We're told that sarcoid is rare in itself; at last count there are 2,182 worldwide. Compare that to 422 million cases of heart disease and you'll see that for every cardiac sarcoid case there is almost two hundred thousand cases of heart disease. But worse yet, there is no cure.

Make that 2,183 now.

"You've been training for this for your entire life. You've got this." I tell him. I'm trying, but I'm a terrible cheerleader right now. I'm no longer working which means I can go with Simon to doctors' visits and help with what his body can't do right now. This is a blessing for both of us. Each day he seems more tired and weaker.

The needed to tell Katherine what was happening was inevitable. By now she knew it wasn't good. This poor child, I kept thinking. I have handed her a litany of devastation to manage over the past five years and she seems to compartmentalize each and move on. When will her little compartments be full? Mine certainly are.

I've always prayed daily. I'm not as good at the church piece, but I attend on a semi-regular basis– enough to be recognized when I do attend. I always feel that my prayers are answered, somehow. I always believe that through all this tragedy a lesson is meant to be learned. As I try to decide what lesson will be learned through our most recent challenges, the phone rings.

"Hey baby."

I recognize his voice instantly. Jaime has been my rock throughout the past two months. He's been checking in regularly and hasn't asked for anything in return. There's been no pressure to meet him in a hotel room or make any decisions. He's been supportive and genuinely caring. The morning I found Simon slumped in the bedroom unconscious, I knew I couldn't go through with my dalliance with Jaime.

I had just returned from a morning run. Simon had been in bed when I left so I assumed this is where I'd find him when I returned. As I started up the stairs to check on him, the darkness confirmed my suspicion that the blinds were still drawn, and he hadn't yet got out of bed. I decided, rather than wake him, to grab a glass of water. It was then that I heard an incredible thump come from our bedroom above. I barely got the glass from my hand before I sprinted up the stairs to the bedroom. The bed was empty, but I quickly saw his body across the room, slumping awkwardly on the floor with half of his limbs and shoulder being held up by the wall leading to our closet. I did the last thing I ever expected me to do. I froze.

Is everyone's journey in life predetermined? I can't help ponder this question as I stood paralyzed with fear, wondering if this is it. Is he dead?

The light danced across the walls precariously, only giving me enough light to make out what was happening. As my eyes adjusted, his limp body bounced into the air with a jolt and landed quickly back down on the hardwood floors. I stared at him, unsure of what I should be doing. Do I touch him? I'm not a doctor, but I wished I was at this moment. My brain flashed of episodes of *Grey's Anatomy* and *The Good Doctor* after I berated myself for not being better prepared. Damn it! I should be doing something. Why isn't he waking?

As the electrodes shock his body a second time, all I can think is he's not coming back to me this time. The real question is: Do I want him to?

I called Jaime the next day after receiving a text from him.

He had sent me one word: "WHEN?"

I knew what he meant. He didn't know what had happened yesterday. He just knew I hadn't picked up his daily call. If he only knew how much I wanted to, how much I needed to talk to him at that moment. The realization that I had needed him made me feel as though I was not only cheating on Simon but meddling in Jaime's relationship as well. Although nothing had happened, it was merely a friendship rekindled, something didn't feel right.

When I saw the simple word he texted, I knew it was anything but simple. Perhaps missing our call yesterday sparked similar fears in him? I turned on my phone, slowly navigated to my contact list, opened Jaime's profile, and touched "call." I would tell Jaime that this was a bad idea. How could I explore a past love while my husband was going to be fighting for his life? "For better or for worse," I promised only three years ago.

When I heard his warm hello on the other end of the

phone, I erupted in tears. Every tear I had held back the night before as I tried to be strong, every tear I stuffed inside while at work, each tear I cried for friends who lived too far away and for my lost savings flooded our call. He was patient with me.

"Where are you? I'll be right there," he whispered.

"No," I gasped.

"Then let it out, baby. Let it out. I'm here for you now, right here."

And, he was. I could feel his love through the phone. He could have written a book on what I needed to hear or how to listen to me. My heart and my brain downloaded every thought through the phone. As I sobbed and struggled to catch my breath, he cooed, "I'm here for you. You're going to be OK. Take your time, baby."

By the end of the call, each detail I hadn't shared before, he learned. He heard every fear and every heart break. No one knew as much about me as Jaime did right now. I was embarrassed that I allowed the flood gates to open, but once they did, I couldn't stop. Margo was struggling with her marriage of fourteen years, I couldn't burden her with more. I didn't want to share the affair with anyone else. Zoe knew enough. Zoe knew more than I wanted her to know. Each friend would know certain parts of my life, but Jaime was the only one who knew them all. Why was it so easy to do?? With this man, a man I had not seen in years, a man I only knew now from distant memory, after twenty years and one phone call?

"Who do you have in New Jersey, Rainey?" Jaime asked.

"My girlfriends will be here when I call," I answered.

"No, Rainey, who lives in New Jersey that you can depend on? A neighbor? A new friend?" he demanded.

I cried softly this time. "No one. I haven't set roots yet. I've just been working to piece together a life for me and Katherine. I decided I'd wait until we move to our final destination before finding friends became a priority." At that, I hesitated and cried harder. Jaime knew me, I thought. He knew that there was nothing in life worse than a social butterfly trapped in a net all alone.

"Okay. Here's what you're going to do next. I know you're busy but go volunteer somewhere. Anywhere where you'll be around other people for at least an hour a day. When we hang up, I want you to find something you love and make a phone call. I'm going to call you at the same time tomorrow to make sure you followed my orders." I couldn't help laughing. He continued seriously, "Rainey, I mean it. I know you, the distraction will be good for you."

I reluctantly agreed and tried to start the conversation about us. He hushed me, "Not now. Let's just get you through the next few days."

The "next few days" turned into the next two months. He called daily to check on me. Sometimes I wouldn't pick up because of guilt and his message would tell me as much.

"I'm not worried about us, Rainey, I'm worried about you," he'd assure me. He'd always leave a threat to ensure I picked up the next day. He'd threaten to call Simon or show up on my door. I knew they were false threats, but I loved him for them. I knew he genuinely cared about me, Rainey Beaufort Bradley.

I did as he said. I reached out to the Greenwood Gardens and volunteered. Greenwood Gardens was a hidden gem wedged between multi-million-dollar homes and a state forest in Short Hills, NJ. The home and gardens where left to the state by the daughter of the Frick family to be used as public gardens. I assume it made no sense financially to upkeep this labyrinth of nature. It seems even the non-profit status and millions in donations couldn't hide the disrepair of the many fountains and overgrown gardens. But still, I found its schizophrenic nature alluring. The gardens were meant to be Italianate in design, but the architect slipped into several different influences as visitors moved from space to space. I couldn't help smiling as I walked it for the first time and left a crumbling Roman fountain to find an Indian teahouse being guarded by Chinese dragons in the adjacent garden. I found each garden a surprise. Even though the hedges desperately begged for pruning, I found sanctuary in its arms.

I warned the curator I was not a gardener but had two able hands and would be happy to support weeding and any outreach she needed. I think I had her at weeding. She asked me to come down the next day.

Jaime was right. For one hour a day I weeded and worked side-by-side with two older women who would teach me the difference between a weed and vernonisa novaborensis. Apparently my first week I was exasperating these women as I'd often be quick to grab the wild looking masses.

"No, Rainey. That's a hibiscus coccineus. You must replant that immediately," Lily scolded. For a non-gardener I did quite a bit of replanting. Lily finally suggested I go somewhere I could do less damage. The next day I was banished to the rose garden. I had confessed it was the only flower I knew anything about tending to, so they were eager to send me off.

"I'm Maude. You must be the hibiscus killer?" I laughed at the greeting I received from my new partner. I laughed not only at her name, but at her humor. Maude was, I would later learn, a "fabulously young eighty-five," and her tongue was quicker than that of most stand-up comics. I loved her, she was just what the doctor ordered.

"Who cares if my only friend is an eighty-five year old, sharp-tongued widow," I reported back, "She makes me laugh, Jamesy."

Our first day together– after she got to know me, maybe it was four minutes in– she stated I "looked sad." She promptly made no hesitation, waited for no response, and followed up with, "It's time for you to get some drugs."

I giggled back and argued, "My therapist said the same thing. But it turns out, you've made me laugh so much in five minutes that I'm not sad any longer."

"Well I'm not sleeping with you tonight so get yourself to the doctor," Maude scolded.

We continued to laugh and on occasion, Maude, the therapist, would jump in and ask questions about my sadness.

I said, "My husband has a rare heart disease and might only have a couple years left."

She'd respond, "Well, thank God for that. Does he have money?"

She had a way of quickly making you laugh as soon as she got her information and every time I'd start getting too serious. But, she always got her information. I had realized by the end of the week, Maude knew everything about me but the affair.

I'm allowing the affair to define me, I thought. I knew it didn't, but it was right now. When would that change?

"So, your only friend in New Jersey is an old woman with a foul mouth and a great sense of humor?" Jaime laughed. We had solidified our ritual of talking each afternoon.

"Don't judge," I said in feigned anger.

"It's a start, at least. How's Simon?" he asked.

This was the first time Jaime had mentioned Simon's name. I guess I knew he had known his name all along. I know I didn't mention it. Every time I'd start to say his name I'd hold back. Maybe I felt guilty? I couldn't pinpoint my feelings but decided that saying his name out loud on the phone to Jaime would make Simon more real, more human. I wanted Jaime to be on my side. I wanted to keep him cheering for me, I suppose. I wanted to keep the possibility of Jaime and me open, although I still wasn't sure I could ever use my hall pass. When he said Simon's name for the first time it was as if the last sliding door closed. Maybe, Jamesy and I were now just wonderful friends?

"He's tired and fat, or so he says. Our waistlines are the only thing in our house that keeps growing." I finally answered.

"Ha! Well, at least you have a good sense of humor about it now. Maybe this Maude is not so bad after all. I'll have to reassess the situation."

I smiled at his subtle way of telling me my attitude was changing.

He continued, “When can I meet her?” he asked. Maybe we’re not just friends?

“Soon enough,” I teased. Then the conversation took a more serious tone.

“Rainey, somehow I love you more today than I did all those years ago. The past few months, your compassion and energy for a man who has hurt you, well, you’re a saint. You’ve moved me beyond words. You don’t have to stay because he’s sick.”

There it was. Permission to leave. Was it his to give, I wonder?

“Jaime...” I started.

“No,” he interrupted, “don’t finish that sentence. The weather is beautiful. Let’s plan a weekend in the Cape. Do Melissa’s parents still have that house up there?”

“Yes, they do.” I answered.

“Call her and tell her you need to escape. I’ll rent a hotel room and you can stay at her parents. If things haven’t changed, they love you like one of their own. It won’t be a problem and you can tell Simon you’re going up for a girls’ weekend. No one has to know. You deserve this. Let me take care of you. No pressure. Stay at her parents’ house or stay with me. You need a break and I... I need to see you.” He had it all planned. How had he remembered Melissa’s parents? I remembered Jaime's text.

"WHEN?"

Dear Diary,

My step-grandparents just left, it was so sweet that they came for Simon's surgery. I think my mom guilted them into it. I don't think they realized how serious Simon's condition was until Mom called them herself. They were going to show up after the surgery, but she called them back and they changed their plans. I heard Mom telling Margo that she started crying the minute she got on the phone with GB (That's what I call him because Grandpa Bradley seems too long) and they called Simon back almost immediately with an earlier arrival.

Mom always gets her way. I couldn't tell you how many of her old workers still visit and call. Sometimes I'd meet some of her clients when we're out. "Your mother is a miracle-worker," they'd tell me. "Pay attention, kiddo, your mother can make anything happen." Why do old people always do that? They feel like they need to sell your parents to you. I already know how lucky I am, I just don't like to tell them!

Last week, Mom slept overnight in a hospital chair after Simon's surgery (he had a defibrillator put in. I guess it's supposed to revive him if he goes into a v-tach rhythm again.) I know it hurt, but she didn't say a word. She didn't want him to be alone. I noticed that she set up some appointments at the chiropractor the next day. She never even complained. When I asked her why she would do that she told me the body rejects it within the first twenty-four hours and Simon was high risk already. She was uncomfortable that he wasn't hooked up to monitors overnight. I knew this really meant she didn't get any sleep in that uncomfortable wooden chair.

When my mother loves someone she will do anything for them. I was freaked out about a test when we first moved to New Jersey. She took the day off from work, bought and read the Midsummer Night's Dream Cliffs Notes, and let me stay home from school the day before my test and helped me study all day. Another time I was really sick, and she waited on me all day. She was so funny. She dressed in all white, made a funny paper hat, and carried around an old silver tray with cool washcloths, raspberry tea, medicine and chicken noodle soup. Even though I thought I was going to die that day, she would make me laugh with the funny way she'd act in her crazy uniform. She also changed her name each time she came to my room. Nurse Nincompoop had glasses with tape on the corners and would pretend to trip. For Nurse Handsy she found a bloody Halloween arm and stuck it from her shirt. She apologized for taking so long between visits, but she had been in surgery and had broken an artery. I can't wait for her to be funny again.

Between Simon being sick, taking care of Mimi (she seems to be on the phone every day with a doctor or the nursing home,) Mimi calling and talking crazy every day, our old house sinking, and my grades; I'm pretty sure we are making her crazy. I told her that she's been forgetting things all the time now. My mother would NEVER forget anything. When I told her, she just started to cry. I felt so bad. I hope she doesn't have Alzheimer's or something.
I was so angry at Simon and Mom when they told me we were moving again. They promised I could stay in Summit. I'm finally meeting people I like!!!! I know they tried, I'm still angry though. At least we'll own a house again. That should guarantee I am at least in the same school till college. Then they can move anywhere they want! I don't care. I wonder if Simon will still be alive then? Poor Simon.

Mom got medicine for her focus. She told me she was having a hard time focusing and she appreciated that I told her about forgetting things. She thought maybe it was her change of life happening. She told me she would be happier and back to normal in six or seven weeks. I don't know why she's always apologizing to me. It's life, right? If anyone has taught me that, it's her. As long as we have our family, we can get through anything. I hope she gets better soon. I miss her.

When will I get to live a normal life????

ALONE OR LONELY?

Starfishing. That's what I called it in the past when Simon would go away on business. On the weekends, Katherine might sleep with me– Oh, how I loved that, too. But during the week, I starfished. I had something of a routine.

Step One: Change every sheet except for his pillowcase.

Step Two: Make the bed perfectly. There is something about bedding when it's crisp and fresh that I love.

Step Three: Don't get in too soon. These steps should be done in the morning, so you can spend the day looking forward to your evening indulgence.

Step Four: Splurge on expensive chocolate and a brilliant bottle of wine.

Step Five: Grab your finest china. I prefer a delicate Spode plate from my great grandmother's dowry. The light weight and dainty flowers of the plate grace my bed tray perfectly. And yes, absolutely grab a bed tray. I have a couple nice wooden trays, but I prefer an antique silver tea tray I picked up at the Brooklyn flea market. It feels more elegant for the occasion. Yes, a beautiful linen napkin as well. Then cut one or two fresh flowers from the garden and you're ready to starfish.

Now the next step in starfishing is completely up to you. I prefer a juicy romance novel, a New York Times best seller. Nothing too heady but it should definitely have a little steam – if you know what I mean. You can rent a movie if you prefer. Simon has always been so agreeable when it comes to movies that there was no luxury in watching one without him. He would watch *Under The Tuscan Sun* with me for the fourteenth time if I asked. A book, well, he would always interrupt me while I read. It was as if he were missing out on something. Eventually I'd learned that if I wanted to read, I had to read aloud when he was with me. That was sweet, of course, but I'd learn he wasn't as tolerant of steamy novels as he was of leadership books. I enjoyed them as well, so that's generally what we read.

On starfish night, however, I would read whatever I wanted. I would do it with such aplomb that I would barely miss him at all.

As soon as Katherine was tucked in, I'd head to the wine cellar where my silver tray beckoned. I'd open one of my favorite bottles, slowly fill my favorite crystal goblet, recork the bottle, and carry my prized tray to the bedroom. Laid out on the bed waiting for me would be my favorite silk robe and a book I'd been eager to crack open. I'd slowly take my clothes off one piece at a time. I'd pay attention to the fabric as it slid down my curves to the floor, then I'd take the next item off. It was like a delicate dance I'd do alone on these nights. Somehow, it made me feel sexy.

Once I was completely naked I'd slip into my robe. My favorite was a chartreuse kimono I had purchased while at the Peninsula Hotel in Hong Kong. I've never much cared for the color, but the romantic twirl of the magnolias in the fabric were both delicate and bold. Like me, I thought. I had splurged on the luxury of it and, had I known how it would feel once it was on, I would have paid twice that.

This was Fuji Silk. Fuji silk has a soft lustre but feels most lavish of all the silks. When I'd put it against my naked skin it was as though it caressed my breasts purposely as I slid it on. I could feel the luxurious fabric smooth just inches past my derriere. It was sexy, and I felt sexy in it. As I would pull the front across my chest I'd notice how my nipples seemed to stand forward, as if begging for more of this fabric. I'd tie the silk tie and move gracefully to the bed.

The magic of the bed was about to occur. Simon would be at a conference, so I knew I had exactly two and a half hours before he'd call to say goodnight. He was an amazing husband, I used to think. So predictable.

I'd pull down the corner of the covers, not disturbing the elegant tray on his side. I'd slip in, carelessly sitting up as if I knew someone was about to photograph me. I would want this life if I were peering through the lens of a camera, I would think to myself. I'd grab the wine I had been thinking about since morning. I usually chose an earthy cabernet to pair with the dark chocolate and sea salt I had showcased perfectly on the small china plate. I'd crack open the book and throw myself into it. As the wine would warm me, the romance novel seemed to come to life. I'd put my wine down and could feel the warmth between my legs as my heroine felt her handsome rogue on the pages for the first time.

There'd be a gentle throbbing, calling me. It would be begging me to bring the pages to life, and I would. I would go slowly, the way Simon used to. I would start by pulling the Fuji Silk from around one of my breasts. I'd stare at my nipple, erect, begging for me to touch it. I'd circle it with my finger gently, throbbing now below. My breath was starting to change, and I'd release the second breast. I put my book down. I cradle my breasts. I love the feel of the fold beneath the weight of my breast. I pull them slightly up, imagining Simon suckling them. I can't ignore the throbbing below any longer. I slowly move my hand down my stomach, my middle finger seemingly knowing the way. The words, the anticipation, I am ready. I need to be touched. I am desperate. My finger glides across my opening, it's warm and wet. My clitoris screams as I pass it gently. I can't stop writhing in pleasure. I want to make this last. First one finger, then two. I need more. My breath is laboring and I think about grabbing the dildo hidden carefully in my nightstand. There's no time. My body bursts. Hot raging flames of lust and desire for my own body extinguished. The perfect ending to the day.

The gift of starfishing is that no one knows what it is but you. Simon always rings predictably at eleven o'clock.

"Are you starfishing?"

"Of course, I have spread out all over your side of the bed. Minus the phone in one hand, I am officially taking up the entire bed."

"I've never seen you sleep like a starfish." I'm not sure why he says that. Is he on to me?

"Well, sneak back home and find out."

"I wish I could." And the recap of the day begins on cue. Meetings, blah blah blah, Micah did this, Paul did that, some Nobel Peace Prize winner spoke– it was more of the same. Perfectly boring conversation as read with my husband's sultry voice. The perfect bedtime story.

I was always surprised that I thought of Simon when I masturbated– proof, I suppose that I was madly in love with him. He had truly swept me off my feet. Before I met him, I would vacillate between George Clooney and Chris Helmsworth. I must admit, I do love watching Thor movies for only one reason, he is beautiful. But no, up until day 838, it was still Simon about whom I would fantasize. That had all changed.

It was day 1022 and Simon had another business meeting. Everything had changed now. It was the day I had decided I would be making my decision. The reality hit me as I thought about starfishing tonight. Did I want to? If I did, I wondered who would fill my thoughts. It was just yesterday that Jaime proposed running off to the Cape to rekindle what we had. Maybe it was simply a test for him as much as an escape for me. I couldn't help thinking of the irony that today would be six months.

Simon was at Salve Regina, a wealthy campus on the bluffs of Newport. He'd be sharing a view of the Vanderbilt's old mansion and ocean bluffs with two hundred other scientists. We were two and a half months away from finding out if his regime of steroids and cancer drugs would reduce the swelling enough to allow doctors a true glimpse of the permanent damage the sarcoid had created. We would know then, we thought, if he would have a year left, or twenty.

I had a tracker on his phone, so I knew where he was. I'd check periodically, wondering if he was arrogant enough to do something stupid again.

No starfishing. I didn't feel sexy anymore. I hated to set a date with Jaime for just that reason. I was a lot heavier than I was when he knew me, and I was also more damaged. I did not feel sexy.

I didn't change the sheets yesterday. I didn't wear Fuji Silk today. No silver tray.

I was glad he was going away though. I needed time alone, to think. The past months have been overwhelming by anyone's standards. It was exceptionally warm in the Northeast this week. Perfect day to be in Newport, I thought. I wondered if any boats were out. It was improbable as it wasn't yet Memorial Day, but I imagined there were. Katherine was at a friend's house for the night, making this the first time I would be completely alone since hell broke loose.

The new house we had finally purchased was almost completely unpacked, minus those boxes that never seem to be unpacked. I had a thousand plans. I would make friends in our new community, I would volunteer more hours with Maude, I would finish the master bedroom, I would get my fucking head together. Tall orders for four days.

I used to love to be alone, I thought. I remembered what it was like in Stepford with all those women jealous of my fabulous life. Was I now just one of them? I thought about my male-haters party that brought Simon into my life. What would they say now? I only talk to the ones I really love. It's been three years since Stepford. It seems like a lifetime. Stepford was home. It was where some of my family members lived, where my college friends all seemed to land, and where I gave birth to my angelic pain-in-the-ass teen.

I wondered if this was God's cruel test. I've been forced to put into practice everything I had advised others to do over the years. He cheated? Leave him! Head up your own ass? YOU control your emotions, snap out of it! I made it sound so easy. What a naïve idiot I had been.

"You've got this!" I'd regularly say. No, not today I don't.

My ability to reason and to think has completely abandoned me. When I took the job in Manhattan, I didn't tell the owners what was really going on, I just needed an escape. The job was simple. I took on one tenth of the responsibility I had in previous roles. They didn't pay much but I could live on one-hundred-fifty thousand a year if I had to. I just needed something to keep me busy. Turned out, I couldn't even do that job. I was a dismal failure. I couldn't read anything more than ten words long without my mind wandering. I looked for the worst in people. That was never me. I kept sneaking into the fire escape for lunch to talk to Jaime as he and Maude were my only sanity these days. Personalities I expertly managed in the past were roadblocks. More so, I was overwhelmed by their idiocy and could think of nothing else. I made silly mistake after silly mistake. I would lose that job, or I would quit. I quit before I was fired. Simon, I could tell, was disappointed. He enjoyed the extra money coming in.

But what could he say?

I worked for a few months and stashed away ten thousand dollars. A little extra to help me when I leave. If I leave. I was reminded that today was the day I had set to decide. Today, the same day I was tracking my husband's whereabouts and planning a reunion with a past love. Today, the same day my husband was dying.

For the past one hundred and nine days I've been a train wreck. No, no one has noticed, no one but Jaime and Maude. If there is one thing we Beaufort women all do well, it's appear strong. Bad ass even. Zoe has kept my secret - I think – and our family has no idea. The women I worked for think I've got my shit together but that I just can't operate without an admin or at this low a level. Everything is fanTAStic.

Tom Hopkins was a famous sales trainer in the eighties. During college I worked for my mother and she would regularly send me to his seminars. One thing he regularly said stuck.

"If someone asks you how you're doing– I don't care if you haven't had a sale in months– you proudly smile and say, "FanTAStic!" I was the master at this. Turns out, so were the other Beaufort women.

"How is the move going?"

"FanTAStic!"

"How is Simon doing?"

"FanTAStic!"

"Is Katherine making friends?"

"Oh, fanTAStic friends."

Here I was. I used to be alone by choice, now, I was lonely. Now I was lonely even when Simon was here.

I looked at the sheets of the bed. They were wrinkled and slightly disheveled. Popcorn, our golden retriever was getting old now. I helped her up onto the bed. Popcorn was a great name in her youth when she bounded around rooms getting into mischief. Now, it brought sadness to me. Popcorn was sad. The sheets were sad. I was sad. Dr. Hoffman said the Zoloft would take six weeks to pull me out of my funk. I was three weeks in and I still couldn't control my emotions. I was still angry. I was angry at everything. I was even angry that I was taking antidepressants.

Dear God, please let these things kick in sooner. Maude was right, I needed drugs.

I looked around. The walls I wanted to decorate seemed hideous to me. I had painted and decorated every room in the house to try to fill my time since I left my job in the city, but I couldn't finish our bedroom. I have always been bold with color. In my house in Stepford, I painted my dining room black and white stripes. I artistically distressed them and had my di ning room set painted white. I did the same with the chandelier. I had rich gold brocade drapes made. Lisa thought I had gone mad.

"Are you sure this won't look like a French whorehouse, Rainey?"

I laughed. I was a risk taker and this risk paid off. A local realtor had heard about my dining room and asked to feature it in his new brochure. I'd see evening walkers slow down as they passed my house and point in. Today though, a variation of beige was the only color I could think to paint this room. Had the color run out of me? Maybe if I repaint it something bold, it will call the old me out?

I was lost in the sheets of our king-sized bed. I was alone. I was alone in so many ways that I hadn't experienced before. I have always been blessed with friendship, and although I still have those friends, they all seem so far away right now. I have had several friends whose husbands had cheated on them. Some left, some stayed. What I knew, though, is once I knew about their affair, I never felt the same about my friends' husbands. Sometimes I never felt the same about my friends. If you stayed, you were weak. I never could look at their husbands again, they disgusted me. I love my friends so much that their husbands may have just cheated on me. I hurt so badly for them. But worse, I pitied them. I pitied these beautiful, glowing, strong women. I couldn't decide if they were different after the affair, or if I was. Did I see them differently? Because I love them, I wouldn't burden them with asking the same questions about me. I wouldn't want them to pity me.

As I pondered this, I realized the truth. I didn't tell them because of my pride. This stupid, stubborn Beaufort pride that has been woven into me since my Scrabble days. The affair wasn't something I did, but it made me less than who I had always thought I was. I used to be a great catch. Today, I was damaged goods. I couldn't even keep a husband happy. We were newlyweds when he cheated. Did he celebrate our second anniversary with a morning romp with her?

These emotions don't go away, I would learn. They're

more like rogue waves. Rogue waves have been part of marine folklore for centuries. They're extreme storm waves that appear randomly in the sea and have been known to swallow ships whole. They have been described by those who have survived them as "walls of water." As I was lying in my crumpled sheets looking at Popcorn, another rogue wave hit. I could no longer open a bottle alone, I was sure I'd devour the entire contents. I cried so hard I couldn't breathe. I decided to check on my husband.

Simon recently got a new Apple watch. The kind that can operate without the wireless capacity of a phone. His phone, I could track. His watch was an excuse to roam free and leave his phone in the hotel room. Was it intentional?

I opened my location app. Yep, Simon had left his phone in the hotel room. Fucking bastard! I didn't believe he would or could be cheating on me there. He was with work colleagues. He had been professing his undying love and we had been working hard on communication over the past six months. But right now, when I should be starfishing, I was crazed with insecurity wondering if he could possibly be cheating on me again.

I had officially become the worst version of myself. I couldn't decide whom I hated more - Simon or me.

My thoughts continued to ricochet in my head. It jumped from the past to the present. It jumped from who I was to who I've become to who I want to be. I thought about my decision to take Rebecca's advice and move to New Jersey.

I had to plan my future after I found out about Portia, so, I created a plan. Originally, I planned to move in with my aunt in Stamford. Audrey would be happy to have us, and I could get a job in the city. Whom did I know to help me get Katherine into a better school? The schools in Stamford were terrible. Did I want Katherine to go to school there until I was financially settled?

"This damn business," I'd think more than once. I had risked everything and the moment when I had nothing, what

I did think I had– love– turned out to be a lie. When Rebecca suggested six months to decide, as we worked through the other options together on paper, six months made as much emotional sense as it did financial sense. Every plan I created meant disrupting Katherine again in high school. Why couldn't I have an aunt with two extra bedrooms who lived in a better school district? I laughed at my ridiculousness. The truth was, moving in with my aunt meant wireless-server-Beaufort would go into action, and my entire family knowing everything within milliseconds. I wouldn't be able to show up at a family function the same way. It wouldn't be fun any longer. I could already see the look of pity in their faces as they looked at me, strong Rainey Beaufort was now scarred and broken, no longer the queen. They'd give me the same look they gave Cecilia when Uncle Tony cheated. I knew I would be Scrabble fodder.

"Oh, poor Rainey," they'd say when I wasn't with them. My pride. Again, my stupid, ridiculous, paralyzing pride. I understand why it's a deadly sin. It was killing me. It had forced me to make a different decision, it had forced me to try to salvage my marriage. Or that's what I told myself.

I sent Jaime a text. "Two weeks from Friday."

MAUDE

I left the house thinking that every conversation I had had with Maude was controlled by Maude. There were days I was convinced she read my mind, but then again, I've never been good at liar's poker. She asked questions and my face always wore the answer. As a result, she had become my confidant and my teacher. That morning, after my night of starfishing, I had more questions, my jealously was more uncomfortable, and my plan– well, was more uncertain. Today, I wanted to lose myself in Maude's world.

I planned my attacked as I passed the Greenwood Gardens' gate and drove up the long, wooded driveway. I wanted to know about her late husband, Harry. I wanted to know about her life. I had imagined the most amazing marriage, her house being filled with laughter, too many parties to count, and friends and family crowding her kitchen.

Maude always wore an oversized gardening hat; blue, with thousands of little flowers and a string that tied under her chin. Her gray hair curled out from under it. It was thin, you could tell, but it begged to be free. Her hands were tiny and frail. You could see her age in her protruding knuckles and the wrinkled backs of her hands, but nowhere else. Every wrinkle always had a laugh attached and every time I saw her, I longed to see the younger woman she once was. I hoped I reminded her of her younger self. I'm sure I didn't, not today at least.

As I descended the broken stone steps, I watched Maude

coddle a large bloom as if it were a small infant. As she held its weight delicately in her small fingers, her nose stayed mere inches away. Her red lipstick turned up at the corners and her lids closed halfway down her bright blue eyes. I almost felt as if I was interrupting.

She sensed me to her left and turned her upward lips toward me.

"I hope I'm not interrupting?" I smiled back.

"I'm just spending time with my friend, Hope."

"Was she talking to you?" I asked almost afraid for the answer.

Maude laughed. "You really aren't a gardener, are you?"

Not sure of the joke, I responded, "No, I only play one on TV."

"Don't worry darling, you'll be funny again once you're feeling better."

I couldn't help but spit a little of the coffee I just sipped at her reply. "Oh my God, Maude. I can't believe you just said that!" At that, we laughed as if we had known each other our entire lives. "Well, I hope you're right," I continued.

Maude returned to the Rose of Hope. She shared how she always starts her day smelling the rose of hope. She took her small hands and lifted two rose heads. At a distance, one looked yellow and the other pink.

"Look at these beauties. Lean in, Rainey."

I leaned forward and tried to smell their aroma. Maude corrected me.

"Look deeper, my love."

I did. The heads were abundant with delicate leaves. The coloring, as you got closer, seemed to be kissed by God. The yellow rose was twenty shades of yellow and graced by specks of red and orange around the outer petals. The pinkish frame the specks created showcased the yellow petals adding to their color, while not overcoming it. The other- the pink rose of hope- was yellow as you closed in with the same red and orange specks. It was kissed deeper by the specks and seemed to protect the yellow core so robustly that the shade of the flower was completely altered.

"So, will they all turn pink?" I asked.

"No, hope looks different for each flower, just as it does for each of us." Sometimes Maude reminded me of Aunt Audrey, sometimes of myself, and sometimes Maude just seemed magical. We were somehow speaking the same language.

"For what do you hope, Maude?" She looked up at me knowingly and grinned her most mischievous grin.

"I hope that Harry and I end up in the same place."

I wasn't sure whether to laugh of cry. I knew she wasn't hoping for death, she was too vivacious and life-loving. It wasn't her time. Was she referring to Heaven and Hell?

"Maude, I think there might be more to your story than I originally expected."

It took a few more directed questions, but finally Maude shared about her and Harry's life.

"It wasn't all roses," she said quietly, "but it was a beautiful bed we tended to." Of all the things she'd share that morning, it was that comment I would hold on to.

Maude told me about how they met and her father's disapproval. As the story moved to her marriage, she answered the questions I hadn't asked.

"Rainey, I don't know if my Harry was unfaithful. Times were different when Harry and I married. I had a wonderful life. And if he were? I'm not sure I wanted to know. I've never worked, what would I have done?"

"You say that as if you've wondered about it?" I wanted to take the words back as soon as they launched from my tongue. "I'm sorry," I tried to retract the statement.

"Rainey, don't be sorry. I did wonder. Things weren't always great, you must tend to a marriage just like these bushes. Harry and I weren't always good at that but we always figured out how to keep it alive. It's impossible for every moment in life to be happy, but it's up to us to create more happy moments than we do sad. Harry and I were happy. Each challenge brought us closer together, so I'm thankful for each one."

"Did you every worry that you wouldn't make it through some of those challenges?"

"Darling, you don't have a real marriage unless you've asked yourself if it's worth it."

I was quieted by her statement. That was my question, or at least one of them. Is it worth it?

Maude continued talking about how hard Harry worked to give her and her daughter what she needed, how her father wouldn't visit them in their home until it was worthy, and how Harry was the one who cried hardest at her father's funeral.

Her stories grew lighter as she laughed about past parties and her part in Harry's business. She called herself "the closer." When Harry would have a particularly tough client, he'd invite them for dinner and would put Maude to work. In her humility, she'd describe her role as the hostess and serving good food as the influencing tool. In truth, you knew that Maude had a way of making everyone and everything around her brighter. She was magnetic and had a funny way of making you laugh when you wanted to cry. She never negated your pain, she just made it a little easier to bear. As we talked, I told her what she meant to me.

"Maude, I'm so thankful for you. It was as if God sent me an angel when I needed one. I love you and appreciate you."

Maude was quiet. It may be the first time I had seen her blush.

"Oh Rainey, I'm just an old woman who prefers good company over the risks you pose to my garden beds." She smiled shyly. I didn't know this side of Maude.

"Well, thank you for putting up with my dark side."

She laughed, "See? You're getting funnier already."

We spent the rest of the morning chatting about nonsense as we clipped and pruned away. Several times Maude would stop and talk to the few visitors who'd stop at the gardens.

I knew she loved her roses but she loved people more. She wasn't like the rest of the volunteers, trying to sell them on the beauty they might see if they looked hard enough. She didn't extol the history of the property or its architectural importance. Maude had her own agenda. Maude wanted to know everything about everyone. She especially loved the teenagers and women. I once asked her why and she simply stated, "They are our future."

"I love you, Maude. See you tomorrow."

GROWING SEASON

Maude was exceedingly chipper this morning. Today, her pale skin had a healthy red glow on the apples of her cheeks and she wore a new shade of lipstick, a color only a woman of her personality could sport.

I had grown dependent on meeting Maude in "our rose garden" each morning. It was really looking beautiful and Maude was a wonderful way to start my day. After we were done in the garden, I'd usually head to the office to dial for donations. I have been secretly putting together a plan for next year that could really change things for Greenwood Gardens, and I had put the finishing touches on the plan last night. I decided to tell Maude about my proposal today and ask her the best way to present it.

Maude was an authority on everything. She didn't work a day in her life but was a brilliant business woman, savvy politician, amazing mother, and outstanding psychotherapist. I'd spend each day being more impressed by her. Her stories never got old and were never repeated - a life well-lived, I'd regularly think. I couldn't ignore her glowing mood today. She was always happy, but today she swayed with glee.

"Margaret's coming!" she beamed. Margaret was her only daughter who lived in Seattle with her children and husband.

"I can't wait to meet her! When is she visiting?" I asked, sharing her glee.

"Visiting? Nooo, she and her girls are coming to live with me!" Her excitement was over the top.

"Coming to live with you? Did she and her husband get transferred here?"

"PFFT!" She got more serious and waved her hand at me as though I was being ridiculous. "She left him!" she blurted.

I was stunned. Maude always bragged about Margaret. She told me about her being offered Partner in her law firm, how beautiful she was, and how she doted on her two beautiful daughters. She told me about her loving husband that was always buying her beautiful gifts and catering to her every whim. I couldn't comprehend why this would please Maude so thoroughly, Margaret coming without him. I froze. He must have cheated. The same as my situation only Margaret was brilliant and beautiful and strong– like I used to be. She left him!

"Well, it's not my business to tell you the details. I will say this, sometimes you can live in the past worrying about what you could have done differently, or you can choose to live in today and celebrate each cherished moment." I imagined reading that in a greeting card. As she said it, I noticed the experience in her eyes.

"Well, when do they arrive and how can I help you get ready?" I asked.

Maude had told me how she hired a "strapping young lad" to clean out the extra rooms and put a fresh coat of paint on. She was proud that she thought to have Margaret go to Benjamin Moore with the girls and help them each choose the perfect color for their new rooms at MeMa's house. I had just seen her yesterday, had all of this happened in just twenty-four hours?

"Well I can't wait to meet them!" I cheered. I realized that at eighty-five, Maude needed no one's help. I thought about my own aunts in their own states of living. They didn't need anyone's help either, whether we liked it or not. I wondered if I was related to Maude in some way, and today, I hoped that I would grow up to be just like her.

"Well, they'll be here Friday." Amazing, Margaret moves as fast as her mother. Moving cross-country in four days is quite some feat. I wondered how she found out.

Maude kept me laughing throughout the morning and I even got her to smile a few times myself. It was nice to be funny again.

Maude asked about the usual things; Simon, Katherine, Popcorn, the house and my new neighbors. It was then she stopped and looked at me quizzically.

"What are you keeping from me, Rainey?"

Suddenly, Catholic school came flooding back and Sister Renna was standing in front of my desk looking down at the note I was about to pass to Lisa. "Nothing Sister Maude," I responded in my best Catholic schoolgirl tone.

We cackled. Oh my God, I cackled for the first time in months.

Maude continued, "I've been noticing lately, a little gleam in your eye. What– Mrs. Bradley– are you holding back?" Now she was one of my girlfriends. Her tone made me giggle.

"Rainey Bradley, you are revolutionizing the Gardens, you're smiling, you're funny– who the hell knew you had <u>that</u> in you– and now, you're even gleaming. Something is going on and I would like to know right now."

I thought about it. I did notice I made her laugh today. I wasn't just sweet Rainey, the volunteer, today. "Maybe it's feeling needed again. I'm busy here, I'm fixing things around the house, and I'm taking care of Simon. Katherine is coming to terms with our move and the school is charming. Maybe being settled and feeling useful has its benefit?"

She wasn't having it. Not one bit.

"There's someone new in your life." She wasn't asking and held a mischievous undertone.

"Maude!" I laughed. That stupid lie detector laugh. Would she know?

Maude knew in an instant, "Raineeey?"

Damn!

I proceeded to tell her everything. I filled in all the blanks. I told her about Simon cheating and I told her about Jaime and my hall pass. I went on for thirty minutes justifying and crying and confessing. At one point the director started across the garden and we heard her shout.

"Rainey, are you okay? Did you get hurt?"

Before I could respond, Maude shook her head, shooed her away and yelled, "Onion weed!"

I roared with laughter and Maude guffawed!

"Is there such a thing?" I asked through my laughing tears.

"Who the fuck knows," Maude answered between laughs.

Once our laughter subsided, I waited to be scolded. Maude had been married fifty-four years when Harry died. Her marriage was the most sacred thing to her, even more so than her daughter. I reminded myself about Margaret as I awaited her judgement.

"Well, is he hot?" said my eighty-five-year-old friend.

"Yes, Maude, he's on fucking fire!"

"Well screw his brains out and fill me in when you get back." We cackled for the next hour making lewd jokes, my New Jersey bestie and I.

Her judgement never came, just more laughter.

I walked in the front door to the common cry of Popcorn's glee. You could leave for fifteen minutes and this dog would greet every return as if you had been gone a week. She was a horrible jumper when she was a pup, but as she matured and was scolded for it, she took on crying as her show of passion. She'd circle and cry at your legs with her tail wagging so fast it would almost disappear. Today was no different, although this time she quickly abandoned my hug to run to the family room. Simon had returned from his meeting before I got home and was sound asleep on the couch. He must be exhausted to sleep through all of Popcorn's commotion. As I stared at him lying there, his eyes opened. A beautiful grin covered his face and he whispered.

"I've missed you."He went to rise, but I quickly motioned for him to stay and walked around to give him a hug.

"Welcome home," I said as I leaned down to kiss him.

"You look beautiful," he said as he admired me.

I looked at my wrists to see a line of dirt starting where my gardening gloves had stopped protecting me. My hair was in a messy bun and I could feel the sweat dripping down the back of my neck. I imagined my face smudged with dirt from wiping my tears with the back of my gloves during my confession to Maude.

"Well, you're either delirious from the medication or you're a man in love." I teased.

Simon quietly said, "In love" and then pulled me near him.

"Let me shower. I'm disgusting," I begged.

"No." Simon was taking control. I didn't expect his strength; he had been so weak. I was surprised to feel my body responding to him.

"Being away from you for four days confirmed my suspicions, I can't live without you, Rainey." He pulled me nearer and started kissing my sweating neck.

"Oh Simon," I moaned, "please let me shower."

"No, I can't wait that long." I felt dirty as I allowed him to take me. We made love on the floor of the family room and my body proved to miss him more than I expected.

After love making, we both shared a shower and he refused to talk about anything but me. I told him stories of Maude and her daughter moving in. He listened as I bored him with details about my job search and how I was going to be volunteering with the Downtown Council of Chatham. Popcorn sat outside the glass shower stall relaxed. She was no longer in charge of protecting me. Her master had returned.

We cooked dinner together and talked about the house–how I would turn our bedroom into a relaxing oasis and other mundane topics. By seven, his overexertion from the afternoon had bested him and he had to go lie down. I brought him a bottle of water for his evening pill cocktail.

When I rounded the corner to our bedroom, I could see his body, naked and spread out across the made bed. I imagined that he would think this is what starfishing was. I leaned against the doorjamb and watched him sleep. His body was sprawled out and depleted from this afternoon's lovemaking. His physique had changed since the defibrillator and the intense treatment. His stomach was slightly distended, and he now sported love handles where there was once a six-pack. I was frozen in front of him, staring grievously at this man I once loved more than life itself. As I looked at him lying on the bed, exhausted and just having given his last bits of energy toward pleasing me, I longed for the days when we could not sit still. We would run, bike, hike and walk together. We dreamed together, and we loved furiously. I wished for the time back when I didn't know about Portia. I longed for him to no longer be sick.

I decided to let him sleep until nine when I would wake him for his medicine. I turned off the light, covered him with a light blanket, and crept back down the stairs to the kitchen. When I picked up my phone, there were three messages. An old friend from Michigan, Margo, and Jaime. Jaime. My heart ached with a strange emptiness and aloneness I still couldn't reconcile. We had missed our time to talk today. Simon's early arrival had made me completely forget about my standing call with Jaime. I texted him a quick message apologizing and promised to speak tomorrow. A simple response came back: Ten Days.

I decided to spend the night reviewing my proposal

for Greenwood Gardens and looking at the agenda for the Chatham Borough Meeting I would be attending next week. Mrs. Smith, my tenth grade English teacher, would say, "Get those juices jangling, girls!"

I decided there was no better juice to jangle than my intellectual Tropicana. I studied and poked holes in my ideas and delivery all night. I used to tell my clients that it was easy to fall in love with your own ideas. Is that what I was doing now?

It didn't matter. My business juices were flowing. I was having fun and it felt great. For once, I lost track of my personal struggles and was able to focus on someone else's. The escape felt good. I'm not sure I thought about the lie I would be telling in ten days.

MARGARET

It was Friday and Maude and I met in our usual place. "You've never told me about your grand plan for Greenwood, darling."

"Why are you here when Margaret arrives, darling?" I nosed with a particular emphasis on the word darling.

"What would Queen Elizabeth do without me? It's a long, harsh weekend when you have to face it unpruned," quipped my bestie. I smiled at the double entendre.

"Don't think I'm not onto you. My guess is that Margaret arrives sometime in the afternoon and you can't bear the thought of sitting and waiting." I said, already knowing the answer.

"Better to stay busy, my dear," was her reply. No truer words were ever spoken. I had become the master of staying busy these days.

I rambled on about my plans for Greenwood as we tended to Queen Elizabeth, Lady Banks, Ingrid Bergman and President Lincoln. My favorite rose was still the cabbage rose, but I was amused by the names. You'd might expect a rose named Mister Lincoln would be lean and lanky but rather, it was a petite tea rose that grew heartily in a bush and was one of the most fragrant in our garden. As I would prune Ingrid Bergman, I'd oft wonder how she scored the deep scarlet red rose while Lady Banks' looked far more plebian in her buds. Could the trellis filled with yellow blooms have reminded the horticulturist of a hat she had worn? As for the Queen Elizabeth, was pink the queen's favorite color?

Of course, Maude knew the answers to my random queries. Although I'm not quite sure of her accuracy, she'd spend hours telling me delightful little tales of history that begged to be challenged. To get her mind off her anticipated visitor, I decided today might be a good day to challenge her creativity and ask her about roses.

"The Ingrid Bergman rose," she would tell me, "was a hybrid created by a family in Denmark."

"Ohhh," I responded to bait her into continuing. She obliged.

"Well, who do you know from Denmark? No one! If you want to become famous you should never move to Denmark, Rainey. There is absolutely no one famous from there. They must be too damn happy over there to want to dream bigger, I suppose. So, these humble gardeners decided that if you're going to name your rose, and you hope it to sell all over the world, you must give it a catchy and nostalgic name. Ingrid Bergman was from Sweden. They figured most of the world was horrible at geography and both countries shared a sea, so why not pretend she was theirs?"

"And Queen Elizabeth?" I goaded.

"Well my love, she was furious that a common actress got a flower named for her, so she demanded the most beautiful rose in the garden be named after the Queen. She would never be outdone. Still won't." She went on about how Elizabeth was most likely the brains behind the #metoo movement next. I loved the way she always twisted current events into her history lessons. It was the way she entwined words like "darling" and "love" with others like "BFF," and "fuck." She could always surprise and entertain.

"What is it about senior citizens making up shit?" I asked. At that I heard a woman's laugh behind me.

"I'm glad nothing's changed since I left, Mum." It was Margaret. I stood to greet her, and she extended her arms to hug me.

"You must be Rainey!"

Margaret seemed slightly older than I but as beautiful as Maude had said she was. She was much taller than Maude, but with the same slender build and casual elegance. Her piercing blue eyes seemed to glow beyond her dark satin hair. I imagined her pulling it back in a smart chignon for court while slaying her opposition. I wondered if the heaviness in her eyes was from the trip here or her recent heartbreak. Both, I understood.

Maude could barely stop smiling. Her hands touched each side of Margaret's face, then jumped to Margaret's shoulders, then her hair. It was as if she was convincing herself this vision was real. I did the same each time Katherine returned from visiting her father. I had to touch her and hug her and squeeze her. And Katherine? Well, Katherine hated every minute of it. At least she pretended to. I wished Katherine could have stayed my little four-year-old sidekick forever, but watching Maude and Margaret reunite, I thought, I wouldn't mind just jumping right past the teen years.

I convinced Margaret that Maude was not needed here and should go back to the house with her and the girls. I had been a very good student these past weeks and promised not to maim any queens or Swedish actresses in her absence. With her frail hand on my cheek, Maude leaned in and kissed me on the other before she left. It surprised me how much this gesture meant to me.

I watched Margaret hold her mother's arm and protect her as she walked her toward the parking lot. Had she any idea how strong her mother truly was? My guess was that Margaret would be leaning on her more than she expected over the next few weeks. I made a mental note to check in and support her as I turned back to Mister Lincoln.

My phone buzzed in my back pocket. "Seven days," was all it read.

I couldn't contain my smile. I remembered Maude's words, "Screw his brains out and fill me in when you get back." When you get back, I thought. Even Maude knew I couldn't leave a dying man. Could I?

As I drove home, I couldn't help thinking of this summer. It seemed like yesterday that Jaime and I made plans to meet. Instead, he had been my rock throughout the spring and into summer. He never did propose to his girlfriend. I hope I hadn't given him false hope. Maybe I wasn't giving him false hope at all. Perhaps he was just being a good friend, and he knew I couldn't leave Simon.

I was still no closer to a decision. In a strange way, I thought I would wait until Simon's follow up PET scan. We'd know then, right? If he only had a few years, I could be there for him. But if we had a long life and hope, how could he spend it with someone who wasn't enough for him? In a strange way, waging this war against Cardiac Sarcoidosis has brought us closer. But still, I can't erase the images of their making love from my mind. He'd never admit it was anything but angry sex, but I knew Simon. They had a relationship. If he loved me, truly loved me as much as I did him, he wouldn't have cheated. If he was going to live a long life, he should be with someone whom he won't cheat on. Feeling sorry for me or guilty for what he had done would only keep him faithful for so long.

As I went down this desperate path of thought, I knew it contradicted everything Simon had told me. But wasn't it time to just be realistic? I would never have cheated, no matter how angry, because that's not who I am. Is that who he is? SeemsLikeANiceGuy. I should have known.

One day at a time, I told myself as I accidentally snipped the head off Ingrid Bergman.

Last week I had challenged Simon to pray. Unlike many scientists, he did believe in God, but he didn't believe in always asking God for favors. My own experiences were evidence enough of His existence. I didn't need a Bible or a priest. I felt His presence when I needed Him. During our conversation, Simon told me he thanked God for me.

His words that followed left me speechless, "I know you're only here because of your beliefs, Rainey. I know you believe that God tells you to forgive me and somehow believe this is your big test. I know you're here because breaking your vow seems worse than living with a broken heart. Maybe God broke my heart because I broke yours. The only thing I would dare to ask God for is the ability to make you happy again and for you to love me as you once did."

I realized he was right. I could tell myself that I was waiting for the right time or that there was a chance I could forgive or that I couldn't leave a dying man, but the truth is that I am not ready to let down God.

When I was living painfully with Katherine's father, sacrificing for a better teen as my therapist Frank had suggested, I prayed regularly for compassion and peace. An unusual event helped me find peace in my role as caregiver. I wondered, was I holding onto this now, all these years later?

I have a dear friend whose husband, Marco, owns a garage. I'd regularly bring my Volvo there for servicing. It was only two years old and didn't need much, but the forty-five-minute drive was worth supporting their goals. One fall, after a regular routine tune-up, I left the garage and started toward the exit ramp to return home. The car made an awful noise. It sounded as though the bottom had fallen to the ground and a bolt was rattling around the engine. I got off the next exit and the sound continued until I finally switched off the ignition in the lot next to Marco's garage.

"Rainey, I don't see anything wrong." His head mechanic came out with him and retightened everything they had touched. I headed off again. Again, as I drove toward home, the noise returned on the entrance ramp.

Marco put the car up on the lift and three of his mechanics went through every possible solution. One found a loose, cracked bolt unassociated with the work they had done. They replaced the bolt and assumed they solved the case.

Back on the ramp, the noise returned. This time Marco asked to keep the car to do errands. He suggested driving it around for a bit might replicate the problem – which no one but me had heard – and, if he could hear the noise himself, perhaps he'd be able to better identify the source. He gave me the keys to his car to go have lunch.

When I got in his car, I was reminded of this beautiful spot only a mile or two from Marco's garage. Our Lady of Lourdes was a breathtaking walking shrine modeled after the Grotto Lourdes of France. It was built in 1958 by the Montfort Missionaries with the hope individuals and families would come to pray to reflect on their own lives, and to imitate Mary's life of faithful discipleship. The winding trail leads you through the wooded hillside, past each of the Stations of the Cross. The "Stations" are a depiction of the fourteen successive incidents during Jesus' last day as a mortal, starting with the condemnation by Pontius Pilate through his crucifixion. The final scene at the summit depicts a larger than life replica of the crucifixion.

I'm not sure there's a more beautiful or moving spot in all of Litchfield County. But that crisp autumn day, I was sure there couldn't be a better way to spend an hour than walking these leaf-covered trails.

I navigated Marco's Infinity up the long driveway and it was as picturesque as I had remembered. At the base of the hike was a stone grotto surrounded by benches where you could observe mass or listen to music. It was small and delicately carved into the mountainside which made it intimate and oddly romantic as candles burned on the empty alter.

I parked the car and decided to walk through the woods and visit each station. It would probably take all of an hour, I calculated. Perfect timing. I started up the path past the first station. I paused for a few moments to acknowledge the suffering depicted and was quickly diverted back to the crunching of leaves as I shuffled through on my way to the second; Jesus accepts the cross. This depicts Jesus carrying the cross on his back. I couldn't recall the accompanying prayers but found peace by stopping at each sculpture. At a couple of the stations, I would sit and silently pray while at others I just slowed and admired.

It would be at the fifth station that an unexpected emotion would sweep over me. I felt as if a giant magnet were pulling me toward it, and I struggled to stay on my feet. I looked around to see if anyone else felt the earth rattling beneath us. As I looked to my left, I saw three nuns and a priest approaching the crest of the path. Did they feel this? Have I gone completely mad? I noticed two sisters looking in my direction but not at me. The third made the sign of the cross while looking upward. Why had she done that? They all looked my way but not at me. The pull was even stronger now. I imagined I looked as though I was going to lose consciousness at any moment, I certainly felt as if I might.

I staggered across the path. Five feet seemed like a mile to me. I grabbed for the bench. Surely this group of four would be here soon asking if I was all right. But they didn't. They mysteriously started toward me and stopped, turned around, and disappeared back over the crest of the path. At that, an uncontrollable burst of crying leapt from deep in my soul. I put my head down toward my lap and tried to get my bearings. I couldn't remember the fifth station, my Catholic guilt raging through me. The pull from my chest was getting stronger. I had an incredible urge to fall to the feet of this statue of Jesus. I didn't.

It was then that I looked up and through my unstoppable tears read, "Simon of Cyrene helps carry the cross." Who was Simon of Cyrene? Thinking of this moment now, the irony that my husband's name is Simon is completely overwhelming.

On the bench in Litchfield I stared at the statue looking

for answers. Why was I having this response? What were the nuns looking at as they glanced my way? I'd ask them when I returned to the bottom of the hill. As I struggled to decipher what was happening, I stared at the stone carvings of Simon and Jesus. It was then that words started rumbling through my head.

"You are Simon, neither prophet nor saint."

The words raged in my brain. It was painfully loud and clear. I looked behind me. Had the priest returned? No one was near– an oddity in itself at this park– yet the voice seemed so close. My head started to hurt, and I sobbed as I stared at the statue. Was that God speaking to me or had I gone completely mad? I didn't remember this station. What was He trying to tell me? Should I be ashamed? I sat silently crying and waiting for more words for what felt like a half hour. No one walked by me. This was odd. It was Jesus and Simon of Cyrene and I in the woods, on this beautiful fall day, having a moment I would never forget.

I could barely find the patience to slow at the last nine stations. I needed to find out more about Simon of Cyrene. I needed to understand why the sisters had turned away and what they saw. I felt like a madwoman, how could I ask that question? They'd for sure think I was mad as well. I looked for the foursome. They were nowhere to be found. I ran to the gift shop and decided to ask the volunteer if she had seen three nuns.

"Oh no, not today. There were two sisters here two days ago, but not today." She was sure of herself. I wondered if I had imagined them as well.

I decided to look for information about the fifth station here. What better place? I looked at every book and postcard, but there was nothing. He was barely mentioned. I couldn't find wi-fi for my phone and the cell service was spotty in the woods. I would have to wait to get back to Marco's. I stared into the mirror to check my face and exited the car hopefully to find my other mystery solved.

Marco greeted me somberly.

"Rainey, I'm sorry. I drove the car for an hour and even went up the same ramp you did four times. I couldn't feel or hear anything wrong. I feel terrible. I called my friend at the Volvo dealership and he's expecting you." I knew then that I was not meant to go home from Marco's that day. I was not meant to get on that entrance ramp without stopping at Our Lady of Lourdes. I knew the car would be fine.

As predicted, I got on the ramp and headed home. Not one peep. I never went to Volvo.

Later I would look up Simon of Cyrene. Simon was an unknown man who was watching along the path Jesus took to his crucifixion. When Jesus started to falter, a guard pulled Simon from the crowd and ordered him to help Jesus carry the cross – neither prophet nor saint. The Cyrenian Movement was started in England and carries the guiding principle of "sharing the burden" in its approach to aiding the homeless and less fortunate. Simon did not help Jesus out of sympathy, he had no choice – he was neither prophet nor saint.

At the time, Katherine's father was completely dependent on me. "I am Simon," I thought. It was not my choice to watch over him, but I obliged. After that afternoon in Litchfield, I gained the strength to carry the burden of her father until Katherine was strong enough to define herself.

Thinking back to when I met my Simon, he also took on my burden. He was appropriately named. Was it now my time to be Simon again? Are Simon and I sharing the burden of each other?

Summer had buzzed by. I got home, and Katherine was busy finishing homework after her first week at her new school. I always knew it was Friday because it was the only day of the week she wasted no time getting her work done. It wasn't because she wanted to eliminate her burden, but because her friends were all allowed to hang out after school on Fridays and she would not miss the opportunity. As soon as she saw me, she jumped up. "Can you bring me to Summit, Mama?" The big blue eyes peeked through her lashes at me.

"How was school?" I decided I'd eventually give in so why not have a bit of fun.

"Mooommmmmm.....pullleeeeaasssse? They can only stay downtown until six."

"Is your ho-" I started.

"Yes! All done!" Before I could finish.

"Well, tell me something that happened at school today." I wasn't done torturing her.

She grabbed her small wristlet and phone and hugged me as she dragged me to the door. "I will. I will. In the car, Mama!" I love this kid.

I drove the five minutes to our old town as slowly as possible. If there was traffic or a light, I would try to hit it. Car time is the most amazing time each day, it's when I hear about Katherine. She'll tell me about school and friends and gossip and boys, but only in the car. It made being her personal taxi enjoyable. She would tell me my fares were extraordinarily high and that she would have called Uber or taken the train had she known she'd have to give up this much dirt. I love this child.

As I pulled to the curb to drop her off, the phone rang through the car speaker. It was Jaime. Katherine hit answer on the console.

"Hello?" Katherine answered.

"Oh. Hey. This must be Katherine?" Jaime responded without skipping aa beat.

"Yes, this is she," she politely responded.

"I've heard a lot about you." Jaime said uncomfortably. I must admit, he did sound a little suspicious as he stumbled through his sentence this time.

"May I ask who this is?" Katherine was cautious and looked at me strangely.

"Oh, I'm sorry. It's Jaime. I'm an old friend of your mom."

"Jaime?" She repeated. The way she said it had a funny ring. Had I told her about Jaime? Could she possibly have remembered an old story like that if I had?

Katherine looked at me, her displeasure unmasked. "I'm sure you didn't call for me. My mom is right here. I'm jumping out of the car, hold on. Nice talking to you– Jaime." She said his name as though she knew who he was, as though she had already known our secret. She looked me in the eyes a little too long and slowly edged her way toward me to kiss me goodbye, never breaking her gaze. I told her I'd pick her up at six, same place. She started to close the passenger door when she stopped it inches from its final destination.

Her slim fingers pulled it back open and leaned in the car, she hit mute on the console, "We'll talk about THIS on our way home." I was speechless. Had she just mothered me?

As the door started to close a second time I yelled out, "We're just friends, Katherine." I laughed nervously at her gumption and unmuted the phone.

"I am not very good at lying, Jamesy."

"You never were, baby."

I got home to find Simon already there, lying on the couch. He looked to be in what was now, his normal state of exhaustion. I felt dirty, but this time not from gardening. Could I slink up the stairs. I hadn't done anything wrong. Yes, we had talked about Friday's meeting. How we'd meet at noon at our favorite beach at Chatham Bars and have lunch poolside before heading to the Atlantic for a long walk. I had a hall pass, I reminded myself. But I hadn't done anything wrong, yet.

Simon lifted his head.

"Hey babe, I missed you. Come here and give daddy a kiss." Why do men say that? I wasn't working. Did that make him my sugar daddy now? I wasn't a girl with daddy issues, so it was always a strange thing to hear. I was always shocked to hear otherwise intelligent men using that phrase. Someone, somewhere, told them it was a good idea. It's not.

"You okay?" he asked.

"Of course, why?" I answered a bit too defensively.

"I need to talk to you, Rainey." Damn. I shouldn't have walked in right after getting off the phone with Jaime. My head was spinning. What could Simon have to tell me now?

"OK," I hesitated.

"No, it's not bad," assured Simon. He continued, "I need you to know that I really love you, Rainey. I feel like things are going back to where we were, before my mistake."

Before your decision, I thought. I stayed quiet.

"You need to know, baby. I am so sorry. I will never risk our relationship again. The last few weeks, well, you've been a saint, Rainey. I am with the woman I want to spend the rest of my life with, however long that may be."

He paused. He got choked up.

He went on, "I am not settling. I am not with you because I want a family. I love Katherine like my own, but you need to know that all the crazy things going through your head are wrong. I am here, right now, because I want to be with you, Rainey Beaufort Bradley. I love you more than I ever knew I could love. The minute I made that mistake, I realized what I had risked. I risked you. I risked us. Every single thing that happened after was because I was trying to protect you from ever finding out, I was trying to protect myself from ever hurting and losing you."

Almost inaudible through my tears, I uttered, "But you did hurt me."

"I know. I'm so sorry. I will do anything to make it up to you."

Then there was a minute of silence. He grabbed me and hugged me as I sobbed but I kept my arms to myself. He rocked and cried with me.

"I love you so much, I'm so sorry," he repeated over and over as we rocked together.

I was shocked by my next words.

"You broke me."

Did I believe that? I did feel broken. The profound sadness I felt was far beyond feeling sorry for myself or feeling trapped. I had felt– inadequate.

Simon pulled back and looked in my swollen, red eyes, "I don't deserve you." Then, his eyes changed. Whatever he was about to say was hard for him. He looked scared and unsure as if to proceed. "What is it, Simon?"

"I want to live for you." There was a silence after he said it.

"No Simon," I corrected. "You want to live for you." He was quick this time.

"No, Rainey, I want to live for you. I don't want to leave you. If you had left me, I'm not sure I would be undergoing treatment right now. I would just live my life the way I was, and one day I'd have a heart attack and die. It would be fast and relatively painless. That's how this disease works. But Rainey, living that way would mean not being with you and laughing with you. It would mean not waking up next to your beautiful smile and watching you sing while you cook and wriggle into the crook of my arm at night to read. I love touching you and looking into your eyes, feeling your body next to mine. The one thing in my life that is more important than everything else, is you. I am fighting this for you. I'm fighting this for me, actually, because I don't want to be without you, ever."

I stared at him like I hadn't in so long. His eyes were locked on mine. For a minute, we were back in Stonington sitting on the jetty staring at each other while the waves broke at our feet. We were in love once. We were madly, passionately in love once.

My phone started ringing. It was Maude.

"Maude has never called my phone before," talking to myself as I automatically answer with concern. I stepped away to answer as Simon looked on with concern.

BUILDING FRIENDSHIPS

"Hi Rainey, it's Margaret, Maude's daughter." I was even more concerned. Maude was feisty and energetic, but she was also eighty-five.

"Hi Margaret."

As if she heard the concern before I could spit it out, she continued, "Oh, you're probably surprised to hear me call on this phone. Everything's okay." She read my mind.

"Well, Maude, I mean your mom, only texts." As I said it, it seemed to tickle my funny bone.

"True, for someone who has as much to say as my mother, she does seem to text and use social media more than my fifteen-year-old. Since I was a child, she's never liked the phone." She imitated her mother, "Margaret, get off that phone and go look in their eyes. It will be far more enjoyable when you make them laugh. She had no idea that advice cost me my virginity!" We both laughed. Margaret may have not inherited all of Maude's looks, but she had absolutely acquired her sense of humor.

"So much more is making sense now," I laughed. I thought about Maude telling me to stop talking to Jaime on the phone and just "go screw him."

"Well, to the reason I'm calling," she definitely had a little

Maude in her, "I'm taking my mother and Lily out for lunch on Monday and I thought it would be great if you could join us?" I pretended to look at my empty calendar and told her I just happened to be free and would be delighted. We discussed a few details about Monday and hung up.

"I love when you laugh," Simon reported as I hung up, "you need to do more of that."

"You're right, I do."

I remembered we had been in a very serious conversation before the phone rang. As I walked across the room to my husband I couldn't pinpoint my emotions. Did I want to continue this? Were we done? I wasn't sure how to respond, yet his words had touched me. I felt each word. I-Want-To-Live-For-You. As I went to sit next to him, he rose and grabbed my legs. He pulled me closer to him and started to unbutton my khakis. As he slipped his face toward the opening I knew his plan. I longed for it. He hadn't done it since I had demanded his compliance in the days leading up to forgiveness Thursday.

"No, Simon." He looked dejected.

"I want to please you, Rainey." He slipped his finger down the front of my lace panties to find that my body was telling him what my words were not.

"You want it," he grinned.

My head was spinning. I had just been on the phone with Jaime, followed by Simon's intense conversation. As his finger touched my clitoris was I imagining Simon's finger or Jaime's? This was wrong. I needed him to stop. My body moved under his touch. I imagined Jaime. I remembered how Jaime's skin was smoother than Simon's. Simon slipped my panties off. I was happy to be wearing something besides the cotton mom underwear I had on the day before. I had decided if I was going to feel sexy again, I needed to start from the inside out.

Their hair was similar, Simon and Jaime's. As Simon's head was between my legs I remembered all those years ago.

"The alphabet," I moaned. Simon didn't know what I

meant. Jaime would trace the letters of the alphabet across my vagina with his tongue and I could never make it through to "J." Something about the anticipation of where he would go next with his tongue would send me into the throws of passion sooner than I would want.

"The alphabet?" Simon asked. I was embarrassed.

"Write your name with your tongue." I felt the "S" snake its way across my clitoris, past my lips, and dangerously close to my anus. I jolted. I was no longer in control. That brief sentence was all the control I could muster. I. Would it be lowercase? As I anticipated the dotting of the 'i' my body raged. M. By the letter 'o' I was breathless. It was Simon between my legs now. My body was giving itself to him. I was not in control. I orgasmed and became insatiable. I needed more. I helped him out of his clothes as quickly as I could manage, almost sheering the buttons off in my haste. We made passionate love on the sofa, in the front room of the house, in front of the picture window, barely masked by the protection of the back of the couch and the front shrubs that guarded our front porch. I could not have enough of this man.

The doorbell rang.

"Oh my God, Simon!" I crouched as low as I could, thankful that my shirt was still on. "Oh, my, God, Simon there is someone at the door!"

"Shit! I forgot I ordered Indian."

"You what? Oh my God, it's a young girl! She had to have seen us. She's looking away. Hurry up and get dressed!"

Simon threw on his shorts and went and collected the Indian food. I kept my face buried in the couch. Oh please Lord, don't let her be anyone that Katherine knows. The door shut, and I peered through the blinds as if I were James Bond.

"She's picking up her phone! She got in her car, Simon, and she is immediately picking up her phone and calling someone! Oh my God! That's exactly what I would do if I just caught two old people doing it on the couch." Simon roared.

"First, we're not old and you're smoking hot. She's probably saying she hopes when she gets married that she's lucky enough to find someone as passionate."

"She's probably saying, damn, I hope that's not what my parents do when I'm at work! Ick!"

We started laughing uncontrollably.

"I love when you laugh," Simon repeated.

"Did you order enough for both of us?"

My mind shifted to picking up Katherine at six. What would I tell her about Jaime?

Monday seemed to take forever to arrive. Usually, I despise Mondays. Katherine goes off to school and Simon to work. Maude only volunteered Tuesday through Friday so I had adjusted my volunteer hours to match her schedule. Monday is generally just me and Popcorn, home alone, applying for jobs or finding random things to do around the house. I'm not sure why the emptiness paralyzed me. Go to the gym, Rainey. Make friends, Rainey. Work, for God's sake, work, Rainey! This behavior was nothing I knew. These were the times I'd tell my friends to choose their attitude, be strong, become who you want to be! But I couldn't. For a while, I couldn't read. I couldn't work. I have every ability to look for consulting clients, but I haven't.

I'm four weeks into the antidepressants and hope they'll help me move out of the pain I stew in at times. I noticed I stopped crying at sad movies and laughing has become easier. A couple weeks ago, I was worried that I would never cackle again. The doctor explained that Zoloft softens the edges and takes away the extremes. Who wants to make it harder to laugh? The first person to create an anti-depressant that doesn't mute the lows AND the highs will be a gazillionaire.

The stillness I am left with after they leave seems to penetrate through my veins like hot oil. I'd try to take my own advice. Sometimes, I'd work outside in the front yard purposely trying to find a neighbor who might be interested in a short conversation. Other times I'd go to a local coffee shop. That was how I had met Margo so many years ago. Finally, I decided I should volunteer. That is the one thing that has made me feel better.

Maude had been my Zoloft the past few weeks. At first it was hard to motivate myself to get in the car to do something I didn't much enjoy when there was plenty of gardening to do here. Maude's laughter and friendship had slowly changed that. I bound out of bed Tuesday through Friday now. I'm needed there, and I think Maude appreciates the company as well. Maude's love of Greenwood inspired me to make a difference and flex an old set of mental muscles I had abandoned this year. I was happy to be thinking about business again, although I knew I was not completely on my game. I ran my ideas past Maude before going to the director who proved to be a worthy partner. With this strange sadness - situational depression is what my shrink calls it - my ability to read people and manage them has escaped me. The very same skill with which I had led teams of thousands and had been given the key to billion dollar businesses had vanished.

As Maude expected, the director would never go for my spring strategy. I followed my new mentor's advice and strategically introduced it when several of the board members were in for a visit. Before I knew it, I was being invited to the city to present my idea at the next board meeting. Maude did some additional plugging as they wandered the gardens.

"Did you hear Rainey's idea? It's fabulous, isn't it?" I heard her going on and on to a board member telling him how they "should put Rainey Bradley in charge of this place."

They did love my strategy for the spring. I knew it was a risk no longer to charge admission. Opening the gardens to the public at no cost would create more foot traffic. The more people who can enjoy it; the more who will donate. My plan to kick off spring with a gardening competition amongst local landscapers would make this an inexpensive garden show for them, would give us plenty of free publicity, and would bring our gardens up to snuff overnight while balancing out the loss from our piddly foot traffic. I also suggested fun ways to collect donations during the event to restore the main fountain, which stands at the center of the property. Unfortunately, it's a visitor's first inclination that the park is in decline. I had a hundred other ideas but would save them. I could thank my new friend and my old beau for helping me reignite that side of my brain.

Today was not a typical Monday. Today, I had a lunch date.

Simon was on to me as soon as he woke up.

"Excited about your girl's day?" he sang.

"It's just lunch with Maude," I tried to underplay it.

"Well, I'm glad you're making friends. You should get a pedicure today while you're out. I know how you love those." Simon always said things like that, especially after I lost my life's savings with the house sinking and the business failing. I was holding onto my small stash from my winter job but was very thrifty when it came to spending money on me. Simon regularly encouraged me to go shopping or treat myself. He had gone out of his way to ensure my understanding that we were a team. His money is our money, he'd say. When he says it, I want to remind him that money was the reason he strayed.

I had to stop doing this! Simon did assume I was using him then. He thought I had married him for his money. I still laugh at the thought. I made more than twice what he did. But that was the past. Why couldn't I let this go? How did Melissa let it go? In my lust for information on healing, I found a quote from Michele Weiner-Davis.

"There's no shame in staying in a marriage, those who do are warriors."

You have to be, I thought. This is the hardest thing I've ever done.

She also suggested that staying with your spouse "delivers a gift to your family by working through the pain," and "may inspire change that was sorely needed." It takes two to ruin a marriage. Maybe this was as much of a lesson as a challenge.

"Four Days," the text read.

I never called Melissa and involved her parents. Simon would never call Melissa to check in on me and I didn't want to lie to anyone else. He might check my location on Katherine's phone, I thought. I would just leave it in the car in a nearby neighborhood or turn it off when I neared the hotel. I'd figure that out Friday. Jaime made reservations at Chatham Bars Inn, one of my favorite places. I was glad to have today's lunch to distract me from the anticipation.

I walked down Springfield Avenue in Summit with a skip in my step. I was surprised how good it felt to be doing something that was a regular part of my routine– albeit with different people– for most of my adult life. Margaret and Maude were like me. They loved being outside. Summit was a metropolitan bedroom community but lacked outdoor dining. There was one street in town, facing the train station, where you could sit outside and eat. As I turned down Maple Street, I was two blocks away from joining my party. By this point, I just wanted to run there. I couldn't believe my excitement.

I chose my outfit carefully this morning. As I walked, I knew I caught the attention of men and women alike. I was going for that carefree, easy elegance that seemed as though I woke up that way. In truth, I'd spent the last ninety minutes creating it. I wore a cream silk blouse that draped magically between my breasts without being provocative and matching wide-legged trousers. I pulled my hair back into a low bun, painted the "natural" look on my face, and grabbed my favorite Jackie-O Chanel sunglasses and an oversized leather tote.

As I turned the corner, I was immediately reminded that I had not met Maude or Lily in anything but their gardening clothes. Maude sat facing away from my direction, but I could tell in an instant it was she. The white curls that were strangled beneath her blue floral gardening hat were finally free. I was surprised to find them longer and thicker than I expected. When she turned, they moved lightly and with a bounce of her curls; she was stunning. Her smile covered her face and her petite frame was draped in a simple cotton button down with a red and navy scarf tied smartly around her neck. She wore tailored navy trousers that were in style yet completely age-appropriate. It was as if Ralph Lauren himself had dressed her.

Margaret was dressed to match. I had wondered if it was intentional. Her flowing mane was pulled back into a neat tail and she wore red capris and a matching white Oxford. Her David Yurman Chatelaine necklace with its deep red garnet stone and surrounding rings of diamonds seemed to make everything else she was wearing seem like an accessory. Lily sparkled in her pale blue top and matching pants in a linen fabric. She had an artsy, somewhat flamboyant pendant that broke the color of her ensemble. It was the kind of outfit that screamed, I don't care if it's after Labor Day, I will wear whatever I damn well please because I've earned it. She wore a hat that I was sure was purchased with the necklace as it had the same colors and zeal.

When they saw me, their true warmth in their faces made me feel as though there was no where I'd rather be. Piattino's was a cozy Italian bistro with an outstanding menu that would make your mouth water as you read it. Unfortunately, their food tasted only half as good as it read but the wine list, friendly waiters, and garden patio made it a great place to lunch. When I made it around to the table, Maude and Lily were almost halfway through their sauvignon blancs and Margaret had just finished her first Macallan. The waiter held my chair as I asked for an Amarone I had grown fond of on a past visit. This propelled us into a conversation about Italy. Maude and Lily were quick to add colorful details about a trip they had taken after Harry had passed. "Our Girls' Trip," they called it.

"I never thought they'd return from it," Margaret said with love. I was trying to make sense of the tales of what they called their "time of dancing, drinking, and inappropriate men." I was sure Maude was madly in love with Harry. Wouldn't she have been heart-broken? This seemed like quite a bit of debauchery from a widow.

"How long ago was this trip where you were taking advantage of these inappropriate men?" I asked.

"Stage Two." Maude said matter-of-factly.

I could tell by Margaret's face that she had been through this conversation before. Margaret raised her hand up for the waiter to return with a third Macallan. I noticed her slightly unravelling. I suggested we order a few appetizers before I followed up on that answer. When the waiter came back with the scotch, a few appetizers turned into "a little taste of everything," as requested by Lily. Lily and Maude ordered eleven appetizers. We had enough food for the rest of the day, a limitless supply of wine and scotch, and we had just started discussing stage two.

At that realization I sent Simon a text that said, "May be late. Can you take care of dinner for you and Katherine?" It was one o'clock.

Lily explained that stage two was the second stage of grief.

"But isn't that anger? It doesn't sound like anger, quite frankly, it sounds like you were having the time of your life." I probed, trying to recall the first stage. Denial! It was denial. Maude helped me understand.

"Anger comes in many forms. The last four years of Harry's life I gave up drinking and dancing, things we loved, because he could no longer join me."

"Mum, don't forget the sex. You had to make up for that as well." Maude looked at her daughter. She knew this was painful for her but chose to continue.

"Rainey, anger manifests itself in different ways for everyone. I was angry at Harry for leaving me. I surprised myself with how I responded. I didn't think it would be like that."

At that, Lily raised her glass and silently toasted her good friend and Harry, I assumed.

"Thank you, Lily,' Maude continued. "When you found out about Simon, I'm sure you were angry? Was your response typical? Oh, I'm sorry darling, I shouldn't have..."

I smiled.

"No, it's okay. When I found out about Simon," I started, trying to decide if she was referring to the affair or his heart disease. "When I found out about Simon, I didn't believe it at first – denial, I suppose – but then I did. I stepped outside of myself."

My head spun as I thought about my demands for sex from Simon. I had become someone I didn't know. The angrier I grew, the more I demanded, and the bolder my requests became. I put an expiration on my anger, Forgiveness Thursday, but now that Maude was saying this, I realize my behavior was not unlike her sexcapade through Italy. As the thought grazed my mind, I laughed at my eighty-something year old friends having sex with random men in Italy. It was almost ten years ago, I thought. Good for them. I choked back a smile.

"What happened with Simon?" I could tell Margaret would never had asked this had it not been for her four glasses of Macallan 25. I thought about her bar bill. That's a two-thousand-dollar bottle of scotch. During my better days, I had bought a bottle of eighteen-year-old Macallan for a thousand dollars for Michael for his fortieth. The twenty-five had to be two thousand. I would not be surprised to see our bar bill over one thousand dollars already. Well, Simon did tell me to go and have a good time, I justified.

"He had an affair," I answered.

Maude was embarrassed for me and for her daughter.

Lily just shrieked, "What? How could he? To you, of all people. He's a fool!"

Margaret's face changed. She grew pensive. Would this be when she confesses why she left her husband? She raised her glass and cheered, "To sinners!"

Maude was furious. I had never seen her even irritated.

"I'm so sorry, darling Rainey. I'm so sorry. I thought you'd mention his illness." At that, Maude admonished her daughter, "Margaret, enough!" She took her small frail hand and with the force of a hurricane she moved the scotch away from her daughter and raised her hand for the waiter. Margaret looked as if she would cry.

"Really, it's okay. Every day I come to terms with it a little more and it gets a little easier. Margaret, are you all right?" I assumed my confession had rattled her. She was white as a ghost.

The waiter interrupted, and Maude stated seriously, "Take this scotch and bring the three of us more wine. We're going to need it to catch up with this one. She'll have a cup of coffee."

I couldn't help laughing. I raised my glass and smiled, "Here's to catching up!"

Maude tried to hold back her smile, but Lily broke it the rest of the way open by patting Margaret's hand while raising her glass and stating,

"Don't worry dear, I'll drink twice for you!"

Our lunch lasted until five o'clock. Margaret seemed to compose herself after a while and Lily seemed to move in the other direction. The stories got more animated from their Italy trip and the four of us covered every topic from Donald Trump to closet organization. There wasn't a quiet moment or lack of laughter the entire afternoon.

Margaret was cautious, I noticed. Something had changed in her since my confession. My heart broke for her. I wondered what stage she was in – denial? Anger? I gathered she didn't have many old friends here still. It sounds like boarding school and summers at the shore made Short Hills only an address she'd use on her paperwork. I decided I'd plan to have her over one afternoon, and we could go walking at Loantaka Park.

"I'd love that," she graciously accepted. Maude's face suddenly read of that same caution consuming Margaret's.

Dear Diary

I love visiting my dad, but it's always nice to get home. I miss my friends and Popcorn.

Simon seems different and he certainly looks different. He must have gained thirty pounds. I'll never forget when my mom showed me a pound of ground beef. Now I was imagining thirty of those stacked up. Could he have gained that much weight in two months? We don't eat meat too often, but my mother can't resist making meatballs and her homemade sauce that she learned from Uncle Michael's mom. They are real Italians. They're salad-after-dinner Italians. I love her sauce. Simon must have never stopped eating it the entire time I was gone! His face is a lot rounder, too.

I'm going to pray for him tonight. Between the weight and his heart acting up more often now, I'm worried the medicine isn't helping. Oh, please God, help him get better. He's more of a father than my real dad. I know he's made some mistakes, but mom and Simon seem better now. I knew their love could conquer all.

I hope my mom isn't going to do something stupid now. Until today, I thought my mom was floating around because she and Simon were doing better. I can't deny I'm a little angry at her. Simon does not seem to be getting healthier. But now, why is Jaime calling her? Oh Mom!! I know who Jaime is! "An old friend," he said. You should have seen my mother's face. He's the only other guy my mother has ever loved. She told me the whole story when I was little. You remember stuff like that. She left a man she loved because he wouldn't let her become who she needed to be. What was he doing back in her life? Especially now!

What if Simon is NOT okay? If he finds out about this, it might kill him. And who is this Maude woman?

I didn't even talk about this week at another new school! Eva's cool, I'm glad for that. High School is way diffs. I met some cool girls, turns out I know them through my Summit friends. Thank God for my Summit friends still. I miss them.

Kate

NEW FRIENDS

Simon and I had started a morning routine since moving to our new home. The three of us would sit and have breakfast together – I should note, this was not Katherine's favorite way to start the day. While Simon and I enjoyed flipping between various news stations and the local news, our burgeoning teenager would much rather spend her morning on Snapchat ensuring she didn't miss any important events after she went to bed the night before. Generally, this news included things like a missed houseparties and things that were said during the group video chat about who likes whom and who did what. This morning it turned out that her friends Kaleigh and Sarah had some type of public row and have unfriended each other. Katherine was distraught that she wasn't in Summit this morning to help these two baes reconcile. Because of this, we had to pry the phone from her hand to get her to the kitchen island to join us. The good news was that she was filled with angst and felt compelled to share more than usual this morning.

Eva still stopped by each morning and was becoming more and more comfortable with us. "Hi Bradley's!" she'd perk.

"Good morning, Eva! Interested in some breakfast while Kate gets her bag?" Eva walked to the counter and grabbed a piece of wheat toast and started jabbering about how she couldn't believe they had so much homework last night and could we believe Demi Lovato almost died of a drug overdose again. The conversation was cut short by Katherine's return and utter dismay at Eva engaging us in conversation. Simon couldn't help letting out a quick laugh.

After we saw Katherine and Eva off, Simon jumped in the shower to get ready for work. I've been uneasy when he's in the shower since he passed out in there a few months ago. Thankfully, he didn't suffer any serious injury, but still. Now, I sit in the bathroom with him and chat about nothing while he showers. It's become a special private time that we both look forward to now. Today we talked about an interview I had scheduled and my walk with Margaret. Last week I had shared with him about Margaret's quick exodus from her marriage and how we shared a similar situation. Needless to say, Simon was quite apprehensive about my new friend and my spending any time with her.

"You're not going to let her talk you into leaving me?" he jested with an undertone of serious concern.

"Simon, I won't dignify that with a response. But yes, yes I will." I smiled. He immediately wiped the condensation from the glass partition to look at my face. He smiled with relief when he saw my smirk.

"Don't do that, Rainey. Don't you know I have a heart condition?"

"Damn, Simon. Are you going to use that excuse for everything?"

"Yes. Yes I will."

I waved to Simon as he drove away while Popcorn joined me on the front porch and I dead-headed the hanging plants. Simon still looked sexy as hell, even with a few extra pounds. He told me this morning the count was at twenty-two pounds. I reminded him it was mostly water retention and to cut back on the salt when he wasn't with me.

"It will fall right back off as soon as you can start working out again," I promised. My heart breaks for him every time he drives away. I wonder if he should even be driving. I am concerned that his heart issues have increased rather than declined.

Margaret pulled up as Simon drove away. I was still on the porch when I saw her. I love starting the day off with a brisk walk and it was nice finally to have someone besides Popcorn to walk with me. I wondered how much she knew. Did she know about Jaime and my hall pass? Did she know Simon was sick? Had we even mentioned that at lunch on Monday? My memory and cognitive abilities were slowly coming back after starting anti-depressants, but little moments like this were still so frustrating.

Margaret rolled down her window and asked if she should drive.

"No, let's leave your car here. We're only a short walk to the trail entrance." She hopped out of her car, still seeming somewhat uncomfortable. I wondered what I was sensing. A woman with her pedigree and from Maude's womb? It didn't make sense.

I introduced her to Popcorn, who I decided should stay home "this time" and welcomed her into my house.

"Can I get you a bottle of water for the walk?" I asked.

"No, I'm good. The only thing my bladder holds up is me. I'll be peeing in the woods the minute it's done."

Laughing at her comment, I said, "I knew I liked you."

"Hey Rainey, I'm so sorry about Monday. I don't normally lose control like that."

I waved my hand at her to suggest the need to apologize was ridiculous, and simply said,

"No need. We've all been there."

Maybe that was the reason for her uneasiness? It was true, we had all been there, especially with what she and I have recently been through. I sometimes wished I could drown my sorrows in two hundred dollar a glass wine and get regretfully shitfaced and forget everything for just one night. As we started walking out the door, I asked if she saw Trump's tweet over the weekend, and she seemed to relax and put a full court press on the politics conversation.

"This could be a dangerous conversation with anyone else," I marveled, "The minute I brought it up I had wished I could suck the words back in." Our forty-fifth president had divided our country. Most of America seemed to stand now on either end of a treacherous battlefield and many Americans were now deciding if they can survive the next two years with any sense of patriotism and unity. Any talk of politics these days could end unpredictably, and here I was, foot in mouth disease on full display.

"I'm glad we're both open-minded," she smiled slyly. It turned out we were on opposite sides of our political tightrope but reveled in conversation that truly would make America great again – if we had it constructively.

She was moving into that cool and breezy woman I met at the Gardens again. We entered Loantaka Recreation area where the parking lot was mostly filled with women much like us. Some were walking. There were a few others with strollers, and you'd see the occasional shirtless stud or gaggle of seniors dappled in amongst the women. Loantaka is a busy scenic, paved bike path tucked in the middle of suburbia. It winds through the woods for two to three miles in each direction, making it perfect for bikes, strollers and conversation. In the summer the tree-canopied walk was cool and you could easily forget you were a couple hundred feet from a planned housing development and the scorching sun in each direction.

As we walked, we moved the conversation from politics to children, then to the #metoo movement and to Maude. We had found the end of the two-and-a-half-mile walk, but it seemed as though no time at all had passed.

Conversation with Margaret was funny, intelligent, and easy. I forgot how nice it was to spend time with "a friend." I could easily see Margaret and me spending more time together.

"Two days," Jaime's text showed on my watch. I saw Margaret's eyes look away embarrassingly.

I snorted, "Oh my God, I do that all the time with Katherine– with Kate." I corrected myself. She was really determined to be called Kate and I needed to give her that.

"I'm sorry, force of habit. I can't even believe I looked." Margaret couldn't hold back her own laughter. "Well now that I'm caught," she continued, "What's happening in two days? Something exciting, I hope?"

Did Maude tell her? Maude's advice rang in my ears. Well, if this woman is going to be my new friend, I might as well disclose. She is Maude's daughter, of course.

I reminded her about my confession at lunch on Monday. Her eyes darted downward. I had clearly struck a nerve. Hesitantly, I continued and explained the hall pass Simon and I agreed on in November.

"But so much has changed since then, Rainey. Does he still think you're going to take advantage of it..." she paused abruptly, "Ohhhhh... Two days." As she was talking she put together the pieces.

"Are you really going to do this?" she asked. I was surprised she asked this.

I'm not sure why I was surprised but simply said, "I think so." There was silence for the first time on our walk.

I broke the silence, finally, with a justification of sorts. I didn't make eye contact as I talked.

"His name is Jaime. He was the first, no, the only man I had ever loved before I met Simon. At my lowest point with depression in March, he called." I tried to spare the extraneous detail as I recapped the events that would lead up to Friday. I continued, "...and as it turned out, he would become my rock for the next six months... through everything." I decided "everything" was too unbelievable so omitted those details. I wanted to share her mother's advice. I wanted desperately to talk about the hall pass again. As I told this story to Margaret, for a reason I would later discover, it was painfully uncomfortable.

Margaret simply said, "Well, it seems your mind is set."

I wanted to scream, "But he cheated on me! You of all people must know!" Why had she turned off? Should I remind her that I had a hall pass. Was she right? Had things changed so much because of Simon's illness? Something wasn't making sense in her response. Should I ask her how she's doing? Should I change the conversation completely? I decided to land in the middle where she could turn the conversation where she wanted it to go.

"How is the move going?" I figured it would be an easy time for her to bring up her husband or to avoid the man conversation altogether.

"The kids are thrilled with their new rooms. We're going furniture shopping tomorrow." As she dodged the heavier topic and kept talking, I decided she must still be in the denial phase. Well, at least she had the courage to leave, I thought.

We walked back to the house, careful not to land on any new landmines in our conversation. I did really enjoy talking to her. We discussed the city, bringing the kids to museums, books, art and current affairs. It was easy. Easy, except for conversations about relationships.

Well, new friendships take time. It would come.

I waved good-bye as she pulled out of my driveway. I thought for sure she'd wish me luck or mention Friday in her parting conversation, but she didn't. I shot Maude a text that I was on my way to Greenwood Gardens to help with the queen and grabbed my gardening gloves and clogs.

"Did she tell you?" was all Maude responded.

When I arrived at Greenwood Gardens thirty minutes later, Maude had just left.

ZERO DAYS AND COUNTING

Katherine never asked me about Jaime after I dropped her off. She had a funny way of turning a blind eye to things she didn't really want to know. She is wiser than her years, that way. Could Jaime be one of those things she doesn't want to know? She did ask me a hundred questions about Simon when she returned from Chicago. Was his weight gain normal? Did the pacemaker have to pace him yet? Had the defibrillator had to zap him yet? Was I cooking healthy for him while she was gone?

The most painful question, "Was Simon getting better, Mama?"

As I said my goodbyes and lied to my family this morning, that was the only question I could hear. The past months have been so hard for him. Was he getting better? No one knew.

The past months have been so hard for me, too. At least that's what my friends and family have told me. The outpouring of love and support was amazing, and minus Margo, no one else knew everything. When someone's life is on the line, what's happening to you doesn't really seem to matter, especially when it's someone you love. However hard I try to stuff that emotion down, I can't deny it. I do still love Simon. But is it enough?

I had become quick friends with Father Peter, our parish priest. During an afternoon break while helping out at the food pantry, we discussed what had been happening in my life over the past several years. For some reason, I shared everything. I told him about my struggling businesses, my house sinking, losing everything, having situational depression, Simon cheating, not being able to focus my thoughts, how the nursing home administration was new and my many trips and daily phone calls to try to get my mother proper care, my mother's dementia, finding out I had tumors that needed to be biopsied (which thankfully turned out to be benign,) being lonely, Katherine's struggle with school, losing my last job, and of course, Simon's rare heart disease that was threatening his life. One box of tissues later and my head was firmly planted on his shoulder. I even surprised myself.

"If my family could see me now," I thought as I cried.

Father Peter was calm, measured, and said the one thing no one else did. He said nothing. He just let me cry and let the flood of emotions roll out. He offered no apologies, no "God is with you, my child." He was just silent. When I had finally let it all out, we sat silently together.

"More tea?" he asked.

A past mentor, Bernie, once told me that the best thing to do in an interview was to be quiet. Your interviewees would either impress you or bury themselves with what they said while they tried to fill the unexpected silence. He was right. I thought of Bernie at that moment. As Father Peter offered me more tea, I had realized I was doing two things that I absolutely hated. I was living in the past and I was being a victim.

What was I doing now as I drove north to meet Jaime? Was I still living in the past? Was I allowing myself to be a victim of my situation and using that as an excuse to do something I would regret?

Was Maude right, or was Margaret?

By the time I hit the George Washington Bridge, I had convinced myself that I deserved this. Simon and I agreed on a hall pass, I wasn't doing anything wrong. Jaime would make me feel sexy, and loved, and lovable again. He was therapy. I needed this, and the truth was I couldn't wait to see him. Jaime was a love lost. All these years later, I never stopped thinking of him either. This was an opportunity to settle the score, get over Simon's indiscretion, and then I could continue building the life I had imagined. This would be my James Covey baptism – a symbolic gesture that puts the past behind you and allows you to start fresh - the end of one era and the start of a new one. It was time to move on.

Simon and Jaime were completely different, but I had loved them both. Jaime was an extrovert who has always wanted to take care of me, something my Beaufort pride would never allow. Simon was an introvert who wanted to spend quiet evenings alone telling me he loved me, to golf together, but had wanted to marry someone with money. Simon grew up poor, so he maintained a hoarding mentality at times. I often wonder if my house and cars attracted him to me first. He wanted to step into my lifestyle and was devastated as much as I when it started peeling away.

Simon, seeing the error of his ways, now realizes "it was miscommunication", now realizes I'll "be successful again", now realizes "money isn't important", now blah, blah, blah. Even last night he begged again for forgiveness and told me how being sick had helped him see how wrong his priorities had been. He told me how it didn't matter if I went back to work or not, what mattered was I. Money wasn't his priority. I was.

God, how I want to believe him.

Simon did like when I was working; I can feel that truth even now between his words. He loved the benefit of buying what he wanted and eating where he wanted as many times a week as he deemed fit. I do, too. But not having that would never be the reason I strayed. Jaime was the opposite. He didn't want me to work. He came from money but, oddly, had simpler needs than Simon. What didn't fit with us then still applies now; I want to work. I need to work. In a way, work delivers accomplishments and challenges that fuel me every day. With that said, I may have defined me by what I do, but it was infuriating to have my relationship assessed by whether I work or not. Didn't Simon realize that I was prideful? Didn't he realize that taking money from ANYONE, even if it were my husband, was devastating to me? I took the risk on the new business because I trusted Simon. We took the risk. And I? I allowed myself to be vulnerable. How did that work out for me? Not very well.

Yes, by the time I crossed the Massachusetts' border I knew I needed this weekend for so many reasons. I thought briefly about how happy Kate and Simon would be when I returned refreshed, ready to face what was still ahead.

I had left at the crack of dawn. I knew from experience, I'd need to hit the Bourne Bridge as early as possible on Friday to avoid the traffic. Even though it was September, you'd still see some traffic on the weekends, especially when the weather promised to be agreeable. This weekend would be very agreeably in so many ways. Damn, I needed this.

As I approached the bridge, the traffic slowed slightly with nary a lit tail light in sight. I rolled down the window in hopes of smelling the ocean breeze as I joined the herd of vacationers crossing the Cape Cod Canal. I looked at the car thermometer. It read seventy-four degrees and it was just past eight. The perfect day. I let my banded finger hang out the window as the warm air massaged my arm and reminded me I would be beachside in less than an hour.

As I crossed into Buzzard's Bay, I awaited the "Welcome to Cape Cod" sign. I was reminded of road trips to the Cape with my aunts and cousins in tow. Eight children and four women crammed into two cars for what seemed like days but was merely a very long, four-hour road trip. This sign was always a promise of the fun ahead. Today was no different.

Jaime wouldn't be meeting me until noon. We decided to

leave my car in a neighborhood in Chatham, a safe community near Melissa's parents' home. It would make it easy for me to check messages but wouldn't raise any concern if Kate and Simon checked my location. We'd meet on a beach we both knew well and would take his car to the inn. I loved the idea of arriving early and having time to myself to soak in the morning sun and take a long walk in a place that held so many special memories.

As I rounded the iconic rotary with perfectly groomed shrubs spelling out Cape Cod, my mind tumbled through the many trips I had taken around this island and all the different passengers who had joined me. My younger cousins asking, "Are we there yet?" and "How much longer?" were replaced with Katherine's similar queries years later. I remembered her little yellow bikini and her squeals of laughter as her toes touched the Atlantic Ocean for the first time at only six months old. I recalled Bryce, an old boyfriend and my discovering a crystal-clear lake on the way to a beach rental. We had pulled over to find a random wooden staircase that led to a private sandy shore. The fear of being caught beckoned with each step down the rickety wooded path. When we found ourselves alone at the bottom with no one in sight, we stripped our clothes with reckless abandon and spent hours floating and skinny dipping in our private pool.

As my friends' children got older, I'd rent a house in Chatham with a fenced in yard, firepit and plenty of bedrooms. It was steps from the beach where I'd host a week-long food and beach fest as an annual sojourn. I loved having a house full of people. It's where my friend Diana taught me to make her famous grilled shrimp - "Lady Di Shrimp" - still a crowd favorite. It's where Melissa's mom would join us and teach us how to make six hearty "lobstah rolls" for the beach out of eight depleted lobsters that we thought were only fit for the trash.

As my memories of the Cape flooded me, autopilot drove me down familiar roads as I found the address where Jaime had thought it best to leave my car. It was a short walk to Lighthouse Beach. I was excited at the prospect of walking the beach before Jaime got here and composing myself after a long drive. I parked within eye sight of the home of Melissa's parents, yet far enough away that they wouldn't see me. I worried that I might be challenged by neighbors, so hopefully knowing someone's name would give me a free pass, if questioned. As I parked my car, Simon's car, I was surprised by how easily I was adapting to this plan. I lied so effortlessly this morning as I kissed Katherine and Simon goodbye.

Who was I becoming?

I decided to bring my phone to the beach with me and hoped to capture some pictures of seals before I would banish it to the car. It had been almost three years since Katherine and I had been to the Cape. Would her memories be as colorful as mine? Kids are funny, they remember the things you'd prefer they didn't.

Margo and Jon, Michael and his girlfriend du jour, and a smattering of short-term visitors throughout the week all joined Katherine and me on our last year at the Cape. Much to Margo's dismay, Jon enjoyed far too much vodka throughout their stay. This was the root of their current problems, she recently confided. Katherine would be quick to remind him of lost flip flops, almost stumbling into the bonfire, and sleeping through an entire beach day because he was too sick to join us. I always tried to get a sitter if I thought there might be too much drinking at a party, but when the gathering was at your beach rental, it was hard to avoid. Katherine and I would always discuss it the next day and try to extract some valuable life lesson, but still, it was one thing I hated for her to witness.

I parked the car and longed for Katherine to be with me. It was easy when it was just the two of us. Maybe it was simply easier because of the affair. Before that, the three of us spent more time together. As I thought about it, in her mind I was safe when I was with Simon. She had always been somewhat protective. She was now a teenager and time together with parents was no longer something she wanted to do.

"Family," she wrote on the kitchen chalkboard last week, "means happiness."

Maybe I'm wrong? Maybe my perspective is askew? As Simon fights for his life, I have been trapped in a cyclone of over-analyzation. "That's just what women do," I once explained to Simon, "We over-analyze everything and have to talk about everything." I explained that he should just accept that as the way it will be because now he had two of us over-analyzing. My recent depression has been eye-opening. I recently looked in the mirror and thought I had gotten prettier. I was so heinously ugly with all this extra weight and crying just a few months ago in the hotel. I scrolled my mom selfies with Kate from January and now to find my appearance hadn't changed at all. The anti-depressants were working and the cloud of depression between my eyes and the receptors in my brain was clearing. How I needed them to kick in now.

I parked the car and continued my pity party. Katherine and I would start new. Fuck Simon and his cheating ways. I'll support him through his illness, but I will also take care of my needs. As the tears started to well, I grabbed for my phone, locked the doors and started walking toward the beach. I hoped my seal and sea glass expedition would distract me from my heartache. At the end of the day, it's heartache. The one person I trusted never to betray me, did.

The end of the street crescendos with the sound of waves hitting the shore of the beach ahead. Lighthouse Beach is unpredictable, and today the shoals and currents sound as though they're busy creating treacherous waters. I wonder if a storm is coming, although the forecast seemed perfectly suited for a beach weekend.

Although you can't see it from the street, the sounds and the smells of the ocean beckoned me. As the road rises, the dune grass creeps from the sand and I'm unsure where the street ends and the sand begins. As I close in on my target. It's a small path I barely remember. It curves gracefully and naturally around the grass, leading to my ultimate reward. The moment my sandals touch the sand, I impatiently remove them. I'm surrounded by true beauty and even more beautiful memories. The sand is warm between my toes and I imagine what I must look like with my hair flailing wildly in the wind.

My blonde hair is longer than it's been. I curled it this morning knowing the curls would loosen after a long drive and the wind would give it a romantic feel as it tousled my hair about. My tortoise shell St. Louis sunglasses that reminded me of the French Riviera, made me feel like a socialite and contradicted just slightly with the gauzy cream sundress with layers of fabric that draped close to my outline. I had a simple matching light weight wrap for my shoulders to keep me warm, but also to sit on if the desire struck me.

As I carried my sandals by the straps in one hand, I drenched my lungs with the sweet air as I crested the dune to the ocean. I forgot how much I loved the beach. It had only been nine months since we left Stonington. Some days that seemed like an eternity and other days like yesterday. The pain from that October evening, however, still seemed so fresh and raw.

As I walked toward the water, I cleared my mind of Simon and reminded myself of the last time I had been here with Jaime. I could almost see him walking toward me with sea glass he had found, excited to deliver this small treasure that would give me great joy as I would add it to my collection. "Every piece of sea glass holds a precious memory of those I love in a place I love." This was my youthful mantra. He walked toward me with a light green, sea worn piece of glass.

"It matches your eyes," I said as I received my gift.

"A new memory," he responded and embraced me in celebration. I laughed at how simple it had been.

I remembered how his dark hair was blowing in the ocean breeze as he held out his open hand. His chest was strong and wide and tan. I loved touching it. His entire body was fit and tone, but his broad chest always caught my attention first.

When you'd move your hands over it, his skin would surprise you with its softness. He had very little hair on his chest and that day, holding out the small piece of sea glass while the sun glistened off the sea behind him, he was my Poseidon. How I had loved him.

My mind moved from the sea glass to lying on the beach with nothing to protect us from the sand but our suits – not caring. Being with him was magical, and safe. Perhaps what I loved most about his chest was the way it enveloped me when he held me. My mind flashed to our hands clasped as we walked down this very beach, dreaming and laughing.

I then remembered the first time, on this beach, when he started naming our children. Four, he had wanted. I wasn't sure what to say. We had never discussed children, and at the time, I didn't even know I wanted any.

"It's too early to have this conversation," I teased. That should have been my clue.

What if? I now wondered.

My mind raced through my incredible life. I've travelled around the globe, twenty-two countries at last count. Some of those with friends, some alone, some with Katherine. I have the most amazing group of friends scattered across the country as I've lived in nine different states. I've climbed the corporate ladder and was a force to be reckoned with for almost twenty years. I started my own business and had a modicum of success when eighty-five percent of entrepreneurs fail. I had found true love twice.

I found true love twice, I thought again. What would have happened if I had said "Yes" to Jaime all those years ago? The sand was getting hotter and I moved closer to the water's edge. Where would I be now? Who would I be now? Does whom you're with, somehow define who you are or who you become?

I jumped back to thoughts of Simon. I had bargained for a hall pass. Stage three, I thought. After winning that hall pass,

I fell into depression. Stage four. Today the one thing I was sure to pack was my Zoloft, my vitamin B, and my vitamin D. I could not leave home without my small drugstore in my purse that ensured my happiness.

What was I doing here? Was Jaime my newest drug?

The Cape was a memory I shared with almost everyone I knew, everyone but Simon. The last time we were in the Cape, Simon had a meeting so couldn't attend. Michael had come up for the last four days of our stay. Michael was like a brother to me. We met when I was nineteen and he was dating my friend. He was slightly older than we, and already owned a house and was determined to teach us his definition of living. He taught us how Frank Sinatra could improve any event (although we were both too young to have heard him on the radio), how cooking dinner with friends could change your life, and how drinking great wine was always worth the investment. It turned out our mutual friend moved to Australia for school and left the two of us behind. We became inseparable. Michael knew my secrets and my pain – and I knew his.

That last trip to the Cape, he and I lay on the bed in the guestroom together talking. I'm not sure where everyone else was. It was just Michael and I. We stared up at the ceiling as we talked and giggled. A serious tone took over him, which was rare in our friendship. Even when he should have been serious, he wasn't. That was the beauty of Michael. He could make everything funny. When Simon was diagnosed, somehow Michael made us both laugh. We laughed hard, too. We knew Michael's heart was breaking as badly as ours from the news, but Michael just had that way about him.

On the bed that day, he wasn't laughing. "QB..." (he had given me that nickname years ago.) Queen Beaufort he called me. "QB, I want what you have. I want the house and the kid and the picket fence. I even want a wife." Michael had been a playboy since I met him. Today he was confessing that he had made the wrong decision. It was that day and that moment when I realized, I did have it all.

I couldn't help wondering, was I risking it all right now?

I looked at my phone, eleven-eleven a.m. Over the course of the past months, I seemed to look always at the time at eleven-eleven. It started to happen every day, morning and night. Eleven-eleven. I decided to ask my good friend Google about it while I sat on the sand waiting for Jaime.

I read everything from make a wish at that time to it being a sign that angels were watching over mw. I could use some angels, right now. The two on my shoulder were having somewhat of a heated brawl as we awaited Jaime's arrival.

And then I read it. How fitting! There were pages and pages on the subject.

In numerology, eleven is the number of transition. It's the time that precedes the coming of a new day. But this wasn't what captured me. There were pages upon pages of references from the Bible.

But the land you are crossing the Jordan to take possession of is a land of mountains and valleys that drinks from rain from Heaven.
Deuteronomy 11:11

11:11 is when God tells the Israelites that they are entering the Promised Land. They would transition into a season in which they were under God's continual blessing from the beginning of the year to the end. Google did not stop there. With every reference of the number eleven in the Bible came a shift of circumstance.

Suddenly, I wasn't alone on the beach. "For better or for worse." I had made a vow. My tears would not be contained. I looked at my tear stained dress. My nose was running, and the bottom of my dress was wet from the splashing waves. Even my dress was crying. I laughed at myself. It was eleven fourteen. Jaime would be here in forty-six minutes. I picked up my phone.

"Hey honey, how was the trip?" Simon's voice was light. He had no idea what would come out of my mouth next. His voice wouldn't be light for long. I couldn't form words.

"Rainey, babe, are you okay?" All he could hear on my end was an eruption of tears. "I'm on my way. Are you okay? Should I call the police? Rainey, where are you?" His words were quick. I could hear his panic. No, this was nothing the police could help us with.

"No." It was all I could say.

He was patient with me. "That's good. You're safe?"

"Yes." I gulped.

Simon was silent. He waited for me to compose myself. He waited, and then finally told me to breathe. He was calm.

"I'm in the Cape. I'm meeting Jaime." There was silence on the other end. I wished I could see his face. Why was I telling him this? What did I want from him?

"You are." His words were slow and deliberate. He wasn't asking the question. I could tell by his tone that he knew who Jaime was. I didn't know where this conversation was going to go. I loved this man and now, I was hurting him. Somehow, I knew I was hurting him more than the sarcoidosis. I could hear it in his breathing.

He finally spoke again. "Rainey, why are you calling?"

"I don't know." Still crying, but for other reasons now.

"I understand. We had an agreement. Do what you have to do, Rainey. I just want you to come home to me." He never calls me Rainey. He wasn't mean or hateful or angry in his tone. He was resigned.

I looked to the sky for an answer. The sun was bright, and strong. It was getting closer to being directly above my head. I looked at my disappearing shadow. He would be here soon.

"I love you, Rainey. I love you so much. I am so sorry I hurt you. I understand that you need to do this." Simon's tone was weakened.

I WILL ALWAYS LOVE YOU

"I'm right around the corner. Please don't leave," pleaded Jaime. "I'm right here, let me just get to you. I just need five minutes. Rainey, please stay. I'm almost there."

I sounded like a lunatic. I had been talking to this man for six months, every day. He had been my rock. He had taken care of me, just as he had promised all those years ago.

We had planned this reunion. We had the perfect hotel suite in the perfect location. And now, after he drove three hours to meet me, I was going to leave before he even arrived.

I remembered Simon's words before he hung up, "Come home, baby."

Simon had once said that the worst part of the affair had been realizing the pain he had caused me. "There was no worse pain than that of hurting someone you love so deeply."

I knew that pain now. Despite everything Simon had done, he was the only man I ever loved enough to marry.

My hands shook as I turned on the car. I wanted to wait for Jaime. I wanted to let him hold me and feel his love. Years had gone by, but I knew, despite it all, we could step back into time together. This weekend could remind me of the woman I was. The strong, desirable woman who had been proposed to six times but only said yes once. The woman who left a trail of broken hearts but only cried for two men. One of these men was about to pull down Dune Drive at any moment.

"Just lunch," Jaime pleaded. His tone wasn't angry. Most men would be angry. Jaime loved me, still. And, I loved Jaime. This was why I had to go. I wouldn't be able to leave once I was with him. I couldn't leave that embrace when I still felt so broken.

Here was my truth. Maybe Jaime and I were meant to be together. Maybe Jaime and I could live happily ever after and Katherine would have two instant big brothers to take care of her and look after her. But I didn't marry Jaime; I married Simon.

I needed to do the right thing.

As I pulled out onto Morris Island Road, I saw him. I kept my head straight, I couldn't look at him. I could feel his beautiful green eyes pleading as he passed. I could feel him begging me to stop from my peripheral view. At this moment, I knew I was hurting the only other man I had ever loved. I pulled my car over to the side of the road.

I heard Jaime's tires screech. Another day I would have laughed at the scene I was creating and ask who that crazy chick was. Jaime did a quick U-turn and pulled up behind me in his Jeep Wrangler, the top off, the tires slightly too big for the vehicle. I laughed that both men drove different versions of the same car. He left his door open as he ran to my window. I couldn't bring myself to put the car in park. I sat frozen, one foot on the brake, the other hovering over the accelerator. What was I doing?

Jaime reached in and put the car in park. My face was wet with tears. He clenched the door handle and slowly opened the driver's side door. He reached in and helped, almost lifted, me out of the car. I could feel his strength beneath his Polo. He was as beautiful as I remembered.

"I know you have to go, baby." He was crying. He was so gentle and careful with me. "I know you, Rainey. I was kidding myself to think I could pull you away from your vows, from a dying man..." His words cut off abruptly. "I'm so sorry, Rainey. I will always love you. I will always be here for you."

I looked up at him. I was tall, but he made me feel petite. I could smell him. He smelled of comfort and love and trust. Why did I trust him? I talked myself into believing for so long that I had dodged a bullet. But this man, I still trusted. We were soul mates. His first marriage was doomed because of his love for me. He had tried to replace me and "fill the gaping hole I had left," he had recently shared. He couldn't marry again because the hole still existed. He had left his girlfriend, the one he thought might fill the hole that still lingered. I reopened that hole over the past six months. I hadn't meant to. I hadn't promised him I'd leave Simon. I was honest. He knew exactly why I was here.

I couldn't form the words I needed as he stood in front of me. I just looked at him. I listened to his words. He pulled me in and I tucked my face against his chest. It felt like home.

"You are still as beautiful as I remember," he spoke softly under his breath. I felt his chest heave against my cheek. His arms tightened around me and I could feel his entire body pressed against mine. It wasn't sexual, it was comforting. I wanted to stay in the safety of his arms. I knew I shouldn't have stopped.

Jaime pulled his head back finally and took his finger around the round of my face and to my chin. He pulled it up slowly to meet his. I felt my lips open and love roll in as I looked in his eyes. I saw the same in his. He gently pulled my lips to his and kissed me softly. How I wanted more from him. Our lips touched each other softly, barely.

"I know I can't have you. Not now." Jaime took control and completed our gentle, loving kiss. I touched my fingers to my mouth, breathless, not with lust. I was breathless with love and heartbreak. I knew I needed to leave soon.

"I love you, Jaime." My heart was breaking just as much as it had twenty plus years ago.

"I will always love you, Rainey. I will always be here." He said.

At that, he opened the car door, took his fingers that held my chin and slowly wiped my tears. His hands were holding my face now, his thumbs trying to make the tears disappear.

"I'm glad you stopped."

"Me, too." I said. He kissed my forehead and helped me into the car as gently as he had helped me out. There were no words left.

"I love you." Were his last words to me as he walked back to his Jeep.

I was in Connecticut before I could stop crying and collect myself.

I am lucky.

They were the only words that would come to me now.

I am loved. I am lucky.

I am surrounded by amazing people. I am lucky.

I thought of my family, the crazy Beaufort family that taught me strength and power and will and determination, those beautiful, loving, strong, bad-ass, women. I am very lucky.

I thought of my father and his family, of having said our final words to each other, of having the gift and balance of my father in my life. I am incredibly lucky.

Katherine. Margo. Zoe. Michael. Lisa. Jen. Melissa. Maude. I am so lucky and loved and thankful.

Over the past few months, I had not thought about how fortunate I was. I had thought about everything I had lost. When I think back, the only one I had lost was myself.

I was near Margo's house now, it would be so easy to stop and see my best friend. I knew I needed to get back to Simon. Besides, I hadn't told her about this trip. She would be hurt that I didn't share it with her. I had told her so much, but now she had her own struggles. She was fighting for her own marriage and she didn't need my misery all these months later.

That was one of the things I loved about her the most. We would laugh at the saying, "Misery loves company."

"No, misery wants to get the hell out of misery so why surround yourself with more?" she would claim.

I spoke to the car, "Siri, call Margo, mobile." I needed to stop and check on her. I'd make an excuse.

Voicemail. Damn. "Hey girl, it's Rainey! Had some windshield time and was thinking of you. Call me, I'll be in the car for a while. I love you. Bye."

The one person who did know everything was my New Jersey bestie, Maude. Maybe I'd check in on the roses. I know she'll be full of her usual questions. "Screw him," she tutored. As the phone rang, I laughed at the disappointment she'd tell me I caused when I'd tell her what happened. Although, she would be discussing HER disappointment. I laughed at my prediction. I screwed him, all right, just not in the way she had mentored me.

"Hey Rainey, it's Margaret. I'm glad you called." I looked at the phone, I thought I called Maude. I did. Maybe she thought I called for her?

"Well, it turns out, I took your advice. I couldn't go through with it. I'm on my way home." "That's good," she responded flatly. Hadn't she heard what I said?

"Is everything OK, Margaret?"

"No. Mum is at Columbia Presbyterian. She was flown in a couple hours ago."

"Is she," my breath caught me. Why would they fly her to the city? It was bad. I didn't need to put her through retelling what happened. I would learn what happened soon enough.

"I'm on my way. What do you need, Margaret? I'm about an hour and a half away, maybe two with traffic."

Columbia Presbyterian was the hospital of kings and queens. Bill Clinton would have his bypass surgery there; sheiks were commonly travelling across the globe to be seen by the doctors here. It was the best. If anyone deserved the best, it was Maude.

I hung up with Margaret. She offered no explanation as to why Maude was there. I knew that couldn't be good. I decided to call Lily. Lily told me she was with Maude when she collapsed at the Gardens. She had called Margaret and met her and the children at Morristown Hospital. Lily was driving the kids into the city as Margaret rode in the helicopter with her mother.

"Her lung collapsed," she explained. "At our age, that's not a good thing, Rainey. But don't worry, Margaret was on the phone and has the best pulmonologist available meeting her at Columbia." I told Lily I was on my way and would meet her there.

I hung up and called Simon.

"I'm glad you didn't stay," he answered.

"Me, too, Simon." I answered. For more reasons than one, I thought.

I explained what was happening with Maude and that, although I knew we had unfinished business, I needed to be there with her. Simon understood and offered to meet me there.

"No, stay with Katherine, ugh, Kate. I'll call you when I know what's happening."

"Ok, babe. Call me if you need me." He was sad. He knew what was coming. I could tell from his voice he knew I would never be able to get over his "mistake." His deliberate, repeated, mistake with Portia.

There was no place you'd least wanted to be than New York City in a car on a Friday night. I would be sneaking in just after five, so hoped to get lucky. I wouldn't stop so I could have a slim chance of beating the rush into the city before theatergoers, diners, dancers, and sports fanatics got in my way. I was thankful this city never slept, which meant, dinner at seven was reserved for early birds and gridlock was generally reserved for later. Still, I knew this would not be a stress-free drive.

I didn't get to Columbia until seven-fifteen p.m. My back hurt, and after over ten hours in a car today, I was exhausted. I valeted my car and ran to the information booth inside the revolving door. They gave me a visitor's pass and I made my way through the maze of elevators and hallways to find a frenzy of activity at the end of what I would learn was Maude's corridor.

As I stared at the room number on my guest pass, I started counting doors to find my way to Maude and Margaret, and I would presumed by that time, Lily and Margaret's two girls.

I shouldn't have been at all surprised to find a room filled with friends who I didn't know. Margaret was sitting next to Maude's bed holding her hand. Lily, as if an angel herself, grabbed my arm and led me back outside of the room before I could make my way through the crowd.

"It's not good, my dear, I'm sorry." Lily was acting her age. She always seemed "more mature" than Maude, and I knew they were close in age. Right now, Lily was acting more like my mother than my wine-drinking, fashion-icon that I had grown to love as much as Maude. "Maude's refusing the surgery," she started, "She said it's her time."

I didn't think I could cry anymore tears after today, but they came. Tears came in torrents down my face.

"Well you know Maude doesn't like all that shit, Rainey. Clean yourself up before you see her." I couldn't help laughing as the Lily I had grown to know over the past several months re-emerged. I excused myself to the bathroom, half laughing but mostly devastated. I would do just that, clean myself up before pushing through the crowd of visitors waiting patiently to do exactly what I would be doing, saying their goodbyes.

There had to be forty balloons: single giant mylar balloons saying get well soon, bouquets of balloons, and pictures of balloons drawn by children she had indubitably touched, as well. They were drawn in red and pink and yellow and white, like Maude's roses, I thought. There were flowers, too, plenty of roses and one single bunch of daisies. I added the roses I had bought at the gift shop to her collection.

"What are you doing here?" I heard the familiar voice scolding me. "YOU, have a hot date," Maude finished weakly. She looked so tiny in the big hospital bed. Was she that small, that frail? Had I never noticed?

"Well, I decided I could be in bed with him or you tonight. I choose you." I smiled as I sat on the edge of her bed, careful not to hurt her. She smiled and grabbed my hand.

"I love you," she said. Then she pulled me closer, "You taught me to say that." She surprised me. I remembered the first time I told her I loved her. It was so easy for me. I noticed it caught her off guard. We had shared those words many times since then over the past months. I never thought it wasn't natural for her.

"Well clearly, my job is done here." I smiled sadly.

"You'd better damn well take care of those roses," she smiled up at me.

"I will, I promise." It wouldn't be the same without her. I looked at the other six faces in the room. Margaret was the only one I recognized. Maude had a stream of visitors.

"Well, how does the story end?" Maude asked weakly, but with a mischievous grin attached. I knew she meant Jaime.

"Well it didn't end in sex," I snorted.

"With divorce?" Maude asked worriedly.

"I don't know," I answered, "I guess it ended with me no longer living in the past." Maude shot Margaret a glance. "I love you, Maude. I really love you. I've loved discovering who you are, and I've loved every story. I've loved meeting your family and your friends." At that I looked around at the room.

Another friend had joined us. I continued, "I don't know how I would have made it through the past few months without you. I love you, Maude. Thank you for being so much more than my friend. Thank you for being my saving grace." Tears began to well in my eyes as Maude's frail hand touched mine.

"I love you, too, Rainey."

At that, a single tear fell. I kissed Maude on her cheek. The last words barely were formed from her lips. I could tell it was almost her time. Her breath was getting shallower. I somehow knew.

I excused myself to go check on the kids and Lily and said I'd be right back. As I left to go get them, I noticed the next friend step up to say her goodbyes. I looked back at the scene I was walking away from. This was a life fulfilled. This was a life well-lived. As I left, I must have made a face that shared my thoughts perfectly. The nurse outside her door simply looked at me and said,

"I know. It's been like that since she arrived. We could barely get the doctor in between the crowds to see her." She smiled at me and then bowed her head.

I went to the cafeteria where Lily was buying a bushel of cookies and ice cream for the girls. "I think we need to go back upstairs and say goodbye to your grandmother. Tell her what she means to you. Tell her you love her." Lily looked at me and nodded. Had she known as well?

The four of us took our bounty of sweets back to Maude's room.

"It's time for just the family. We sent the others away." The nurse was sullen, but also very matter-of-fact. I walked in with the children. As I rounded the curtain, I heard Margaret say to Maude, thinking they were alone, "The only good thing that came from me cheating on David was that he kicked me out in time for me to be here with you. I love you, Mum."

I stood frozen at the curtain. Margaret looked at me, her eyes red and horrified. I pushed the kids toward her and quietly said,

"Fill the air with everything you love about your grandmother. She will love that. Share all of your favorite stories of her and funny times together. Listen carefully, too. She's had a life well-lived with you two, and she loves you beyond words." The kids looked at me and nodded dutifully, I think, happy that they had some direction at this awkward time.

Margaret mouthed, "I'm sorry, Rainey." She stretched her arms toward her daughters.

I left the room with Lily. We linked arms as we cried together on the walk to the waiting room. Lily barked at the nurse, again un-Lily-like,

"Let us know when the time comes. We'll be right here for the family."

In the waiting room, Lily and I spoke very little. We cried together. We remembered together silently, shoulder against shoulder. We didn't need to speak. We knew this woman had left an indelible imprint on our souls. Every few minutes, Lily would reach over and pat the top of my hand. That was a memory of the three of us, I would think as she did it. Finally, breaking the comfortable silence, I would say, "I wish I had met Harry."

Lily looked at me, "He was just like your Simon."

The nurse arrived almost an hour later, "I'm sorry."

"Thank you," I replied. Lily and I didn't have to speak, we both quietly rose and walked toward Maude's room arm in arm. Lily entered first. I was still in disbelief that Margaret– and Maude– had kept such an important piece of Margaret's story from me. Lily ran to comfort Margaret immediately. I took my cue and went to the children. I had only known them for a short time, but they grabbed around my neck and both held tight as their tears released. I wrapped my arms around both little bodies and thought of Katherine. Maude's body was still in the room. I thought about my father and how he had left his body before he passed. For some reason, I could still feel Maude's presence. She wasn't done watching over her flock. I asked them if they had said everything they wanted.

The littlest said, "I forgot to tell her that she was the best Grandmum in the whole, wide, world."

"Well, somehow I think she just heard you." I smiled and looked up. I held them as we cried.

Margaret would soon join us. She touched my back. "Thank you, Rainey. Thank you for being here. I'm so sorry–" I held my hand up to signal it was all right. Now was not the time for me to be upset about her commonality with my husband.

"I wanted to tell you sooner. I wanted to tell you before the Cape. I knew what this mistake had meant for me. Promise we'll talk later?"

There was something so sincere about her words. I was holding her children. Her mother had just passed only minutes ago, and she wanted to make amends– for something that really had nothing to do with me?

"Of course."

Lily would stay with Margaret while they managed through paperwork and details that needed to be wrapped up before she left. I took the kids with me to get my car. I knew that what was to come could take twenty minutes or two hours. I told Lily to text us when they were done and I'd meet them at the entrance of the hospital. I would give them a little tour of the city at night to preoccupy them.

The valet had the car ready by the time we got down the elevator. I tipped him generously knowing we'd be in his way when we returned and thankful not to have to wait on a Friday night outside the busy emergency area. I waited for the girls to get buckled in the back seat before I headed for the West Side Highway. Margaret's youngest reminded me of Katherine with her excitement, "Can we see where the ball drops? We've never been there."

I was surprised to hear this when her sister chimed in, "Yes we have, idiot. It's Times Square."

"I'm gonna tell Mom."

"Go ahead."

"Well, we've never been there at night. So there!"

I could have interjected. I always found siblings fighting as a pleasant reminder of why God didn't give me a second. It was exhausting. How did parents manage this day in and day out? Katherine once said after a weekend at a friend's house, who happened to have three siblings, "Ahhh.... It's so nice and quiet here, Mom." I'm not sure I was wired for more than one child.

"Well, let's see what's new since you've been there last," I compromised. It took ten minutes to get the six miles to forty-second street and twenty minutes to get the next eight blocks. I kept hoping it took as long as I had imagined for Margaret to do the paperwork.

The girls could have cared less about the time. The big lights of the city had captivated them. Their heads were wrenched out the window when I thought better to open the sunroof. The Audi had one of those long sunroofs that made admiring skyscrapers far less dangerous than their strategy – putting their little necks as far out the window as they could while taxi drivers perilously maneuvered away from clipping an ear.

"Is that a prostitute?"

"Who eats meat on a stick?"

"That smells good."

"P. U. That's disgusting!"

"Did you see her outfit?"

"Does that man with a guitar have any clothes on?"

"That's not the real Mickey Mouse!"

Their questions and observations tickled me. I missed Katherine beyond words right now. I still had to get home and have the inevitable conversation with Simon. I wondered what David had said to his daughters as he let Margaret whisk them across the country. I could never let Katherine out of my custody. How did he allow her to take them, especially after what she had done? I guess she was a fierce lawyer. I thought about how she was quiet when I talked about Jaime.

"To sinners!" she had cheered in her drunken awkwardness at lunch. No wonder Maude was so angry.

But, it got her here, when she needed to be here.

As I headed back toward the West Side Highway my phone buzzed. I knew that meant our timing would be perfect. Lily had taken the girls in by Uber so she could console them. I couldn't imagine Lily navigating the traffic in her big, black Mercedes. Her head barely cleared the steering wheel and the big sedan, a gift from her husband, was presumably designed to protect her more so than anyone with whom it came in contact. I laughed as she showed me the most recent scratches from a sign she backed into in the parking lot. She was going to write to the town council. There was no need for the base of a parking lot sign to be so deceptively large. She was sure many drivers had done even worse damage than she had because of the sign's ridiculous design.

As we drove up to the hospital, Lily and Margaret were just exiting the front doors. I pulled up and Lily immediately started bantering about how they made her wait for everything.

"They should be prepared, this is a very delicate time." Margaret jumped in the back seat with her girls and hugged them.

"Thank you for driving us home, Rainey."

The girls told them about the naked man and the fake Disney characters as we crossed the George Washington Bridge.

"Oh, so the Naked Cowboy lives on?" Margaret chuckled. "How I've missed New York."

Twenty minutes later we were pulling up to Maude's house. The Georgian brick colonial seemed bigger than I remembered. I hurt with how much I missed her right now.

Jaime's kiss seemed like years ago.

"I'll pick you up in the morning and we can get Maude's car, I mean your mom's car, at the Gardens and then I'll help you with the arrangements." I got out and hugged them each and said goodnight as they walked away. Lily waved from the passenger's seat and blew kisses. She was exhausted. We all were. It was close to 1:00 A.M. after an emotionally taxing day. I got back into the car with Lily once they all safely made it to the front porch.

"Lily, you are an angel. You've been so strong today, but I know you lost your best friend." My heart broke as I said those words. Who was my best friend? I couldn't help my selfish thoughts.

"You, too, my dear. You, too. Now take a right at the end of Maude's drive."

Lily lived four houses away from Maude in an even bigger colonial. Her husband, whom I never really remember her mentioning, had left the light on for her and opened the door as the car's headlights curved around the circle drive. Lily leaned over and kissed my cheek,

"Good night, my dear."

"Good night, Lily." The age had wrangled its way into Lily's vocabulary. Yesterday, it was hard to remember they were in their late eighties. Today, it wasn't.

When I pulled up to the house, the front porch light and lamp post in the front yard were lit. Both lights. He must want me home. I sat in the driveway for a bit. I had hoped Simon might greet me like Lily's husband had. No sign of Simon. I had sent him a text before we left the city, around midnight, but he hadn't responded. I looked at my phone, eight messages today. Four numbers I didn't recognize. Margo tried twice, Zoe and my mother. No Simon. Maybe he was sleeping?

NEXT STEPS

There was no movement in the house, no glow of the television coming from a window or anyone waiting for me in the front room. Could Simon have fallen asleep? Should I wake him? What would I say? I sat in the driveway staring at the house. All my plans, six months and I would decide. He was sick, and I begged God to help me help me forgive him. I tried, but when I would expect it the least, a vision of them together ricocheted through my brain.

I asked Father Peter about forgiveness once. He said, "people forgive when they're ready to forgive."

Zoe called me the other day with a heavy heart. She confessed that she had been going through the motions when she was around Simon, but she had still been so angry with him. She then shared when she saw him this past visit, she had truly forgiven him, finally, and she wanted me to know. She loved Simon again as a brother-in-law and as a friend, she told me. She had finally come to terms with his re-acceptance into our family. I asked what made the difference for this change of emotion, and she said,

"Well, I realized that if you could forgive him, then who was I to stand as judge?" I couldn't tell Zoe that I hadn't forgiven him.

I decided to leave my bags in the car and creep into the house and try not to wake anyone. The front door was unlocked. I quietly dropped my purse at the door and decided to wash my face in the first-floor bathroom and use a guest toothbrush to brush my teeth. This was the best chance I had to not wake everyone up. Simon was a light sleeper, I didn't want to wake him for a multitude of reasons. I was exhausted and depleted, and I didn't want to have this conversation right now. I had allowed his affair to strip me of my power and I needed to take it back. This would not be an easy message to deliver.

As I walked past Simon's office I saw a small book I gave him for Valentine's Day two years ago. I hated that book. It represented the Valentine's Day he was with another woman, the Valentine's Day and the anniversary when I thought I was the happiest woman on earth and my husband was busy making someone else happy.

He had been reading it.

The cover of the book read, *The Reasons I Love You*. Simon had left the book opened, faced down on his chair. I almost missed it, but Simon was notoriously neat, he would never leave something lying out like that. I picked up the book and looked at the page he had been reading. The book was a journal of sorts. It guided you through documenting moments in your relationship that embodied your love for each other.

I picked up the book and saw my own handwriting facing back.

"I love how safe you make me feel," it said on the left page. On the right page, the words screamed at me, "I love who I am when I'm with you." The two things he took away from me, side-by-side in this dumb little book that had represented nothing but lies and deceit when I looked at it now.

I was so fucking happy. I just want to be happy again.

I held the pages to my chest as I cried. I went to pull the book away and close it when I noticed one of my tears had landed on the page. When I wiped it, I noticed yet another stain next to mine. This stain had dried. Was this Simon's tear?

I thought about the words where both our tears had dropped, "I like who I am when I'm with you."

The words couldn't be less true right now. But did I love myself less because of who I had become because of the affair, or had I stopped loving myself before that? Did I link my success in business with my confidence in life? Simon cheated on me because he fell in love with who I was and was disappointed with who I wasn't. I wasn't a real estate magnate or a business prodigy. I no longer made three hundred and fifty thousand a year but rather, barely covered my own expenses. I would get another job, but should that define our relationship? Do I want to be with someone whose values don't align?

I tried to understand why money was so important. I guess he came into it thinking I would contribute financially, and I didn't. I tried. I took risks with him, but it didn't work out well. There was the unexpected: the house sinking and losing over a hundred and fifty thousand dollars in equity, the depression that had taken away my ability to see, and think, and consume any information.

I was dying inside, not supporting myself. I wanted to be successful. I had worked hard my entire life to be comfortable when I retired. Didn't he realize that every time he mentioned money, he was pouring acid into my veins? When you're beating yourself up about your lack of success and you find out your marriage depends on it as well, well, that's a lot of stress to put on anyone.

I had to fix me before I could be the leader that could support me. And suddenly, I was sure of where I needed to start. I needed to start at the top of the stairs. It was time to take my power back.

DAWN

'It is always darkest just before the Day dawneth.'
Thomas Fuller, 1650

I woke up next to Simon still sleeping. His breathing seemed different this morning. I had become an expert on his breathing. I had also become an expert on when his heart was paced by his new bionics, the multiple similarities, and how and when he slept. It was as if, with my pedestrian education, I could outwit the doctors because I just paid more attention. I dreamed of finding the missing clue that had kept researchers away from a cure. If I only pay attention, I'm sure I could uncover something helpful.

Was his breathing more labored because of the stress I had put him through yesterday? I know he's getting worse, but I keep fabricating silly– but believable– hypotheses so he'll stay optimistic. I know I shouldn't have called him, I just needed him. I needed to hear his voice. For the first years of our marriage, he had been my best friend. Now, I would vacillate between my moral obligation to my vows and my moral obligation as a human being, versus the person I am to my core, a Beaufort. I had let his "mistake" take away my self-respect, my dignity, and most importantly the bad-ass woman I spent a lifetime fueling. It was time to take that back, regardless of his health.

It was Saturday and I didn't want to have this conversation in front of Kate. As Simon slept, I slipped out of the bed unnoticed and went to Kate's room. I needed this child right now. It didn't matter that it was six-thirty in the morning. My heart ached for the one person on earth that meant more than all others.

I opened her door to find her asleep. She moved slightly as I opened the door. Her long blonde hair was splayed across the pillow and the bed looked as though she spent the night wrestling in it. I wondered why she had such a restless night.

I jumped into the full-size bed and rested my head on the pillow facing hers. I watched her shoulders rise and fall with each breath and her long eye lashes and plump lips that still held a small bit of residue from the mascara and lip gloss she started wearing. She was becoming more beautiful every day. Could I do this to her again? By leaving Simon to make myself whole, was I hurting her or teaching her selflove? It pained me to create any more pain for her.

I lay next to her thanking God for keeping her safe and well. It was then I heard that familiar groan,

"Moooommmmmmmm– Why do you do this?" I brushed her hair from her face and responded,

"One day you'll understand. I love you, angel."

"Okay, Mom. I love you, too. Now can I go back to sleep? It's Saturday!"

I laughed at myself, to quote my only child, I was so annoying. If she wasn't so tired she may have told me herself. I was. I love this child more than life; it's a love you don't fully understand until you have a child.

I told her quickly about Maude and that I needed to go to help Margaret and the kids. I'd probably be back by early afternoon. She put on her sad face without opening her eyes for the news about Maude and then said,

"Sorry, Mom." She then seemed to think about what this meant and added, "Don't be too late. Simon wasn't doing well last night. I think he was zapped a couple times."

"Okay baby, call me when he wakes up and let me know

how he's doing. If I need to be back sooner – for either of you – I will be. I love you."

"Okay. Love you." At that she rolled over in her bed and fell back to sleep.

Margaret is an early riser. I was confident I could show up at seven a.m. with two non-fat lattes and be warmly received. I also bought some scones and cake pops for the girls for when they'd wake up later. As I drove to Maude's house, I thought about the scene at the hospital the night before. There was a line of people waiting to pay their last respects. Maude had touched each of our lives. She had made us laugh right to the last minute. She was strong, not only in life, but for all of us at the end of hers.

I walked around to the kitchen door where I had greeted Maude and recently Margaret many times before. As expected, Margaret was sitting alone at the small island. Her laptop was open, but her eyes were elsewhere. I rapped quietly on the door not to wake the kids or startle her. She stood up quickly and moved to my arms for a long hug.

"Oh Rainey." She started crying as I hadn't yet seen. Her shoulders shook as I hugged her back.

"I'm so sorry," I whispered. She kept me in her arms like a favorite teddy bear. It was then I realized I was all she had here now. She had been brave for the girls, but Maude was why she was here. She left her old life in Seattle just as I had left mine in Connecticut.

When she unclamped her arms, she smiled weakly and looked at the coffee and pastries I had barely got on the counter before she reached me.

"Thank you." She grabbed one of the lattes and sat back at the counter where she cleared an opened newspaper and her laptop in a way of welcoming me to the seat. I sat down next to her. I was like Maude in these situations, I loved to fill the air and bring lightness into the room, but I knew now was not the time. Margaret just kept shaking her head as tears streamed into her latte. I put my hand on her arm as if to say without words that I was here for her. When Margaret finally started to speak, it was a hoarse whisper.

"My mother knew everyone in town. Everyone loved her." She paused. "I loved her. I wasn't ready for her to leave me. I needed her." Her tears were even heavier.

"I know I can never replace your mother but let me be here for you. I know how lonely it can be." I tried to console her but wondered if I was really consoling myself.

"Rainey, I see the hurt in your eyes with what you're going through. I see the hurt that Simon caused you and I know, I did the same to David. I know you must see everything you hate in Simon in me."

"No, I don't." I really didn't. It was the first time I realized that I didn't hate her for what she'd done to her husband. My heart broke for a man I don't know, but hating her? No, I didn't. She was easy to forgive. I could see the pain in her eyes. I could see the gut-wrenching regret that she wore sadly in her expression. I didn't know what it was when we first met. I had known that expression before, but couldn't place it. I now knew I recognized it as the same expression Simon wore every day.

"You and David will get through this." I couldn't believe those words came from my lips. Margo had said the same to me nine months ago. Why was everyone always cheering on reconciliation? Even I! I hadn't known how true the words I shared with Katherine would be. It was harder to stay with someone than to leave. But it was also important to follow your heart.

"David will be here for the girls tomorrow. I'm going to beg him to take me back." Margaret didn't shock me with her words. I surprised myself with my next question.

"Are you sure you want him back? I mean, there's a reason why you strayed, right?"

Her youngest trudged into the kitchen, still wearing her

clothes from the night before. Her hair was a brilliant bonnet of curls and knots and sleep. She shuffled over to Margaret where her head and arms landed around her mother's waist. Margaret picked her up to her lap and held her close to her chest. She looked at her youngest thoughtfully, and then looked back at me and responded. "Yes."

Lily showed up with a basket of muffins at the same door I crept through forty minutes ago. They smelled as if they had just left the oven and the light floral napkin covering them almost lifting itself at the hands of its aroma. It took two entire seconds for Margaret's lap to be cleared and a small hand to enter the basket and break the muffins from their loving prison. She smiled as the warm blueberry muffin came toward her mouth. We all laughed, and Lily walked to the coffee pot.

"Now I'm going to stay with the girls. I already called Mr. Salvarone at the funeral home, I know Maude wanted to use him. I told him you'd both be there within the hour. I told him everything Maude wants so there should only be small details for you to agree on."

I looked at Margaret in astonishment. Had Lily and Maude had some secret pact? I wondered.

Lily continued, "I sent you an email this morning with the obituary. I didn't know if you wanted David included. Just send it back to me and I'll ensure it gets to all the right people. Now, about the reception. After the funeral Maude wanted an Irish celebration here at the house, like she had for Harry. There would be no crying, only celebration. I've already called the caterer and you just need to pick out the food. He's emailing you a list this morning. You pick three things from each category. I will take care of the rest."

"Lily!" I couldn't help but exclaiming. "How did you?"

Margaret ran to Lily and hugged her. It was so quick, I thought for sure she'd be wearing the coffee Lily held in her one small hand.

"Okay you two, run off. Mr. Salvarone is waiting," Lily choked back her tears.

As Margaret ran upstairs to change, Lily pulled me aside. By this time, both girls sat indulging in the warm muffins. Lily handed me a set of keys.

"Maude wanted you to have these."

I was shocked. What kind of keys would Maude have wanted me to have? And why was Lily giving them to me?

"What are these?" I asked.

Lily explained, "Maude has a summer home on Lake Hopatcong. There's four bedrooms, a pool, and a beautiful porch that overlooks the lake. It's the nicest home on the lake. She was afraid you were going to leave Simon and wanted you to have someplace to go. She put your name on the title a few weeks ago. I don't know how she knew, God bless her soul." Lily got lost in her grief momentarily. "It's thirty minutes from Katherine's school so you could commute and she would be no worse for wear. Maude even suggested you could sell it and buy something sweet in Chatham."

I was overwhelmed. "But what about Margaret?"

Lily was all business. "Margaret knows, and don't you worry, Maude had plenty to pass around. This is a vacation home for you and your family or a new home for you and Katherine." I was speechless.

"I couldn't," I started.

"It's too late. Maude took care of everything. The taxes are paid through next year. You could, and you will." There was bossy Lily again. Who knew?

I was overwhelmed.

"I have all the paperwork back at my house. Stop by when you wish and I'll walk you through it." Lily said as Margaret returned, looking as if she had never shed a tear. Margaret looked at the keys and smiled.

"You'll love it. My mother loved you, Rainey. She wanted to do this for you."

The tears started once again. As I wiped them, my voice broke as I thanked Margaret.

In the car we were silent. So much had happened in the past twenty-four hours. I think we both needed time to prepare for what was next. We rounded the corner to Salvarone's Funeral Home and pulled into the driveway. An older gentleman, maybe Maude and Lily's contemporary, stood at the door on a red carpet under a carport. He motioned for us to pull up to the carpet and when I did, signaled for a young man to join him. They each met us as the car stopped and opened our doors. Just as Lily had told us, Mr. Salvarone was awaiting our arrival.

The carpeted hallways were surrounded by large white sets of double doors, beautiful but heart-breaking. As we followed our host to the "Tea Room," I stared at each door wondering if someone's loved one was lying in wait on the other side, waiting for mourners to fill the seats and to kiss their embalmed bodies in grief. Rainey, pull yourself together. My mind was everywhere. Which door did our beloved Maude lie behind? Rainey!

Once in the Tea Room, a lovely young woman brought us a tray of biscuits and a two silver pots. Presumably one held hot water and the other coffee. Mr. Salvarone explained that Maude had already made her arrangements and he had only a few questions for Margaret. He explained that Maude believed a funeral was for the living, not the dead. She knew there'd be some things the family would want, and Margaret was free to change any of the details.

After ten minutes, it was clear that Maude left no stone unturned and knew what her daughter had wanted as well as she knew how to care for roses. Everything was perfect.

"There is one thing," added Mr. Salvarone. He looked at me, "Rainey, I was asked by the deceased to give this to you. She had hoped you would read it as it's written, during the service?"

"Of course," I responded, and took the envelope.

The morning went fast. Faster than I wanted, in fact. I knew the inevitable lay ahead for me at home. It was the hardest decision I would ever make. I would say goodbye to a man I loved and– thanks to Maude– I now knew where I was going.

As I drove up the driveway to Greenwood Gardens, Margaret and I couldn't stop talking about everything that her mother had prepared. As I pulled next to Maude's Ingrid Bergman red, Audi S5 convertible, I couldn't help smiling. Margaret looked over at me and back to the car, "She was never going to age gracefully, was she?" She smirked.

"I need to know," Margaret asked again, "How can you so easily forgive me and hope for David to take me back when you can't forgive Simon?" I wasn't prepared for her question. I wasn't sure if her question was about me, or her.

"I don't know. Maybe because you didn't hurt me?" I answered.

Margaret didn't slow, "What happened in Cape Cod yesterday? What happened with Jaime?"

I felt like a witness in a murder investigation suddenly. My heart thumped in my chest, I felt like an idiot. How could I have done that to either of these men? I let Jaime drive all the way there, I called Simon from the beach, I was horrible and hurtful to both men. My actions weren't intentional, but as I was trying to heal they were being stabbed.

I told her everything. I told her about how I was driving away before Jaime got there, I shared how attracted I was to him still, I told her how much I loved him, and I shared how I called Simon from the beach.

I told her Simon's last words to me, "Come home, Baby."

She cried with me. As we cried together, Margaret put her hand over mine.

We sat for a few minutes longer before Margaret pierced our silence, "What did you need from Simon when you called him from the beach?"

I didn't think about it before answering.

"I needed to talk to my best friend."

Margaret got in Maude's car and blew a kiss as she pulled from the lot. Her dark hair was released from its smart ponytail and was free in the breeze. She looked beautiful. I looked down at my phone - three messages, all unknown numbers. I assumed all the calls yesterday and today were from friends of Maude whom we knew from the Downtown Committee or the Gardens. I would have to call them back soon. Now that we had a date, it would be easier. Katherine hadn't called yet. They were sleeping late, it must be almost eleven, I thought. I looked at the time; eleven-eleven a.m.

I decided to walk to the rose garden and read what Mr. Salvarone handed me. I walked down the tiers of stone steps in need of repair and through the tall hedges to the rose garden where Maude and I met. I sat next to the Queen Elizabeths. All the roses were gone now, just the nicely pruned greens remained. I opened the package.

The first page was a note from Maude with few words that read:

My darling Rainey,

Meeting you has been one of the highlights of my life. You have brought me love, happiness and joy. You have been a second daughter– minus those painful teenage years! I hope this finds you with the answers you've been seeking because you taught me the only one that really matters – Love.

Rainey, you are still that bad-ass woman you reference. She's not gone, she's just hiding.

I will be in your heart always, as you are in mine,

Maude

PS. See if you can convince that Garden to name a rose after me! LOL!

I laughed out loud at her last line. She was always telling the Director that she should have her own rose. Laughing to the end, I thought. I loved how she incorporated "young words" into her note. She was always practicing and stopping young people in the Gardens asking them to repeat some phrase she loved. "Young words," she'd say to me when they'd leave, "I love them!"

I pulled out the pages behind her note.

Dearly departed, and I say that because you are so dear to me. You must know that I love you all or you wouldn't have taken the time to show up, I suppose. I have asked my dear friend Rainey Bradley to read this to you for two reasons. First, because I know my beautiful Margaret is a hot mess right now weeping in a pew somewhere near the front of the church. More importantly, because Rainey Bradley taught me one of my finest life lessons at eight-five years old; to say I love you.

You should know Rainey. Everyone should know Rainey. She loves so deeply, but because she does, she hurts so deeply as well. Right now - keep it together Rainey - she's probably trying to hold her shit together so she doesn't break out in tears.

Here's what I want you to know, all of you.
This is what I've learned from Mrs. Rainey Bradley.

You get one life, and I've been gifted a marvelous one. I have had a life of generosity and giving. My dear Harry has ensured that even in his absence, my time could be spent doing for others. He knew giving was the secret of great joy, as are children.

But one thing I wouldn't understand until later, was that it isn't just giving of yourself that shows love, but it's the words you don't say that should never go unsaid.

So, as my dying wish, I ask you all never to hold back the following, from those you love.

Never hold back...

A touch, during good times and bad.
A smile that says, no matter what, I am here for you.
A thank you, no matter how late or expected the gifts or words may be.
An apology, even when you're not the one who's wrong.
Forgiveness, because we all have made mistakes.
A second chance, because everyone deserves at least one.
Self love, because you are also worthy of forgiveness.
And most importantly,
Never hold back the words "I love you" because it's not until you truly give them away that you will be able to fully receive it in return.

To my dearest Margaret, I love you more than the sun rises and the stars shine.
Elisa and Madison, my darling granddaughters, I will fly to Heaven propelled on my love for you, alone.
David, you are our family, and I love you.
Rainey, thank you my dear, for loving me back.
And Lily, my dearest Lily, I'll have the chardonnay waiting my dear friend. I love you.

Now, it is time to stop crying and start celebrating. Remember, I'm with my Harry now. So please, join us as our spirits dance with you back at our home. Toast to us and laugh with us. I love you each and all.

With all my heart, Maude

Well, she nailed it. I read the words over again. Was she sending me her final message? I adored this woman, and she knew me as well as Margo and Lisa, yet I had only known her half a year. Maude was patient with me. She never gave me advice about Simon, never. I wondered if it was because of Margaret and David? Had she and Harry been through something similar?

I looked at the eulogy I would read. She was still giving, even in her death. I don't know that I had truly taught her all those things, but was honored she thought so. Was this her way of telling me to practice what I preach?

Margaret had asked not why I called Simon from Cape Cod, but what did I need from Simon. The affair hurt because Simon was my best friend.

I may have talked myself into believing that I had stayed in this marriage because of my vows, because Katherine loved him, because it was the right thing to do for Katherine, or because he was dying; but I know now why I really stayed. I stayed because I love him. I had lost myself because I had loved Simon more than me, or who and what I thought I was.

I needed to get home right away. I knew what I would say.

I could barely stay focused on the voicemails I was listening to. I was so prepared to be giving out details about the arrangements for Maude that I'd find myself completely shocked as call after call was a referral for me to consult. Word had gotten out about my help with the Gardens and the Downtown Council and work was flooding in. I couldn't wait to tell Simon. I couldn't wait to tell him about Maude, the letter, the new business and so much more.

Truth was, Simon was still my best friend and I still loved

him.

I pulled in the driveway and almost ran to the front door. Katherine was sitting in the family room watching TV with Popcorn lying across her lap. Popcorn, our ten-year-old Golden Retriever, knew love. This dog could show love more genuinely than anyone in our house. Katherine held her back as she tried to run and greet me.

"No, Popcorn, stay!" Kate whined, "She was so snuggly, Mom." I gave Popcorn a big hug and walked over to Katherine. I kissed her on the head,

"I love you." I thought about Maude's note. "Where's Simon?" I asked casually. Katherine shrugged her shoulders,

"I haven't seen him yet." Simon had been an early riser for the past year, up before seven. When we met, he loved to sleep until nine or ten, I guess we've all changed a little.

I started to feel a strange fear come over me. I raced up the stairs to our bedroom. Something wasn't right. I went to push the bedroom door open but a weight on the other side held it back.

"Simon? Are you up?" I tried the door again. The handle turned but the door wouldn't budge. Was he holding it shut? "Simon! Open the door!" I felt vomit rise in my throat. What was the noise I was hearing? Was someone talking? Was he on the phone? "Simon! What are you doing?"

I finally fell to my knees. Was he hiding something, someone, from me again? Maybe I wasn't the only one planning on spending the weekend with someone else? Who was talking? Who was saying his name? I heard a woman talking on the phone. In desperation, I looked beneath the crack of the door. It was then I knew something horrible had happened.

No light shone through the crack except to a small space to the right side of the door. I could see his skin. Simon was lying against the door. It was then that I saw the blood. There was so much blood near his body. I screamed for Kate to call nine-one-one.

His body was lying against the inside of the door. With no shirt on and two hundred and thirty pounds of skin, I could barely budge it. I knew it had to hurt. I had to get in there.

"Simon, Simon, are you okay??? Wake up, baby! Simon, I love you! Kate, did you call nine-one-one?"

She was standing behind me with the phone to her head.

"What happened?" Her face was filled with fear. Her giant blue eyes were scared and wet. I heard another voice.

"Rainey, is that you?"

It was from the other side of the door. I realized someone was on the phone still. Katherine opened the closet door and the next thing I know a giant cloud of baby powder plumed in the air.

"What are you doing?" I screamed.

"Mom, his body is sticking to the floor. We need to open it. Oh my God, Mom. Is he alive?"

ACCEPTANCE

Kate took her thin, strong hand and pushed the powder under the weight of his body. As she pulled her hand out, she noticed the blood covering the tips. I wish I could have taken that terror from her. I hadn't realized she didn't see the blood.

"I know, baby. I know. We've got to get this door open. Let's push it firmly, but slowly. Maybe we can push him away without doing anymore harm." Together we pushed the door until Katherine could squeeze through the opening. I hadn't planned it, nor had I expected her to throw her thin body through the opening. She shrieked in horror.

"Oh my God, Simon! God, please don't let him be dead, please don't let him be dead..." Her voice trailed in tearful pain.

"Katherine, help me get in there. What do you see? Katherine, what is happening?" The panic enveloped me. I was no longer rational.

"I'm pulling his arms-" was all I could hear through her tears. I heard the ambulance outside.

"Up here!" I screamed in panic. Please God, please don't let me bury two of my best friends today.

The voice on the phone kept yelling, "Rainey? Rainey? Kate, are you there? What's happening?"

I had managed through the door and Kate and I had pulled Simon's limp body away from the door. I guessed that the gash on his forehead came from hitting the corner of the dresser as he fell. But why did he fall? How? He had a pacemaker and a defibrillator. They were supposed to keep him alive.

"His chest!" Kate yelled. Neither of us were any good at forming words in an emergency. We learned this today. I expected another gash but saw his chest move instead. He was alive still. The paramedics entered the room.

"He's going to need blood," one said.

"How long has he been out?" the other asked.

"I, I don't know," I was overwhelmed. The phone. It had become silent. Was the woman still on the line? Who was it? Whom had he been talking to?

I picked up the phone.

"Hello, are you there?"

There was no answer. I looked at the number, it wasn't linked to a contact. It was a Connecticut number. I found "Recents" at the bottom of his phone and I tapped it. No contact information but the words "New London" were in gray beneath the number. It was the third call from this number today. There was one at nine-thirty-three a.m., another at ten-fifty-two a.m., and this last one at twelve-fifteen p.m. I clicked the information icon to the right of the twelve-fifteen call. Outgoing call, eighteen minutes, it read. I looked at the paramedic through my tears and said somberly, "no more than eighteen minutes." I went back a screen and looked at the duration of the ten-fifty-two call. Incoming call, missed. The same for the nine-thirty-three call. Missed. I scrolled down his phone. There were no other recent calls showing. He had deleted them.

As they loaded Simon into the ambulance, he was groggy but conscious. His defibrillator had gone off as he was walking out of the bedroom. The jolt had apparently thrown him to the floor, and on the way there, he hit his head. He had lost a lot of blood, but he was conscious.

I walked to the back door of the ambulance with Simon's

phone in hand. I pushed the Connecticut number with my thumb. Simon looked at me, strapped helplessly on the gurney.

"Portia," I said calmly, "Simon will be at the Morristown Medical Center in Morristown, NJ. He should still be alive when you get there."

I placed the phone on the gurney, turned and put my arm around Kate, and walked back into the house.

SPRING

Kate was running around in a frenzy. "Mom, everyone will be here soon, we're not ready!!" I laughed. Had it been that long since we had entertained?

"Get in here and chop," I laughed. Kate had invited her new boyfriend over to meet the family. I suggested he come earlier than everyone, so he didn't catch the whole brood at one time.

"You know, Mom, Uncle Trevor can be brutal! Please don't let him be mean to Ethan. Please, Mom."

"It will be fine," I assured her. I looked over at Ethan who was trying to be calm, but Kate's energy was starting to make him nervous. He had met several of our new friends before, including Margaret, but Kate had him a little nervous about the aunts and uncles. I couldn't help giggling.

I had met Ethan when I had dropped Kate off at a basketball game. He was a string bean of a boy, but sweet. He would eventually grow into that body, I thought. His sandy blonde hair was parted at the side and was easily moved by the breeze from the lake. It was the perfect day for a party, I thought. And the way he looked at Kate? Well, that was perfect as well.

I handed Ethan a knife and asked him if he knew how to cut onions. Kate shot me a death stare, knowing that I would soon have some joke ready about boys crying. I acknowledged the stare and smiled.

The front door opened, and our first guests arrived. I wasn't sure if they'd make it this early, but I was glad they had. Kate expertly greeted our guests like the perfect hostess. She hadn't skipped a beat, greeting and asking to take their bags. I love that child. They gave her giant hugs and politely refused her offer. Instead they followed her upstairs where she would show them where to put their things down. As they made their way back down the steps, Michael threw open the door and yelled.

"Where's QB?!?"

He saw Kate bouncing down the stairs and she jumped in his arms as if she was still seven.

"Hi, Uncle Michael!" He told her how beautiful she was while they blocked the other guests from getting to the ground floor.

"Where's this new boyfriend?" Michael asked. Trevor bounded in behind him with Jen, Melissa, Lisa and Zoe.

"New boyfriend? What new boyfriend? Where's Rainey? Rainey, do you know about this?" Trevor teased.

"Uncle Trevorrr," Kate warned and gave him a big hug.

"Yes, he's in here and we've already made him cry. Come in here and meet Ethan!" I called from the kitchen. "The wine has been breathing for far too long."

Our first guest came up behind me while I was chopping. He put his hands on my shoulders and up to my neck where he gently positioned my lips to kiss them. I couldn't help staring happily into his eyes, forgetting we had an audience.

From the foyer I heard Michael, "As I live and breathe! Jaime O'Brien?!? How the hell are you?" I smiled as I heard the reunion but he needed no introduction to the man standing behind me. Ethan was safe. It was I that would be under the spotlight this weekend, but I didn't care. I was happy.

Jaime's arms moved behind me and he put his arms around my waist while I finished chopping. He bent down and kissed my head, lingering to breathe in my scent. He suddenly grabbed one of my hands as if using it as a pointer. We pointed to his two sons, six feet three and younger versions of the Jaime I knew. He then pointed to Kate and Ethan standing next to them. "One, two, three, four," he whispered loud enough for the room to hear. "I finally got my happily ever after."

I looked around the room- my room- my kitchen- and saw my family. I saw Margaret and Lily. Two of my aunts were just arriving through the front door. I saw all of Kate's pseudo aunts and uncles. Zoe had her arms full. The room was filled with everyone I love.

"Yes, I certainly did get my happily ever after." I agreed.

Today, was officially a new day; Day One.

Made in the USA
Middletown, DE
05 June 2019